Disney

365 Stories

A story a day

PaRragon

Bath · New York · Cologne · Melbourne · Delhi
Hong Kong · Shenzhen · Singapore · Amsterdam

Winnie the Pooh characters are based on the 'Winnie the Pooh' works by
A. A. Milne and E. H. Shepard.

The movie THE PRINCESS AND THE FROG Copyright © 2009 Disney,
story inspired in part by the book THE FROG PRINCESS
by E.D. Baker Copyright © 2002, published by Bloomsbury Publishing, Inc.

101 Dalmatians is based on the book *The Hundred and One Dalmatians* by Dodie Smith,
published by The Viking Press.

This edition published by Parragon Books Ltd in 2015

Parragon Books Ltd
Chartist House
15–17 Trim Street
Bath BA1 1HA, UK
www.parragon.com

ISBN 978-1-4723-7710-4

Printed in China

Disney
101 DALMATIANS

New Year's Day

It was the first day of the new year, and Pongo and Perdita were out for a walk with their pets, Roger and Anita. The morning fog was beginning to part, and the air was clear and cold. "Oh, Pongo," Perdita sighed happily. "What a wonderful year we've just had – 15 puppies to be thankful for!"

"Yes, darling, and think of all we have to look forward to this year," said Pongo.

"Can you believe they all stayed up till midnight last night to ring in the new year?" Perdita cried. "And still awake when we left! I do hope they don't tire out dear, poor Nanny."

"Yes, that was quite a party we had at the flat last night," Pongo agreed. "And Lucky would have spent the whole night watching television if we had allowed him to."

"Perhaps we should be getting home now," said Perdita. "I am so afraid that Cruella De Vil may come around while we're out. I dread the way she looks at our puppies."

"I suppose we should," said Pongo. "But I'm sure Nanny has been taking good care of them." Pongo and Perdita gently pulled on their leads to let Roger and Anita know it was time to go home. The four of them walked towards home just as a new sprinkling of rain began to gently fall.

"Nanny! Puppies! We're home!" called Roger as he and Anita took off their muddy boots and Pongo and Perdy brushed off their paws on the mat in the hall. But no one answered.

"Pongo!" exclaimed Perdita, her panic rising. "Where are the puppies?"

Pongo raced up the stairs and began searching the rooms one by one. Perdita went to check the kitchen. Roger and Anita exchanged concerned looks, but tried to remain calm.

Pongo hurried into the sitting room to rejoin Perdita, who was on the brink of tears. "Oh, Pongo!" she cried. "Where can ..."

"Hush, darling," said Pongo, his ears pricked intently. The two dogs fell silent. Then they both heard it: a tiny snore coming from the direction of the couch. There, nestled among the cushions, the puppies were sound asleep!

"I found Nanny!" Roger called. "She fell asleep in her chair!"

Perdita was busy counting the sleeping puppies. "... 12, 13, 14 ... Oh, Pongo! One of the puppies isn't here!"

But Pongo had trotted into the next room. "Here he is, darling!" he called. "It's Lucky, of course. He's watching the New Year's Day celebration on television."

An Icy Secret

The kingdom of Arendelle was a busy and happy place, nestled among the mountains and fjords of the far north. At night, the northern lights often lit up the sky with beautiful patterns.

But the King and Queen lived with a secret worry. Their eldest daughter, Elsa, had a magical power – she could freeze things and create snow and ice with her hands!

Anna, their younger daughter, adored her big sister. One night, Anna convinced Elsa to create a winter wonderland in the Great Hall!

But while the girls were playing, Elsa accidentally hit Anna with a blast of icy magic. The little girl fell to the ground, unconscious. A white streak appeared in her hair.

Frightened for her sister, Elsa called out for help. The King and Queen rushed the girls to the realm of the trolls.

The trolls were mysterious healers who knew about magic. A wise old troll was able to cure little Anna and change her memories so she couldn't remember Elsa's magic. He also warned that Elsa's powers would grow stronger.

"There is beauty in it but also great danger," he said. "Fear will be her enemy."

Back in Arendelle, the King and Queen locked the castle gates to keep people out. No one would discover Elsa's secret.

Anna played alone while Elsa worked hard to control her powers. But whenever Elsa had strong feelings the magic spilled out. The King gave her gloves to hold it back, but Elsa was afraid she might hurt someone by accident. She even avoided Anna, in order to keep her little sister safe.

Anna missed her sister. As the years went by she kept asking Elsa to play, but Elsa always said she was busy.

Then, when the girls were teenagers, the King and Queen were lost in a storm at sea. The sisters felt more alone – and apart – than ever.

When Elsa came of age it was her duty to become Queen, but Elsa was worried about being the centre of attention. What if her powers accidentally came out?

On a summer's day, the gates of the castle were opened for one day only for the Queen's coronation. It was to be a glorious celebration for the people of Arendelle, but Anna was the most excited. She was thrilled at the chance to meet new people – and, maybe, she thought, she might even fall in love!

DISNEY·PIXAR
FROM THE MOVIE **INSIDE OUT**

Inside HQ

One day, a little girl called Riley was born. At that very moment, Riley's first Emotion, Joy, stepped up to a console in Headquarters inside Riley's mind.

Joy saw Riley's parents on a screen as it flickered to life.

"Hi, Riley," Joy heard Mum say.

Joy touched the console and Riley smiled with happiness.

In Headquarters, a golden memory sphere suddenly came rolling across the floor towards Joy, and she picked it up. It replayed the moment of Riley's first smile. The sphere was gold because the memory was happy. Joy turned and stored the sphere on an empty shelf at the back of Headquarters.

She returned to the console, which was covered in buttons and levers that could control Riley's feelings and reactions. Just then, Joy noticed somebody standing next to her.

"I'm Sadness," said the newcomer.

Sadness touched the console and baby Riley began to cry.

"Can I just …?" Joy asked, and she took control again. "I just want to fix that. Thanks."

As Riley grew older, Joy and Sadness were joined by three more Emotions – Fear, Anger and Disgust. Each Emotion helped Riley in their own special way.

Joy was the leader of the group, and all she wanted was for Riley to be happy.

Fear helped keep Riley safe. He worked hard to keep Riley far away from potential hazards.

Disgust protected Riley from things that looked, smelled or tasted gross. Like broccoli – eww!

Anger cared very deeply about things being fair for Riley. Most of Riley's tantrums happened when Anger was at the console.

Finally, there was Sadness. Her job was not as obvious as Riley's other Emotions. In fact, Joy wasn't sure why Sadness was there at all.

Over time, the shelves in Headquarters were gradually filled with coloured memory spheres – blue for Sadness, purple for Fear, red for Anger and green for Disgust. But, mostly, the shelves were full of happy golden memories. As the shelves filled up, the older memory spheres were sucked up through tubes to another area of Riley's mind called Long Term Memory, where they were stored until Riley needed to remember them again.

Together, the Five Emotions made important choices for Riley. But with Joy in charge most of the time, everything was perfect. Riley was a happy, contented little girl. Joy saw no reason why anything should change.

Disney · PIXAR
FINDING NEMO

Marlin's Story

"P. Sherman, 42 Wallaby Way, Sydney ... P. Sherman, 42 Wallaby Way, Sydney." Dory kept muttering the address. She and Marlin were searching for Marlin's missing son, Nemo. They had just escaped an angry anglerfish, and now they were trying to find someone who could give them directions to Sydney. That's where Nemo probably was.

"P. Sherman, 42 Wallaby Way, Sydney ... P. Sherman, 42 Wallaby Way, Sydney," Dory continued to chant.

Marlin had the address memorized and thought he would go crazy if he had to hear it again. "Dory!" he said with a sigh. "I know you just want to be helpful, but do you really need to keep talking?"

"I love to talk," said Dory. "I'm pretty good at it. Hmm ... what were we talking about?"

"I just want to find Nemo," Marlin said.

"That's right, Chico," said Dory.

"One time, Nemo and I ..." Marlin began.

"Go on," Dory said. "Is this going to be exciting?"

"Yes, it's an exciting story," said Marlin, relieved that he had got her to stop reciting the address. "Well," Marlin began, "one time, I took Nemo to the other side of the reef, to visit a relative of mine who was known as the fastest swimmer of all the clownfish, in his day.

But when we visited him, he was getting on in years."

Dory yawned. "When's the good part?"

Marlin sighed. "I was just about to get to it!" he said. "So, anyway, on the way back home, guess what we ran into?"

"What?" asked Dory.

"A huge jellyfish! It was hovering in the water, blocking our way through two big tufts of sea grass."

"Uh-huh," said Dory. She seemed to be trying to remember something. "P. Sherman ..." she muttered softly.

"For a moment there I thought we were goners," said Marlin. "But then ... a huge sea turtle swam up and swallowed the jellyfish in one gulp!"

"Did you say thank you to the sea turtle?" asked Dory, who seemed back on track.

"Well, no," Marlin replied. "I was afraid he would eat us, too, so Nemo and I hurried on our way. But, ever since then, I have been fascinated with sea turtles. And I hope I never have to meet another jellyfish!"

"Say, I've got a story too!" said Dory excitedly. "It takes place at 42 Wallaby Way, Sydney. At P. Sherman. Now, at P. Sherman, 42 Wallaby Way, Sydney, there was this, um, fish ... and ... well ..."

Marlin just groaned and kept swimming.

THE
LION KING

Scaredy Cats

"Nala!" Simba whispered. "Are you awake?"

"Yes," Nala whispered back, stepping out of the dark cave where she slept with her mother. "Why are you here? You're gonna get us in trouble ... again."

Earlier, Simba and Nala had gone to explore the forbidden Elephant's Graveyard, where they'd been trapped by hyenas. Simba's father, Mufasa, had rescued them.

"Come on," Simba hissed. "Follow me."

Soon the two cubs were on the dark savannah near the base of Pride Rock.

"What do you want, anyway?" Nala asked.

"I just wanted to make sure you weren't still scared," Simba said.

Nala scowled at him. "Scared?" she exclaimed. "*I'm* not the one who was scared!"

"What?" Simba cried. "You're not saying *I* was scared, are you? Because there's no way I'd be scared of a few stupid hyenas. I wouldn't have been scared even if we ran into *ten* hyenas."

"Well, I wouldn't have been scared even if we found *20* hyenas and an angry water buffalo," said Nala.

"Oh yeah?" Simba said. "Well, I wouldn't have been scared of *30* hyenas, an angry water buffalo and a – "

"FURIOUS HORNBILL?" a new voice squawked from the darkness.

"Ahhhhhh!" Simba and Nala cried, jumping straight up in the air.

Just then, a brightly coloured bird stepped out of the shadows. It was Zazu, Mufasa's most trusted adviser.

"Zazu!" Simba cried. "You scared us!"

"I wasn't scared," Nala put in indignantly.

"Me neither!" Simba added quickly.

Zazu glared at both of them over his long beak. "Not scared, were you?" he said drily. "That certainly explains the shrieking."

"You just startled us, that's all," Nala mumbled.

Zazu fluffed his feathers. "Listen up, you two," he said. "There's no shame in admitting you're scared. Even King Mufasa wouldn't deny that he was terrified when he found out you were missing. And, if it's good enough for him, it's good enough for a pair of scrawny cubs like you. Right?"

"I guess so," Simba said as Nala shrugged.

"Everyone gets scared," Zazu went on. "It's how you respond to it that counts. That's where *true* bravery lies. Get it?"

"Got it," Simba and Nala said.

"Good." Zazu marched towards Pride Rock. The sun was coming up and it was time for breakfast. "Now let's get you back home posthaste ... or I'll *really* give you something to be scared of!"

TinkerBell

Tinker Bell is Born

One winter's day in London, a baby laughed for the very first time. That laugh floated up and away to meet its destiny. It would become a fairy, just like all first laughs. It flew straight for the Second Star to the Right, and passed through it in a burst of light. On the other side was … Never Land!

The laugh floated towards a magical place in the heart of the island. This was Pixie Hollow, home of the fairies. Vidia, the fastest flying fairy of them all, guided the arrival into the Pixie Dust Tree. There, a dust-keeper named Terence sprinkled it with pixie dust, and it took the shape of a tiny fairy.

Clarion, queen of the fairies, helped the newcomer unfurl her two gossamer wings. The new fairy flapped her wings and realized she could fly!

Queen Clarion waved her hand, and several toadstools sprung up around the Pixie Dust Well. Fairies immediately fluttered forwards to place different objects on the pedestals. Rosetta, a garden fairy, brought a flower. Silvermist, a water fairy, carried a droplet of water. Iridessa, a light fairy, placed a lamp on her pedestal.

"They will help you find your talent," the queen explained to the new fairy.

The youngster timidly placed her hand on a beautiful flower. Its glow instantly faded. She reached for a water droplet, but that, too, faded. The fairy moved on without touching anything else – she was afraid to fail again – but then something amazing happened. As she passed by a hammer, it began to glow. Then it rose up off its pedestal and flew straight for her!

"I've never seen one glow that much before," said Silvermist.

Vidia glowered. She had one of the strongest and rarest talents in Pixie Hollow, and she wasn't looking for competition.

"Tinker fairies," called the queen. "Welcome the newest member of your talent guild – Tinker Bell!"

A large fairy named Clank and a bespectacled fairy named Bobble came forwards to greet Tink. Then they whisked her off for a flying tour of Pixie Hollow. It was almost time for the changing of the seasons, and they could see everyone getting ready.

Finally, the trio landed at Tinkers' Nook. Tink looked around and saw fairies fixing and fashioning all kinds of amazing, useful objects. She knew she would enjoy living here, and was excited about discovering her unique fairy talent.

A Tiny New Friend

It had been a week since Cinderella's step-mother had forced her to move out of her bedroom and into the attic of the old house. But still Cinderella was not used to her new sleeping quarters. It was a cold, bare, lonely little room. The only other soul around to keep Cinderella company was a skittish little mouse who she had seen scurrying in and out of a hole in a corner of the room.

She had always been fond of animals, and mice were no exception. But how could she let the little fellow know that he shouldn't be afraid of her?

Well, thought Cinderella, he must be cold ... and hungry.

So one day, at suppertime, Cinderella slipped a piece of cheese into her apron pocket.

And that evening, when her work was finished, Cinderella hurried up to her room and pulled out her sewing basket. She used some scraps of fabric to make a mouse-sized suit of clothing: a red shirt and cap, a tiny orange coat, and two brown slippers.

"A tiny outfit for my tiny friend," she said.

Cinderella carried the clothes over to the mouse hole and knelt before it. She pulled the cheese out of her pocket and placed it, with the clothes, in the palm of her hand. Then she laid her open hand just in front of the mouse hole.

"Hello in there!" she called.

A mouse cautiously poked his head out of the hole and sniffed the air. Seeing the cheese, he inched out of the hole and over to Cinderella's hand. He paused and looked up at her questioningly.

"Go ahead," she said kindly. "They're a gift just for you."

Seeming to understand, but still skittish, the mouse scampered onto her palm, picked up the cheese and the clothes, and hurried back into the mouse hole.

Cinderella chuckled, then waited patiently for a few minutes, still kneeling in front of the hole.

"Well," she called after a short while, "let me see how they look on you!"

Timidly, the mouse came out in his new outfit. Cinderella clapped her hands.

"Perfect!" she said. "Do you like them?"

The mouse nodded. Then he jumped, as if an idea had just occurred to him. He scurried back into the mouse hole. Cinderella frowned. Had she frightened him?

But her worries vanished when the mouse reappeared – along with several other mice, who followed timidly behind him.

"More friends!" Cinderella cried. She hurried to get her sewing basket, delighted to have found the warmth of friendship in the cold attic room.

A Visit in the Night

It's not easy to read with a broken arm! Alone in his room, young Carl was trying to turn a page without letting go of his torch.

Suddenly, he heard a gentle rubbing noise. Then a blue balloon forced its way through his bedroom curtains!

"Ouch!" cried Carl, as he knocked his plaster cast against the bedside table.

A merry little face, framed by a mop of red hair, appeared at the window and Carl let out a second cry.

"It's me! I thought you might need a little cheering up!" whispered Ellie, his new friend, before she leaped down onto the floor.

She slipped quickly under the cover that Carl had made into a tent.

"Look!" she said, showing him a small notebook. "I'm going to show you something I've never shown to anyone else. Swear you won't tell anyone; cross your heart!"

Carl promised and Ellie opened up the book. A photo of the explorer Charles Muntz had been stuck on the first page.

"It's my adventure book! When I grow up I'm going to be an explorer too. And I'll go to South America, to Paradise Falls!"

Carl looked admiringly at the beautiful waterfalls, next to which Ellie had drawn the little house where they'd met each other that same afternoon.

"Obviously it'll be tricky to move the clubhouse all that way!" said Ellie, who had noticed Carl's look of surprise.

The boy didn't say a word, but couldn't stop his eyes from looking up to the shelf where his collection of miniature airships stood, including a model of Muntz's *Spirit of Adventure*. Ellie immediately understood.

"But of course!" she cried out. "You can take us there in an airship! Promise me you'll do it! Promise!"

Carl promised. He could see no reason not to. Ellie was a true adventuress!

"See you tomorrow, right?" she said, getting up. "You're one hell of a chatterbox, you know?" she added, laughing, before straddling the window and disappearing into the night.

"Wow!" murmured Carl, totally bowled over by his new friend. Just ten minutes in Ellie's company was one of the biggest adventures of his life!

That night, as he slept, he dreamed of a colourful little house perched at the top of Paradise Falls....

A Fairy Tale Kiss

Once upon a time in New Orleans, two young girls named Tiana and Charlotte were unlikely friends.

Charlotte believed in fairy tales and wishing on stars, but Tiana knew that wishing could only help her if she worked hard to make her dreams come true.

One night, Tiana was visiting with her mother, Eudora, who worked as a seamstress for Charlotte's family.

Tiana loved visiting Charlotte's big house and went there as often as she could.

That night, her mother was sewing a new dress while telling them a fairytale about a prince who had been turned into a frog – Charlotte's favourite story.

"... and the beautiful princess was so moved by the poor frog's desperate pleas that she leaned forwards ..."

"This is my favourite bit!" Charlotte whispered in Tiana's ear.

"... she drew closer, moving her lips to his, and then ..."

"Yes, do it, princess!" whispered Charlotte under her breath.

No, don't do it! thought Tiana, looking disgusted.

"Smack! She kissed the slimy frog, which turned into a charming prince. They married and lived happily ever after!" said Eudora with a smile.

"Hurray!" exclaimed Charlotte. "Please tell us the story again!"

"Sorry, but it's late," said Eudora gently. "We must go home soon."

As Eudora was putting away her sewing things, Tiana said to Charlotte, "There is no way in this whole wide world I would ever, ever, ever – I mean never – kiss a frog!"

With that, Charlotte picked up a frog puppet and put it on the head of her kitten. The little animal tried to get away, but Charlotte held it up to Tiana saying, "Well, go on, kiss it, your prince charming!"

"Yuck! No way!" protested Tiana.

"Really?" asked Charlotte, surprised.

"I would kiss a hundred frogs if I could marry a prince and be a princess!" said Charlotte. She planted a big kiss on the nose of the kitten, who leaped away in horror!

"It's the frog who's disgusted by the princess!" cried Tiana, laughing. "You're going to have to brush up on your fairytale kisses, Lottie!"

And the two girls rolled round on the floor laughing! They had no idea of the adventures the future would bring.

Beauty $_{and\atop the}$ Beast

The Castle

In a sleepy little village there lived an eccentric inventor named Maurice and his beautiful daughter, Belle.

Gaston, a strong and handsome young man who also lived in the village, had decided that he wanted to make Belle his wife. "After all," he told his friend Lefou one evening while they were drinking in the tavern, "she's the best-looking girl in town."

When Gaston arrived at Belle's house the next morning, he was confident that she would

agree to marry him. But, when he asked her for her hand, Belle refused him without even a second thought. She knew she could never marry someone as arrogant and conceited as Gaston!

The following day, old Maurice set off for a fair with his latest invention. But as night fell, he lost his way and had to seek refuge in a castle. In the village it was said that a huge beast lived in the castle, but Maurice desperately needed shelter, and so he had to knock on the door.

Maurice was welcomed by some friendly enchanted servants, including a candelabra named Lumiere, a clock named Cogsworth, a teapot named Mrs Potts and her son Chip, a little teacup.

But the Beast was furious when he discovered a stranger in his home and he threw Maurice into the dungeon.

When Maurice's horse returned home alone that night, Belle set off at once to search for her father. Eventually she came upon the castle.

"Oh, Papa," Belle cried when she found Maurice huddled in the freezing dungeon, "we must get you out of here!"

Sensing danger, Belle turned round. There was the Beast, coming towards her and growling loudly.

"Please let my father go," Belle pleaded with the Beast. "I'll take his place here instead."

The Beast agreed to the deal at once. He dragged Maurice out of the cell and sent him back to the village. Then the Beast showed Belle to her room.

"You can go anywhere in the castle," he told her, "except for the West Wing. That is forbidden!"

The enchanted servants could see that poor Belle was miserable, so they prepared a wonderful meal for her and tried to cheer her up with their singing and dancing.

Belle tried to enjoy herself, but deep down she was still lonely and missed her father greatly. She wondered if she would ever see her home again....

Disney
Lady and the TRAMP

Spaghetti and Meatballs

Tramp had just escaped from the dogcatcher – again. He'd taught that dogcatcher who was boss! Tramp could smell wood burning in fireplaces, dinner cooking ... his stomach suddenly rumbled. Escaping from the dogcatcher always made him work up quite an appetite!

But where would he go for dinner tonight? He usually stopped by the Schultzes for some Wiener schnitzel on Monday, he had corned beef and cabbage with the O'Briens on Tuesday ... but what he was really craving was some spaghetti and meatballs.

So, Tramp headed to Tony's Restaurant. He scratched at the back door, as was his custom.

"I'm coming! I'm coming!" Tony shouted. He appeared at the door wiping his hands on a towel. He pretended not to see Tramp, as he always did.

"Hey, nobody's here!" Tony shouted. "It must be April Fools' Day!" He pretended to think for a moment. "No, it's not the first! It's not even April! It's January!"

Tramp couldn't take it any more. He was so hungry! He barked.

"Oh, there you are, Butch my friend," said Tony. Tramp, aka Butch, jumped up and down. "I'll get your dinner," said Tony. "Relax, enjoy yourself."

Tramp sat down and looked around the cluttered alleyway. This was the life!

Just then Tony appeared with a plateful of pasta. He had given Tramp two, no make that *three* meatballs! This was quite a special night.

Tony stood and chatted with Tramp as he ate his meal, telling him about his day – the late delivery of fish, the customer who had complained that the tomato sauce was too garlicky, the trip that he and his wife were planning to take....

Tramp finished eating and gave the plate one last lick. It was sparkling clean.

"That reminds me," said Tony. "There's something I've been meaning to talk to you about. It's time you settled down and got a wife of your own."

Tramp gave Tony a horrified look and began to back out of the alleyway.

Tony laughed so hard his sides shook. "Goodbye, Butch!" he called. "But mark my words, one of these days, you're going to meet the dog you can't resist! And, when you do, I have a good idea – you bring her to Tony's for a nice romantic dinner!"

Tramp barked his thanks to Tony. He walked down the block, shaking his head. He was footloose and collar free! Settle down? That was never going to happen!

Peter Pan

A Never Land Story

It was a cold winter night, and John and Michael just couldn't get to sleep. They climbed onto the bed of their older sister, Wendy.

"Oh, tell us a story, Wendy!" said Michael.

"Yes, please. A Peter Pan story!" pleaded John.

"Certainly," said Wendy. "Have I told you about the time that Peter Pan outsmarted the evil Captain Hook?"

"Yes!" said Michael eagerly. "And we want to hear it again!"

Wendy laughed and began her story. "Well, one night, Captain Hook moored his ship in a secret cove close to the island of Never Land. He and his men rowed ashore quietly, for he was intent on discovering the hiding place of Peter and the Lost Boys. Captain Hook hated Peter Pan because the boy had cut off his hand in a duel and fed it to a large crocodile. And now that crocodile was determined to swallow up the rest of him. Luckily for Captain Hook, however, this crocodile had also swallowed a clock, so the pirate would always be alerted to the crocodile's presence by the sound of the ticking clock.

"Fortunately for Peter Pan," Wendy continued, "his dear friend Tinker Bell learned of Captain Hook's evil plan ahead of time. She flew to Peter and warned him that the pirate was coming. 'Oh-ho!' laughed Peter. 'Well, we shall be ready for him then!' He found a clock just like the one the crocodile had swallowed. He whistled up into the trees, and a group of his monkey friends appeared. 'Here's a new toy for you!' Peter shouted, and tossed the clock up to them. 'Stay out of sight, now!' Peter told the monkeys, and then he and the Lost Boys hurried to their hiding places.

"When Hook came to the clearing, the first thing he heard was the ticking clock. The sound seemed to be coming at him from all sides! The monkeys were having a grand time, tossing the clock back and forth, and creeping up behind Hook. Seized with terror, Hook and his men raced to their boat and rowed madly back to their ship."

Just then, the Darling children's parents came in to check on them. "You're not telling more of these poppycock stories about Peter Pan, are you, Wendy?" their father asked.

"Peter Pan is real, Father!" cried the children. "We know he is!"

As the parents kissed their children goodnight, they didn't see that a boy in green was crouching just outside the nursery window. He had been listening to the story, and he would be back again – soon.

Winnie the Pooh

Say Ahhh, Pooh!

"Christopher Robin says it's time for my animal checkout," said Pooh.

"Checkout!" cried Piglet. "Oh p-p-poor P-P-Pooh – you're sick!"

"Sick?" asked Pooh. "No – I'm fine. Though I must say I am feeling a bit rumbly in my tumbly."

"Let's go together," said Piglet. "It's so much more friendly with two." So, Pooh and Piglet climbed the ladder up to Owl's house.

"Christopher Robin, why do I need an animal checkout, anyway?" asked Pooh once they had arrived at Owl's house.

"Silly old bear," said Christopher Robin. "Not an animal checkout – an annual checkup. We need to make sure you are healthy and strong. And this time, Owl will give you a special injection to help keep you well." Pooh's tummy flopped and flipped.

"It's okay," said Christopher Robin. "It will only hurt for a few seconds, and the medicine in the injection will keep you from getting mumps and measles and things like that."

Rabbit called for Pooh to go into Owl's room. Piglet wished him good luck. Once Pooh and Christopher Robin were inside, Owl entered with a flourish. "Well, if it isn't Winnie the Pooh!" he exclaimed. "Splendid day for a checkup, isn't it? I say, how are you feeling?"

"A bit flippy-floppy in my tummy, actually," said Pooh. Then Owl felt Pooh's tummy. He felt around Pooh's neck and under his arms and said that everything seemed to be right where it should be. Pooh was glad. Then Owl pulled a small rubber hammer from his bag. "Reflex-checking time!" he said grandly.

"What's a reflex?" asked Pooh. Owl tapped Pooh's knee – and his leg gave a little kick. "Oh do that again," said Pooh. "That was fun." So Owl tapped Pooh's other knee, and that leg gave a little kick, too. And it didn't bother Pooh in the least when Owl said: "Sit right here in Christopher Robin's lap. It is time for your injection."

"I know it will only hurt for a moment, and it will keep me from getting bumps and weasels," Pooh said bravely.

"That's mumps and measles, Pooh," said Owl.

Piglet came in and sat right next to Pooh while he had his injection. When Owl was done, Rabbit popped back in with a plaster.

"Wow," said Piglet. "You didn't even cry!"

"An annual checkup is no problem for a brave bear like Pooh," said Christopher Robin.

I'm just that sort of bear, thought Pooh with a smile.

THE LITTLE
MERMAID

Sebastian's Big Day

It was Sebastian's big day. As composer for the court of King Triton, he had been working very hard on a new piece of music, and that evening he was going to conduct the royal orchestra as they played his song before everyone for the first time. At last, thought Sebastian, his true genius would be fully appreciated!

That afternoon, in preparation for the concert, Sebastian went over every detail. He perfected the positioning of the musicians' chairs on stage. He prepared extra copies of the music in case any of the musicians forgot their own. He even had his bow tie washed and pressed.

Then, just before the curtain went up, the musicians began to gather backstage. Music filled the air as the trumpet fish and the conch shell players tuned their instruments.

Benny the octopus, the orchestra's drummer, was the last musician to arrive.

"Sebastian!" he exclaimed, rushing over to the conductor. "I – I can't play tonight!"

Sebastian stared at Benny in shock. "What do you mean? You *have* to play!"

"You don't understand," Benny replied. "I *can't*. I took a nap this afternoon and fell asleep on my tentacles, and now they're all tingly! I can't hold my drumsticks!"

The gravity of the situation hit Sebastian hard. "What am I going to do?" he exclaimed, looking around at the musicians. "My composition calls for eight drums. Benny has eight tentacles – one for each drum. Where will I find enough hands to take his place?"

Just then, Ariel and her six sisters swam backstage to wish Sebastian luck.

"Ariel!" Sebastian cried. "Am I glad to see you!" He explained his problem to Ariel and her sisters. "Could each of you help by playing a drum in the concert?" he asked.

"Of course!" the mermaid sisters replied.

Sebastian breathed a sigh of relief. "Okay, we have seven drummers. We just need one more!"

All the musicians stared at Sebastian.

"*Me?*" he said. "But I am the composer and conductor! This is the day my true genius will finally be appreciated. I cannot be hidden in the drum section. I must be front and centre!"

But, wouldn't you know it, when the curtain went up minutes later, there was Sebastian, drumming away. His day in the spotlight would have to come another time. As he played, he shrugged and smiled.

"Well, you know what they say," he whispered to Ariel, who drummed at his side.

"The show must go on?" Ariel guessed.

"No," Sebastian replied. "A true genius is never fully appreciated in his own lifetime."

16

Pongo Carries a Tune

"I don't know what we're going to do," Roger Radcliffe told his wife, Anita. "We have all these puppies to feed, and I don't have *one* song to sell!"

"Don't worry," Anita told him. "I'm sure you'll be inspired soon."

"I'm glad *you're* sure!" said Roger. "Because all I've got is a bunch of used paper." He pointed to the overflowing wastebasket.

"Don't give up," said Anita. "I know that you can do it."

After Anita left, Pongo watched his pet pace in front of his piano.

"Pongo, old boy, I must have written ten songs in ten days. But they're all terrible," said Roger, pointing to the wastebasket. "What am I going to do?"

Pongo wanted to help his pet, but he didn't know how.

That night, Pongo talked to Perdy about Roger's dilemma. They sat in the middle of the living room, surrounded by puppies.

"Roger has already written ten songs," explained Pongo. "He just doesn't think they're good enough to sell. But I know they are – I've heard him play them, and you don't have a songwriter for a pet without developing a good ear for hit songs. The songs are right upstairs, stuffed inside his wastebasket."

Perdy saw what he was thinking.

"Do you know the way to the music publisher?" she asked.

Pongo nodded. "I've taken Roger for walks there dozens of times."

"I think you should try it," said Perdy.

After Roger and Anita had gone to sleep, Pongo padded into the music room and gathered up the sheet music from the wastebasket. Then he sneaked out of the house, carrying the music to the publisher's office. Pongo pushed all the pages under the door, then trotted back home.

The next day, the phone rang. Roger answered.

"You what?" Roger said into the receiver. "You did ... ? But how did you ... ? Oh, I see ... well, thank you. Thank you!"

Anita rushed over. "Who was that?"

"My music publisher," said Roger. "He's buying ten of my songs."

"Ten songs!" cried Anita. "I thought you didn't even have *one* to sell."

Roger scratched his head in confusion. "I didn't think I did."

"So, what happened?" asked Anita.

Perdy looked at Pongo and barked. Her husband could carry a tune too – all the way across town to Roger's publisher!

Tangled

Once Upon a Flower

Once upon a time, in a land far away, a single drop of sunlight fell to the ground. It grew into a magical golden flower with special healing powers.

The only person who knew the location of the flower was a vain and selfish old woman named Mother Gothel.

Mother Gothel kept the flower secret. She used it to keep herself looking young and beautiful.

As centuries passed, a glorious kingdom was built close to the cliff where the flower grew. The forever youthful Mother Gothel watched from the shadows – guarding her precious flower from the people of the kingdom.

One day the kingdom's beloved queen fell gravely ill. Everyone in the kingdom wanted to help. They had heard stories about a magical flower with healing powers.

The people of the kingdom searched far and wide – until, at last, they found the magical golden flower.

As Mother Gothel looked on in horror, a royal guard dug up the flower and took it back to the palace.

The Queen drank a potion containing the flower, and instantly recovered! Soon after, she gave birth to a beautiful baby girl.

The King and Queen, and the whole kingdom, launched flying lanterns into the sky to celebrate the Princess's birth.

One night an aged and vengeful Mother Gothel crept into the nursery. While she stroked the baby's hair and sang softly, Mother Gothel became young again! The flower's magic lived in the baby's hair!

Mother Gothel greedily cut off a lock of the baby's hair – but the hair instantly lost its power and turned brown. The only way Mother Gothel could remain young was to keep the child with her, always. She snatched the baby and vanished into the night.

Everyone in the kingdom searched, but no one could find the Princess.

The King and Queen were heartbroken. But they remained hopeful that one day their daughter would return to them. Each year on the Princess's birthday, they released lanterns into the night sky.

They hoped their light would guide their daughter home....

But Mother Gothel was raising the Princess, who she named Rapunzel, in a high tower in a hidden valley. She loved the girl only for her hair and treated Rapunzel as a prized possession.

Would Rapunzel ever be able to return to the kingdom where she belonged?

A Winter's Tale

One bright, sunny January day, Winnie the Pooh was trudging through the Hundred-Acre Wood on his way to visit his good friend Piglet. Piglet was ill in bed with the sniffles. Overnight it had snowed heavily, and the woods were blanketed in beautiful, fluffy snow.

"Poor Piglet," Pooh said with a sigh. "What a shame he can't come outside to play in this lovely snow." His boots crunched on for a few more steps, and then the bear of very little brain came up with a perfectly wonderful idea. "I know!" he exclaimed. "I will bring some snow to Piglet!" He scooped up a mittenful of snow and formed a snowball. He dropped it into his pocket, and then he made another, and then another. Soon he had three snowballs in each pocket, and another on top of his head, underneath his hat. He hurried on to Piglet's house. When he was nearly there, he passed Tigger, Rabbit, Roo and Eeyore, heading the other way.

"Hello, Pooh!" called Roo. "Come and build a snowman with us!"

"I'm sorry, but I can't," said Pooh wistfully. "You see, I am bringing some snowballs to Piglet, who is sick in bed with the sniffles." He said goodbye and hurried on his way.

Piglet was indeed not well, but he was very happy to see his friend. "Hello, Booh," he said snuffily. "I'b glad you cabe. *Ah-choo!*"

"Poor Piglet," said Pooh. "I'll make tea." He was just putting the kettle on when a large drop of icy water rolled out from underneath his hat and down his nose. This reminded Pooh of something.

"I brought you a present, Piglet!" he cried, snatching off his hat. But there was nothing there. Puzzled, Pooh ran to his jacket, which he had hung on a hook near the door. There were no snowballs in either of the pockets! But there was a sizeable puddle of water on the floor underneath Pooh's coat.

"I don't understand it!" Pooh remarked, scratching his head. "I brought you some snowballs, but they seem to have disappeared."

"Oh d-d-d-dear," Piglet said with a sigh. "Well, thanks for thinkig aboud be. I do wish I could go outside and blay. Could you bull back the curtains so that I can see the snow?"

Pooh hopped up and did what his friend had asked. Both of them gasped when they looked outside.

There, just below Piglet's window, Tigger, Rabbit, Eeyore and Roo had built a beautiful snowman, just for Piglet!

"Oh, friends are wonderbul!" Piglet said happily. "*Ah-choo!*"

Snow White
and the Seven Dwarfs

A Bedtime Story

It was bedtime in the little cottage in the woods. Snow White kissed each Dwarf goodnight and tucked them into bed.

"Wait! Wait!" called out Happy before she blew out the candle. "Please tell us a story!"

"Very well," said Snow White, smiling. She settled down at the foot of the beds and began....

"Once upon a time, there lived a happy little princess – or rather, a mostly happy little princess, but for a single person: her stepmother, the Queen."

"Bah!" grumbled Grumpy with a sneer.

Snow White sighed. "You see, no matter what the Princess did – no matter how hard she worked or how good she tried to be – the Queen did everything in her power to make her sad."

"Poor Princess," murmured Bashful.

"Oh, but don't worry," Snow White assured him. "Mostly, the Princess was jolly! She found that if she whistled and sang while she worked, her work would fly by and her mood would be sunny. And then, there were always her daydreams – for she truly believed that if she wished for something hard enough, it surely would come true."

"What did sh ... she ... *ah-choo!* ... wish for?" asked Sneezy.

"Well," began Snow White, "for one thing,

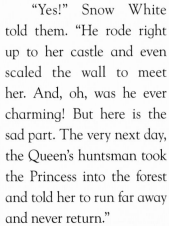

she wished for a charming and dashing prince to find her and whisk her away. And then, one day, a prince did find her!"

"Really?" exclaimed the Dwarfs.

"Yes!" Snow White told them. "He rode right up to her castle and even scaled the wall to meet her. And, oh, was he ever charming! But here is the sad part. The very next day, the Queen's huntsman took the Princess into the forest and told her to run far away and never return."

"So, did she?" Sleepy asked sleepily.

"Yes," Snow White replied. "She ran until she could run no farther. Only then did she realize she was terribly lost and lonely – with no friend in the world and no place to go."

"Poor Princess," whispered Bashful.

"That's what the Princess thought too," Snow White said. "For just a minute. But then she discovered she wasn't alone at all. There were chipmunks and squirrels and deer and rabbits and birds ... all sorts of forest creatures there to help her. They took her to the sweetest little cottage you ever did see, and the most faithful friends a princess could ever have."

"And what happened next?" asked Grumpy.

"Well, they lived happily ever after, of course!" Snow White replied. "What did you think?"

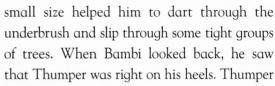

The Race

"Good morning, young Prince," Thumper greeted Bambi one bright winter day.

"Good morning, Thumper," Bambi said.

"I have a great idea, Bambi. Let's have a race," Thumper said. "We'll start from here." He drew a line in the dirt. "And whoever makes it to that big pine tree over there first, wins the race."

"But it would be silly for us to race," Bambi told his friend.

"Why's that?" Thumper asked, confused.

"Because I'll win," Bambi said.

"What makes you so sure?" Thumper challenged, puffing up his chest.

"Because I'm bigger and faster than you," Bambi explained.

"If you're so sure you'll win," Thumper said, "why are you afraid to race me?"

Bambi paused to think about this. He didn't want to hurt the little rabbit's feelings. "Fine," he said at last. "Let's race!"

"Great!" Thumper exclaimed. "Ready?"

"Ready!" Bambi said.

"Okay," Thumper said, crouching down. Bambi crouched down too. "On your marks. Get set. Go!" cried Thumper.

They both took off as fast as they could. Bambi, with his long legs and big, wide stride, immediately took the lead. But Thumper's

small size helped him to dart through the underbrush and slip through some tight groups of trees. When Bambi looked back, he saw that Thumper was right on his heels. Thumper took the opportunity to hop past Bambi. Bambi paused to jump over a tree that had been knocked down, blocking the path. Thumper was able to wriggle under it. He popped up in front of Bambi and took the lead.

Bambi took longer and longer strides, running faster and faster. Soon he had passed Thumper. But, in his hurry to go as fast as he could, he got tangled up in a bush. As Bambi struggled to free himself, Thumper hopped past him again.

They were quickly approaching the big pine tree. Bambi was running as fast as he could, jumping over logs and bushes. Thumper hopped as quickly as his bunny legs would carry him, ducking and weaving through whatever obstacles were in his way. As they crossed the finish line, they were in a neck-and-neck tie.

"See!" Thumper said, panting. "Little guys can keep up!"

"You are absolutely right!" Bambi said, also panting.

And the two friends, both winners, sat down together to catch their breath.

The Missing Slipper

"Oh, what a lovely morning!" cried Cinderella as she sat up in her bed in the royal palace. The sun was shining. The birds were singing. And the delicious smell of freshly baked cinnamon buns was drifting up from the royal kitchen.

"Mmm, breakfast," said Cinderella. She smiled down at the mice gathered on her satin bedspread. Then she stretched over and slipped on the dressing gown that lay at the foot of her bed. "Now, where are those slippers ... ?"

"Here's one, Cinderelly!" said Jaq, jumping down to drag a silvery bedroom slipper closer to Cinderella's foot.

"Thank you, Jaq, dear," said Cinderella as she slid her toes inside. "But ... where's the other one?"

Jaq turned and looked around. "I don't see it, Cinderelly!" Quickly, he bent down and peeked under the bed. Still nothing. Uh-oh!

"Mert! Bert!" Jaq shouted to his friends. "Has anybody seen Cinderelly's slipper?"

The other mice shrugged and shook their heads.

"Don't tell me I've lost my slipper," Cinderella said with a sigh. "Not again!"

"Don't worry, Cinderelly," a mouse named Suzy told her. "We'll find it."

Together, Cinderella and her friends searched her room from top to bottom. They peered under tables, behind bookcases, inside wardrobes and dressing tables – everywhere a missing slipper could possibly be.

"I'm beginning to think it walked away," Cinderella said sadly.

"Hmm," said Jaq. "That slipper was here last night...." Suddenly Jaq stopped. "Gus-Gus!" he exclaimed, smacking his forehead. "That's right!"

"What's right?" said Cinderella.

"Follow me, Cinderelly," Jaq said.

With one slipper on, Cinderella followed Jaq as he tiptoed across the room and nodded towards a little mousehole. "Look here, Cinderelly," he said.

Curious, Cinderella knelt down and peered inside ... and sure enough, there was her missing slipper – with a soundly sleeping Gus nestled cosily inside.

"Oh," said Cinderella, "what a little dear."

"Wake him up, Cinderelly!" said Jaq.

"Oh, no!" replied Cinderella. "Let's let him sleep."

"But Cinderelly needs her slipper!" he cried.

Cinderella thought for a moment. "Actually, no!" she told her mouse friends as she kicked off her other slipper. "I've just decided it's the perfect day for breakfast in bed!"

Sleepless Beauty

"Oh, there, there, little Aurora. There, there," cooed Flora, trying to calm the crying, fussy baby princess. Flora and her fellow fairies, Fauna and Merryweather, stood huddled over the cradle of tiny Aurora and looked down anxiously and helplessly at their royal charge.

But Aurora's cries only grew louder. In fact, she had not stopped crying since the three fairies had arrived with the baby earlier that day at the secluded cottage in the woods.

"Oh, goodness!" cried Fauna. "What have we got ourselves into? We promised the King and Queen that we would hide Aurora out here in the woods, and raise her without magic. But we don't know the first thing about taking care of human babies!"

Flora gave Fauna a comforting pat on the back. "Now, now, don't panic, Fauna," Flora said. "It may be harder than we expected. But this is the only way to keep the Princess safe from Maleficent."

Merryweather and Fauna knew Flora was right. So, one after another, they tried different things to get the baby to stop crying and go to sleep.

"Well," said Flora, "fairy babies are soothed by a sprig of dandelion root placed in their cradle. Let's try that!" Flora hurried out of the cottage and returned minutes later with the sprig. She laid it at the baby's feet.

But the baby cried on. "Perhaps she needs to be entertained!" suggested Fauna.

So, Flora, Fauna and Merryweather locked arms and danced a little jig. They kept it up for quite a while, until they were out of breath. But baby Aurora took no notice and carried on crying.

"Come on," Fauna said to the others, "let's use a little magic. Just to help her sleep. I can't bear to see her so upset!"

"It's too dangerous!" cried Merryweather.

"Oh, fiddle-faddle!" shouted Fauna, who began to wave her wand over the sleeping child.

Just then, Fauna accidentally nudged Aurora's cradle, causing it to rock gently back and forth. Soothed by the rocking, the baby's cries slowly grew softer and softer.

"Fauna!" cried Flora. "You've done it!"

"Look how much she likes the rocking!" added Merryweather.

So, the three fairies continued to rock the cradle gently back and forth, and soon Aurora drifted off to sleep.

"Well," Fauna whispered to the others, once the baby was sleeping soundly, "that wasn't so hard, now, was it?"

Where's Pluto?

"**M**innie!" cried Mickey over the phone. "Goofy promised to walk Pluto while I'm at my dentist's appointment but he hasn't arrived yet. Can you come over?"

"Sure," Minnie said.

Minnie and Pluto were playing in the park when Daisy came along, then the three of them headed back to Mickey's house together.

Then there was a cry.

"Help! My cat is stuck in a tree!" cried Mickey's neighbour, dragging Minnie and Daisy away.

"Wait," Minnie cried. "What about Pluto?"

"Your dog?" said the neighbour. "He can't come – poor Fluffy will never come down!"

"We won't be long," Minnie promised Pluto, hooking his lead to a tree.

But when Minnie and Daisy got back a little later, Pluto was gone! He'd been dognapped!

Minnie and Daisy raced down the street, questioning everyone they met.

"I passed a dog with a man in a red hat," said an elderly man. "They went that way."

Minnie and Daisy raced away and found a man in a red hat walking a bulldog.

"That's not Pluto," Daisy cried. "We forgot to say that he's a golden-brown dog."

"You're looking for a golden-brown dog?" asked a girl. "One was tied to a postbox, over there."

Minnie and Daisy ran towards the postbox.

"It's got to be Pluto," Daisy cried. "How many golden-brown dogs could there be around here?"

Daisy and Minnie turned the corner and saw that the dog had golden-brown fur, but he wasn't Pluto.

"Well, there are at least two golden-brown dogs around here," said Minnie.

Minnie asked a passing postman if he'd seen a dog with golden-brown fur.

The postman nodded. "I saw one dog. The guy walking him was carrying a yellow ball and they were heading to the park."

"A yellow ball!" Daisy exclaimed. "The dognapper stole Pluto's toy, too!"

"I think I know who took Pluto," Minnie said to Daisy as they ran.

Sure enough, there was Pluto, with ... Goofy!

"Goofy was the dognapper," said Minnie.

"Dognapper?" Goofy asked.

"We thought someone had stolen Pluto from Mickey's garden," Minnie said.

"Gawrsh, sorry," Goofy said. "I saw Pluto tied to that tree and figured he was waiting for me. I promised to walk him, but I was late."

"How did you work it out?" Daisy asked.

"A dognapper wouldn't take the ball," Minnie said. "But a dog walker would!"

Pluto barked and Minnie laughed. "That's Pluto's way of saying that three dog walkers are better than one."

ALICE
in
WONDERLAND

A Tiny Tale

One day, Alice was sitting in the garden, listening to her older sister read a book out loud. It was lesson time and, as her sister's voice droned on about the ancient Greeks, Alice's mind wandered. She wondered if it was nearly teatime. She had smelled scones baking earlier, and her stomach rumbled in anticipation. She watched a little caterpillar climb a blade of grass, its tiny body scrunching and straightening as it moved up the leaf.

"What must it be like to be as tiny as that?" Alice wondered to herself.

The next thing she knew, she *was* that tiny! In an instant, the garden had grown higher and higher until the grass towered over her head, as tall as trees. The caterpillar, now half as long as Alice, waved its antennae at her and continued its climb.

"Oh, my!" cried Alice. "I must get back to the house. If I don't start out now, I shall never be back in time for tea!" She began to make her way through the forest of grass, until she arrived at the garden path. The path, which formerly had seemed to slope ever so gently, now appeared as a mountain in front of her, and the house was not even visible.

"I shall never get home in time for ... *WHOOPS*!" Alice felt herself suddenly on her back, travelling feet first up the path.

She looked down and gasped. Three ants were carrying her on their backs! "Put me down at once!" she said to them crossly, but the ants took no notice of her. With a quick twist of her body, she managed to tumble to the ground. The ants appeared not to realize that their load had vanished, and continued up the hill.

"Well, at any rate I am now a good deal closer to home," said Alice, gazing up at her house.

She found herself standing at the edge of a huge puddle. "However shall I get across?" she wondered. Then a large leaf blew off a tree and landed in the puddle directly in front of her. She stepped onto the leaf and let the breeze blow her across. "I am nearly there!" she said triumphantly. But, a moment later, a huge blackbird swooped down and plucked her up by the sleeve of her dress. She felt herself airborne. "Oh, bother, now I shall never get home for tea," she said.

The next thing she knew, her sister was plucking her sleeve. "Wake up, Alice! You've fallen asleep again!" With an exasperated sigh, her sister stood up. "We may as well end the lesson for the day, as it's time to go in and have our tea."

Enormously relieved to be her usual size again, Alice followed her sister up the garden path and into the house.

The Mind World

Riley's Five Emotions – Joy, Sadness, Fear, Anger and Disgust – loved working in Headquarters inside Riley's mind. The Emotions helped Riley through every day of her life. They protected her, cared for her and always tried to keep her happy!

Over the years, the shelves in HQ became filled up with coloured memory spheres, which eventually got moved into Riley's Long Term Memory. But when something really important happened to Riley, a special extra-bright memory sphere was created.

These spheres were core memories, and they were stored in the core memory holder inside Headquarters.

Each core memory powered one of Riley's Islands of Personality. Riley had five Islands – Goofball, Friendship, Hockey, Honesty and Family. Each Island was connected to HQ by bridges called lightlines. The Islands were like mini theme parks inside Riley's head, and as long as the core memories stayed in their holder in Headquarters, the Islands of Personality would shine brightly.

Riley loved to mess around and be silly – that's what kept Goofball Island running. Friendship Island was brighter when Riley spent time with her best friend, Meg. Hockey Island was created when Riley scored her first goal playing ice hockey. Riley's parents taught her never to lie and Honesty Island helped her remember this. But Family Island was probably the most important one – there was nothing Riley cared about more than her family. These Islands of Personality made Riley ... Riley!

One night, just after Riley had turned 11 years old, the Emotions in Riley's head gazed at the screen as her parents tucked her into bed.

As Riley fell asleep, the screen went dark.

"Woo-hoo! Another perfect day!" Joy called happily.

"All right, we did not die today," said Fear. "I call that an unqualified success."

Joy looked at the wall of brand-new, happy, golden memories. "Nice job everybody! Now, let's get those memories down to Long Term," she said. Joy pulled a lever and a tube dropped down from the ceiling of Headquarters. The new memories were sucked up the tube, and Joy watched from the window as the colourful spheres were taken out across Riley's Mind World, to be stored in her Long Term Memory.

"We love our girl," Joy continued. "She's got great friends, a great house; things couldn't be better. After all, Riley's 11 now. What could possibly happen?"

Disney · PIXAR
BRAVE

Legends are Lessons

Long ago, there was a kingdom called DunBroch in the Scottish Highlands. Though the kingdom was young, the land was ancient – a place full of magic ... and danger.

King Fergus and Queen Elinor had brought peace to the clans of the kingdom. They were also raising their own clan: triplets (Harris, Hubert and Hamish) and one teenaged, adventurous princess called Merida.

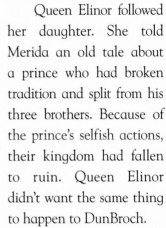

Queen Elinor had high hopes for Merida. She thought a princess should be well rounded ... knowledgeable about her kingdom ... and above all, perfect in every way. In Queen Elinor's eyes, Merida had much to learn.

But Merida lived for her rare days of freedom, when she could grab her bow, climb onto her horse, Angus, and spend the day in the forest. Merida was a skilled archer and rarely missed a shot.

One day, Merida returned to the castle to find her family eating dinner. King Fergus was telling his favourite story: how he had fought a bear called Mor'du and lost his leg! Mor'du hadn't been seen since. They'd all heard the story a hundred times.

Just then, some letters arrived from the lords of three neighbouring clans. At the Queen's invitation, they would each present a son to compete for Merida's hand in marriage!

Merida was horrified. She didn't want to marry!

"I won't go through with it!" she shouted, and ran from the room.

Queen Elinor followed her daughter. She told Merida an old tale about a prince who had broken tradition and split from his three brothers. Because of the prince's selfish actions, their kingdom had fallen to ruin. Queen Elinor didn't want the same thing to happen to DunBroch.

"Legends are lessons," Elinor told Merida. "They ring with truths."

Merida was not convinced. She saw marriage as something that would take away her freedom. She had so many more adventures planned!

"I don't know what to do," Queen Elinor said to King Fergus later. "If only she could try to see that I do this out of love!"

Meanwhile, Merida was complaining to Angus....

"I don't want my life to be over. I want my freedom! I swear, Angus, this isn't going to happen," she vowed.

Merida was determined to follow her own path in life. The last thing she wanted was to be like her mother.

Would Merida ever learn to understand Queen Elinor's point of view?

101 DALMATIANS

Thunderbolt Patch

Every evening, Pongo, Perdita and their 15 Dalmatian puppies would gather around the television to watch the heroic adventures of Thunderbolt the dog. The puppies would stare wide-eyed as Thunderbolt saved the day from all sorts of thieves and villains. Patch wanted to be just like Thunderbolt!

After the programme, it was time for the puppies to go to sleep so Pongo and Perdita could go for a walk with their humans.

But one night, Patch had other ideas. "Can't we stay up a bit longer?" he pleaded.

"It's time for sleep now," Perdita replied, as she and Pongo left for their walk.

But Patch didn't want to go to sleep. He wanted to go on a great adventure, just like Thunderbolt! And when the puppies heard a strange scurrying sound, Patch saw his chance.

"Look!" whispered Patch, pointing to a small mouse sitting near the puppies' basket. "It's a big bad bandit! We've got to catch him!"

The puppies all wanted to play pretend, so they scampered out of bed and sneaked upstairs after the fearsome outlaw.

"Follow me," Patch whispered, pretending to be Thunderbolt. "That nasty scoundrel is heading towards the music room."

Before the puppies could catch the bandit, they heard someone coming up the stairs.

It was Nanny! If she caught the pups, they would be in big trouble.

"Hide," whispered Patch. The pups quickly scampered into the music room and found hiding places.

"Now, what's all this noise?" asked Nanny, looking around the apparently empty room.

As the pups held their breath, Patch spied the scoundrel slipping back downstairs. When the coast was clear, the puppies resumed their chase.

"That burglar must be in here somewhere," said Patch as the puppies searched the empty kitchen.

"There he is!" shouted Rolly, suddenly.

Rolly darted towards the bandit … but he knocked over a bag of flour. The flour covered Rolly, turning him white!

"That pup doesn't have any spots," Patch said, pointing to his brother. "He must be the *REAL* intruder!" Patch pretended.

The puppies all pounced on Rolly, but soon Pepper saw Pongo and Perdita outside.

"Mother and Father are coming!" Pepper exclaimed. "Everyone back to bed!"

"Come along, chaps!" shouted the leader of the pack. "Thunderbolt Patch will save the day!"

When Pongo and Perdita peeked in on their precious puppies, they found them … curled up in bed – just as they had left them!

Disney
MICKEY
& FRIENDS

The Scavenger Hunt

One morning, Minnie found someone had slipped an envelope under her front door!

"What's this?" Minnie wondered, opening it. "A secret scavenger hunt! The first item on the list is a picnic basket."

Minnie opened the cupboard and pulled out a basket and a blanket.

Minnie headed outside and checked the list again. "Item number two: three cucumbers," she read.

Minnie picked the vegetables from her garden and put them in her basket.

Minnie read the next item on her list. "A long stick. There's only one place to go for that!"

Minnie was heading for the woods when she ran into Goofy.

"Hiya," Goofy said. "What are you doing?"

Minnie was about to show Goofy when she remembered that the scavenger hunt was a secret. Then she noticed that Goofy was hiding some blueberries behind his back. Maybe he was part of the scavenger hunt, too!

"Just out for a walk," Minnie replied. "See you later, Goofy!" She hurried off into the woods.

Soon Minnie had found the third item on her list. Then she heard rushing water. "I wonder what that is," she said.

A few minutes later, Minnie reached a stream. Nearby was a patch of plants.

"Strawberries! The next item!" Minnie cried.

The next item on her list was five smooth stones. Minnie waded into the stream and found them in no time.

Minnie had one item left: a yellow flower.

But Minnie had wandered too far into the woods and now she was lost!

"I'll never finish the scavenger hunt if I can't get out of the woods!" she said.

Suddenly, Minnie saw something on the ground. "Blueberries! They must have fallen out of Goofy's bag."

Minnie followed the blueberry trail back to the path – and a daffodil patch!

"A yellow flower!" Minnie cried. "That's the last item on my list!"

Minnie added one to her basket.

As she arrived at the park, Minnie saw her friends appear with their own baskets.

"Surprise!" Mickey cried. "You each had a list of items to collect. Now we can combine them!"

Minnie laid down her blanket. Donald tied balloons to a tree. The friends added the flowers they'd picked to Daisy's vase. Mickey cut up the berries and vegetables for lunch.

Then they played in the park. Donald used Minnie's stick to hit the piñata Mickey had brought. They all played hopscotch with Minnie's stones and Daisy's chalk. Goofy made a funny hat from Donald's newspaper. It was a wonderful party!

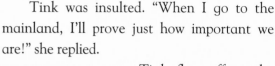

A Tinker's Talent

Tinker Bell had not long arrived in Pixie Hollow and was being shown around her new home. Two fairies named Clank and Bobble couldn't wait to show her all the handy things that tinker fairies made.

Soon Fairy Mary – the no-nonsense fairy who ran Tinkers' Nook – arrived. She noticed the new fairy's dainty hands. "Don't worry, dear, we'll build up those tinker muscles in no time," she exclaimed. Then, after reminding Clank and Bobble to make their deliveries, she was gone.

A little while later, they were on their way, with Cheese the mouse pulling the wagon. There were rainbow tubes for Iridessa – she explained she would roll up rainbows, put them in the tubes, and take them to the mainland.

"What's the mainland?" Tink asked.

"It's where we're going to go for spring, to change the seasons," replied Silvermist.

Next the tinkers stopped at the Flower Meadow, where Vidia was vacuuming the pollen out of flowers with her whirlwind.

"Hi! What's your talent?" Tink asked.

"I am a fast-flying fairy. Fairies of every talent depend on me," answered Vidia. She made it clear that she didn't think much of tinker fairies.

Tink was insulted. "When I go to the mainland, I'll prove just how important we are!" she replied.

Tink flew off to the beach, where she discovered several wonderful treasures buried in the sand! Clank explained these were Lost Things, which washed up on Never Land from time to time. Fairy Mary whisked the trinkets away. The queen's review of the springtime preparations was that night, and there was a lot to do. Tink decided this was her chance to prove to Vidia just how important a tinker's talent really was!

That evening, the Minister of Spring welcomed Queen Clarion to the review ceremony. Suddenly, Tinker Bell interrupted the proceedings. "I came up with some fantastic things for tinkers to use when we go to the mainland!" she told the queen excitedly.

Tink pulled a homemade paint sprayer out of the wagon and demonstrated it on a flower that needed colouring. But it exploded!

"Has no one explained?" Queen Clarion said gently. "Tinker fairies don't go to the mainland. The nature-talent fairies do all of those things. I'm sorry."

From this moment, Tinker Bell decided she would change her fairy talent for good.

An Excellent Cook

After returning to her cosy home, Tiana decided to help her father, James, cook dinner. Her father was an excellent cook, and just like James, the little girl loved to cook.

"What are you going to make for us, sweetheart?" asked her mother.

"Gumbo!" replied Tiana. This was her father's speciality. He even had an enormous pot, which he kept especially for his gumbo! So little Tiana sat perched on a stool stirring, seasoning and tasting! "I think it's done," Tiana announced and watched her father anxiously as he took a spoonful.

"Let's see," said James, as he put the spoon to his mouth. "Delicious, sweetheart! This is the BEST gumbo I've ever tasted!" He then gave it to Tiana's mother to taste, who also thought it was delicious!

"You have a gift, Tiana! A gift this special just has to be shared!"

And with that, the family invited the neighbours to enjoy the gumbo on the porch outside. The night air filled with the sounds of clinking spoons, conversation and laughter.

"You see," said Tiana's father, "food brings folks together from all walks of life. It warms them right up and puts smiles on their faces."

When bedtime arrived, Tiana's mother and father came to tuck her in. Tiana pointed at a star that was shining much brighter than all the other stars in the sky.

"I was told that if we wish hard enough, the Evening Star will make our dearest wishes come true."

Both of her parents encouraged the little girl to wish on the Evening Star. "But remember," added James, "you've got to help it along with some hard work of your own." Then, thinking of the night filled with good food, family and friends, he said, "Just never lose sight of what's really important."

Tiana looked at the picture that her father had once given her. It was of a beautiful restaurant. It was her father's dream to open a restaurant in the old sugar mill. Well, now it was Tiana's dream too, and she was ready to work hard to achieve their dream, with the help of the Evening Star.

"Our restaurant will be called 'Tiana's Place', and we will serve your gumbo to our customers," said James, giving Tiana a kiss goodnight.

I will make our dream come true! Tiana promised herself as she went to bed that night. She fell asleep peacefully, knowing she would have the courage to succeed.

Tangled
The Girl with the Magic Hair

Rapunzel's hair had magical powers. Upon a single touch it could cure an illness or make you young again. This is why Mother Gothel stole the little girl soon after she was born: she needed her hair so that she could stay young forever.

Mother Gothel didn't want Rapunzel to ever leave, so she locked the child away in a tall tower. Mother Gothel brought her up to believe that she was her mother and that the world outside was full of danger.

Rapunzel grew into a beautiful young woman, who loved to fill her time with activities. She played the guitar, brushed her long, long, long hair and did her chores.... But what she liked to do best was paint. She covered the walls with paintings of the countryside and the stars, which she could see from her window.

On the day before her eighteenth birthday, Rapunzel wanted to break her usual routine. Throughout her life, Rapunzel had seen mysterious lights floating up into the night sky on her birthday. She felt they were meant for her. More than anything, she wanted Mother Gothel to take her to see them.

"Rapunzel! Let down your hair!" Mother Gothel called when she arrived at the tower.

"Right away!" The young girl leaned out of the window. She unwound her long hair until it touched the ground. Mother Gothel took hold of it and Rapunzel hoisted her up.

"Pull, pull harder!" It was very difficult, but Rapunzel never complained.

"Hi. Welcome home, Mother!" Rapunzel said as soon as she'd finished pulling her up.

"Oh! Rapunzel, how do you manage to do that every single day without fail?" Mother Gothel asked. "It looks absolutely exhausting, darling!"

"Oh it's nothing, Mother," the young girl replied politely.

"Then I don't know why it takes so long, Rapunzel!" Mother Gothel cried.

Rapunzel was confused. Was Mother Gothel joking? There was a moment's silence.

"Come now, dearest! I'm just teasing!" Mother Gothel finally said, laughing.

Phew! Rapunzel thought. *Because, if Mother Gothel hadn't been joking, it really would have been unfair!*

Sometimes, Rapunzel didn't understand Mother Gothel's jokes. But she loved her mother very much all the same.

Rapunzel took a deep breath, ready to ask Mother Gothel for the one thing she wanted more than anything....

The Beast and the Witches

The Beast stood in his garden. His mind was filled with images of the beautiful young woman inside his castle: Belle, so brave and noble – willing to take her father's place as a prisoner in the castle dungeon. What sort of woman would do that – sacrifice her freedom for his?

He stood staring at the castle, trying to recall how it had looked back before the witches' curse. It was like a prison to him now. When he was human, he had spent

much of his time stalking wild beasts for sport, for fun. But since he had been turned into something to be hunted, he had shut himself away. Only now his fate was in Belle's hands.

He heard the odd sisters approach. They were an indistinguishable trio of witches, each with a little doll-like face and bird-like gestures.

Lucinda was the first to speak. "So, you've managed to capture yourself a pretty little thing at long last."

"We're surprised, Beast," said Martha.

"Yes, surprised," spat Ruby. "We dreamed of hunters tracking you down."

"Why, you're even wearing clothes. Holding on to the last shred of your humanity, are you?" they said in unison.

The Beast did nothing. He wanted to kill the witches and everything else in his path, but he had to keep control.

Martha spoke up again. "Just in case you've forgotten, here are the rules: you must love her, and that love must be returned with true love's kiss."

Lucinda cackled. "It won't be long now...."

"Not long at all, Beast," echoed Martha. "Soon the last petal of the rose will fall and you shall remain in this form with no chance of transformation to your former self."

"And on that day ... we will dance! Dance!" they cried.

The Beast finally spoke. "And what of the others?" He was talking about his servants. "Are they to remain as they are, doomed to enchantment as well?"

Ruby's eyes widened in wonder. "Concern? Is that what we detect? He never used to give them a second thought, unless it was to punish them."

"I think he's afraid of what they might do to him if he doesn't break the curse."

And with that the sisters turned on their heels and clickety-clicked their way out of the garden.

101 DALMATIANS

Rolly's Midnight Snack

"Time for bed!" called Pongo.

"Aw, Dad," complained Patch, "we're not tired!"

"No arguments," said Pongo. "Little puppies need their rest."

With a sigh, Patch joined the line of puppies climbing the staircase.

"I'm hungry," Rolly complained as the puppies settled down for the night.

"You're always hungry," said Patch.

"And you always want to stay awake and have adventures," said Rolly.

Patch sighed. "Too bad we never get what we want."

Hours later, Rolly felt a tap on his shoulder. "Is it morning?" he asked with a yawn.

"No," said Patch. "It's midnight. Wanna explore? I'll get you a snack."

"A snack!" cried Rolly excitedly.

"Shhhhh!" said Patch. "Come on."

Rolly followed Patch to the kitchen.

Patch nodded towards the table. "After dinner, I saw Nanny put some juicy bones up there. She's saving them for tomorrow's soup."

"Soup!" cried Rolly. "What a waste! Bones are for chewing on!"

So, Patch and Rolly came up with a plan.

First, Patch climbed onto Rolly's shoulders to reach the table.

Everything went fine until Patch threw down the first bone and it landed in the dustbin. Rolly took off after it and leaped inside!

Rolly was stuck. Patch tried hard not to panic. He thought and thought until he came up with another plan – a Rescue Rolly Plan!

Patch went upstairs and woke Lucky and Pepper. The two puppies followed Patch into the kitchen. Then Patch found his father's long lead and tossed one end into the dustbin.

"Take hold of the lead!" Patch told Rolly.

"Okay," said Rolly.

Patch turned to the other puppies and said, "Now, let's all pull on this end of the lead, on the count of three."

The three puppies pulled. The dustbin fell over and Rolly tumbled out onto the kitchen floor.

"Thanks!" said Rolly.

The puppies licked their brother, and they all returned to bed.

Before Rolly drifted off to sleep, he whispered to Patch, "Guess you finally got your adventure."

"Yeah," said Patch. "But I'm sorry you didn't get your snack."

"Sure, I did," said Rolly. "While I was waiting for you to rescue me, what do you think I was doing? I was eating that juicy bone. And, boy, was it good!"

Groundhog Day

Winnie the Pooh pounded on Piglet's front door. "Wake up! Wake up!" he called to his friend. "Today is Groundhog Day!"

Piglet dressed quickly and, moments later, the two friends were hurrying to the homes of their other friends who lived in the Hundred-Acre Wood.

"Today is Groundhog Day!" shouted Pooh and Piglet together as they woke Tigger, Rabbit, Owl, Eeyore, Kanga and Roo. Then the whole group proceeded to Christopher Robin's house to wake *him* as well.

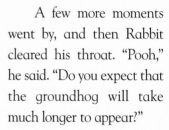

But where are we going to find a groundhog? wondered Piglet. Soon, they arrived at the Thoughtful Spot, and everyone sat down to wait.

"Um, exactly what is it that we are waiting for?" asked Piglet after a few moments.

"Why, groundhogs, of course!" said Pooh.

"But what is it that is supposed to happen on Groundhog Day?" Piglet persisted.

Being a bear of little brain, Pooh was unsure how to answer. He looked expectantly at Christopher Robin.

"There is an old tradition," Christopher Robin began, "that says that 2 February is the day that the groundhog comes out of his hole after a long winter sleep, to look for his shadow. If he sees it, he decides that there will be six more weeks of winter and returns to his hole.

If he doesn't see it, he decides that spring will soon be here, and stays above ground."

"I see," said Pooh, who, truth be told, did not really see at all.

A few more moments went by, and then Rabbit cleared his throat. "Pooh," he said. "Do you expect that the groundhog will take much longer to appear?"

"Oh!" Pooh replied, looking at his friends. "I haven't got the faintest idea how long it will take to see a groundhog, as I don't know any groundhogs personally."

This news came as a bit of a shock to the group. But, all of a sudden, Gopher's head popped up from the ground in front of them.

"Aha!" shouted Pooh triumphantly.

"It's only Gopher," said Rabbit.

"I believe Gopher will do quite nicely today," said Christopher Robin. "Gopher, do you or do you not see your shadow?"

Gopher blinked in the sudden sunshine, then looked down at the ground. "I sssssay," he said. "I ssssuppose I do ssseee my ssshadow."

"Well, that's that, then," said Christopher Robin. "Six more weeks of winter. Thank you very much, Gopher."

"You're welcome," replied Gopher, who seemed a bit confused by the whole thing. "Happy ssspring, everyone!"

Frozen Fjords

On a warm summer's day in the kingdom of Arendelle, the palace gates had been opened for Queen Elsa's coronation. Her sister, Anna, was very excited because it was the first time since childhood that she had been allowed out of the castle, and that visitors had been allowed in.

Anna slipped outside alone. She strolled around the kingdom, exploring every street, meeting new people – she just couldn't understand why the palace gates had always been kept closed.

Suddenly, a handsome man accidentally bumped into her on his horse. He introduced himself as Prince Hans of the Southern Isles and Anna was instantly smitten with him.

At the coronation Elsa had to remove her gloves to hold the royal orb and sceptre. She was worried because, without her gloves, she might lose control of her magical power. She didn't want to freeze the orb and sceptre, but, more importantly, she didn't want anyone to know she could freeze whatever she touched!

Anna stood by Elsa's side, sneaking glances at Hans.

At the Coronation Ball Hans and Anna spent the whole evening laughing, dancing and talking. It was love at first sight ... so they decided to get engaged!

Elsa couldn't believe it. "You can't marry a man you just met," she scoffed.

"You can if it's true love," Anna insisted.

"My answer is no," Elsa said firmly. Now that she was Queen and head of the family, she had the right to stop the marriage.

Elsa started to leave the room, but Anna grabbed her hand – and accidentally pulled off Elsa's glove.

Anna kept arguing. "Why do you always shut me out?" she asked Elsa. "I can't live like this any more!"

"Enough!" Elsa cried. She threw her arms up in frustration, forgetting that Anna had removed her glove. A freezing blast shot from Elsa's bare hand, sending a sheet of ice across the ballroom! Everyone stared in disbelief.

Elsa fled the castle, terrified that she might hurt someone. "Stay away from me," she warned the townspeople.

Everything she touched turned to ice as she ran. Even the fjord froze as she stepped on to the water. All the ships became trapped in the ice as she ran towards the mountains.

The kingdom was in an uproar as ice spread everywhere, but at least Anna finally understood why Elsa had kept herself closed off from everyone for so many years.

It was clear to Anna that she had to follow Elsa. She was concerned for her sister, but also for the kingdom. Anna had to get Elsa to return so she could thaw out everything that she had frozen.

So, Anna set out after her big sister, leaving Hans in charge.

Tink's Trinkets

Tinker Bell had decided she wanted to change her unique fairy talent, so she could visit the mainland. Tinker-talent fairies were not allowed to go. Reluctantly, the other fairies agreed to help. No fairy had ever changed his or her talent before!

Fawn, one of the animal fairies, tried to show Tink how to teach baby birds to fly. Unfortunately, Tink's baby bird seemed terrified. Tink then saw a majestic bird soaring in the sky. She decided she would ask it to help her. But the bird was a hawk!

Tink quickly escaped and flew straight into a fairy called Vidia. They jumped down a tunnel inside a tree. When Vidia reached the end of the chute, she stopped in the nick of time – but Tink accidentally slammed into her and sent Vidia shooting out of the tree. The hawk opened its beak, ready to strike. Luckily, the other fairies were able to chase the bird off, but Vidia was furious, and Tink felt awful.

Tink soon realized her friends didn't want her to change her talent. Desperate, she went to visit the only fairy she thought might be able to help – Vidia.

But Vidia was in a bad mood, and had an idea to get Tink in trouble! She suggested that Tinker Bell prove she was a garden fairy by capturing the unruly Sprinting Thistles.

Tink knew this was her last chance to get to go to the mainland. She tried hard to herd the thistles, but Vidia cheated by blowing open the corral gate. All of the Thistles ran right out. It was a stampede! The Thistles trampled over the carefully organized springtime supplies, and Tink was devastated.

Queen Clarion soon appeared and scolded Tinker Bell. Tink decided she must leave Pixie Hollow forever, but she couldn't go without one last visit to the workshop – she had to admit that she did love to tinker.

At the workshop, Tink noticed some trinkets she had found on her first day in Pixie Hollow. Then, she had an idea....

That night, clever Tink showed the Queen how she had designed speedy machines using the trinkets, to fix what the Thistles had trampled. Vidia was furious!

Queen Clarion looked sharply at Vidia and sent her to capture the Thistles. The other fairies worked all night using Tink's machines. By morning, the fairies had more springtime supplies than they had ever seen! The fairies cheered.

"You did it, Tinker Bell," congratulated Queen Clarion.

Cowgirl Minnie

Minnie was excited – she, Mickey and Goofy were going to the Lucky Star Dude Ranch for a few days!

Goofy was excited about riding a horse. As soon as they reached the ranch, he hopped on the first horse he saw. But he jumped on it backwards!

"Uh-oh!" Goofy cried as the horse bucked.

Luckily, Minnie had brought some carrots to feed the horses. She held one out and the horse happily trotted over to it.

"Thank goodness you were here!" Goofy gasped.

The owner of the ranch came out to meet them. "Howdy, cowgirl," he said to Minnie. "I'm Cowboy Bob. How 'bout we get you up on that horse?"

In no time Minnie was riding like a pro!

"Cowboy Bob, can you teach me how to lasso?" Goofy asked.

"Sure," Cowboy Bob said. "Just swing the rope over your head, aim and then let go!"

Goofy followed Cowboy Bob's instructions. "I'm going to lasso that post," he said.

Goofy whirled the lasso and let go. But he lassoed his foot!

"You could use some more practice, Goofy," Mickey said.

Minnie giggled. "Mickey and I are going for a ride. See you when you get yourself untangled."

For three days, Minnie, Mickey and Goofy learned how to be cowboys. On their last morning at the ranch, Minnie and Goofy watched a rodeo.

"I wonder where Mickey is," said Minnie. "He really wanted to see this!"

But Mickey was asleep! Then the noisy crowd woke him up and he looked at the time. He had to hurry or he would miss all the fun!

Mickey quickly raced across a field, jumped over a fence … and landed on a bucking bronco in the middle of the rodeo!

Everyone cheered as Mickey held on tightly. "This is sort of fun!" he cried.

As Mickey waved his hat to the crowd, the announcer called out, "Mickey has just broken the ranch record for the longest-ever bronco ride!"

Just then, the bronco bucked and Mickey slid off him.

"We have to help Mickey!" Minnie cried.

"I'll lasso it for you, Mickey!" shouted Goofy. But instead of lassoing the bronco, he lassoed Mickey!

Meanwhile, Minnie led the bronco safely back to his stall.

The crowd cheered as Cowboy Bob presented the rodeo ribbons.

Minnie won for taking care of the horses. Mickey won for his bronco riding. And Goofy won for trying to lasso everything in sight!

That night, the friends sat by the campfire. "This has been so much fun," Minnie said.

Just then, she spotted a shape against the moon. "Look, a coyote! Now I really feel like a cowgirl!"

The Induction

Nemo still had a satisfied smile on his face from the previous night's induction ceremony. I'm part of the club! he thought.

"So, Shark Bait, what did you think of the ceremony?" Gill asked.

"It was the best!" Nemo exclaimed.

"If only we could get Flo to be part of the ceremony," Deb mused. "But she never seems to want to come out at night."

"So, kid, what was your favourite part?" Jacques wanted to know.

"I think my favourite part was swimming to the top of Mount Wanna ... wannaha ... ha ..." Nemo tried unsuccessfully to pronounce it.

"Wannahockaloogie," Bloat said.

"Yeah," Peach reminisced. "I have a soft spot for my first climb too."

"I wonder," Nemo said. "Who came up with that name?"

Bubbles pointed at Gurgle, who pointed at Bloat, who pointed at Peach, who pointed at Deb, who pointed at Flo.

Deb shrugged. "I guess we came up with it together," she said.

"Why do they call it the Ring of Fire if there's no fire?" Nemo asked.

"Well, you see, it's like this – I don't know," Peach had to admit.

"But who made it up, then?" Nemo asked.

"I think Bubbles came up with the Ring of Fire," Gurgle offered.

"Aren't they beautiful?" Bubbles mused.

"I find it very unsanitary to swim through others' bubbles," Gurgle complained. "Which is why I came up with the chanting part of the ceremony. It's very cleansing both for the body and the mind, and circulates carbon dioxide through the gills."

"That makes sense," Nemo agreed, although it really didn't.

"And don't forget about the kelp fronds," Peach piped up.

"Oh, there's no big secret there," Deb confided. "I just like giving a good whack with the old kelp fronds every now and then." And she demonstrated by whacking Bloat, who immediately began to swell up.

"Was that really necessary?" Bloat asked as he floated away.

"What can I do in the next ceremony?" Nemo asked eagerly.

"Hopefully, we won't have another one. Not if we break out of here first, Shark Bait," Gill answered.

"Well, you never know," Deb said forlornly. "Maybe Flo will come around."

Everyone rolled their eyes at that, including Nemo.

Making Dreams Come True

Tiana lived in New Orleans in the 1920s. She was a very pretty and clever young girl. She hadn't had the good fortune to be born as rich as her best friend Charlotte, but she had inherited her father's gift for cooking.

Even though her father had passed away, she still wanted to make their dream come true for both of them – Tiana was determined to open the restaurant they had always dreamed of owning.

But Tiana didn't have much time for fun. She worked hard as a waitress, trying to earn as much money as she could. She hoped to one day buy the building she'd found that would house the restaurant of her dreams.

One morning, Tiana was serving breakfast at Duke's Diner when Charlotte's father, Big Daddy, came in for a bite to eat.

"Good morning Mr La Bouff!" Tiana greeted him. "And congratulations – I hear you were voted king of the Mardi Gras parade!"

"Caught me completely by surprise ... for the fifth year in a row!" chuckled Charlotte's father. "Now, how about I celebrate with –"

"Some beignets?" guessed Tiana, with a full plate already perched on her arm. "They've just come out of the oven!"

Just then, Charlotte burst into the restaurant. "Oh, Tia! Have you heard the news? Prince Naveen of Maldonia is coming to New Orleans!"

Charlotte showed Tiana a picture of an attractive young man, adding, "And Big Daddy invited him to our masquerade ball tonight!"

Charlotte's eyes shone with excitement. She would do anything to become a princess ... including marrying the first prince that came along!

"That's wonderful, Charlotte," said Tiana. "I've got a little word of advice – my mother always says that the quickest way to a man's heart is through his stomach!"

The girl turned to her father who was busy feasting on beignets. He looked as if he was in heaven. Her friend was right!

"You're a true genius, Tiana! I am going to order five hundred of your man-catching beignets for this evening!"

Charlotte handed her a bundle of notes, and Tiana almost exploded with happiness. This was enough to finally allow her to make the first payment on her restaurant!

It just shows, she thought. *Charlotte and I have very different dreams ... but they might each help the other to come true!*

Disney
THE
LION KING

Tag!

Early one morning, Simba woke up ready to find Nala and continue their game of Tag. The night before, when their mothers had made them stop ("Time for bed, Simba!" "Time for bed, Nala!"), Simba had been It – which is a terrible way to go to bed! – and he was eager to tag Nala and make *her* It as soon as possible. But, when he arrived at the pride's meeting place, everyone, it seemed, was there except for Nala.

"Where's Nala?" he asked his mother.

"Oh, I heard her mother say she wasn't feeling well," she replied. "So they're staying in the cave and resting until she's better."

"But she has to come out," protested Simba. "I'm It and I have to tag somebody!"

His mother smiled. "I'm afraid you'll just have to wait, little Simba," she said.

"But that's so boring!" Simba groaned.

"You can play by yourself, Simba," she reminded him.

"Aw, all right." Simba sighed. First, he tried hunting grasshoppers. But they jumped so high and so far – and so fast! – he soon grew tired and frustrated.

Then he tried climbing trees. But the birds didn't much like a lion cub messing around among their branches and shooed him away.

Finally, he tried just lying down and finding pictures in the clouds. But that was Nala's favourite game, and it made him miss her.

He rolled over and swatted a bright wildflower with his paw. "Tag, you're It," he said half-heartedly. Then, suddenly, an idea popped into his head. What if he picked some wildflowers and took them to his sick friend? It might even make her feel better!

With newfound energy, Simba picked as many flowers as he could carry in his mouth and made his way back to the pride's cave.

"Dees ah fur Nana," he said, dropping the flowers at Nala's mother's feet. "These are for Nala," he repeated. "I hope she feels better really soon."

"Oh, thank you, Simba," the lioness said. "But why don't you give them to her yourself? She seems to be feeling much better. Nala!" she called. And out came Simba's friend, smiling and looking very glad to see him.

She sniffed at the pretty flowers. "Are these for me? Gee, thanks, Simba." Then she turned to her mother. "Can I go out and play with Simba now, Mama?"

"I don't see why not," said her mother.

"Grrreat!" said Nala.

"Yeah, grrreat!" said Simba. Then he reached out and gently tapped her with his paw. "Tag! You're It!"

Cinderella

Dear Sisters

"I had the strangest dream," Cinderella told her mouse friends one morning while she was getting ready for another day of drudgery. "My Fairy Godmother sprinkled happy dust over Anastasia and Drizella, and they were so nice to me."

"But that was only a dream," Jaq warned her.

"I know," Cinderella told him, "but it was so nice, that I think I'll try to pretend that it really happened. Whenever they're horrid to me, I'll pretend they actually said something sweet and kind."

"They don't seem so sweet and kind to me," Jaq told Gus as the three went downstairs. Gus nodded in agreement.

"Wash my dresses." Drizella threw her laundry at Cinderella.

"And polish my shoes." Anastasia opened her wardrobe door. "All of them."

"Do the dishes!"

"And mop the floor!"

"Draw the curtains!"

"And clean the rugs!"

"Right away, sisters!" Cinderella sang out, as sweet as you please. "Thank you!"

All day long, Drizella and Anastasia barked orders at Cinderella. But, no matter what they asked her to do, Cinderella always sang back, "Right away, sisters!" or "You're too kind!"

Finally, Anastasia pulled Drizella aside.

"No matter what we tell Cinderella to do, she stays happy," Anastasia said. "She acts like we're doing her a favour. It's making me nervous!"

"Do you think she's gone mad?" Drizella asked. Anastasia looked worried. "She could be! Who knows just what she's capable of!"

Just then, Cinderella walked in. She stopped, surprised to see her stepsisters looking at her as though she were crazy.

"Why, my dear sisters, whatever can be the matter? I do hope you're not ill," she said.

"D-d-d-dear sisters?" quavered Anastasia. "You called us your dear sisters?" She and Drizella edged towards the door.

"Of course," said Cinderella. "I adore you both. I'm the luckiest girl in the world to have such kind, caring siblings."

That did it. Convinced that Cinderella had lost her mind, the two stepsisters turned and ran. Cinderella listened as her sisters' doors slammed shut. Then she smiled at Gus and Jaq, who had been watching the whole time.

"They may not actually be caring or good-natured," Cinderella said to the mice, "but they'll be too frightened to come out of their rooms for at least a few hours. Who's up for a game of hide-and-seek while we've got the run of the house?"

The mice squeaked happily, and the friends spent a lovely afternoon together while Anastasia and Drizella cowered under their beds.

Carl and Ellie's House

After their first meeting, Carl and Ellie became best friends. Every day they would meet at Ellie's clubhouse to play and dream together about exploring the world.

One sunny morning, they decided there was no two ways about it — one day, they would go to South America and live next to Paradise Falls.

The years passed and Ellie grew up to be a cheerful and rather talkative young woman. Carl grew into a dependable and quiet young man.

Their friendship grew into love, and they got married when they were both aged 19. They bought the little empty house they had played in as children and set up home there.

Of course, the old house needed doing up! Ellie busied herself filling in the holes in the roof and Carl fixed a new weather vane.

They also patched up the walls, the windows and the floors. Finally, they painted the whole house in bright colours, exactly as it looked in Ellie's adventure book.

One morning, the only thing left was the letterbox. Ellie decided to paint it, but she had hardly given the metal its first lick of colour when Carl leant carelessly against it!

Ellie burst out laughing at the big mark left by his hand. She then pressed her own hand to the side of the box. When she lifted it off, the two prints seemed to be joining as if to hold hands....

To earn enough money for their journey to South America, the couple found jobs at the town zoo. Ellie looked after the animals and Carl sold balloons to the children.

When they returned home in the evening, they were pleased to get back to their pretty house.

Ellie painted a superb picture of Paradise Falls, which she stuck above the fireplace. In front of it she placed a piece of pottery and a small statue of a tropical bird.

Carl added a pair of binoculars and his *Spirit of Adventure* model. Then he put a jar on a table in which, every month, they put aside some money for their trip.

Unfortunately, whatever they managed to save steadily disappeared! They had to buy new tyres for the car, pay for a plaster cast for Carl and then replace the roof of the house.

But over the years they continued to dream, enjoy themselves and, in the evenings, dance together in their lounge.

Neither of them was worried. They knew that one day they'd leave and live out their big adventure.

Beauty and the Beast

The Curse

To hear the sisters tell the tale of the curse would be to hear a story filled with examples of what a terrible person the Beast had been. But for him times had been good. He was just an arrogant young prince who loved hunting, drinking and stealing kisses from ladies. If he wasn't in the forest, he was in the tavern.

"Drinks are on me tonight!" his friend Gaston had shouted. "To celebrate the prince's engagement!"

But not long after, Gaston found out that the prince's fiancée, Circe, was secretly from a poor farming family. At first the prince didn't believe him. No pig farmer's daughter could be as beautiful and well dressed as Circe. But Gaston kept on. So they rode to the farmhouse, and there was Circe, standing in the pen feeding the pigs.

The prince was enraged. "How dare you keep such a thing from me!"

Circe crumpled in tears. "You never asked about my background! Why should it matter? We love each other!"

"Love you? Look at yourself – covered in muck! How could I possibly love you? Come on, Gaston, let's leave this place."

And the two men rode off, their horses kicking up dust which covered the poor maiden.

That evening, Circe went to see him.

The prince sighed with annoyance when he saw her looking so pathetic, holding a single red rose. Her eyes were red from crying and she had a ratty shawl round her shoulders that made her look like an old beggar woman.

Her small voice was hoarse from crying. "Surely you didn't mean the things you said to me."

"I cannot marry you, Circe," he said.

When Circe looked up at him, her shawl fell back and her face was no longer splotched and red from crying. Her skin glowed like moonlight and her hair shimmered like stardust.

Then voices climbed out of the darkness:

"Farmer's daughter?"

"Our little sister?"

"Why, she is of royal blood."

Circe's witch sisters stepped into the light and stood behind her.

"I see now you only loved my beauty," said Circe. "And I will ensure no woman will ever want you! Not as long as you remain tainted by vain cruelty."

She handed the prince the single red rose. "Since you would not take this token of love from the woman you professed to cherish, let it then be a symbol of your doom...."

Disney

Lady and the TRAMP

A Lady's Touch

Late one night, Lady's ears perked up and her eyes flew open with a start. The baby was crying! Lady had grown to love the new baby in the house, and she was very protective of him. If he was crying, she was going to find out why. She climbed out of her basket, pushed open the swinging door with her nose and tiptoed up the front stairs.

Meanwhile, Jim Dear and Darling were trying to calm the baby. "Oh, Jim, I just don't know what's the matter with him!" said Darling. She was holding the baby in her arms, trying to rock him and soothe him, but his little face was a deep red and covered with tears. Jim Dear sat groggily at the edge of the bed and looked at his wife helplessly.

"Well, we know he isn't hungry," said Jim Dear, "since we've just given him a bottle." He massaged his temples as though they hurt. Then he noticed Lady, who had walked tentatively into the bedroom. "Hello, Lady," he said to her.

Lady took a few steps closer to the cradle, where Darling was laying the baby down. His little fists were closed tight, and his shrieks had turned to loud sobs.

"We just don't know what's the matter with the little guy," Jim Dear said wearily to Lady. "We've fed him and changed him, and I've sung him every lullaby I know. Maybe you can figure out what's bothering him!"

That was all the invitation Lady needed. She jumped up onto the bed and peered into the cradle. The baby's eyes were squeezed shut and his cheeks were wet with tears. His little legs were kicking the covers. Lady reached in and tugged at the covers to smooth them out. The baby opened his eyes and looked at Lady. His cries dropped to a whimper, and he reached out to touch her. His tiny hand grabbed hold of her ear and tugged. Lady winced but held still. With her chin, she began to rock the cradle and, with her furry tail, she beat a rhythmic *thump, thump, thump* on the bedcover.

"Ga!" said the baby as he broke into a gummy smile, his big blue eyes looking like wet forget-me-nots. Still holding Lady's ear, the baby giggled.

"Oh, look, Jim Dear!" cried Darling delightedly. "Lady has got him to stop crying!"

"I just don't know what we'd do without you, Lady!" Jim Dear said gratefully.

Rock, rock, rock went the cradle. *Thump, thump, thump* went Lady's tail. Soon the baby's eyelids grew heavy, and then his eyes closed. Tears still streaking his little round cheeks, he relaxed his grip on Lady's ear, smiled and fell asleep.

On the Move

All was well inside Riley's Mind World. Joy, Sadness, Fear, Anger and Disgust – Riley's Five Emotions – worked hard to keep their girl happy. Riley had great friends, a great house – things couldn't have been better.

But one day, just after Riley had turned 11 years old, her parents told her that the whole family was moving from their home in Minnesota, across the country to San Francisco over 1,900 miles away!

"Wha…." Joy said, shocked by the news.

"Aiiiiighh!" screamed Sadness, Disgust, Anger and Fear.

"Okay, not what I had in mind…." said Joy, as she tried to find the positives.

During the long car journey, Riley's family drove past fields and city suburbs, on mountain roads and seemingly never-ending highways. While the other Emotions were panicking, Joy tried to cheer everyone up.

"Hey, look!" she said, as they arrived in San Francisco. "The Golden Gate Bridge! Isn't that great? It's not made out of solid gold like we thought, which is kind of a disappointment, but still!"

Riley tried to imagine her new house, but, when the car finally arrived there, her new home was not at all how she'd hoped it would be. Riley's Emotions were speechless. The house looked dark and dreary.

Riley decided that checking out her new room might make her feel better. It didn't. Her room was small and dark with a sloped ceiling. Joy tried to help by picturing where all of Riley's stuff would go. All she needed was her bed, her desk and a few other things, and the place would soon feel like home. Riley's butterfly curtains would certainly brighten it up!

Minutes later, Riley's parents told her the bad news. The removal van carrying the family's belongings was lost. Riley would have to sleep in a sleeping bag until her bed arrived!

Through all of this, Joy desperately tried to keep Riley happy. She stepped up to the console in Riley's head and helped her look on the bright side.

Riley picked up a broom and started to play goofball hockey with her dad. Before long, even Mum joined in. The family collapsed into a hug, and soon after, yet another happy memory rolled into Headquarters.

Mum smiled at Riley. "Thank you," she said, "Through all of this confusion you've stayed our happy girl."

Perhaps things wouldn't be so bad in San Francisco, after all.

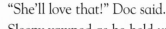

Snow White
and the Seven Dwarfs

Happy Valentine's Day

"Whatcha doin', Doc?" Happy asked.

Doc was hard at work carving a heart out of a piece of wood. "I'm making a present for Snow White," he replied.

"A present for Snow White?" Happy exclaimed. "Oh, dear! Did I miss her birthday?"

"No, silly," Doc said. "It's Valentine's Day."

"Valentine's Day?" Happy turned to Dopey. "Have you ever heard of Valentine's Day?"

Dopey shook his head.

Doc cleared his throat. "Valentine's Day," he began,

"is a very special tradition that gives people the opportunity to let loved ones know how important they are."

"I'm giving Snow White these handkerchiefs," Sneezy said as he sneezed into one of them. "Well, maybe not *this* one."

"That's very thoughtful," Doc answered. "I'm sure she'll be able to use them."

"If he has any left," Grumpy moaned.

Then Bashful shyly held out a paper flower he had made.

"Wonderful! And you?" Doc asked Dopey.

Dopey held up a paper aeroplane he'd just made for Snow White.

"You know what I'm going to do? I'm going to juggle for Snow White for Valentine's Day," Happy offered.

"She'll love that!" Doc said.

Sleepy yawned as he held up a pretty card he made.

"And you?" Doc asked Grumpy.

"Well, all right," Grumpy confessed. "I wrote Snow White a poem."

"A poem! Really? Can we hear it?" Doc asked.

"Don't push your luck!" Grumpy snapped.

Just then, the cottage door opened. Snow White had arrived!

"Happy Valentine's Day!" the Seven Dwarfs sang, each holding up his gift for Snow White to see.

"What a wonderful surprise!" Snow White exclaimed. She was holding a bundle of valentines – pretty red and pink hearts on lacy doilies – and handed them out to the Seven Dwarfs, placing a kiss on each of their cheeks. The Seven Dwarfs all thought they were the most beautiful valentines they had ever seen. Even Grumpy was pleased. Bashful blushed an especially bright shade of red as Snow White kissed him on the cheek, and Sleepy started yawning before Snow White could hand him his card. Then Sneezy sneezed, blowing his card into the air. Happy laughed, and Dopey smiled too.

If you asked any of them, he'd tell you it was the best Valentine's Day ever!

FROZEN

A Spectacular Scene

In a frozen Arendelle, Queen Elsa was climbing high into the mountains. With no one else to worry about, she let all her powers loose. A blizzard flew round her as she created ice sculptures, made a snowman and even transformed the way she looked.

As she neared the top of the mountain Elsa created a magnificent shining ice palace. She felt like the person she was always meant to be! She may have been alone, but she was, at long last, entirely herself.

Anna, meanwhile, couldn't wait to be reunited with her sister. Now that Elsa's secret was out, they could finally be close again!

The storm made Anna's journey difficult, though – especially when her horse threw her into the snow and ran away. Luckily, she spotted a small building up ahead.

The building was Wandering Oaken's Trading Post and Sauna. Inside, Anna gathered up boots and some warm clothes.

Just then, a young man named Kristoff trudged in. He was an ice harvester and very unhappy that the surprise snow storm was ruining his business!

Kristoff mentioned that the storm was coming from the North Mountain, so Anna pestered him with questions. She wanted information to help her find Elsa.

But Kristoff was busy bargaining with Oaken. "Back up while I deal with this crook!" he told Anna.

An insulted Oaken threw Kristoff out!

That gave Anna an idea. She found Kristoff in the stable with his reindeer, Sven, and gave him the supplies he needed. In return, she asked that he take her up the North Mountain.

After giving it some thought, Kristoff agreed. "We leave at dawn," he said.

"No," said Anna. "We leave right now."

As they travelled further up the mountain and deeper into the forest, Anna explained to Kristoff what had happened in Arendelle. It all sounded strange to him, but he hoped Anna could convince Elsa to bring back summer so that people would need his ice again.

Suddenly, they heard wolves howling. Kristoff turned to see a pack of wolves chasing their sled!

Anna helped Kristoff fight off the wolves, but Sven was forced to leap over a deep gorge to escape. The sled crashed on to the rocks below, but Anna, Kristoff and Sven were safe.

When dawn broke, Anna and Kristoff could see Arendelle far below at the bottom of the mountain. To their dismay, the kingdom was still locked in winter.

They hiked further into the forest, where Elsa's powers had created a spectacular scene.

Anna was in awe. "I never knew winter could be so ... beautiful," she said with a sigh. Even though Anna knew that Elsa's powers were dangerous, she couldn't help but be impressed by what they could create.

Fish-in-the-box

"Ariel?" Flounder called out timidly, poking his head inside Ariel's secret grotto. Ariel had told Flounder to meet her there, but she hadn't arrived yet. "I guess I'll wait for her inside," Flounder said to himself. He swam around slowly, gazing at Ariel's collection of things from the human world. The rock ledges were filled with various objects the Little Mermaid had found in sunken ships and up at the surface – everything from a clock to a music box to a knight's helmet. It was Ariel's favourite place.

But, without Ariel there, Flounder found the place lonely ... and quiet ... and ... creepy.

"Yikes!" Flounder screamed, startled by the sudden appearance of another fish as he swam past a piece of a broken mirror. When he realized it was just his own reflection, Flounder breathed a sigh of relief. "Oh, Flounder, don't be such a guppy," he told himself, repeating the line Ariel always used on him.

Flounder swam past one object that he had never noticed before – a square metal box with a handle on one side.

"I wonder what that thing does," said Flounder, staring at the handle. After a few moments' hesitation, Flounder summoned his courage. By flapping his tail fin and pushing the handle with his nose, he managed to turn it around once ... twice ... three times. Nothing happened. Flounder was halfway into the fourth turn when – *Boing!*

The latch to the top of the jack-in-the-box released and the spring-loaded jester inside popped out of the box and lunged at Flounder.

"Ahhhhhhhhhhhh!" Flounder screamed as he raced backwards away from the jack-in-the-box and collided with the lid of an open treasure chest.

The force of the collision caused the lid of the chest to slam shut, trapping Flounder inside.

Moments later, Ariel swam through the door of the secret grotto.

"Flounder?" she called. "Are you here yet?"

From inside the chest, Flounder yelled to Ariel. *"Mm-nn-eer!"* came the muffled cry.

Ariel followed the sound of his voice and swam over to the chest. Lifting the lid, she found her friend inside. "What are you doing in there?" Ariel asked with a giggle.

Thinking quickly, Flounder replied, "I'm about to do my imitation of that thing." He pointed at the jack-in-the-box. Then Flounder sprang suddenly out of the chest, raced out of the door ... and kept on swimming.

He'd had enough of Ariel's secret grotto for one day!

The Perfect Birthday

Mother Gothel was a wicked old woman, who stole a princess when she was just a baby. Though she pretended to love the girl, Rapunzel, she truly only loved Rapunzel's magical hair, which kept the old woman forever young.

Mother Gothel had convinced Rapunzel that she needed to protect her magical hair by never leaving the tower.

But being stuck in a tower didn't change Rapunzel's spirit.

She and her friend Pascal, the chameleon, were busy every day, doing lots of activities, including her favourite – painting! But Rapunzel had one dream that she longed to make come true.

Throughout her life in the tall tower, Rapunzel had seen strange lights floating up into the night sky on her birthday. She felt they were especially for her. More than anything, she wanted Mother Gothel to take her to see them.

On the day before her eighteenth birthday, with Pascal urging her on, Rapunzel decided to tell Mother Gothel what she really wanted on her birthday.

"I want to see the floating lights!" she blurted out, revealing a painting she had done of them.

"Oh, you mean the stars," Mother Gothel lied. She wanted Rapunzel to forget her wish.

"That's the thing," countered Rapunzel, "I've charted the stars and they're always constant. But these? They appear every year on my birthday – only on my birthday. I have to know what they are."

"Go outside?" asked Mother Gothel in shock.

Mother Gothel said that the world outside was far too scary for a weak girl. There were ruffians, quick-sand and snakes!

"Rapunzel, I'm only thinking of you. If you want a perfect birthday, don't ever ask to leave this tower again!" Mother Gothel insisted.

Rapunzel fell silent. She put her arms around Mother Gothel's neck. She understood why her mother wanted to protect her.

Unseen by Rapunzel, the wicked woman gave a sly smile. "Let's put this silliness behind us," Mother Gothel said, patting Rapunzel on her head.

Rapunzel sighed and smiled weakly. *After all. What more could I want?* Rapunzel wondered. *I have everything I could dream of right here.*

Rapunzel knew that she should have been happy with what she had. But she just couldn't give up on her dream.

Disney
Bambi

Growing Up

One day, Bambi and Thumper were playing in the meadow.

"Look, Bambi!" exclaimed Thumper.

A herd of stags was thundering towards them.

"I wish I could be a stag!" Bambi exclaimed.

"Well, you know what my father always says," said Thumper.

"I know," said Bambi. "'Eating greens is a special treat. It makes long ears and great big feet.'"

"No, not that!" said Thumper. "I mean, he does say that, but he also says, 'If you want to hop well, but your hop is all wrong, then you have to practise all day long!'"

"I have to hop all day long?" asked Bambi.

"No!" cried Thumper. "If you want to become a stag, you have to practise!"

Bambi glanced back at two big deer. They suddenly ran towards each other, locking horns to test their strength. They looked so powerful and majestic. Bambi wanted to be just like them!

"Okay," Bambi told Thumper.

"Okay," said Thumper. "Follow me."

Thumper hopped to the edge of the meadow. He stopped by a big oak tree. "Lower your head," he told Bambi.

Bambi lowered his head. "Now what?" he asked, staring at the ground.

"Run straight ahead," said Thumper.

Bambi ran straight ahead – towards the trunk of the old oak tree! But, before he got there, a voice cried, "Stop!" Bambi did, skidding to a halt only a few inches from the tree trunk.

Thumper and Bambi looked up. Friend Owl looked down at them with big curious eyes. "Bambi, why were you going to butt my tree trunk with your head?" asked Friend Owl.

"I'm practising to become a big stag," said Bambi. "Stags butt heads to show their strength."

Friend Owl laughed and said, "Bambi, the stags have antlers to protect their heads! And becoming a stag is not something you can practise. It's something that will happen to you with the passing of time."

"It will?" said Bambi.

"Of course!" Friend Owl assured him. "Next summer, you'll see. You'll be bigger and stronger. You'll also have antlers – and, I hope, enough sense not to butt heads with an oak tree!"

"Yes, sir," said Bambi.

"Now go on, you two," said Friend Owl. "And don't be in too much of a hurry to grow up. You'll get there soon enough, I promise you!"

"Okay," said Bambi and Thumper. Then the two friends returned to the snowy meadow to play.

Disney · PIXAR

WALL·E
A New Friend

If you lived back in the 29th Century, you would live off in space with all the other people from Earth.

Long ago, Earth had been evacuated because it was too polluted. No one could live there until someone cleaned up the planet. And there was someone left behind to do that work.

WALL•E was a Waste Allocation Load Lifter, Earth-Class. He didn't mind his lonely job of compacting rubbish. He looked at it as a sort of treasure hunt. He never knew what he would find each day in the trash.

But WALL•E wanted more in life. He didn't ask for much, he just wanted to hold hands with someone – someone he loved. He had seen this watching his favourite film over and over. It was his dream.

One day, WALL•E was out compacting and cubing trash when he found something special. It was a plant. His pet cockroach chirped, knowing that his friend would be really interested in this green thing. Neither one of them had ever seen anything like it before. WALL•E took it home to keep with his other treasures.

Soon afterwards, another robot landed on Earth. WALL•E was very excited to have some company! WALL•E fell in love with the sleek new robot at first sight. Her name was EVE, and WALL•E watched her in awe.

Over time, WALL•E figured out that EVE was looking for something. But she wouldn't tell him what it was.

WALL•E took her to his home and showed her all the treasures he had collected from the trash. He was very proud of the things he had found.

But when WALL•E showed EVE the plant, she immediately grabbed it from him and stored it in a secret compartment in her chest! Then she shut down. She slept and slept, no matter how hard WALL•E tried to wake her up.

Before long, EVE's ship returned to take her away.

No! WALL•E loved her. He didn't want her to leave.

As the ship prepared to fly away with EVE inside, WALL•E decided he couldn't let her go. He latched onto the outside of the ship.

WALL•E had finally found someone he wanted to hold hands with, and he was not going to let her leave without him.

And so, WALL•E followed EVE into space....

Wendy's Music Box

Tinker Bell had been trying to learn a new fairy-talent since she arrived at Pixie Hollow. She wanted to visit the mainland and tinker-fairies could not. Tink tried to be an animal fairy, a light fairy, a water fairy and a nature fairy. But she was not good at any other talent.

Tinker Bell sat on the beach. "Great," she muttered. "At this rate, I should get to the mainland right about, oh, never!"

She angrily threw a pebble and heard a *CLUNK!* Tink went to investigate and found a broken porcelain box. By the time her friends found her, Tinker Bell was putting her discovery back together. The final touch was a porcelain ballerina that fit into the lid. Tinker Bell gave the dancer a spin, and to her delight, the box played music!

"Do you even realize what you're doing?" asked Rosetta. "Fixing stuff like this – that's what tinkering is!"

"Who cares about going to the mainland anyway?" Silvermist added.

Later that day, Tink saved the fairies' springtime supplies by tinkering and making wonderful new tools. Tink realized that her talent was very important after all. The fairies were very pleased with Tink and wanted to help her.

"Queen Clarion," said Silvermist. "Can't Tink come with us to the mainland?"

"It's okay," Tink protested. "My work is here."

Fairy Mary – the no-nonsense fairy who ran Tinkers' Nook – flew over, looking sternly at Tink. "I don't think so, missy!" she said. She gave a little whistle, and Clank and Bobble led in the wagon. Tink's music box was inside, all polished and shiny.

"I'd imagine there's someone out there who's missing this. Perhaps a certain tinker fairy has a job to do after all … on the mainland," said Fairy Mary.

So the nature fairies and Tink went to London to deliver their springtime magic. Tinker Bell found the home where the music box belonged, and tapped on the windowpane. A little girl named Wendy Darling poked her head out of the window. Tink watched from her hiding place as Wendy's face filled with happiness at the discovery of her long-lost treasure. The girl took a small key from a chain around her neck and turned it in a slot. The music box began to play!

Soon the fairies' work was done and it was time for them all to return to Never Land. Tink couldn't wait to get home – she had lots of tinkering to do!

Chaos in the Kitchen

"Now, now, dearie," said Aunt Flora to little Aurora, "it's time for your nap." Flora had just given the baby (who was now named Briar Rose) her bottle and settled her in her cradle.

"Time to make supper!" Flora said to Fauna and Merryweather, turning away from the snoozing baby princess and clapping her hands together purposefully.

Flora, Fauna and Merryweather gave each other uneasy grins. It was the first meal the three fairies had to prepare in the little cottage in the woods, where they would live until Aurora's 16th birthday.

The King and Queen had sent their beloved daughter into hiding to try to protect her from a curse laid on the princess by the evil fairy Maleficent. In order to be sure to keep Aurora well hidden, the three fairies had vowed to give up their magic wands and live as ordinary humans. None of them had ever cooked, cleaned or cared for a baby before. This was going to be quite an adventure!

"Now, remember, dearies," said Flora firmly, "we're to use no magic when preparing this meal!"

The three fairies sighed. This was not going to be easy!

"I shall cook a stew," said Merryweather. The others thought that was a wonderful idea. What a cosy meal for their first night in the cottage! Stew sounded hearty and delicious!

"I'll bake some blueberry biscuits and mash the potatoes!" said Flora.

"Are you sure you know how?" asked Fauna.

"How hard could it be?" said Flora. "Fauna, why don't you make a salad?"

"I'll try!" said Fauna brightly. So Merryweather chopped meat and vegetables, Flora mixed flour and water, and Fauna chopped and diced the salad vegetables.

But, an hour later, dinner still wasn't ready. Merryweather's stew smelled like old boots. Flora opened the oven and pulled out her biscuits, which were as flat as pancakes. The mashed potato was terribly lumpy. And somehow most of the salad vegetables had ended up on the floor.

The three fairies looked at each other in dismay. "Back to the drawing board, girls," said Flora. "But let's not be too hard on ourselves – after all, we've got 16 years to learn how to cook without magic!"

"And that's how long it's going to take!" replied Fauna.

Merryweather laughed. Fauna was obviously joking – wasn't she?

Writing a Poem

One day in Wonderland, Tweedledum and Tweedledee decided to write a poem about writing poems. So, they put their heads together and set to rhyming. Soon they had quite an amusing poem composed. It even had a title – "So You Want to Write a Poem". The only thing they just couldn't agree on was how to end it.

"Read what we have so far, would you?" said Tweedledee. So Tweedledum began:

So you want to write a poem.
You do? Is that true?
Writing poems is usually
Easy to do.
Sun rhymes with fun;
Dew rhymes with shoe;
End sounds like friend,
And other words too.
Breezy is easy;
It rhymes with queasy.
Pet sounds like net;
That one's no sweat.
Many a word
Will rhyme with day,
Like hay and say
And even bouquet.
Words with long 'e' sounds
Are always a cinch.
Bean tree and sweet pea
And flea, at a pinch.
But then there are toughies

Like cousin and buzzin'.
There are rhymes for them,
But they're not dime a dozen.
Also tricky is icky
And apple and stronger.
Although you can rhyme 'em,
It may take you longer.
There's whoozit and whatsit
And hogwash and hooey.
You try to rhyme those,
And your brain goes kablooey.
So, when writing a poem,
Keep one thing in mind:
Avoid all the hard words
And you'll do just fine!
This poem is over.
This poem is penned.

This poem is finished,
So this is the ...

Tweedledum looked up. "That's it," he said.

Tweedledee racked his brain. "What rhymes with 'penned'?" he said. "'Bend'?" He tried it out: "'This poem is finished, so this is the *bend*.' No, no, that doesn't seem right."

Tweedledum took a stab at it. "There's 'pretend'. 'This poem is finished, so this is *pretend*.' Nah, I don't like it."

Tweedledee sighed. "We'll never think of a good rhyme for the end of this poem."

"You're right," said Tweedledum. "I guess we'll have to leave it unfinished."

So that's what they did.

And that was the end.

The Masquerade Ball

"Where could she be?" Cinderella asked. She looked around the grand ballroom. Hundreds of happy citizens were gathered there, each dressed in a splendid costume.

Cinderella and her new husband, the Prince, were holding a Masquerade Ball. Cinderella had sent a special invitation to her Fairy Godmother, who had promised to come.

But the ball had started almost an hour ago, and Cinderella still hadn't seen any sign of the cheerful little woman.

"Don't worry, my love," the Prince said. "I'm sure she'll – what's this?"

A messenger handed Cinderella a note.

Never fear –
I'm here, my dear.
Just seek and you will find
Which mask I am behind!

Her Fairy Godmother was playing a trick on her! "I'll find you," Cinderella whispered.

Was her Fairy Godmother wearing that beautiful unicorn costume? Was she the princess with the pink mask? The dancing harlequin clown? The fuzzy brown bear? Cinderella felt a little dizzy as she turned around and around. How would she ever find her Fairy Godmother in the crowd?

Cinderella stared at a masked milkmaid with twinkling eyes standing near a fountain.

Could that be her? she wondered.

Cinderella looked around thoughtfully. When she turned back to the fountain, the milkmaid was gone! Instead, someone in a butterfly mask was standing there.

"Looking for someone, Princess?" the butterfly said in a deep voice.

"No – never mind," Cinderella said.

She wandered away, still searching. But she kept thinking about the twinkling eyes behind the butterfly mask. Then she remembered something – the milkmaid had the same twinkling eyes! Could it be.... ?

She hurried back to the fountain. But there was no sign of the milkmaid or the butterfly. The only person standing nearby was wearing a beautiful white swan costume.

"Oh, dear," Cinderella whispered.

She stared at the swan. Mischievous eyes twinkled behind the feathered white mask.

Suddenly, Cinderella laughed out loud. "Aha!" she cried. "I caught you!"

She pulled off the swan mask. Her Fairy Godmother smiled back at her. "You win!" she exclaimed. "How did you find me?"

"I almost didn't, the way you kept magically changing costumes," Cinderella said. "Then I remembered how you magically changed *my* outfit not too long ago – and I figured it out!"

THE JUNGLE Book

Go Fish!

"Okay, small fry," said Baloo the bear. "Today I'm going to teach you to fish like a bear!"

Mowgli was delighted. He loved his new friend Baloo. Unlike Bagheera the panther, who kept insisting that Mowgli should live in the Man-village for his own protection, Baloo made no such demands on Mowgli. Baloo was much more interested in having a good time living in the jungle, and so was Mowgli.

"Now, watch this, kid," said Baloo as they arrived at the riverbank. "All ya gotta do is wait for a fish to swim by and then...."

Whoosh! Quick as a flash, Baloo held a wriggling silver fish in his paw. "Now you try it!" he said to Mowgli.

Mowgli sat very still, waiting for a fish to swim by. Then – *splash*! – he toppled headfirst into the water.

"Hmm," said Baloo after he had fished Mowgli out and set him down, dripping. "Now I'll show you my second technique."

Baloo and Mowgli walked towards another part of the river. This time, the fish could be seen occasionally leaping out of the water as they swam down a little waterfall. Baloo waded a few steps into the water, waited for a fish to jump, then – *whoosh*! – he swiped a fish right out of

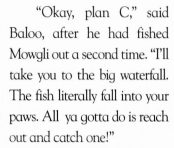

the air. "Now you try, buddy."

Mowgli waded in just as Baloo had done. He waited for the fish to jump and then leaped for it. *Splash*!

"Okay, plan C," said Baloo, after he had fished Mowgli out a second time. "I'll take you to the big waterfall. The fish literally fall into your paws. All ya gotta do is reach out and catch one!"

Mowgli followed Baloo to the big waterfall. Sure enough, silvery fish were jumping all the way down the fall. Catching one would be easy!

In the blink of an eye Baloo held up a fish for Mowgli to admire.

"I'm going to do it this time, you watch me, Baloo!" said Mowgli excitedly. He scrunched up his face with concentration. Then – *flash*! – for an instant, Mowgli actually had a silvery fish in his hands. But, a second later, the fish shot out of his grasp and jumped into the water again. Mowgli looked down at his empty hands with a sigh.

"You know what, kid?" said Baloo, clapping a huge paw on Mowgli's skinny shoulders. "I think you're working too hard. That's not how life in the jungle should be! It should be fun, happy and carefree. So, come on. Let's go shake a banana tree instead!"

And Mowgli cheerfully agreed.

TinkerBell
AND THE
LOST TREASURE

Tinker Bell and the Moonstone

Pixie Hollow was abuzz with excitement! The fairies were preparing to celebrate the arrival of autumn, and Tinker Bell had been asked to make the sceptre that would hold the precious moonstone – which helped to make blue pixie dust and restore the Pixie Dust Tree.

Bursting with joy, Tinker Bell rushed to tell Terence the good news. He offered to help, but before long the little fairy began to get irritated with him getting in the way. Eventually, Tink lost her temper and accidentally broke the moonstone! Tinker Bell was in despair; she didn't know what to do.

That night, at the theatre, a fairy named Lyria told a story of lost treasure. Far away, on a forgotten island, there was a mirror, hidden in a boat, with the power to grant one wish. Tinker Bell decided to go in search of the mirror to put right her silly mistake. She set to work building a hot-air balloon and gathering her supplies.

Along the way, Tinker Bell met Blaze, a little firefly. One morning, the two new friends were surprised by a violent storm! When the fog cleared, they realized the balloon was stuck in a tree. Tink flew down to the ground, and the balloon drifted away and was carried far beyond their reach.

Tinker Bell was sad, but luckily Blaze and some new little bug friends were there to help her. Tink realized how much she missed Terence, her best friend who always did his best to be there for her.

Tink finally caught sight of the lost boat and discovered, at the bottom of the wreck, the magic mirror!

But, annoyed by Blaze's buzzing, Tinker Bell hastily asked for silence – instead of a new moonstone. And her wish was granted! Tinker Bell had just thrown away her last chance!

Tinker Bell started to think about Terence again, and she started to feel very bad about getting angry with him.

Then, as if by magic, Terence appeared behind her! He had flown all night long and had even found her balloon.

Back in Pixie Hollow, the Autumn Revelry was about to begin. They had no time to waste!

During the journey home, Terence helped Tinker Bell to make a new sceptre out of the shattered fragments of moonstone. They arrived for the ceremony just in time.

The blue harvest moon lit up the strangely beautiful sceptre, and blue pixie dust started to fall from the sky. Hurray! Tinker Bell had succeeded – with a little help from her friends!

A New School

When Riley and her parents moved to San Francisco, things didn't go smoothly. The removal van filled with their stuff got lost, and the new house wasn't as nice as their one back in Minnesota. But despite this, Joy tried to keep all Riley's Emotions feeling positive – as long as Riley was happy, everything would be fine.

Soon it was time for Riley to start at her new school. In Headquarters, Joy gave each of the Emotions an important job to do. She carefully drew a chalk circle round Sadness's feet.

"This is the Circle of Sadness," Joy explained. "Your job is to make sure all the sadness stays inside it."

At school, the teacher asked Riley to tell the class something about herself. Smiling shyly, Riley shared a happy memory of playing hockey with her family. Then, suddenly, her smile faded.

In Headquarters inside Riley's mind, Joy realized that Sadness had touched the hockey memory sphere – and it had changed from a happy, golden memory to a sad, blue memory!

"Sadness, what are you doing?" Joy cried.

"Oh no, I'm sorry," Sadness said, confused. Riley began to cry in front of her new class. While the other Emotions tried to stop the sad memory playing in Riley's mind, Sadness was alone at the console. As Riley cried, her first-ever blue core memory was created.

In a panic, Joy grabbed it as it rolled across the floor. She pulled a lever and a tube came down from the ceiling, ready to vacuum up the memory.

"Joy, no!" cried Sadness. She tried to grab the blue core memory back from Joy. As they struggled, they knocked the core memory holder. The five golden core memories, which powered Riley's Islands of Personality, fell out! The Islands – everything that made Riley who she was – went dark.

"Ahh!" Joy scrambled to collect up the core memories.

In the chaos, Joy, Sadness and all six core memories got sucked up the vacuum tube! They all travelled through Riley's mind and were dumped out in Long Term Memory. Joy knew they had to get back to Headquarters to get the Islands of Personality working again, before Riley forgot about everything she loved.

But the closest route back was across the narrow lightline bridge that connected Goofball Island to Headquarters.

"If we fall we'll be forgotten forever!" said Sadness.

"We have to do this. For Riley," Joy answered. "Just follow my footsteps."

Pinocchio

Follow Your Star

Jiminy Cricket was a wanderer. He loved the independence, the excitement and the simplicity of his way of life. For many a season, he had roamed the countryside, stopping to rest in towns along the way, and moving on when he grew restless.

But lately, Jiminy Cricket had noticed that there was one thing missing from his vagabond lifestyle: a purpose. Camping one night by the side of the road, he sat on his sleeping bag and gazed into his campfire.

"I wonder what it would feel like to be really helpful to someone," he said.

Jiminy lay on his sleeping bag and tried to get comfortable on the hard ground as he gazed up into the starry night sky. As his eyes scanned the many tiny points of light, one star to the south jumped out at him and seemed to shine brighter than all the rest.

"Say, is that a Wishing Star?" he wondered aloud. Since he couldn't know for certain, he decided it would be best to make a wish on it, just in case. "Wishing Star," he said, "I wish to find a place where I can make a difference and do a bit of good."

Then, his wish made, Jiminy Cricket suddenly felt a strange impulse: an urge to get up, gather his things and follow that star – the Wishing Star. He couldn't quite explain the feeling, but he felt it just the same.

So do you know what Jiminy Cricket did?

He put out the campfire. He gathered his things. And he took to the road. He followed that star all through the night. He walked for miles along highways and byways, across fields and over hills. He walked until the sun came up and he could no longer see the star to follow it. Then he made camp and he slept.

He did the same thing for several more nights and several more days.

Then, one night, he came to a village. Looking up at the Wishing Star, Jiminy Cricket noticed that it seemed to hang directly overhead.

It was very late at night as Jiminy Cricket walked into the village and looked around. Every window of every house was dark – except for one window in a shop at the end of a street. So Jiminy Cricket hopped over to the window. Peering inside, he saw that it was a woodcarver's workshop, dimly lit by the embers of a fire dying in the fireplace. It seemed a warm and pleasant place to stop for the night.

Little did Jiminy Cricket know that it was the home of Geppetto, a kind old woodcarver who had just finished work on a puppet he called Pinocchio.

And little did he know that he had just found a place where he would do more than just a bit of good.

No Work for Tinker Bell

Tinker Bell and her fairy friends from Pixie Hollow were on their way to bring summer to the mainland.

Summer was the busiest of all the four seasons – which meant the fairies would be away from home for months instead of days.

Tinker Bell was so excited! She had heard that the fairy camp where they'd be staying was an amazing place.

Once Tink and the others arrived, the nature fairies got right to work.

Vidia, a fast-flying fairy, made the summer grasses sway. Iridessa, a light fairy, bathed flowers in sunshine.

Rosetta, a garden fairy, helped bees find their way to the flowers' sweet nectar. Fawn, an animal fairy, greeted birds while Silvermist, a water fairy, frolicked with tadpoles.

Meanwhile, Tink landed in a peaceful clearing with her friend, Terence – a dust-keeper fairy.

"Where is everyone else?" she asked him.

Terence pulled back a tangle of leaves beneath a huge oak tree, revealing the busy fairy camp. Tink couldn't wait to get right to work!

"Don't worry, you'll find something to fix," Terence told her. Then he flew off to make pixie dust deliveries.

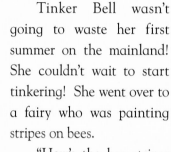

The fairy camp was even more incredible than Tink had ever imagined! Hidden beneath the tree, an entire fairy community bustled with activity.

Tinker Bell wasn't going to waste her first summer on the mainland! She couldn't wait to start tinkering! She went over to a fairy who was painting stripes on bees.

"How's the bee striper working? Need any tweaks?" she asked.

The animal fairy shook her head. "It's working fine, Tink," she replied.

Tinker Bell was glad that her inventions were working well, but she really wanted something to fix. Her tinkering nature meant she only felt truly happy when she was busy fixing something.

Since there wasn't anything that needed to be repaired just yet, Tink decided to go and look for lost things.

The other fairies reminded Tink that she needed to stay hidden from humans. They couldn't believe that Tink wanted to get *closer* to the humans – they knew that it could be very dangerous if a human discovered a fairy.

But Tinker Bell – as curious as ever – was determined to do some exploring while she was on the mainland.

FROM THE STORY
Disney
FROZEN

Elsa's Palace

Anna was amazed by what her sister Elsa had created – it was the most beautiful winter landscape she had ever seen.

"But it's so white," came a voice from behind her. "How about some colour? I'm thinking crimson or chartreuse."

Anna and Kristoff whirled round. There, standing behind them, was a living snowman!

"I'm Olaf," he said, and he explained that Elsa had made him.

Anna asked Olaf to lead them to her sister. "We need Elsa to bring summer back to Arendelle," she explained.

"I've always loved the idea of summer," said Olaf, smiling. "The warm sun on my face ... getting a gorgeous tan...."

But Anna and Kristoff both had the same thought: summer would not be good for a snowman!

Back in Arendelle, the man Anna wanted to marry, Prince Hans, was trying to keep everyone calm. One of the visitors, a duke, was especially angry that his ship was stuck in the frozen fjord. It meant that he was unable to leave the kingdom.

Just then, Anna's horse showed up without her. Hans was worried. What could have happened to Anna?

"Princess Anna is in trouble," Hans called out. "I need volunteers to go with me to find her!"

The Duke insisted that his men join the search party.

Meanwhile, the path up the mountain was getting very steep for Anna, Kristoff and Sven. Luckily, Olaf found a stairway made of ice that led straight to Elsa's palace.

"Whoa," said Anna as they reached the top. The palace was amazing! There were large rooms with high ceilings, and staircases and archways all sculpted from ice.

But Elsa wasn't happy to see Anna. She was afraid of hurting her again with her icy powers.

"You should go, Anna," Elsa warned. "I'm too dangerous." But Anna explained that Arendelle needed Elsa's help. The kingdom was freezing and no one knew what to do.

Now Elsa was frightened. She admitted that she couldn't unfreeze the kingdom because she didn't know how! Anna was sure they could figure it out together, but Elsa just grew more upset. Frustrated, she cried out, "I can't!" And an icy blast shot across the room and hit Anna in the chest!

Kristoff rushed to help Anna. "I think we should go," he said.

"No! I'm not leaving without her!" insisted Anna.

"Yes, you are," Elsa replied, conjuring up a giant snowman.

"Hey, you made me a little brother," Olaf said happily. "I'm going to name you Marshmallow!" But Marshmallow wasn't little – or friendly! Anna, Kristoff and Sven took one look at him and prepared to run!

Curious Tinker Bell

Tinker Bell arrived in Pixie Hollow last spring, where she had discovered her talent as a tinker fairy. Now, she was on a mission on the mainland, the world of humans, where the fairies were setting up summer. But Tinker Bell couldn't find anything that needed to be repaired, so she wanted to look for lost things.

The other fairies reminded Tinker Bell that they needed to stay hidden from humans – because humans could be dangerous to fairies.

Just then, a loud *CRACK* went through the fairy camp! Fawn was startled and knocked over some paint she was using to decorate butterfly wings. The splattered butterfly took off.

The loud noise made Tinker Bell very curious. The other fairies hid, but Tinker Bell went to see where the noise came from. She was intrigued by the sight of a car making its way down the winding road – and took off after it! Tinker Bell had never seen a car before.

Tink followed and watched as the car stopped at an old house in the country.

Then she saw a little girl, her father and their cat get out.

"Could we have a tea party in the meadow? Please?" Lizzy, the little girl, pleaded.

"Not today," Dr Griffiths said wearily. "I have quite a bit of work to do."

After the three had gone inside, Tink flew under the car to examine it. Suddenly, Vidia appeared. "You shouldn't be this close to the house!" she scolded.

But Tinker Bell was already poking around the engine. She found an interesting-looking lever and turned it. Outside of the car, Vidia got showered with water! She was furious! Tink knew fairies couldn't fly with wet wings!

Moments later, Lizzy and her father returned to the car – and the fairies froze in fright. Luckily, the humans were busy examining a strange-looking butterfly.

"I guess that's just the way the fairies decided to paint it," Lizzy said.

"Fairies do not paint butterfly wings, because fairies are not real," Dr Griffiths insisted as he captured the creature with a net. Lizzy sighed. Her father was a scientist and he didn't believe in magic or fairies. He was also often too busy to spend much time with her.

Tinker Bell had heard the humans' conversation and she almost wanted to prove fairies existed right there and then! But she knew that could be dangerous, so she stayed hidden – for the moment.

The Prince and the Sorcerer

Prince Naveen was completely unaware of it, but New Orleans was a city of magic, good and evil. Bad experiences might be waiting just around the corner – particularly if you were a carefree young prince! On top of that, Naveen's parents had cut off his income. They wanted him to take responsibility for himself.

But this didn't bother Naveen. His only thought was to enjoy himself and have fun!

When he got off his ship, he put on his crown and began to sing, dance and play the ukulele all round the town. Lawrence, his faithful valet, tried to make him see sense....

"We must go to this masked ball, my Prince! Your hosts are waiting for you!"

"But first, Lawrence, it's my round of drinks!" Prince Naveen declared.

"That's all very well, but you've got nothing to pay with!"

However, Naveen refused to look for work. There was just one solution: to marry a rich young girl. But marrying would deprive him of his freedom, and he didn't much like the idea of that either!

Just then, a sinister character passed by the Prince in the street....

"What an excellent stroke of luck for me!" he laughed. This was Dr Facilier, a fearsome sorcerer who had his sights set on taking Naveen's place and seizing his wealth.

"Delighted to meet you, your Highness!" Dr Facilier greeted Naveen as he went by. "Let me introduce myself: Dr Facilier. I can tell your fortune, read your future ... and make your dearest wishes come true!"

Careless of any danger, Naveen followed him into his den, at the end of a dark alleyway. Terrifying whispers haunted the place. Scary masks glared down from the walls and shadows danced everywhere.

The sorcerer said, "Trust me! I know how to solve your money problems!"

Naveen was hearing exactly what he wanted to hear! He was fascinated. Facilier took his chance. He waved a magic talisman, pricked Naveen's finger with it and filled a vial with his blood! Naveen began to shrink and shrink, and was transformed into a frog!

"Welcome Prince Frog!" Dr Facilier cruelly roared with laughter.

Poor Naveen! It was true, money wouldn't be a problem for him from now on, but what would happen to him? He had no idea what life as a frog would bring.

Tangled
Flynn Rider

While Rapunzel was getting ready to celebrate her eighteenth birthday, hidden away in her tower, a thief called Flynn Rider was escaping into the forest with his latest stolen prize, a royal crown, and his two partners in crime, the Stabbington brothers. Suddenly, Flynn stopped in front of a WANTED poster. He frowned.

"Heh! It doesn't look a bit like me! Have you seen the nose they've given me? It's outrageous! I'm much better looking in real life!"

"We couldn't care less, Flynn!" the Stabbingtons grumbled. "We've got to get out of here!"

Too late – the royal guards appeared at the top of the hill. The thieves ran off as fast as they could but soon found themselves trapped in a dead end, up against a stone wall! There was only one way out – to climb over the top! Flynn turned to his accomplices.

"Give me a leg up chaps. Once I'm up there I'll pull you after me."

But the Stabbingtons didn't trust him. Flynn had a reputation for being a bit of a rogue – sly as a fox, crafty as a monkey! They shook their heads.

"If you want us to give you a leg up, first of all give us the satchel with the crown, just in case you decide to run off without sharing it!"

"Oh, great! Nice to know you trust me!" said Flynn, pretending to get cross. "When I think of everything we've been through together and now this. Here's the satchel! Will you help me now?"

The Stabbington brothers agreed, and with their help Flynn was over the wall in a flash. They then asked Flynn to help them climb it, but he refused and burst out laughing.

"Sorry chaps, I've got my hands full!" He waved the satchel that contained the crown in the air.

The Stabbingtons were furious. Flynn had managed to get hold of the crown without them seeing!

"You're right. I had no intention of sharing it with you!" added Flynn as he made off. "Good luck in prison!"

He was glad to be rid of them – they were too ruthless and dangerous to be trusted.

Flynn raced off into the woods but the royal guards were already hot on his heels.

Suddenly, Flynn realized that Maximus, horse to the captain of the guard, was even more determined to catch him than the guards were. How was he going to escape capture now?

The Den of Doom

"Where are we going, Baloo?" Mowgli asked. He and Baloo had been travelling through the jungle for a while now.

"Have you ever heard of the Den of Doom, Man-cub?" replied Baloo in a hushed voice.

Mowgli gasped. "The Den of Doom? They say that the Den of Doom is a giant cave filled with bears who will eat anything – or anyone! They say that those bears can hear for miles and see in the dark! They say that even Shere Khan is afraid of them!" he exclaimed.

"Mmm-hmm," said Baloo. "They do say that. They *also* say that all of the bears in the Den of Doom are over eight feet tall, that their teeth are green and razor-sharp, and that their battle cry is so loud that the whales in the ocean hear it and shake with fright. They say all that, and much, much more."

"And we're *going* there?" Mowgli squeaked. "We can't! Baloo, those bears aren't like you! They're dangerous!"

"Too late, Man-cub," Baloo said with a grin. "We're already there!" He picked up Mowgli, whose knees were knocking together so hard he could barely stand, and strode right into a thicket. The bear ducked under a huge palm frond and emerged into a large, sunlit clearing in front of an enormous cave. Baloo put Mowgli down. The boy looked around in complete and utter surprise.

Mowgli had expected to see hundreds of fierce, angry bears. Instead, he saw hundreds of relaxed, happy bears having a really good time. Bears were swimming in a small pond, splashing and laughing. Bears were resting in the cool shadows of the cave. Bears were playing tag out in the clearing and chomping on piles of ripe, delicious fruit. It was, in short, a bear party.

"I don't understand," Mowgli said to Baloo. "This is the Den of Doom?"

"Yep," Baloo said happily, grabbing a palm frond and fanning himself with it. "It used to be called the Den of Delights, but we had to change the name. See, everyone in the jungle knew that the Den of Delights was the most fun place around. We bears never turned anyone away from our party. But then it got so crowded that it just wasn't any fun any more. So we spread a few rumours, changed the name, and *presto* – it's the Den of Doom! Now no one bothers us bears any more."

"But what about me?" Mowgli said anxiously. "I'm not a bear."

"You're an honorary bear, Mowgli," Baloo replied with a smile. "You sure have enough fun to be one!"

Disney
DUMBO
Float Like a Butterfly

One day, Dumbo's best friend, Timothy Q. Mouse, found Dumbo looking sad. "What's the matter, little guy?" the mouse asked the elephant. "Have people been teasing you about your ears again?"

Dumbo nodded. The little elephant looked totally miserable.

Timothy shook his head. The two were very good friends and did everything together. He didn't mind one bit that Dumbo had large ears. In fact, he thought they were great.

Timothy was trying to think of a way to cheer up his dear friend. And then he saw something. "Look, Dumbo!" he cried, racing over to a nearby fence post. Hanging from the fence was a large cocoon. "It's a butterfly cocoon!" Timothy said excitedly.

Dumbo came over to examine it.

"And look – it's about to hatch into a butterfly," said Timothy. He looked thoughtful for a moment, and then he turned to Dumbo. "You know what? You are a lot like the little caterpillar that made this cocoon."

Dumbo looked at Timothy quizzically.

"Yep, it's true. You see, a caterpillar is something nobody really wants around much. They think it's kind of plain looking, and it can't really do anything very interesting. But then one day, the caterpillar turns into a beautiful butterfly, and everyone loves it. And you know what? I think

you're going to be that way, too. When you get older, everyone is going to admire you rather than tease you!"

Dumbo smiled gratefully at his friend, and wiped away a tear with one of his long ears.

Suddenly, it started to rain. "Oh no!" cried Timothy. "The butterfly is going to get its new wings all wet. It won't be able to fly if it gets rained on. What'll we do? We need an umbrella!"

As Timothy looked this way and that for an umbrella, Dumbo smiled and unfurled his long ears. He draped them over the fence post so that they made a lovely roof for the insect, protecting it from the falling droplets of rain.

"Great idea!" said Timothy admiringly. The two friends stood there during the downpour, which didn't last very long. While they waited, they watched the beautiful new butterfly emerge from its cocoon and unfurl its colourful wings. When the rain stopped, the butterfly spread its wings (which were quite dry, thanks to Dumbo) and flew away.

"You know, my friend," said Timothy as they watched it fly away, "I think someday you're going to be a big success. You'll be like that butterfly – happy, carefree and floating along. Well, not floating for real, that's impossible. Imagine that, a flying elephant!"

Disney · PIXAR
FINDING
NEMO

Homesick

Nemo still couldn't believe everything that had happened to him. First, he'd been snatched up by a scuba diver in the ocean. Then, he'd travelled a long way in a big water cooler. Finally, he'd been dumped in a fish tank in a dentist's office. The other fish in the tank seemed nice, but Nemo missed his dad and his old home. He couldn't think about anything except getting back to the ocean. But would their plan to escape really work? It seemed hopeless....

"Hey, kid." Bloat the blowfish swam over to him. "Are you okay? You look a little down in the gills."

"I'll say," said Nigel the seagull.

Peach the starfish glanced over from her spot on the tank wall. "He's just upset," she said. "It's only natural." She smiled kindly at Nemo. "It's okay, hon. We know how you feel."

"How could you know?" he muttered, feeling sorry for himself. "You weren't grabbed out of the ocean, away from your dad."

"Well, no," a fish named Gurgle admitted. "But we all had families back where we came from. We all miss them."

"Really?" Nemo blinked in surprise. He hadn't thought about that.

"Sure," Peach said. "The lady who sold me over the Internet kept lots of us starfish in her basement." She sighed sadly. "I still wonder where all my brothers and sisters ended up. I'd give two or three of my arms to see them again."

"I hear you," Bloat agreed. "I was hatched in somebody's garage. They sold me and a whole school of my brothers and sisters and cousins to Bob's Fish Mart. Just when we made friends with the other fish there, he came in and bought me." He waved a fin towards the dentist in the office outside the tank. "It could be worse, though," Bloat continued. "You guys are the best friends I've ever had."

A fish named Deb nodded. "I'm lucky he bought me and my sister together. Right, Flo?" She smiled at her own reflection in the glass of the tank. When the reflection didn't answer, Deb shrugged. "I guess Flo is too choked up to talk right now. But I can tell by her smile that she agrees. We don't know what we'd do without each other. But we still miss the rest of our family."

"Wow," Nemo said, looking around at his new tankmates. "I guess you guys *do* know how I feel."

Even though he was sad that the other fish had been taken from their families, it made Nemo feel a little less alone. At least they understood how much he wanted to find his way back to his father. Now, a little braver and more determined than ever, Nemo was ready to escape from the tank – no matter what.

The Pet Show

"Mickey! Morty! Ferdie!" Minnie cried, racing into Mickey's garden. "I'm chairperson for the Charity Pet Show. Isn't that exciting? We're raising money to build a new shelter for stray animals."

"We should enter Pluto in the pet show!" said Ferdie.

"We can teach him to do tricks," said Morty. "Can we, Uncle Mickey? Please?"

"All right," Mickey said. "It's for a good cause."

Mickey and Minnie watched as the boys started to train Pluto.

"Roll over, Pluto," Morty said. But Pluto just wagged his tail.

All week, Morty and Ferdie tried to teach Pluto new tricks. He fetched, he rolled over and he shook hands ... but only when he wanted to.

"At least he's doing *some* tricks," said Mickey.

Finally, the day of the pet show arrived. Minnie was at the ticket booth when Mickey and his nephews arrived.

"Guess what!" said Minnie. "We've already made enough money for the new animal shelter!"

"That's great!" said Mickey.

What wasn't great was Pluto's performance. He shook hands when he was told to sit. He rolled over when he should have jumped. And he barked when he was supposed to lie down.

Worst of all, when Police Chief O'Hara was choosing the Best Pet of the Day, Pluto growled at him! The chief was standing right where Pluto had buried a bone!

Chief O'Hara was just about to announce the winner when the crowd heard Minnie scream from the ticket booth.

"Stop!" she cried. "Thief!"

"Oh no! The ticket money!" Morty and Ferdie shouted.

By the time Chief O'Hara, Mickey and the boys reached the booth, Pluto was sniffing around the scene.

"I turned away for just a minute," said Minnie, "and someone ran off with the cashbox."

Suddenly, Pluto stopped sniffing and ran into the woods. A moment later, Minnie heard a shout and the thief came running out. He was holding on to the cashbox – and Pluto was holding on to him!

Pluto tugged the thief to Chief O'Hara.

Later that afternoon, Chief O'Hara presented Pluto with the Four-Footed Hero medal. "Thanks to Pluto, every animal will have a place to go – and a chance to find a good home," he said.

"You know," said Minnie later when they were back home, "it's okay that Pluto isn't a show dog. He's something better. He's a hero!"

Mickey, Morty and Ferdie agreed. And then, without being told to, Pluto shook hands with everyone because, this time, *he* wanted to.

THE
LION KING

Just Like Dad

"Dad, when I grow up, I want to be just like you," Simba said to his father.

Mufasa nuzzled his son's head gently. "All in good time, son," he said.

Just then, Simba's friend Nala bounded up to them. "Come on, Simba!" she called. "Let's go play by the river!"

On their way, Simba stopped abruptly. "Listen to this," he said. He threw back his head and roared as loudly as he could. Then he looked at her expectantly. "Do I sound like my dad?"

Nala tried to suppress a giggle. "Not quite," she said.

Soon they reached the river. The waters were high as a result of the recent rains. Simba found a quiet pool at the side and stared down at his reflection. "Do you think my mane is starting to grow?" he asked Nala.

Nala sighed. "Maybe a little," she replied. "But, Simba, what's the big rush? Let's just have fun being young!"

Simba was eyeing a tree branch that extended over the raging river. "Well, I may not be as big as my dad yet, but at least I'm as brave as he is!" he shouted, and raced up to the tree. Climbing its gnarled trunk, he began walking along the branch over the water.

Nala hurried over. "Simba!" she yelled. "Come back here! The branch is going to break!"

But Simba couldn't hear her over the loud waters. Nala bounded away to get help.

Simba felt the branch begin to sag. "Uh-oh," he said to himself.

Suddenly the whole thing broke off and Simba tumbled into the water. The current was strong, and he struggled to swim towards the shore. He was running out of strength, and he realized he might not make it.

Then he felt himself being lifted out of the water and tossed onto the bank. Dripping and coughing, he looked up – right into the angry eyes of his father.

"Simba!" thundered Mufasa. "There's a big difference between being brave and being foolish! The sooner you learn that, the better chance you will have of growing old!"

Simba hung his head. Out of the corner of his eye, he saw Nala, pretending not to overhear. "I'm ... sorry, Dad," he said softly. "I just wanted to be brave like you."

His father's gaze softened. "Well," he said. "As long as we're soaking wet, why don't we go to a quieter part of the river and do some swimming?" He looked over to where Nala was sitting. "Come on, Nala!" he called. "Come with us!"

"Yippee!" cried the cubs, and they all went off together.

Cinderella
Chore de Force

Cinderella watched as a blue-and-pink-tinted bubble floated up from her bucket. "Isn't that pretty?" she said as she watched the bubble float higher and higher and finally pop into nothingness. Gus and Jaq and all the rest of Cinderella's mouse friends nodded in agreement.

"I bet it would be fun to float around in a bubble all day! I could see whole cities at a time, bounce on clouds and soar with the birds," Cinderella said dreamily. Her bird friends chirped happily. They liked the idea of sharing the skies with her.

"What am I doing?" Cinderella suddenly said. "I should stay focused on my chores." She finished cleaning the windows and prepared to mop the floor.

Cinderella plunged the mop into a bucket of soapy water, then dragged it across the floor. At first, she felt worn out. Then it occurred to her, as the mop slid across the slippery floor, "This is like dancing! How I love to dance!" Gus and Jaq copied Cinderella as she twirled around the room with the mop. "What fun!" she cried happily.

"Oh, my," Cinderella caught herself. "Did I say that aloud?" Maybe I just need to get away from all these bubbles, she thought. Ironing should do the trick!

She was ironing away and humming merrily to herself when she realized how dark the sky had grown.

"Look at the time!" Cinderella exclaimed. "I've been daydreaming the day away and haven't even started dinner."

Cinderella hurried to the kitchen where she chopped and minced and grated and stirred. "I don't know where this day has gone," she fretted as she added ingredients to her stepsisters' favourite soup. "I've got absolutely nothing done!" And, just then, Cinderella's stepsisters, Anastasia and Drizella, barged into the kitchen.

"Where's my laundry?" barked Anastasia.

"Done," Cinderella said.

"And my ironing?" Drizella added.

"Done," Cinderella replied again.

"Did you mop the floors?"

"Wash the windows?"

"Make our dinner?"

"Done, done, done!" Cinderella said gaily.

The sisters marched out of the kitchen muttering with displeasure.

And there Cinderella stood, all alone in the kitchen once more. As she stirred the pot of soup, she thought, I guess I did get a lot done, after all! She twirled across the room in celebration – and Jaq and Gus and the rest of her mouse friends joined her.

Disney · PIXAR

BRAVE

I Choose Archery!

Merida was a young and adventurous princess who lived in the ancient Scottish Highlands, in a kingdom called DunBroch. Merida's mother, Queen Elinor, wanted Merida to marry a son from a neighbouring clan. This would help to keep peace between the lands.

Merida, however, didn't feel ready to marry. She wanted to go on great adventures and follow her own path in life. Elinor and Merida couldn't see eye to eye.

Soon, the clans' ships sailed into DunBroch. Queen Elinor dressed Merida in a formal gown, ready to greet them.

"I can't move," Merida complained. "It's too tight."

"It's perfect," her mother said, smiling. But Merida wasn't happy at all.

The royal family welcomed the lords and their clans in the castle's Great Hall. Lord MacGuffin, Lord Macintosh and Lord Dingwall, the heads of each clan, stepped forward to present their sons.

Merida was unimpressed by all three of the young lords. She desperately tried to think of a way out of the marriage.

Alas, the peace among the clans proved fragile. A few insults were all it took to set them brawling. Luckily, Queen Elinor soon restored order.

The queen clarified the rules. Only the first-born of each of the leaders would compete for the hand of the princess. The princess herself would determine the challenge.

First born? Merida's eyes lit up as an idea formed in her head. She leaped to her feet, crying, "I choose archery!"

The competition began at high noon. Young MacGuffin took the first shot – and nearly missed the target completely. Young Macintosh's shot was slightly better. His attitude, however, was not. He stomped angrily on his bow. Wee Dingwall was the clumsiest of them all. But to everyone's amazement, he hit the bull's-eye!

Just then, Merida strode onto the field. "I am the first-born descendant of Clan DunBroch!" she declared before the stunned crowd. "And I'll be shooting for my own hand!"

"Merida! I forbid it!" the queen cried. Merida ignored her and raised her bow.

One by one, Merida fired her arrows at the targets. She hit all three bull's-eyes! Queen Elinor was furious! Merida might have just ruined the peace between the clans.

The Prince Chooses a Bride

At first there was no sign of Circe's curse taking hold. She had said that, unless the prince changed his ways, his ugly deeds would ruin his handsome face and everyone would see him for the beast that he really was. She had cursed the whole castle and all the servants, too. But none of this had come true, and the prince saw no reason to believe it would.

So, life went on and it was good. He noticed little changes in his appearance – but it was only when his friend Gaston said that he looked five years older that the prince gathered his courage to look in the enchanted mirror Circe had given him.

At first glance he didn't seem much changed.

"Look closer, prince." It was a witch's voice.

The prince's heart started to pound like thunder, and laughter surrounded him. His vision became narrowed, and soon everything closed in on him. Suddenly, his world became black.

When he woke up, his loyal servant Cogsworth was there, looking tired.

"You're awake, sir!" Cogsworth said. "You were very ill, suffering from a severe fever. I found you lying on the floor." The prince had been asleep for a long time.

Gaston decided the only remedy for the prince's increasing anxiety was a party. At first the prince didn't share Gaston's enthusiasm, but all the staff were behind the idea, and if the prince found the young woman of his dreams, all the better.

On the night of the ball, the only girl to catch the prince's eye was a girl with auburn hair.

"Gaston, who is that?"

Gaston realized the prince was talking about Belle – the girl that he adored himself; the girl that *he* wanted to marry!

"You wouldn't be interested in her, trust me!" Gaston replied. "She's lovely, yes, but her father is the laughing stock of the village! No, dear friend, we need to find you a princess! Someone like Princess Morningstar over there."

"Yes, bring over Princess Morningstar. I'd very much like to meet her."

Princess Tulip Morningstar had long golden locks, a milk-and-honey complexion and light blue eyes. Everything about her sparkled, except her personality. But that didn't bother the prince. He had enough personality for both of them. It wouldn't do to have a wife who took attention away from him. She was his perfect bride.

Lady and the TRAMP

Don't Mock Jock

Aunt Sarah had only just arrived to look after the baby while Jim Dear and Darling were away, but already her Siamese cats, Si and Am, had caused nothing but trouble. When they made a huge mess in the living room, Lady had been blamed for it, and Aunt Sarah had taken Lady to be fitted with a muzzle!

Meanwhile, left alone in the house, Si and Am had discovered the doggy door that led out to the garden.

"What works for doggies, works for kitties, too," hissed Si.

They slunk out to the garden. They dug in the flower beds, scared the birds at the birdbath and chased a squirrel up a tree.

Then they found a small hole in the garden fence. They poked their heads through the hole and spied Jock snoozing by his kennel.

"Time for a wake-up call?" said Am.

Si smiled and nodded. They squirmed through the hole and stole silently across the yard until they were sitting on either side of the sleeping Jock. Then, at the same moment, they let loose a shrill, ear-splitting yowl.

Jock awoke with a start. By the time he had identified the culprits, Si and Am were halfway across the lawn, heading for the fence.

Jock tore after them, barking. But, in a flash, the cats squirmed through the small hole and were out of Jock's reach. The opening was too small for Jock. He had to be content with sticking his head through and barking at the cats as they strolled casually up the back steps of Lady's house and through the doggy door. Then they collapsed in a laughing fit on the kitchen floor.

"Dogs are so dimwitted," Si cackled.

They waited a while, then crept out through the doggy door again, itching to try their trick once more. Peeking through the hole in the fence, they spied Jock, eyes closed, lying in front of his kennel. They squirmed through the hole and crept towards him.

But, this time, Jock was ready for them. When the cats got within five feet of him, the feisty Scottie leaped to his feet and growled. The cats gave a start, wheeled around and raced for the fence, only to find the way blocked by Jock's friend, Trusty the bloodhound, who stood, growling, between the cats and the hole.

Jock and Trusty chased Si and Am around Jock's garden until Jock was confident they had learned their lesson. Then they allowed the cats to retreat through the hole in the fence.

This time, they didn't stop running until they were up the back steps, through the doggy door, and safely inside.

And inside is where they stayed.

Tink Never Gives Up

While they were setting up summer on the mainland, the fairies based their camp under a large oak tree, so that no humans would see.

But shortly after Tinker Bell arrived, a car had backfired with a bang as it was driving past on a nearby road.

The noise had made everyone jump and Fawn accidentally spilled paint on a butterfly's wing!

The other fairies hid, but Tinker Bell just had to see what had made the noise. Vidia went after her, trying to get Tink to come back. But Tink wouldn't listen.

The car had stopped outside of a country house. A little girl, Lizzy, and her father had got out of the car and gone into the house with their bags.

Tink had flown into the car's engine to investigate and had accidentally showered Vidia with water! Vidia was upset, because she couldn't fly with wet wings.

Just then, Lizzy and her father returned to finish unloading the car. Tink and Vidia froze, but the humans' attention was focused on a butterfly – the very one that had been splashed with paint when the car backfired.

Lizzy thought that fairies had decided to paint the wing differently, but her father,

Dr Griffiths, disagreed. He didn't believe in fairies. He caught the butterfly in a jar to show to the museum.

If Vidia hadn't stopped her, Tink would have flown out and proven that fairies existed right then and there!

Meanwhile, Lizzy was pulling a little fairy house out of the back of the car. She hoped a real fairy would come to live in the tiny house one day.

Lizzy asked her father to help her set it up in the meadow, but – as usual – he was too busy. He had to get ready for a meeting he was having at the museum the next day.

When the humans had left, Tinker Bell apologized to Vidia for getting her wet.

"Maybe if you spent less time causing disasters," Vidia snapped, "you wouldn't have to help everybody so much."

But Tinker Bell wouldn't listen. She was too excited! The pair set off together into the meadow, where they soon spotted Lizzy's fairy house! Tink flew over for a closer look.

"Tinker Bell, we're not supposed to go near human houses!" warned Vidia.

"Human houses are a lot bigger," Tink replied.

Vidia sighed, knowing Tink wouldn't give up on her plan to explore.

Lizzy's Fairy House

Tinker Bell was a very curious tinker fairy. She always wanted to investigate everything – and nothing interested her as much as the mainland. Humans had such unusual inventions!

The fairies were bringing summer to the mainland. Almost as soon as Tink arrived, she saw a car speeding past on the road. She couldn't help but follow it to take a closer look.

Soon the car stopped in front of a house. The driver was a scientist called Dr Griffiths and he had a little girl called Lizzy.

Vidia had followed Tinker Bell, trying to get her to come back to the fairy camp. The two set off into the meadow near the house, and Tink spotted a row of buttons lined up like stepping-stones. She started picking them up to take back to camp.

"I'm not carrying this human junk...." began Vidia, but then she spotted something that made her stop in her tracks. It was a fairy house that Lizzy had made!

Tinker Bell was excited.

"Tinker Bell, we're not supposed to go near human houses!" warned Vidia.

"Human houses are a lot bigger," Tink replied. She went inside and looked around, delighted by the tiny furnishings.

"It's perfectly safe," Tink called.

"Oh, really?" asked Vidia. To teach Tinker Bell a lesson, she whipped up a gust of wind that slammed the door shut!

Tink didn't mind. She was having fun exploring.

But suddenly, Vidia saw Lizzy approaching in the distance. She pulled on the door to let Tink out – but it was jammed shut!

"Tink, someone's coming!" cried Vidia. "Get out of there!"

Tink ignored her. She was sure Vidia was just trying to scare her.

Vidia hid, watching as Lizzy got closer. "Oh, no! What have I done?" she cried as the little girl peeked into the house.

"A ... a ... a fairy ..." Lizzy whispered.

Tinker Bell saw Lizzy's huge eye staring at her through the window. It was terrifying! Lizzy snatched up the fairy house and raced back home. Vidia followed at a safe distance.

Dr Griffiths was busy studying a butterfly he had captured earlier. "Now, dear," he said. "What did you want me to see?"

"Um, never mind ..." Lizzy answered. She worried that her father might try to study the fairy the way he was studying the butterfly.

Lizzy ran upstairs to her room with the little fairy house and Tinker Bell inside. What would happen to the curious fairy now?

THE LITTLE MERMAID

The Wrong Gift

"Wow, Flounder, everyone's here!" cried Ariel. Mermaids and mermen had come from all over the ocean to wish Ariel's sister Aquata a happy birthday.

Unfortunately, Ariel still needed to pick out a gift for her sister. So, Ariel and Flounder left the party and swam to her secret cave.

Together they looked over Ariel's vast collection of bells, clocks, jewellery and other human knickknacks she'd scavenged from shipwrecks.

"How about this?" asked Flounder, swimming around a ship's wheel.

"Too big," said Ariel.

"Or this?" suggested Flounder, nudging a single gold earring.

"Too small," said Ariel.

Suddenly, Ariel noticed a music box.

"This is it!" she cried. "The perfect gift! I've listened to this one again and again, and it plays a really beautiful song."

Ariel swam back to the celebration. Beside King Triton, Aquata sat on a clamshell, and, one by one, the guests presented her with their birthday gifts.

While Ariel waited her turn in line, Sebastian the crab swam by. "Hello, Ariel," he said. "What gift do you have for Aquata?"

When Ariel proudly told Sebastian, his jaw nearly dropped to the ocean floor. "Are you out of your mind?" he cried.

Ariel's eyes widened. Sebastian was right! King Triton hated humans. And Ariel was not supposed to have anything from their world. That's exactly why she'd kept her cave a secret!

Just then, King Triton's deep voice bellowed, "Ariel, you're next."

Ariel hid the present behind her back.

"What gift do you have for your eldest sister?" asked Triton.

"Uh ..." Ariel began.

"A song!" Sebastian announced.

Ariel racked her brain for a song to sing, and then she hit on it! She opened her mouth, and sang the melody from the music box.

When she finished, Flounder swam behind her, replacing the gift in her hand with a beautiful starfish for Aquata's hair.

"It's beautiful!" said Aquata. "And so was your song!"

King Triton smiled approvingly, and Ariel sighed with relief. How she wished her father would change his mind about humans!

"I'd give almost anything to see what the human world is like," she told Flounder. "Do you think my father will ever understand?"

"Maybe when he finally sees what it means to you," said Flounder, "someday he will."

Bagheera Bears Up

Mowgli danced around, humming happily to himself.

"What are you doing, Mowgli?" Bagheera asked from his perch in a nearby tree.

"Practising being a bear," Mowgli told him. "You should try it."

"Me?" Bagheera said, stunned. "I couldn't possibly do such a thing."

"Why not?" Mowgli wanted to know.

"Well, I'm a panther and I happen to like being one," Bagheera replied. "Why on earth would I want to be a bear?"

"Are you kidding?" Mowgli exclaimed. "Bears have the life! They hang out all day long, and they eat ants!"

"Eat ants?" Bagheera asked. "And that's a good thing?"

"Sure!" Mowgli said. "Well, truthfully, they tickle your throat at first. But you get used to it soon enough."

"Have you?" Bagheera asked.

"Not yet," Mowgli confessed. "But I will!"

"Whatever you say, Mowgli," said Bagheera.

Mowgli thought for a moment. "And if you were a bear, you would eat fruit and drink coconut juice, and you would relax, just like us!"

"If you ask me," Bagheera said, "I don't see anything so bad about being a panther. In fact, I like it very much."

"I think you're scared," Mowgli told him.

"Absolutely not!" Bagheera protested. "What on earth would I have to be scared of?" He stood up, stretched and gracefully jumped out of the tree and onto the ground.

"Exactly," Mowgli said. "So, why not try it?"

"You've got to be kidding me!" Bagheera said.

"You know what your problem is?" Mowgli said.

"I'm afraid to ask," said Bagheera.

"You're like a beehive," Mowgli told him. "You work too hard." He stared at Bagheera. "Come on, dance with me!" he cried, grabbing Bagheera's paw and prancing around the panther. After a bit, Bagheera began to dance too, moving his feet and twitching his tail.

"That's it!" Mowgli cheered.

"You know what?" Bagheera admitted. "This isn't so bad after all."

"Now you're getting it!" Mowgli exclaimed. "Now you see why being a bear is so great!" The Man-cub stopped dancing and threw himself on a soft patch of moss. "It's not so bad, is it?"

"Actually," Bagheera said, scratching his back against a rock, "it's sort of fun!"

"One more time!" Mowgli cheered, and they began dancing again.

Jasmine

Jasmine's Treasure

Jasmine flipped through her parents' wedding album. She was happy to be marrying Aladdin but wished her mother were still alive to share the moment.

Jasmine studied every detail, and made a decision. "I want my wedding to be exactly like my mother's," she said. "Then she will be a part of my wedding!"

So she selected the same flowers her mother had chosen. She asked the chef to prepare the same menu and bake the same cake that her parents had. And she showed her mother's wedding dress to the royal seamstress.

"Your mother would be touched that you are honouring her like this," the Sultan said, handing Jasmine an envelope. "She wrote this letter to you many years ago."

My dear Jasmine,

I am writing this letter to give to you when you are to be married. I'm sure you are busy with the preparations. The most wonderful part of my own wedding was my treasure of all treasures. I am so happy that you have found yours!

All my love,

Mother

Jasmine imagined her mother dressed up, with her 'treasure of all treasures'.

"It must have been a truly breathtaking jewel!" Jasmine decided. She had to find hers.

Jasmine studied the wedding album again, but her mother wasn't wearing a priceless jewel.

She found her father with the Genie. "Do you remember Mother's treasure of all treasures from your wedding day?"

The Sultan had never heard of it, but the Genie summoned diamonds, rubies and emeralds. "Choose your very own treasure of all treasures!" he exclaimed.

Jasmine knew none of the jewels was the treasure. "Thank you," she said. "I'll know it when I see it."

Jasmine shared her troubles with Aladdin.

"We'll find it, I promise!" he said.

Jasmine and Aladdin searched in all the store rooms, but they didn't find the treasure.

"I'll keep searching," Aladdin told her.

The day before her wedding, Jasmine read her mother's letter again and her eyes fell on a sketch of her father, drawn by her mother.

Suddenly, Jasmine understood. Her father was her mother's treasure of all treasures!

Aladdin entered. "I'm sorry," he said. "The treasure – I haven't found it."

"I had my treasure all along!" Jasmine said. "It's *you*, Aladdin!"

Their wedding was perfect. Jasmine's dress was lovely and the food was delicious. But, most importantly, Jasmine had Aladdin, her treasure of all treasures, by her side.

A Blustery Day

"Oh dear," said Pooh as the wind whipped around him. "It's very windy. Are you sure this is a good idea, Tigger?" He and Tigger were carrying Pooh's kite out into a clearing in the middle of the Hundred-Acre Wood.

"Don't be silly, Pooh Boy," Tigger responded. "Today is the perfect day to fly your kite. After all, what else is wind for?"

"Yes," Pooh replied. "I suppose you're right." He leaned into a particularly strong gust to keep it from blowing him over as they walked on. Winter was on its way out of the Wood, and spring was on its way in – and it seemed the wind was rushing in to fill the space in between, for it was one of the blusteriest days Pooh could remember.

At last, struggling against the wind, Pooh and Tigger reached the middle of the clearing and got ready to launch the kite. Pooh unrolled some kite string while Tigger held the kite.

"Okay, Pooh," said Tigger. "Get ready! You hold on to the string, and I'll toss the kite up into the wind. One ... two ... THREE!"

With that, Tigger tossed the kite and it was immediately seized by the strong wind and carried high into the air where it danced and darted this way and that.

Meanwhile, Pooh struggled to hold on to the roll of kite string.

"Let out some more string, Pooh!" Tigger suggested. "Let's see how high we can fly it!"

So Pooh let out some more string. The kite sailed higher into the air and, blown around by stronger and stronger gusts, it tugged harder and harder on Pooh's end of the line.

"Fly it higher, Pooh!" exclaimed Tigger.

So Pooh let out more and more string until he had let it all out. He clung tightly to the end of the line as the kite soared, seeming almost to touch the low clouds.

Then, all of a sudden, a tremendous gust of wind blew through the clearing. At the end of the kite string, Pooh felt his feet leave the ground as the wind grabbed hold of the kite and carried it sharply upward.

"My goodness!" said Pooh, realizing that he was being lifted up. Then, before he could be carried too high, he let go of the kite string and tumbled gently to the ground.

But the kite sailed on – up and away, dancing on the breeze for what seemed like forever, until it came to rest at last in the high branches of a very tall tree at the edge of the clearing. Pooh wondered how he would ever get it down.

"Oh well," said Tigger, patting his friend sympathetically on the back. "Guess you flew it just a little too high there, Pooh Boy."

Carl's Promise

Carl and Ellie had been best friends since they first met as children. They grew up, got married and dreamed of becoming explorers.

But Carl and Ellie didn't become explorers. They both worked at the zoo. However, they still dreamed of travelling to Paradise Falls in South America. They saved all their spare money in a jar to pay for the trip. But they could never quite collect enough.

The years went by, and Carl and Ellie grew older. After Ellie passed away, Carl kept all her things just as they had been. But it wasn't the same. He missed Ellie. To make matters worse, the neighbourhood around their beloved home was being torn down to make room for tall, modern buildings.

One day, Carl heard a knock at his door. A boy in a uniform was standing on his porch.

"Good afternoon," said the boy. "My name is Russell, and I am a Junior Wilderness Explorer. Are you in need of assistance today, sir?"

"No," replied Carl. He didn't want help. He just wanted to be left alone.

But Russell wouldn't leave. He wanted to help Carl so that he could earn his Assisting the Elderly badge.

"If I get it, I will become a Senior Wilderness Explorer," Russell explained.

To get rid of Russell, Carl gave him a task. He asked him to find a bird called a Snipe. "I think its burrow is two blocks down," Carl said.

Russell eagerly set off to find the bird, not knowing that it didn't really exist. Carl had made the whole thing up!

Not long after that, Carl received some bad news. He was being forced out of his house and sent to live in a retirement home. Carl didn't want to leave his house. All his memories of Ellie were there.

That night, Carl sat in his living room, looking through Ellie's adventure book. He remembered Ellie's dream of going to South America. He had promised her he'd take her there in an airship.

The next morning, two nurses arrived to drive Carl to the retirement home. "I'll meet you at the van," he told them. "I want to say one last goodbye to the old place."

As the nurses walked back to their van, a huge shadow fell over them. They turned to see thousands of balloons tied to Carl's house! A moment later, the whole house rose into the air!

"So long, boys!" Carl yelled out of the window. He was going to South America!

Bambi

Spring Has Sprung!

Spring had come at last to the forest. *Sniff, sniff* – Bambi could smell the change in the air. The days were growing longer. The nights were getting shorter. The ice and snow were quickly melting away. Crocuses and daffodils were pushing new green shoots out of the ground.

And the forest didn't feel quite as lonely as it had during the cold weather. In just the last few days, Bambi had noticed that there were more animals peeking their heads out of their holes and burrows and dens.

As he took a walk through the forest very early one morning on the first day of spring, Bambi came upon Mrs Possum and her children hanging upside down by their tails from a tree branch. She and Bambi had not seen one another in a long while. But Mrs Possum recognized him just the same.

"Well, hello, Bambi," said Mrs Possum.

"Hello, Mrs Possum," Bambi replied. "I haven't seen you since autumn. Where have you and your family been all winter long?"

"Oh, we like to spend most of our winter indoors," Mrs Possum replied. "But now that spring is here, it's so nice to be out in the fresh air again." Then Mrs Possum and the rest of her family closed their eyes and dozed off, because they liked to spend most of their days sleeping, you know.

Walking on through the forest, Bambi stopped by a tree filled with twittering birds.

"Hello, Bambi," said one of the birds.

"Hello," Bambi replied. "And where have you birds been all winter long?"

"Oh, we fly south for the winter, to warmer places where we can find more food," the bird explained. "But we are so happy it is spring once more. It is lovely to be back in the forest."

Then the bird joined her voice with her friends' twittering tunes. After so many months without it, the chirps and tweets were sweet music to Bambi's ears.

Bambi walked further, meeting old friends at every turn. He came upon mice moving from their winter quarters back into their spring and summer homes. He noticed the squirrels and chipmunks snacking leisurely on nuts, no longer storing them away in their winter stockpiles. He heard a woodpecker rapping at a pine tree. And he spotted the ducks out for a swim on the pond.

Yes, thought Bambi, it had been a long, cold, difficult winter. But somehow the arrival of spring made him feel that everything would be all right. Everywhere he looked there was life, there were new beginnings ... and, most importantly, there was hope.

Snow White
and the Seven Dwarfs

Home Sweet Home

As the sun rose above the Seven Dwarfs' cottage, Snow White was already thinking about what to make for supper that evening. She had arrived at the cottage just the day before, after her evil stepmother, the Queen, had driven Snow White from the palace and the Queen's huntsman had left her alone in the forest. Luckily, a group of helpful woodland creatures had befriended Snow White and led her to the Dwarfs' little cottage. Now, for the first time in a long while, she felt safe and happy.

She was so grateful to the Dwarfs for sharing their cosy home with her, she wanted to give them a special treat.

"Perhaps we'll have berry pie for supper tonight!" she said to her furry woodland friends after the Dwarfs had gone to work. The little animals nodded in agreement. Together they left the cottage and headed to the forest to pick berries. With all her friends helping, Snow White quickly filled her berry basket. Then she sat down among the sweet-smelling flowers with a sigh.

"How different life has become," she said to her friends. "I don't miss the grand castle at all. I love living in this funny little cottage. A home does not need to be grand to be a happy one! Remember that!"

The animals exchanged looks with one another. They began tugging at her skirt to pull her to her feet.

"What is it, dears?" she asked them. "Oh! Do you want to show me where all of *you* live? I would love to see!" she said delightedly.

Two bluebirds were first. Twittering excitedly, they fluttered around their nest, which had been built in a cosy nook of a nearby tree.

"What a lovely nest!" cried Snow White. The birds looked pleased.

The fawns were next. Pulling at her skirt, they brought Snow White to a sun-dappled clearing in a warm glade.

"How cosy!" exclaimed Snow White. The fawns flicked their tails happily.

Next, the chipmunks and squirrels showed her the hollow in an old tree where they lived. Then the rabbits proudly showed her the entrance to their burrows.

"You all have such pretty little homes," said Snow White, as they made their way back to the Dwarfs' cottage. "Thank you for showing them to me. We are all lucky to live where we do, aren't we?" she said with a smile.

And with that, she skipped the rest of the way back to the cottage to start preparing her pie. She could hardly wait until the Dwarfs got home!

An Icy Blast

Queen Elsa ordered her giant snowman, Marshmallow, to escort Anna and her companions off the mountain. She didn't want Anna to stay at the palace because she might accidentally hurt her again, and she couldn't go back to Arendelle because she didn't know how to undo the icy damage she had done.

Marshmallow started to guide the friends out of the door, but Anna hit him with a snowball, so he decided to chase them instead!

Anna, Kristoff and Olaf ran as fast as they could until they came to a cliff edge. The only way was down! They dropped a rope over the edge and began to lower themselves down, but Marshmallow grabbed the rope and pulled them back up. Panicked, Anna did the only thing she could think of: she cut the rope!

Luckily, Anna, Kristoff and Olaf landed safely in a soft snowdrift. Kristoff's reindeer, Sven, rushed to see if they were okay – he was especially concerned about Olaf's carrot nose. As Kristoff pulled himself out of the snow, he realized something was wrong with Anna: her hair was turning white.

"It's because Elsa struck you with her powers, isn't it?" Kristoff asked. He was right. When Anna had refused to leave the castle without her sister, Elsa had become angry and lost control of her powers. She had accidentally shot an icy blast across the room that had hit Anna in the chest.

Concerned about Anna, Kristoff came up with a plan. "We need to go and see my friends," he said. "They can help."

Back at her ice palace, Elsa paced back and forth. She was trying to work out how she could unfreeze Arendelle and bring summer back to the kingdom. She felt very upset, which made her powers even more difficult to control. As Elsa became more emotional her powers grew stronger, which made the storm even worse.

Meanwhile, Prince Hans and a group of other important visitors, who had been trapped in Arendelle by the ice, were making their way up the North Mountain. As they climbed higher, they saw the snow storm growing over the ice palace.

Night fell as Kristoff led Anna, Olaf and Sven into a remote and rocky valley. Kristoff said that his friends lived there.

Suddenly, Anna thought she saw some of the rocks move. "Trolls!" she exclaimed.

Kristoff had spent a lot of time with the trolls, so he was practically family to them. He knew they could help Anna.

The trolls were very excited to see Kristoff and even more excited to meet Anna. They lifted them up on their shoulders and carried them along to see the old troll.

The trolls thought Anna was Kristoff's girlfriend and that it was a great match. They were so happy, which goes to show that love brings out the best in everyone!

Tangled
A Big Girl Now

Flynn Rider, the thief, was escaping from the palace guards through the forest. In his bag was his precious stolen prize – the royal crown! Guards and bowmen were following him, and even Maximus, horse to the captain of the guard, was determined to catch him.

But Flynn was cunning. The thief swung on a vine, knocked the Captain off the horse, and landed in the saddle himself. Flynn clung to the satchel as Maximus snorted furiously, twirling until he finally sunk his teeth into the bag.

"Give me that!" yelled Flynn. As he yanked the satchel free, it went flying into the air.

The satchel snagged on a tree branch that extended over a cliff's edge. But that didn't stop Flynn or Maximus. They both made their way out onto the branch. Flynn reached the bag just ahead of Maximus. "Ha-ha!" the thief crowed triumphantly. CRACK! The tree branch splintered and they both toppled into the canyon below.

Flynn instantly took off. As he felt his way along a rock face, he was thrilled to discover a hidden entrance to a cave and soon emerged to an astonishing sight. There, in the centre of a hidden valley, stood an enormous tower. It was the perfect hiding place! "There's not even a door!" he remarked.

Using two arrows, Flynn climbed the tower and into the open window at the top. Finally, he breathed a sigh of relief. He had his satchel and he was safe from that manic horse.

CLANG! Suddenly, everything went black.

Rapunzel had seen Flynn climbing the tower and hit him with a frying pan! He was out cold.

Using the frying pan, she opened his lips. His teeth weren't pointy. In fact, nothing about this man seemed ugly and scary, as Mother Gothel had warned. He was actually very pleasant looking.

Quickly, she stuffed him in a wardrobe and propped a chair against it. Then she stopped to consider her situation. She had just defended herself from an outsider. Rapunzel felt exhilarated! Surely this act of bravery would prove to Mother Gothel that she could handle herself in the outside world.

"Too weak to handle myself out there, huh, Mother? Well ..." she laughed, "Try telling that to my frying pan!" Rapunzel boldly brandished the frying pan above her and WHAM! She accidently hit her own head!

"Oh no!" she moaned, upset. It was a good thing Mother Gothel hadn't seen that.

Disney
Sleeping Beauty

Berry Picking

Once upon a time, in a forest far away, there lived a lovely princess who did not know she was a princess, and three good fairies who pretended to be mortal. (Of course, you know exactly to whom we are referring ... so let's get right to the story of Briar Rose and her three 'aunts'.)

One morning, Flora called the group together to suggest they go out to search the forest for berries.

"What a wonderful idea," said Briar Rose.

"Yes, indeed," said Merryweather. "If we pick enough, we can make a berry pie."

"If we pick enough," declared Fauna, "we can make enough jam to last us through the whole year."

"Well, we'll never have enough if we don't get started now," said Flora. And so they gathered their berry baskets and set out.

They followed a shady path through the forest until they came upon a thicket bursting with berry bushes. And, without delay, the four berry-pickers got to work. But, as you will see, just because they got to work, doesn't mean their baskets actually got full.

Merryweather, for one, had a terrible time keeping her basket upright. Every time she bent to pick another berry, her basket tipped and out spilled all but two or three.

Fauna, on the other hand, had an entirely different problem keeping her berries in her basket – somehow they kept finding their way into her mouth!

And as for Briar Rose, her heart and her mind were miles away from her berry basket ... dancing instead in the arms of a handsome stranger.

"All right, dearies," Flora called as the sun began to sink. "It's time to start back to the cottage. Let's see what you've got."

"Um, well ..." said Merryweather. "I don't seem to have many berries in my basket."

Flora rolled her eyes and moved on to Fauna. "Let me guess ..." she said as she looked from Fauna's empty basket to her purple mouth.

"Ah, yes ..." Fauna said as she guiltily dabbed at a drop of juice on her lips. "Berries ... delicious!"

Flora sighed. "And you, Briar Rose?" she asked hopefully.

But Briar Rose just looked down sheepishly at the empty basket in her hands. "I'm sorry, Aunt Flora," she said. "I guess I got a little bit distracted."

"Well," said Flora, shaking her head, "no berry pie for us this week, I guess." Then she shrugged. "But we can always have chocolate cake instead!"

THE
PRINCESS
AND THE
FROG

The Masked Ball

The masked ball was in full swing at Charlotte's house. All of the important people from New Orleans were there! All apart from Prince Naveen.

"It's just not fair! I never get anything I wish for!" Charlotte complained to Tiana.

"There are still some latecomers due to arrive," Tiana tried to console her.

"No, he's not coming!" sobbed Charlotte. "It's my fault, I didn't wish hard enough on the Evening Star!" Charlotte gazed up and pleaded, "Please, please, please –"

Tiana let out a sigh – her friend still believed in fairy tales.

Suddenly the doorman announced the arrival of the Prince, and Charlotte hurried to welcome him. Tiana was amazed. She was just wondering if the star really had granted her friend's wish, when she spotted the estate agents from whom she was supposed to be buying the old mill, to turn into her restaurant.

"Have you brought me the contract to sign?" she greeted them cheerily.

"No, our agreement has been revoked, madam. Someone has just offered us a better price."

Tiana was so disappointed that she fell against the food and ruined her costume!

Charlotte arrived to help. "Oh, my dear Tia!" she consoled her friend. "Come with me, I'll lend you one of my princess gowns!"

She led her to her room and Tiana quickly changed. She looked beautiful, but she was too upset to return to the ballroom with her friend. Tiana went out onto the balcony alone to watch the night sky.

"My dream of opening my own restaurant will never come true," she whispered to herself. "Unless ... I cannot believe I'm doing this," she said. And she started to wish on the Evening Star! She closed her eyes and concentrated.

When Tiana opened her eyes again, a frog had appeared on the balcony!

"Great," said Tiana ironically. "So I'm supposed to kiss you, I assume?"

"Kissing would be nice, yes!" exclaimed the frog, smiling.

"A talking frog?!" Tiana shrieked and ran back into Charlotte's bedroom. Really, what a ridiculous evening. First, she had wished on a star and now she was seeing things!

"I'm going to end up believing in the impossible!" she panicked.

Tiana thought she was starting to believe in fairy tales, just like Charlotte did, and she couldn't think of anything more terrifying!

Beauty and the Beast

The Change Begins

The prince arranged for a portrait to be painted of him with his new fiancée, Princess Tulip Morningstar. But when he saw it, the prince was alarmed. His eyes looked cruel and his mouth looked thinner and more sinister than it had looked before. The portrait painter would pay for such an uncharitable act!

"I need a favour," he said to his friend Gaston. He wanted the artist killed! "The incident cannot be traced back to me, you understand?" the prince warned Gaston.

And that was just the beginning of the prince's awful deeds. When Princess Tulip returned to the castle, she hoped the prince would treat her with kindness and love. But his smile turned to a scowl as soon as he saw her. "You are in quite a state from travelling. I'm surprised you didn't make yourself presentable before showing yourself."

The staff tried to cover up their master's meanness, but his behaviour didn't improve.

And then the servants started to turn to stone! It was the curse – and the prince had to break it. Marrying Tulip was the only way. She loved him, so all he had to do was make the witches believe he loved her, too. He had to seal their love with a kiss.

Lumiere arranged a romantic evening so love could blossom. Flowers were moved from the hothouse to the garden to recreate the joy of spring, and the princess was overwhelmed with happiness. She kissed the prince, but the prince's mood shifted from glee to panic when he heard a noise that sounded like an animal.

The prince looked serious. "Stay here. I'm going to check it out."

When the prince came back, he had been badly clawed and was angry. When Lumiere greeted them at the door, he told them that Cogsworth was missing. And the next day, Mrs Potts went missing too.

The prince turned on Tulip. "If you loved me, none of this would be happening! Mrs Potts and Cogsworth would be here! The animals in the maze wouldn't have attacked me, and I wouldn't look like this!"

So that was it. The transformation from prince to beast was almost complete. He had broken another girl's heart, and he was behaving more and more like an animal. Only Lumiere had avoided the curse, but the prince soon turned on him too, and then the Beast was alone.

Disney
ALICE
in
WONDERLAND

The Silent Treatment

The Queen of Hearts loved to shout orders at her royal subjects. She shouted so much, in fact, that it wasn't surprising when she came down with a terrible case of laryngitis.

"There, there," said her husband, the diminutive King. "Rest your voice and let me do the ruling for you, my dear." The Queen hardly let the King get a word in edgeways, so he was looking forward to being in charge for a change.

As they strolled through the royal garden, the Queen noticed that the fence was painted pink instead of the required red. "Off! Off!" the Queen croaked. She wanted the King to punish the royal gardeners with her favourite order, "Off with their heads!"

Instead, the King said, "The Queen decrees that you may have the day off!" The gardeners cheered as steam escaped from the Queen's ears. "You must relax, sweetheart," the King warned her, "or you simply won't get well."

Soon the couple paused to play a game of croquet. The Queen hit the hedgehog ball with the flamingo mallet, and the hedgehog rolled willy-nilly across the lawn. The playing-card wickets knew better than to let the Queen make a bad shot. They jumped all over the grass, making sure the ball passed underneath them. "I'm undefeated!" the Queen rasped triumphantly.

"What's that, dear?" asked the King.

He couldn't understand exactly what his wife was saying. "The Queen says she cheated!" he finally announced.

The entire royal staff gasped. Those nearby ducked as the Queen swung a flamingo at the King's head.

"That's enough croquet for today," crooned the King soothingly. "You don't want to tire yourself out."

He led his wife to a bench in the shade. The Queen sat down, pointed to the servants hovering nearby and acted out drinking a cup of tea.

The King stood up and announced, "You're all invited to have tea with the Queen!" Of course, this was not what the Queen had in mind at all.

A table was laid with tea, fancy cakes and sandwiches. Everyone ate, laughed and had a wonderful time. The Queen, ignored by everyone, seethed with anger.

She grabbed one of the flamingo mallets, then charged the table. Unfortunately, she didn't see the croquet ball in her path. As she tripped, the flamingo's beak plunged into the ground, causing the Queen to pole-vault up and over the table of guests and through her open bedroom window.

"A splendid idea, my dear!" called the King. "A nap will do you good!"

Dance, Daddy-o!

Deep in the jungle at the temple ruins, the monkeys and their ruler, King Louie, were always looking to have a swingin' time.

"Let's have a dance-off!" King Louie suggested to the monkeys one evening.

"Hooray! Hooray!" the monkeys cheered.

"What's a dance-off?" one monkey asked.

"You know, a contest," said King Louie. "An opportunity for everyone to get down, strut their stuff, cut a rug! And whoever lays down the smoothest moves is the winner!"

"Hooray!" cheered the monkeys.

King Louie rubbed his chin. "The first thing we need is some music," he said, pointing at the monkey musicians. "Hit it, fellas!"

The musicians blasted out a jazzy tune, blowing through their hands like horns, knocking out a beat on some coconuts and drumming on a hollow log. Soon, all the monkeys were gathered around the musicians, tapping their toes and shaking their tails.

"Now," said King Louie, "who will dance?"

All the monkeys raised their hands. King Louie looked around. "Let's see," he said scratching his head, "I choose ... me!"

"Hooray!" the monkeys cheered. They were disappointed not to be chosen. But, after all, King Louie *was* their King.

So King Louie moved his hips from side to side. He waved his arms in the air. He closed his eyes so he could really feel the beat.

"Dance, Daddy-o!" one monkey cried.

King Louie boogied and bopped like he had never boogied and bopped before. Then, when the song was over, King Louie stopped dancing and scrambled onto his throne. "Now it's time to choose the winner!" he said.

"But King Louie...." one monkey began to object. All the other monkeys were thinking the same thing: didn't you need more than one dancer to have a dance-off?

"Oh, silly me," said King Louie with a chuckle. The monkeys looked at each other and smiled, expecting that the King had realized his mistake. But, King Louie said, "Of course, we need a judge! Who will judge?"

Everyone raised their hands. King Louie looked around, then said, "I choose ... me!"

"Hooray!" the monkeys cheered.

"And as the judge, I will now choose the winner of the dance-off," King Louie continued. He looked around at all the monkeys. "Now, let's see. I choose ... me! Let's hear it for the winner!"

"Hooray!" the monkeys cheered, because, after all, King Louie was their King – and a pretty swingin' dancer, too!

Fairies to the Rescue

Tinker Bell has been captured by a little human girl called Lizzy! The fairies were bringing summer to the mainland, and Tink had flown off to investigate a car that had passed by the fairy camp.

The car stopped at a country house, and Tink watched as the humans spotted a butterfly with a paint-splattered wing. Lizzy's father, Dr Griffiths, was amazed, but wouldn't believe Lizzy when she said the fairies must have painted it that way. Dr Griffiths was a scientist and didn't believe in fairies.

Vidia, who had followed Tink, was upset. She knew humans could be dangerous and she wanted to go back to the fairy camp. But then Tink had found a little fairy house that Lizzy had made. She went inside to explore and Vidia, wanting to teach Tink a lesson, slammed the door shut with a gust of wind.

Just then, Vidia had seen Lizzy approaching, but the door of the little house was stuck! Vidia could do nothing but hide as Lizzy picked up the fairy house and spotted Tinker Bell.

The little girl was so excited, she took the house – and Tink – straight up to her bedroom. Lizzy placed the fairy house on the bed and peeked in one of its windows.

But Tinker Bell was nowhere to be seen. "Where have you gone?" wondered Lizzy. She took the roof off the house and *ZIP!* Tink darted out.

Mr Twitches, the family cat, immediately lunged for the fairy. As Vidia watched at the window, Lizzy put Tinker Bell in a birdcage for safekeeping.

"Don't worry," Lizzy told her. "Mr Twitches won't bother you as long as you're in there."

Vidia knew that she had to free Tink, but she couldn't do it alone. She flew as fast as she could towards fairy camp, but a rainstorm slowed her down.

When Vidia finally arrived at fairy camp, she explained to her friends what had happened. She said that Tinker Bell had been captured in a cage, and that they had to go and save her.

"We can't fly in the rain," Fawn said. "And the meadow's already flooded!"

Clank and Bobble weren't worried, they had a plan. They were going to build a boat!

With Clank and Bobble's help, the entire camp set to work creating a hull out of bark, a mast out of reeds and twigs, and a sail out of a lily pad.

It was going to be a challenge, but the fairies were determined to rescue their friend.

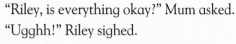

No More Goofing Around

Things were not going well inside Riley's Mind World. Sadness had touched a happy memory, changing it to a sad one – and made Riley cry in front of her new classmates! Even worse, Joy, Sadness and Riley's core memories had accidentally been sucked out into Riley's Mind World and ended up in Long Term Memory. They had to get the core memories back to Headquarters quickly before Riley forgot about everything she loved!

While Riley was having dinner with her parents, Anger, Fear and Disgust were up in Headquarters trying not to panic. Disgust was driving the console, trying her best to keep Riley acting normal.

"I've found a junior hockey league," Mum said to Riley. "And get this: try-outs are tomorrow after school. What luck, right?"

"Oh yeah," Riley said sarcastically. "Sounds fantastic."

Mum looked at Riley in shock. In Mum's Headquarters, her Emotions figured out something must be wrong.

"How was school?" Dad asked.

"It was fine, I guess. I don't know...." Riley answered grumpily.

Riley's parents were surprised. They couldn't understand why their daughter wasn't her usual happy self.

"Riley, is everything okay?" Mum asked.

"Ugghh!" Riley sighed.

"Riley," Dad said sternly, "I do not like this new attitude."

Inside Headquarters, Anger took over the console. "Oh, I'll show you attitude," he said, pushing buttons and levers.

At the dinner table, Riley lost her cool. "Just leave me alone!" she screamed.

"That is it!" Dad shouted, pounding the table. He pointed upstairs. "Go to your room! Now!"

Riley stormed upstairs.

Later, there was a knock on Riley's door. Dad opened it and stepped into her bedroom. Riley was lying on her sleeping bag in silence.

"Do you want to talk about it?" asked Dad. Riley said nothing.

Dad tried to start up their goofball act, making noises like a monkey, but Riley simply turned away. Giving up, Dad left the room.

In Riley's Mind World, Goofball Island made a terrible groaning noise. It was collapsing! Riley had stopped goofing around with her dad – that part of Riley's personality was crumbling away!

Joy and Sadness ran back to the solid ground of Long Term Memory. They watched as Goofball Island fell into the darkness.

Then it was gone.

The Missing Daffodils

One spring day, Daisy went to Minnie's house to help in the garden. But when the two got outside, they found a big surprise.

"My daffodils are gone!" Minnie shrieked.

"It must be a flower prowler!" Daisy cried.

Minnie and Daisy searched for clues.

"What's this?" Daisy asked, pulling a few strands of fuzzy white hair off a bush near the daffodil patch.

"Maybe the flower prowler left it," Minnie said.

A moment later, Minnie's doorbell rang. Mickey was standing there with a big bunch of daffodils tied with a fluffy white ribbon!

"Mickey!" Minnie cried. "How could you cut down my daffodils?"

"What do you mean?" Mickey asked, confused. "I bought these at the flower shop!"

Minnie put the flowers in a vase. She was glad that Mickey wasn't the flower prowler.

Minnie, Daisy and Mickey decided to look around town for the thief.

They headed to the park and found Goofy. He had a daffodil pinned to his waistcoat.

"Hiya," Goofy called. "Do you like my flower? Mr Power has a daffodil sale on today!"

"Hmmm...." said Minnie. "That's quite a coincidence."

They peeked through the window of Power's Flowers. The shopkeeper had a fuzzy white moustache and his shop was full of daffodils!

The friends burst inside. "Where did you get these daffodils?" Minnie demanded.

"From Mrs Pote, the farmer," Mr Power replied. "She delivers daffodils every day, but today she brought dozens of extras!"

Mr Power pointed the way to Mrs Pote's farm. "You can't miss her," he said. "She has fuzzy white hair."

Mrs Pote's farm was called Pote's Goats.

"Yes, I delivered extra daffodils today," Mrs Pote told Minnie. "My favourite goat, Flower, eats a lot of them as soon as they bloom but she must not have been very hungry today."

Mrs Pote led the friends to Flower's pen but there was no goat inside!

"She must have escaped!" Mrs Pote cried.

"There's a hole in the fence," Mickey said.

"Not only are Minnie's daffodils gone, but so is Mrs Pote's goat!" Daisy said.

"These two mysteries are connected," said Minnie. "I know who the flower prowler is!"

She pointed towards a trail of footprints.

They followed the footprints to Daisy's garden. There was Flower, happily munching away on Daisy's flowers.

"There's our flower prowler," Minnie said. "If we could only train her to like weeds!"

Tangled

Who's Tricking Whom?

Rapunzel was feeling very pleased with herself. A stranger had climbed in through the tower window and she had managed to knock him out and lock him in her wardrobe!

Now Rapunzel noticed the satchel Flynn had dropped when he fell.

She reached inside and pulled out a gold crown covered with jewels.

Pascal looked on curiously as Rapunzel inspected the strange object – she had never seen such a thing before. She tried slipping it over her wrist, but it fell right off. Then she placed it on top of her head. It fit perfectly!

Rapunzel gazed into the mirror. Something seemed familiar –

"Rapunzel! Let down your hair!" Mother Gothel called out.

Quickly Rapunzel hid the crown. Then she threw her locks of magic hair out of the window so that Mother Gothel could climb up into the tower.

"I've got a surprise for you!" the wicked woman exclaimed. "This evening I'm going to make you your favourite soup!"

"I've got a surprise for you too," mumbled Rapunzel staring at the wardrobe.

Then Rapunzel turned to Mother Gothel and spoke confidently, "You know you said I mustn't leave the tower because I would never be able to manage on my own outside? Against all the dangers, Mother? Well, don't worry any more – I've just –"

"That's enough!" Mother Gothel suddenly roared angrily. "You're not leaving this tower! EVER!"

Rapunzel was shocked. Realizing she would never get out of the tower unless she took matters into her own hands, Rapunzel quickly asked for another birthday present.

"Oh, of course." Rapunzel said. "I just wanted to tell you that instead of leaving the tower I would much rather have some mother-of-pearl paint for my birthday."

Mother Gothel frowned. To make this paint she would have to collect shells from a shore far away, three days' walk.

"Yes, I think I'd rather stay here in safety and get the paint I need to finish my pictures," the young girl insisted.

"It's a deal," Mother Gothel agreed and sighed with relief. "I'll be back in three day's time." She went off smiling – she had tricked Rapunzel!

From the top of her tower, Rapunzel watched her heading off into the distance. She was smiling too ... because, in her own way, she had managed to trick Mother Gothel.

The Witches' Confession

At the top of a hill was a gingerbread-style mansion. Its roof stretched skyward, like a tall witch's hat. Inside, the witches were having their morning tea. Martha was bringing in a tray of scones when she heard Lucinda squeal with delight.

"She's here! She's here!" Lucinda cried.

Circe came into the room to see why her sisters were in such a tizzy. "Ah," she said. "Pflanze has finally come home!" She stroked the cat on the head. "And where did you get to, pretty girl?"

Circe's older sisters looked at each other fearfully.

"Or should I be asking what you've been doing?" Circe put her hand on her hip, waiting for her older sisters to answer.

"Pflanze has been with the prince, keeping an eye on him for us."

Circe rolled her eyes. "I told you to leave him alone!" But she couldn't help asking, "What did you see?"

"Nasty, terrible things! He drove a girl to jump off the cliffs...."

Ruby explained. "He's turned into the Beast, as we thought he would. And he almost killed Gaston while stalking in the forest."

Circe looked disappointed. "But he didn't kill him, so there's still hope?"

The sisters were aghast. Was she still in love with him?

"I'm not in love with him. I had just hoped he would have changed his ways and made a better life for himself!"

Lucinda smiled at her little sister. She wasn't like them. She cared about people. They only cared about her. They delighted in the downfall of people.

The sisters told Circe about Tulip.

"So, she threw herself off the cliffs?" Circe asked.

"She did, my dear, but was saved by Ursula."

Circe glared at her sisters. "And what did the sea witch demand in return?"

"How would we know?" said Lucinda innocently.

But they did know, and Circe guessed what it was – the sea witch had taken Tulip's beauty! Circe was furious. She was going to Morningstar Castle first thing in the morning to sort this out.

Lucinda went to the pantry and returned with a little drawstring bag. "Give Ursula this. Tulip's beauty will be returned."

Circe smiled and thanked her sister. "Don't get into any trouble while I'm away."

The Good Thing About Rain

"Rise and shine!" cried Pongo. One by one, he nudged each of his 15 Dalmatian puppies with his nose.

The puppies yawned and stretched.

But Rolly just rolled over and slept on.

"Aw, come on, Rolly," Pongo whispered in the pup's ear. "It's morning! Don't you want to go out?"

At the mention of the word 'out,' Rolly was instantly wide awake!

Rolly was not alone. As if by magic, the sleepy group had become a pack of jumping, barking puppies. They raced together through the kitchen to the back door, where they jumped up and down, waiting for Nanny to let them out into the garden.

"Okay, here I come," said Nanny, as she made her way across the kitchen. Then she flung the door open wide and stepped out of the way to let the puppies race past.

But they didn't move. It was raining!

"Oh, go on," said Perdita, trying to nudge the pups out the door. "It's only a little water."

But they wouldn't budge.

The next morning, Patch awoke with a start. With a few sharp barks, he helped Pongo wake the other puppies. Within seconds, all 15 were crowding around the back door.

Nanny rushed to open the door again.

And once again, the puppies were very disappointed to see raindrops falling.

"Well," said Pongo with a sigh, "April showers bring May flowers!"

The next morning, the puppies weren't in any hurry to go outside. After all, it was probably still raining. They thought that all they had to look forward to was another whole day spent inside.

So, when Nanny opened the door on a sunny morning, the puppies were so surprised that they didn't know what to do.

Then, springing into action, they tumbled over one another in their rush to get out the door. They raced off in different directions, ready to sniff, dig, roll and explore.

But then, almost at once, all 15 puppies froze in their tracks. They looked around at each other, then down at themselves. What was this stuff getting all over their spotted white coats? It was brown. It was wet. It was squishy. It was mud! And it was FUN!

From the doorway, Pongo and Perdita looked out at their muddy puppies and laughed.

"You know what this means, don't you?" Pongo asked Perdita.

Perdy nodded. "Baths."

Pongo smiled, watching the frolicking puppies. "Let's not tell them – just yet," he said.

Minnie's Easter Bonnet

It was a perfect spring day and Minnie was spending it in the perfect spring way – she was making a new Easter bonnet!

"Not bad," Minnie said, admiring her new hat in the mirror. "But it's not quite right."

Minnie searched through her wardrobe and her dresser until she found an old bag of balloons. Minnie quickly blew up two – one pink and one yellow. Then she removed the feathers from her Easter bonnet and tied the balloons to it with pretty lavender ribbons.

As Minnie was putting the final touches to her creation, she spotted Mickey through her window. "Yoo-hoo, Mickey!" she cried, running outside. "I want to show you something!"

Suddenly, a gust of wind took the balloons and Minnie's bonnet up into the sky!

Minnie quickly jumped into Mickey's car. "Follow that hat!" she cried.

Mickey and Minnie drove through town, keeping their eyes on the floating bonnet.

"Oh no!" Minnie cried. She watched as a curious crow flew towards her bonnet! The bird began pecking at the pink balloon and … POP! The startled crow flew off.

There was only one balloon left, but the bonnet was still floating high in the air.

Mickey and Minnie drove to the edge of town, following the bonnet as the wind carried it further and further away.

Soon they reached a farm and Mickey spotted a rope hanging from a fence post. Mickey grabbed the rope and made it into a lasso.

One … two … three times he tossed the lasso into the air, but the bonnet was still out of reach.

The hat zigged and zagged over the farm until the yellow balloon snagged on a weather vane on top of a barn. POP!

Minnie watched the bonnet drop into the branches of a tall tree. "We've got it now!" she cried. "Help me with this ladder, please, Mickey!"

While Mickey held the ladder, Minnie carefully climbed up and found …

… a robin sitting in her hat!

"Shoo! That's not a nest!" Minnie said.

But the robin was comfortable and wouldn't budge. Then it was joined by another robin.

"Oh, I see," Minnie said, smiling at the happy couple. She tried to be very quiet as she climbed back down the ladder.

"I should have suspected that it would end this way," Minnie sighed.

"What do you mean?" Mickey asked.

"After all," Minnie said with a laugh, "what's an Easter bonnet without a few Easter *eggs*?"

Make Believe

The fairies were bringing summer to the mainland. Curious Tinker Bell had left the safety of fairy camp to follow a car along a road – she wanted to see how it worked.

Vidia had followed Tink, trying to get her to come back. She knew fairies weren't supposed to go near humans. But Tink hadn't listened. The car soon stopped at a house, where a girl, Lizzy, and her father had got out. Lizzy believed in fairies, but her father, who was a scientist, did not.

Tink found a fairy house that Lizzy had made. Tink was exploring it when Vidia accidentally trapped her inside! Lizzy found Tinker Bell and was very excited – she had finally found a fairy. She took the fairy house, with Tink inside, up to her room. To keep Tinker Bell safe from the family cat, Lizzy put the fairy inside a birdcage.

Vidia watched from the window and thought Lizzy was keeping Tink prisoner! She rushed back to fairy camp to get help and the fairies built a boat in order to rescue Tinker Bell – it was raining, so they couldn't fly.

Back at the house, Lizzy let Tinker Bell out of the cage and showed off her collection of fairy artwork. But as Lizzy described what was going on in each picture, Tink realized that the little girl had her fairy facts all wrong!

Tink tried to tell Lizzy, but all Lizzy heard was a jingling sound. "So that's how fairies speak!" she exclaimed. Tink went over to the fairy house to fix the door.

"Why, you're quite the little tinker, aren't you?" asked Lizzy.

Tink pointed to herself, then rang the little house's fairy bell. "Tinker Bell?" Lizzy cried. "What a lovely name!"

Just then, Lizzy's father came upstairs to fix some leaks in the roof. "Lizzy," he said, "it sounds like you're talking to ... a fairy?"

Tinker Bell hid. Lizzy quickly held up a fairy drawing to show her father. "Oh, yes, but she's make-believe," she replied.

"Quite right," her father said. "For that reason, I would like to see you spending less time in the fantasy world and more time in the real world. This summer you have an excellent opportunity to learn all sorts of wonderful things. Here is a blank field journal. I'm sure you'll be able to fill it with your own scientific research." Satisfied, her father went back to repairing the house.

Lizzy sighed. She hadn't wanted to put Tinker Bell in danger by telling her father about her. But she hoped one day she could convince her father that fairies really did exist!

DUMBO

You're Gonna Be Huge!

Dumbo sat in the corner with a big frown on his face.

"What's the matter, kid?" Timothy asked.

Dumbo just shook his head.

"You've got nothing to be sad about," Timothy continued. Dumbo didn't say anything.

"Well, if you're not going to tell me what's bugging ya, I guess I'll just have to figure it out for myself," Timothy said. "I know!" he exclaimed. "You're hungry?"

Dumbo shook his head.

"Thirsty?" Timothy asked.

Dumbo shook his head again.

"Concerned about the June-bug population in Saskatchewan?" Timothy suggested.

Dumbo shook his head doubly hard.

"Well, then," Timothy concluded. "It can only be one thing. It pains me to say it, but I think you have a case of 'feeling sorry for myself-itis'."

Dumbo's large ears pricked up.

"Yes," Timothy continued. "It's a dangerous disease that has affected many of us. Even the strongest cannot avoid it."

Dumbo looked to his left and to his right, then pointed to himself.

"Yes, that's right – you!" Timothy said. "I bet I know what's got you down – your above-average ear size."

Dumbo nodded.

"And the fact that people make fun of you," Timothy continued.

Dumbo nodded even more.

"And, on top of all that," Timothy said, "you've been separated from your mother."

A tear started to form in Dumbo's eye.

"Don't feel sorry for yourself!" Timothy ordered. Dumbo looked up, surprised.

"You know why?" Timothy asked. "Because one day you're gonna be huge!"

Dumbo blinked in disbelief.

"We're talking autographs, your name in lights. They're gonna eat their hats for the way they treated you," Timothy predicted.

Dumbo looked nervous.

"I don't mean eat their hats for real," Timothy explained. "It's just a figure of speech. Not that some of them wouldn't deserve having to eat their hats. But that's not what we're talking about. They're gonna be really sorry they treated you so bad, understand?"

Dumbo nodded his head.

"All right then," Timothy said. "Feeling better?"

And Dumbo nodded doubly hard as visions of success, happiness – and being with his mother again – filled his head.

A Frozen Heart

The trolls were carrying Anna and Kristoff aloft in celebration, thinking that Kristoff had brought her to meet them because she was his girlfriend. But the truth was that Anna had been hurt and Kristoff was hoping that the old troll would be able to help her.

When he saw her the old troll realized that Anna's sister Elsa had put ice in Anna's heart. He told them it would make her freeze solid within a day, but he did give them hope. "An act of true love can thaw a frozen heart," he explained.

Kristoff, Sven and Olaf, their little snowman friend, decided to take Anna back home to Prince Hans. Hans and Anna were planning to get married, so surely he could break the spell with true love's kiss.

Meanwhile, Hans was searching for Anna. He and the Arendelle search party arrived at Elsa's ice palace. Marshmallow, Elsa's giant snowman guard, tried to stop them and protect the Queen. But the mob attacked him and burst into the palace to find Elsa.

Whenever Elsa was worried or afraid her powers increased and now she unleashed them, full force, on the men trying to capture her. She created a huge wall of ice and icy spikes to defend herself. Some of the soldiers were pushed back and trapped on a balcony, while others were pinned down by ice spikes so they couldn't move.

Hans was alarmed. "Don't be the monster they think you are!" he shouted to Elsa.

Elsa realized her magic had gone too far. She let her hands drop, and the men were safe. But then one aimed a crossbow at Elsa! Hans pushed it aside so the arrow struck a large ice chandelier. It fell in a crash and landed on top of Elsa, knocking her out.

Hans instructed the soldiers to take Elsa back to Arendelle in the hope that she could undo the icy damage.

When Elsa woke up she realized she was in one of the castle's cells. Gazing out through the window, she was shocked to see how her storm had damaged the kingdom. When Elsa asked for Anna, Hans explained that her sister hadn't returned.

Outside, Sven was hurrying down the mountain carrying Anna and Kristoff on his back. Anna was in Kristoff's arms and it was clear to him that she was getting weaker and weaker.

When they finally reached the castle gates, he passed Anna to the royal servants. As the servants took Anna inside and the castle gates closed, Kristoff felt a sudden great sadness.

Kristoff was starting to realize that he cared deeply about Anna, but he knew that her true love, Hans, could make her well again. He just hoped that they had reached the castle in time. Little did he know that Prince Hans wasn't who he seemed to be....

A Change of Scenery

Dr Sherman had left for the day when Gill called everyone together for a Tank Gang meeting.

"We need to make some changes around here," Gill began. "We've all been living in this glass box for how long now? And every day we stare at the same scenery – the same volcano, the same sunken ship, the same treasure chest and tiki hut. Well, seeing as how we can't change what's in our tank, I propose we rearrange things a little. Who's with me?"

"Great idea!" cried Peach the starfish.

"I'm with you," said Deb. "And Flo is too," she added, pointing at her reflection.

Everyone agreed. "We can completely transform the place," said Bloat.

"All right!" said Gill. "Then how about we start with the tiki hut? Bloat, you hoist it up. Gurgle and I will help you move it. The rest of you guys tell us where you think it should go."

Gill, Bloat and Gurgle swam over to the tiki hut. Bloat wriggled his body underneath it and blew himself up, hoisting the hut a few inches off the gravel. Meanwhile, Gill and Gurgle stationed themselves on either side of the hut and prepared to push.

"Let's try it over there," said Peach, pointing to a far corner of the tank.

With blown-up Bloat acting as a cart underneath the hut, Gill and Gurgle pushed the tiki hut into the corner.

"Oh, no," said Deb, "that's all wrong. Can we see what it looks like over there?" She pointed to the opposite corner of the tank.

So Gill, Gurgle and Bloat worked together to move the tiki hut again.

"That's a disaster!" exclaimed Jacques.

"Yeah, he's right," said Nemo.

Gill, Gurgle and Bloat were getting worn out by all the moving. "Can we all just agree on where it should go?" said Gill. "And quickly?"

"Ooh! I know!" said Deb. "Bring it over this way." She led Gill, Gurgle and Bloat over to a shady spot next to some plastic plants. "Put it down here," she said. So they did.

"I like it!" exclaimed Peach.

"The perfect spot," said Jacques.

"Mmm-hmm," said Bubbles.

Gill stepped back and looked around. "Guys, this is where it was in the first place!"

"Is it?" asked Peach.

Deb giggled. "Well, no wonder it just seems to fit here!"

The other fish nodded – except for Gill, who sighed in frustration. And that was the end of the tank redecoration for the evening.

Pictures in the Stars

Ever since Mufasa had died and Simba had left the Pride Lands, Timon and Pumbaa had been Simba's only friends – but what fun the three of them had together. One of their favourite things to do after their evening meal was to lie on their backs in the tall grass and gaze up at the night sky, looking for shapes in the stars.

"Okay, okay, I got one," said Pumbaa, lifting a foreleg to point to one area of the sky. "See, over there, that long, thin, curving outline? It's a big, juicy, delicious slug!" Pumbaa licked and smacked his lips, imagining the taste of a slug snack. "Mmm-mmm!"

Simba chuckled. "Pumbaa, how can you still be hungry? We just ate!"

Pumbaa shrugged. "It's a gift," he said.

Timon cleared his throat. "I hate to disagree with you, Pumbaa my friend, but that's no slug you see up there. That's an elephant's trunk. If you follow that curving line of stars, you see it connects with the elephant's head at one end. And there are the ears," Timon said, tracing it all out with his finger, "and there are the tusks."

Simba chuckled again. "Somebody still has his mind on that elephant stampede we almost got flattened by this afternoon," he said.

"Hey ..." Timon said defensively, "what's that supposed to mean?"

"Oh, no offence, Timon," Simba replied.

"I just think it's funny that the things you and Pumbaa see in the stars just happen to be the same things that are on your mind at the time."

"Ooh! Ooh! I've got another one!" Pumbaa interrupted. "A big bunch of tasty berries right over there," he said, pointing at a grouping of stars. "Don't they look good?"

"See what I mean?" Simba said to Timon, gesturing at Pumbaa.

"All right, all right, Mr Smarty-Pants," Timon replied. "So what do you see in the stars?"

"Well, now, let's see," said Simba, gazing intently at the tons of tiny points of light twinkling down at them. There were so many that you could see practically any shape in them that you wanted to. It all depended on how you looked at them. But just to get Timon's goat, Simba wanted to find something really bright – something really clear. Something Timon couldn't deny that he saw too.

Just at that moment, a shooting star streaked the entire length of the night sky.

"I see a bright streak of light rocketing across the sky!" exclaimed Simba.

"Ooh! Me, too!" said Pumbaa. "Timon, do you see it?"

Timon had to admit that he did. "Yeah, yeah, I see it," he muttered grudgingly. "Ha-ha. Very funny, Simba."

Piglet's Pink Eggs

Winnie the Pooh had dropped in to visit Piglet, who was busy dyeing Easter eggs. "Easter is coming up, you know," Piglet explained.

On Piglet's kitchen table were six little cups. Pooh peered inside them. Each one held a different-coloured dye: blue, green, red, yellow, orange and pink.

Then Pooh noticed a basket filled with some eggs Piglet had already dyed. Every one of them was pink.

"Would you like to dye the last egg, Pooh?" Piglet asked.

"Oh yes," Pooh replied. "I would like that very much."

So Piglet showed him how to place his egg in the wire dipper, and how to use the dipper to dip the egg into the cups of dye.

"What colour should I dye my egg?" Pooh asked.

Piglet smiled. "That's the fun of it, Pooh," he said. "You can choose any colour you want!"

Pooh looked over at Piglet's basket of pink eggs. Then he looked back at the cups of dye.

"You don't seem to have a yellow egg yet," said Pooh. "So I think I will dye mine yellow."

"Good idea!" Piglet exclaimed.

Pooh dipped his egg into the cup filled with yellow dye. He let it sit in the dye for a few minutes, then lifted it out again.

"It worked!" cried Pooh. "Piglet, look! What do you think of my yellow egg?"

"Oh Pooh, it's great," Piglet said. "It's b-bright ... a-and it's sunny ... and i-it's very, very yellow, isn't it?"

Piglet was quiet for a moment. Then he cleared his throat.

"D-do you think ... I don't know for sure, mind you. But do you think it could maybe use a little bit of, say, pink?" Piglet said.

"I think you're right," Pooh said. So he dipped his egg into the cup filled with pink dye. He let it sit there for just a few seconds before lifting it out. The little bit of pink dye on top of the yellow dye made the egg look pinkish-yellow.

"Hmm," said Piglet. "That's very pretty. But – if you don't mind my saying so, Pooh – I think it could use just a little more pink."

"Okay," said Pooh. So he dipped the egg back into the pink dye. This time he let it sit for five whole minutes before lifting it out. More pink dye on top of the yellow-and-pink colour made the egg look as pink as pink could be.

"Well, what do you think?" asked Pooh.

"Perfect!" Piglet exclaimed.

They let Pooh's egg dry. Then Piglet put it in the basket with all the other pink eggs.

"Well, what do you know," said Piglet. "It fits in so nicely!"

Of Mice and Rice

"Cinderella! Help!" shrieked Drizella. "And hurry!" yelled Anastasia.

Cinderella dropped the broom she was holding and rushed down the hallway. "What is it, stepsisters?" she called.

"We're stuck!" yelled Anastasia.

Cinderella hurried to the parlour. She had to suppress a giggle at what she saw. Her two stepsisters were stuck in the doorway, so hasty had they both been to leave the room first. Their grand hoop skirts were wedged tightly in the doorway! With a bit of tugging and pulling, Cinderella managed to free the sisters. Smiling to herself, she headed back to the kitchen.

"Meeeeeowww!" came a cry.

"What on earth...." said Cinderella. She hurried into the kitchen. Lucifer the cat was howling at the top of his lungs. "What is the matter, Lucifer?" she said, running over to the fat feline. "Oh! You silly thing! You've got yourself stuck too!" Cinderella laughed and tugged him out of the mouse hole he had wedged his paw into. With a haughty look at Cinderella, the cat strode away.

"Oh, that naughty cat!" she said. "He got himself stuck chasing after you poor little defenceless mice, didn't he?" She peeked into the tiny mouse hole.

The mice crept cautiously out of their hole.

"You little dears," Cinderella said softly. "Why, you're all shaken up! Well, do you know what I do when I feel sad or afraid? I find happiness in my dreams." She picked up her broom. "You see this broom? I like to pretend that it is a handsome prince, and the two of us are dancing together!" She and the broom began gliding around the room.

The mice squeaked with delight, and then they suddenly dashed for their hole. Someone was coming!

It was Cinderella's stepsisters. "What on earth are you doing, Cinderella?" said Drizella.

"I was just, uh, sweeping," Cinderella replied quietly, blushing.

"Well, you looked as though you were having too much fun doing it!" snapped Anastasia. Then a nasty smile appeared on her face. Picking up a bowl of rice from the table, she dumped it onto the floor. "Perhaps you need something else to sweep!" she said with a mean laugh. The two sisters left.

Cinderella's mouse friends rushed out and began to pick up the grains of rice. That gave Cinderella an idea. "Why don't you take the rice for yourselves?" she said. The mice squeaked happily, and Cinderella smiled. "You know," she said, "I think we'll be just fine if we all look out for each other."

THE PRINCESS AND THE FROG

Two Frogs Instead of One

Tiana had just discovered a frog on the balcony of her friend Charlotte's room. Then the frog had started to talk! Tiana ran back into the room in terror – she couldn't believe it. It was a lot of nonsense, like something from a made-up fairy tale!

"I didn't mean to frighten you," apologized the frog. It jumped onto a piece of furniture to take a closer look at Tiana, who was dressed in Charlotte's clothes and looked like a princess.

"Please allow me to introduce myself," he said. "I am Prince Naveen of Maldonia. I was very handsome and very charming, until I was transformed by an evil sorcerer!"

Terrified, Tiana grabbed a large book from a shelf. "If you're the prince, then who was that waltzing with Lottie on the dance floor?" She had seen Prince Naveen dancing at the ball downstairs. She got ready to throw the book at the frog.

"Wait! I know that story!" the frog interrupted, looking at the cover of the book. "It's the story of the Frog Prince!"

Naveen leafed through the pages of the book, and turned from a picture of a frog to one of a prince. "Don't you see?" he asked. "It's just like the fairytales. If you kiss me, I'm bound to turn back into a prince!"

Tiana grimaced in disgust, but the frog Naveen insisted.

"I don't kiss frogs," refused Tiana.

"You might like to know that as well as being fabulously attractive, I have a fabulously wealthy family! Help me to regain my appearance and, in exchange, I will give you whatever you want...."

Tiana thought. This might be her only chance of finally being able to own the restaurant she and her father had dreamed of.

"Just a kiss, then?" she murmured.

"Several if you wish, my dear!" smiled the frog.

Tiana closed her eyes. She took a deep breath and – *smack!* – she planted a quick kiss on the frog's pursed lips.

When she opened her eyes again, nothing had happened. Apart from one thing – she had turned into a frog too! "Aaaaaah!" she screamed when she caught sight of her reflection in the mirror.

"Don't panic!" begged Naveen. "I know, getting two frogs instead of one wasn't exactly what we had in mind. But at least we've got company!"

Tiana, mad with rage, did not reply. She tried one of her new talents, and leapt – *boing!* – at Naveen's throat!

Tinker Bell
AND THE
GREAT FAIRY RESCUE

Something to Fix

All the fairies knew that Tinker Bell was too curious for her own good! That explained why she went into the little house made by Lizzy, a little girl from the mainland. Then Vidia played a joke and accidentally trapped Tink inside!

Lizzy found Tinker Bell and was very excited. She took the fairy up to her bedroom and put her in a cage – so that the family cat couldn't catch her. Vidia had watched safely from the window and then quickly flown back to fairy camp to get help.

But then a storm had begun! The fairies couldn't fly in the rain and the meadow was flooded, so they decided to build a boat. As they set off to rescue Tinker Bell, Silvermist, Rosetta, Fawn and Iridessa remembered that with 'faith, trust and pixie dust', anything was possible. As Bobble steered them in a fast-moving current, Rosetta looked out at how far they had to travel, hoping that Tinker Bell was safe.

But Tinker Bell was fine – and being questioned non-stop by an excited Lizzy about what it was like to be a fairy. Lizzy couldn't understand Tink's tiny voice, so Tink answered with hand movements.

Next, Tink opened a blank field journal that Lizzy's father had given her – he didn't believe in fairies and had wanted Lizzy to record her research about 'real' things in it. But it was perfect for her fairy facts!

Lizzy wrote the words "Scientific Fairy Research" on the first page. Then Lizzy asked questions and Tinker Bell acted out the answers.

Soon the journal was filled with drawings of Tink's fairy friends and Pixie Hollow, and descriptions of the fairies' special talents.

Now that Lizzy's fairy field journal was complete and the rain had eased off, it was time for Tink to go and find her friends. Tinker Bell was sad about leaving Lizzy, but excited about going back to fairy camp.

Tink flew out of the window, but stayed and watched while Lizzy tried to show her father the journal they had made.

"I made it especially for you, father. It's just like your field journal, it's filled with lots of facts...."

But Dr Griffths was too worried about the leaks in the roof to look at her book. He had to fix them to stop water damaging their house.

Tink saw how sad Dr Griffiths was that he couldn't spend more time with his daughter. She decided she had to stay and help them. After all, fixing was her talent!

Wolves and Witchcraft

The Beast woke up on the floor next to the enchanted rose given to him by Circe. Its light was hazy and its petals were few.

He heard Belle outside the door. She wasn't allowed in the West Wing!

Belle came into the room, drawn to the rose and spellbound by its beauty. The Beast jumped out and growled at her: "This room is forbidden! Get out!"

Belle stuttered, trying to find words to defend herself, but fear took hold and she ran out of the castle and deep into the forest. That was it! She no longer cared about her promise to stay in her father's place. She wanted to go home. Together they would find a way to defeat the Beast.

The odd sisters laughed and stomped their boots in happiness when they saw what was happening through Pflanze the cat's eyes. The Beast had chased away any hope of breaking the curse. They danced and sang: "The girl is going to die!"

If Circe were there, she'd help Belle, but her older sisters had asked Ursula the sea witch to keep Circe with her for as long as she could manage. They didn't want their little sister meddling in their plans.

Lucinda sprinkled a purple powder into the fireplace and black smoke rose up in the form of a wolf's head. "Send the wolves into the wood, scratch and bite until she bleeds, kill the beauty in the wood, make him regret his evil deeds!" she chanted.

The witches laughed and watched as the wolves began to advance on Belle, chanting the words together.

Soon the wolves were upon her. But then something flew past Belle. She didn't know what was happening, but the sisters did. It was the Beast! He attacked the wolves and killed them all. Belle wanted to run but she saw the Beast was hurt. He had saved her life, and now he needed her help.

The odd sisters watched in shock, realizing their mistake. They should never have sent those wolves to kill Belle! This would bring them together! The witches' only hope was that Belle had seen the Beast for what he was. "She will be repulsed by him! Sickened by the death that surrounds him!"

But they could see the look of concern on Belle's face.

"It's time to send Pflanze to see Gaston. I'm sure he would like to know where his dearest Belle is!"

If anyone could destroy the Beast, it was Gaston.

Disney
Lady and the TRAMP

Tony and the Tramp

Tramp licked the last of the tomato sauce from his chin. "So, what do you think, Pidge?" he asked Lady.

"That was the most wonderful meal I've ever had," Lady gushed.

"What did I tell ya?" Tramp boasted. "There's no one in the world who can cook up a meal like Tony!"

"I couldn't agree with you more," Lady said. "Can I ask you a question?"

"Sure thing," Tramp said. "Ask away!"

"I was just wondering," Lady began, "how you and Tony met."

"How I met Tony?" Tramp laughed. "Now that's a story!"

"I bet!" Lady said.

"Well, see, it goes like this," Tramp began. "It was a cold and snowy night. I don't think it had ever been that cold before, and I know it hasn't been since. I had been walking uphill for miles. Icicles were hanging from the tip of my nose."

"Wait a minute!" Lady interrupted. "You were walking for miles – uphill? In this town?"

"That's right!" Tramp said. "You've never seen the likes of it."

"Exactly!" Lady told him. "You know why?"

Tramp shook his head.

"Because it isn't possible! There are no big hills around here!" Lady said.

"Not possible?" Tramp said. "Okay, you're right," he confessed.

"So, then, what's the truth?" Lady asked.

"The truth is," Tramp began, "I wasn't always the slick, handsome devil you see before you."

"Is that right?" Lady was amused.

"And this one afternoon I was being harassed by a group of mangy mutts who outnumbered me ten to one. So, I took off as fast as my paws could carry me. And as they were chasing me, along came this dogcatcher!"

"Oh, no!" Lady cried.

"Exactly!" Tramp continued. "The mutts scattered out of sight, so I didn't have *them* to worry about any more. But now the dogcatcher was closing in! I thought I was a goner!"

"What happened?" Lady asked.

"Then Tony came running out with a bowl of steaming hot pasta," Tramp explained. "He told the dogcatcher I was his dog. The dogcatcher didn't believe him. But, when Tony put the bowl of pasta down in front of me, he had no choice. Let me tell you, I thought I'd died and gone to heaven."

"I can relate to that," Lady said, recalling the meal.

"And the rest," Tramp said, "as they say, is history!"

"And a tasty one at that!" Lady concluded.

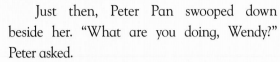

Should I Stay or Should I Go?

Wendy sat watching Michael and John play with Peter Pan and the rest of the Lost Boys.

"John and Michael seem so happy," Wendy said to herself. "And why wouldn't they? Never Land is such a beautiful place, and the flying is so much fun!

"Still," she had to admit, "it is also dangerous. Who knows what sort of trouble we could get into, especially with Captain Hook running about?

"And," Wendy said, "I don't think that Tinker Bell likes me very much."

Wendy considered this, then burst out, "What am I talking about? I'm making it sound like it's an awful place, but the truth is, Never Land is the most wonderful place on earth!

"Perhaps that explains it!" Wendy suddenly realized. "Maybe I really want to stay in Never Land, but in my heart of hearts I know I shouldn't. After all, Mother and Father must miss us terribly. And we miss them too! Oh, and what about Nana?" Wendy began to fret. "She must worry about us endlessly!

"That settles it!" Wendy stood up abruptly. "We must leave for home immediately.

"But if I stay – " Wendy stopped herself. "I'll never have to grow up!

"Then again, I always wanted to be an adult someday," she concluded.

Just then, Peter Pan swooped down beside her. "What are you doing, Wendy?" Peter asked.

"Oh, nothing," Wendy told him.

"Then why don't you come join us?" he suggested.

"I will," Wendy told him. "In a minute."

"All right! But last one there is a rotten – " Peter took off before he could finish his sentence.

"How can I ever leave Peter and the Lost Boys?" Wendy wondered. "They need me so much.

"But so do our parents," she quickly reminded herself. "Should I stay?" she wondered aloud. "Or should I go?"

Wendy's eyes fell upon a daisy. She bent over and pulled it out of the ground. "Should I stay?" she asked as she pulled a petal from the daisy. "Or should I go?" she asked as she pulled a second petal from the daisy.

Wendy did this over and over again until there was only one petal remaining on the daisy.

"Well," she said, "this flower says we should go back home. And I suppose it's right. We'll go back ... but maybe not just this minute."

Wendy stood up. "Hey, Peter, wait up!"

And with that, she flew off after Peter, her mind at ease at last.

THE LITTLE
MERMAID

Ariel Changes the Tune

Sebastian rapped his claw on a piece of coral and cleared his throat. But the mermaids kept talking as if the little crustacean were not even there. With a heavy sigh, Sebastian grabbed a huge conch shell. After a lot of effort he managed to hoist it to his mouth and blow.

The shell sounded like a giant horn. The mermaid princesses looked startled, and, to Sebastian's relief, they stopped talking.

"Shall we begin?" the small crab asked calmly. He was anxious to start rehearsing. King Triton's daughters had amazing singing voices, but they still had not decided on the right song to sing for their father's birthday. And there were just a few days left before the celebration!

Sebastian raised his claw and was about to bring it down to start the vocal warm-up when Aquata interrupted him.

"Ariel's not here," she said.

"Oh, Ariel!" Sebastian cried. Ariel was constantly swimming off on her own and holding things up.

"Do you want us to find her?" Arista asked.

"No." Sebastian sighed dramatically. "Then you will all be lost, and I don't know what I would tell your father."

"We wouldn't get lost," Attina protested.

"We *always* show up on time," Adella added. The other sisters nodded their heads in agreement.

"Why do we have to sit around and wait for her?" Alana grumbled. The rest of her sisters nodded angrily.

"Girls, girls!" Sebastian said, trying to calm them. He wished they could go ahead without Ariel, but her voice was by far the most beautiful.

Suddenly, Ariel swam up with Flounder.

"I hope you weren't waiting for me," she said sweetly.

"Ariel!" Sebastian didn't know whether he should be angry or relieved.

"Where have you been?" Aquata put her hands on her scaly hips.

"We still don't have a song for father!" Attina added.

"We do now!" Ariel said cheerfully. She couldn't tell them, but she had been to the surface. It was forbidden. But she had got something very special from her seagull friend Scuttle today. A new song! Ariel began singing the human tune. After only a moment, Ariel's sisters began to sing along.

Sebastian closed his eyes and listened. The song was perfect! "Where did you learn it?" he asked when they were done.

Ariel looked at Flounder. "A little bird told me," she said with a wink.

Disney · PIXAR
BRAVE
A Gammy Spell

Deep in the ancient Scottish Highlands, in a kingdom called DunBroch, lived a princess called Merida. Her mother, Queen Elinor, wanted Merida to marry a son from one of the neighbouring clans, in order to keep peace among the kingdoms.

But Merida didn't want to marry. She wanted to keep her freedom and choose her own destiny. So, when the suitors came to compete at archery for her hand, Merida took her bow and beat them all.

"You don't know what you've done," the queen told Merida.

Merida was very angry. She couldn't understand her mother's point of view. "You're a beast!" she shouted. "I'll never be like you!"

Angrily, Merida slashed the family tapestry between the images of her and her mother. Hurt and angry, Merida fled from the castle on her horse, Angus. She was crying too hard to watch where they were going.

Suddenly, Angus stopped, sending Merida flying. When she got to her feet, she saw that she was standing inside a ring of giant stones. She saw strange blue lights flickering. They seemed to beckon Merida forward. The lights formed a chain leading deep into the forest. Merida followed the blue lights. They led her to a small cottage in the woods.

The cottage belonged to an old woman who seemed to be a wood-carver. But it didn't take long for Merida to realize the woman was actually a witch.

Merida explained, "If I could just change my mum, then my life would be better."

The Witch told Merida about a prince who had asked, long ago, for the strength of ten men. Merida would get a similar spell. The Witch set to work, throwing things into her cauldron. When she was done, the Witch pulled out a cake and handed it to Merida.

Back at the castle, Merida gave the cake to her mother. Elinor took a bite.

"Now, why don't we go upstairs to the lords and put this behind us," Elinor said.

But just then, Elinor stumbled. She was feeling dizzy. Merida helped Elinor upstairs and into bed. The next thing Merida knew, a huge shape rose up from the sheets!

"Mum, you're a bear!" Merida cried. "That scaffy witch gave me a gammy spell."

Hearing this, Elinor-Bear let out an angry roar. Merida had wanted to change her mother's mind, but the spell had changed Queen Elinor completely!

All that Merida cared about now was saving her mother from the witch's spell!

Disney
Beauty and the **Beast**

Belle and the Beast

Belle was tired of being trapped inside the castle. It was too cold to go outside, so she sat idly in the small study next to the fire, wondering when she would see the Beast.

She was less cross with him since he had saved her from the wolves, but she couldn't forget about his terrible temper. She played the scene in her head over and over. The wolves, the woods, the Beast, the blood. She had almost died that night because of his rage, and why? Because she had touched his precious rose? Her anger and fear hadn't stopped her mending his wounds, though, had it?

She didn't know the Beast was watching her. She didn't know that he might have killed her if the wolves not been there to distract him.

The Beast was deep in thought. Imagine it; imagine if he had killed her. It would have been the final act of evil and he would have lost himself completely. But Belle was his last chance.

How could he possibly make her love him? He was loathsome. He saw that now. He saw how horrible he'd become, and knew he deserved Circe's punishment.

Belle looked up at him and smiled.

He hadn't expected that. "Belle, will you come with me? There is something I want to show you."

She followed him cautiously until they came to a door.

"Close your eyes," he said. He took her by the hands and led her into the room.

She heard a swish and then felt warm sunlight on her face. "Now can I open them?"

The Beast found himself smiling for the first time in ages. "All right, now!" he said, and she opened her eyes, which widened at the remarkable sight of the library.

"I can't believe it! I've never seen so many books in my entire life!"

The Beast hadn't expected to feel this way; hadn't expected how it would feel to make someone happy.

"You like it?" he asked.

"It's wonderful!" she said, happier than he'd ever seen her before.

"Then it's yours." And he felt something completely unexpected. What had started out as a way to bring them closer together for the sake of breaking the curse had now turned into something else – something he didn't understand.

He loved making her happy.

The Prettiest Flower

One morning, Bashful went out to pick the prettiest flower he could find. Suddenly, he heard a noise just over the hill.

"*Ah-choo!*"

Bashful climbed the hill and saw his friend on the other side.

"These darn flowers are making me sneeze," said Sneezy. "But it's worth it – because I've picked the prettiest flower for Snow White's hair." He showed Bashful the white orchid he'd picked.

"That sure is pretty," said Bashful. "But I've got a flower for her too. It's even prettier."

Bashful showed Sneezy the rosebud he'd picked. Then he blushed pinker than its petals.

"*Ah-choo!* Yours is pretty too," said Sneezy. "Let's go home and see which one Snow White likes best."

On the path back to their little cottage, Sneezy and Bashful came upon Doc, Happy and Sleepy. They were all arguing about something.

"Snow White bikes liolets," insisted Doc. "I mean she likes violets!"

Happy laughed. "No. She likes daisies!"

"I think she likes muuuuuums," said Sleepy with a yawn.

"You *would* think that!" grumbled a voice behind them. It was Grumpy. He held a long stem with small pastel blossoms.

"That's the perfect flower for you, Grumpy," said Doc. "Snapdragons!"

"Very funny!" Grumpy snapped.

When they all arrived at their house, they saw Dopey.

"Dopey, what do you have behind your back?" Doc asked.

Dopey showed them a single yellow tulip.

"*Another* flower!" cried Happy.

When the Seven Dwarfs went inside, they found Snow White in the kitchen.

"We all wanted to thank you for being so good to us," said Doc. "So we each picked a flower for your hair."

"Now it's *your* turn to pick the flower you like best," said Grumpy.

Snow White felt terrible. She loved all the Dwarfs and she didn't want to hurt any of their feelings by choosing one flower over another.

"I have an idea," she told them. "Put all of your flowers down on the table, and go outside for five minutes. When you come back in, I'll be wearing the flower I think is the prettiest."

The Dwarfs went outside. When they came back in, they gasped in surprise. Snow White had made a flower crown.

She'd found a way to wear all their flowers!

"I love every one of your flowers!" she told them. "Just like I love each and every one of you!"

A Muddy Rescue

Tinker Bell's curiosity had led her to a human house and to a little girl named Lizzy. Lizzy lived with her father, a scientist called Dr Griffiths who didn't believe in magic or fairies and was often too busy to spend time with his daughter – even though he wanted to.

Another fairy, Vidia, had tried to stop Tink from exploring – she knew humans could be dangerous – but Tink had ignored her. When she saw Tink get caught by the girl, Vidia had raced off back to fairy camp to get help.

But a storm had started and fairies couldn't fly in the rain! So, they built a boat and set off to rescue Tinker Bell.

What the other fairies didn't realize was that Tink was fine! She was having a lovely time with Lizzy, who loved fairies.

Tink had decided to stay and help Lizzy spend more time with her father. She had an idea – if she could help Dr Griffiths with the house repairs, he would have more time to spend with Lizzy!

Meanwhile, back on the fairy boat, the rescuers were in a panic. They were heading straight for a waterfall!

"Hang on, we're going straight down!" yelled Bobble.

Then Silvermist, a water fairy, reached into the waterfall and made the water rise up so that the drop wasn't as steep. After a wild ride, the boat crashed onto the shore.

The fairies were all fine, but the boat was ruined. They had no choice but to continue their mission on foot.

Vidia finally spotted the muddy road that led to Lizzy's house. Vidia helped her friends across, but then got stuck in the mud herself! Silvermist, Fawn, Rosetta and Iridessa grabbed onto her and pulled.

Then, suddenly, they saw the lights of a car coming towards them! "Pull! Pull!" cried Rosetta – but Vidia was trapped.

Iridessa knew what she had to do. She walked towards the car, then held up her hand and bounced the headlight beams back at the driver. He thought another car was coming straight for him and slammed on his brakes.

Moments later, the driver got out of his car. "Hello? Is somebody out there?" he asked.

Fawn grabbed his shoelace and instructed the others to hold on tight. When the driver turned to leave, he pulled them all out of the mud!

The fairy friends were so relieved. They made sure everyone was okay, then continued on their way to rescue Tinker Bell.

Bambi

First Impressions

Bambi was just discovering the wonders of the forest. His mother had brought him to a little clearing in the woods. The sudden sunshine and bright green grass surprised and pleased him, and he bounded around on his still-wobbly legs, feeling the warm sun on his back and the soft grass under his hooves. While his mother grazed nearby, Bambi began to explore.

He found a patch of green grass and clover, and he bent down to eat. This was not an easy feat, as his long legs made it difficult for his little neck to reach the ground. When his nose was just a few inches from the tips of the grass, he suddenly leaped backwards in alarm. A leaf had just sprung up from the patch of grass and had landed a few feet away. A hopping leaf? he wondered. He followed it and, as soon as he drew close, the leaf hopped away from him again!

Bambi looked around at where his mother stood, still grazing. She seemed to think they were in no great danger. So, he followed the leaf all the way to the edge of the clearing, where a wide brook babbled over craggy rocks.

Bambi's fascination with the hopping leaf faded as he approached the brook. Water cascaded smoothly over the rocks, bubbling and frothing in shallow pools. He took a step closer and felt his foot touch a rock at the edge of the water.

Suddenly, the rock moved! It shuffled towards the water and then – *plop!* – jumped right in and swam away.

Bambi was dumbfounded as he watched it dive beneath the surface and vanish. He stared at the spot where the rock had been for a moment, and then stooped down to have a drink, widening his stance in order to do so.

Suddenly, he jumped back in alarm. There in the water, staring right back up at him, was a little deer! Cautiously he approached again, and there it was!

Bambi turned and bounded back across the clearing to his mother.

"Mama! Mama!" he cried breathlessly. "You will never guess what I have seen!"

His mother lifted her head and gazed at him with her clear, bright eyes.

"First," he said, "first I saw a jumping leaf. Then, I saw a rock with legs that walked right into the water and swam away! And then," he he continued in amazement, "and then I saw a little deer who lives right in the water! He's right over there, Mama!"

His mother nuzzled her son, thinking over what he had said. Then she laughed gently.

"Darling," she said. "I think you have just seen your first grasshopper, your first turtle and your very own reflection!"

A Question Of Charm

Rapunzel had been kept in a hidden tower her whole life by a woman she thought was her mother – Mother Gothel. Rapunzel had managed to make Mother Gothel leave the tower for a few days, and she decided to ask the stranger she had locked in her wardrobe if he would do her a big favour. She held up a frying pan, ready to hit him if he turned dangerous. Then she opened the wardrobe.

Wham! The intruder fell out onto the floor. Rapunzel tied him to a chair with her enormously long hair. Then her pet chameleon, Pascal, licked his ear to awaken him.

"Huh?!" the stranger said, astonished. "Is this real hair?"

"What do you want with my hair? To cut it? Sell it?" Rapunzel exclaimed.

"No!" shouted the stranger. "Listen, the only thing I want to do with your hair is to get out of it, lit-er-a-lly!"

Rapunzel looked at him suspiciously. "Who are you, and how did you find me?" The young man suddenly smiled. His most attractive smile. "I know not who you are, nor how I came to find you, but may I just say … Hi. How ya doin'?"

Rapunzel didn't react. The intruder finally answered. "My name's Flynn Rider, blondie!"

"I'm Rapunzel, not blondie."

"Hey! Where's my satchel?" asked Flynn, who had noticed that his bag containing the stolen crown was missing.

"I've hidden it!" Rapunzel said. "Something brought you here, Flynn Rider. So I've got a deal to offer you."

Rapunzel showed him the picture she had painted. It was of the floating lanterns in the sky that only appeared on her birthday each year.

"Tomorrow evening, these lanterns will appear in the sky. I want to know where they come from. If you take me there and then bring me back, I will give you back your satchel!"

Flynn shook his head. "I can't be seen hanging around the castle right now."

"In that case, bad luck: you'll never see your satchel again!"

Not knowing what to do, Flynn tried to charm Rapunzel once again. "All right, listen! I didn't want to have to do this, but you leave me no choice. Here comes the smoulder." Rapunzel just stared at him and, before long, it was Flynn who gave in. "OK, blondie. I'll take you to see the lanterns."

Rapunzel was delighted. Finally, after all these years, she was going to leave the tower. Her birthday wish had come true. She was going to see the floating lanterns!

Disney
PRINCESS

Cinderella

The Heart of a Champion

Life at the palace was a dream come true for Cinderella. She particularly loved that her dear old horse, Frou, lived there too. He had been her faithful friend since she was a child.

One day, an invitation arrived. "You are hereby invited," read the Grand Duke, "to attend this year's annual Royal International Horse Show, to be held exactly one week from today. Please choose one member from your royal household to represent you in the competition."

Everyone decided that Cinderella should compete!

Although there were lots of fine horses to choose from, Cinderella wanted to ride her old friend, Frou.

"My dear," said the king, turning up his nose. "If none of my horses suit your fancy, I can have another hundred champions here by morning!"

"Frou may be old," said Cinderella, "but he has the heart of a champion!"

And with that, she saddled Frou and swung herself up. "Come on, Frou," she told him. "Let's show them what you've got."

Every day for a week, Cinderella and Frou trained for hours. But Frou kept making mistakes. No matter how sweetly Cinderella urged him, he missed every jump.

At last, it was the night before the royal horse show. "Please don't worry," Cinderella told Frou. "You're going to be wonderful."

But Frou didn't quite believe her.

Just then, Cinderella's Fairy Godmother appeared! "My dear," she whispered, "you know Frou can win, and I know Frou can win, but our friend Frou doesn't know it at all. What he needs is a reason to feel confident."

And with that, she raised her magic wand and waved it at Frou. To Frou's amazement, a glass horseshoe appeared on each of his hooves!

"With these horseshoes, you'll never miss a step," she told Frou, sneaking a wink at Cinderella. "And while I'm at it," she added, waving her wand again. Instantly, a golden saddle appeared on Frou's back and Cinderella's simple dress became a beautiful riding outfit.

The next day at the horse show, Frou looked like a true champion! He held his head up high and cleared every jump with ease. And it was all thanks to the magical glass horseshoes – or so Frou thought. Cinderella knew better, though. The horseshoes just gave Frou the confidence he needed to be the great horse he always had been.

Cinderella and Frou came first! The Princess was very proud of her oldest friend.

Disney
Sleeping Beauty

Fairy Medicine

Deep in the forest, in a humble cottage, the three good fairies had been secretly raising Briar Rose for many years. One morning, the girl woke up with a terrible cold.

"We must nurse her back to health," said Flora.

Fauna and Merryweather agreed. So, while Briar Rose stayed in bed, Flora brought her a bowl of soup. Fauna fetched her a cup of tea. And Merryweather gave her a dose of medicine.

"Ooooh!" said Briar Rose, wrinkling her nose. "That tastes awful!"

"Most medicine tastes awful, dear," said Merryweather. "Just drink it down."

"Would you like anything else?" Flora asked.

The princess blew her nose and gazed out her window at the beautiful spring day. "What I really want is to get out of bed," she said.

"Oh, no, dear," said Flora. "You're far too sick."

Then the fairies left Briar Rose and went downstairs.

"I feel bad for the sweet girl," said Fauna. "Staying in bed all day is boring."

"What can we do?" asked Merryweather.

"I know!" cried Flora. "We'll entertain her!"

"Splendid!" said Merryweather. "I'll fetch my wand and conjure up some fireworks, a puppet show, and – "

"And perhaps that clever dog who jumps through hoops!" added Fauna.

"No!" Flora cried. "We all agreed to give up our fairy magic until Briar Rose turns 16 and she's safe from Maleficent's curse."

"Not even a little magic?" asked Fauna. "Just a few fireworks?"

"No!" Flora said again, stomping her foot.

"Well," said Fauna, "how do mortals entertain themselves when they're sick in bed?"

"I know!" cried Flora. She brought out a deck of cards. "We'll play card games! That will be fun!"

The three fairies then went up to Briar Rose's room and played card games with her all afternoon. Briar Rose won almost every game, too, which really cheered her up.

After a while, Briar Rose yawned and said she was ready to have a sleep. So the fairies went back downstairs.

When Flora went outside to do some gardening, Fauna approached Merryweather. "Tell me the truth," she whispered. "Did you use magic to let the princess win?"

"I just used mortal magic," confessed Merryweather. "No harm in a little sleight of hand. After all, you must admit, if you're feeling down, winning is the best medicine!"

A Chilling Plan

When Kristoff handed Anna over to the servants at the castle gates, they rushed her to the library where Prince Hans, Anna's fiancé, had been meeting with some of Arendelle's most important people.

Shivering, Anna explained that her sister Elsa's icy blast had hit her and frozen her heart. She thought that his kiss would cure her.

"Only an act of true love can save me," she said.

"Oh, Anna," Hans sneered. "If only someone loved you."

Anna was shocked and confused. What was he talking about? She thought he *did* love her!

Hans went over to the fire and doused it with water to make the room even colder. Then he explained to Anna that he had only pretended to love her in order to take over Arendelle! All that was left to do, he told her, was to get rid of Elsa. "Summer will return and the kingdom will be mine!"

"You can't," gasped Anna, before collapsing on to the floor as the ice slowly spread through her body.

Hans left her and locked the library door so that Anna couldn't get out and no one could get in to help her. Alone, Anna realized how reckless she had been. In trying to find love, she had doomed herself *and* her sister.

Hans returned to the meeting with Arendelle's important people. He told them, with great drama, that Elsa had killed Anna! He continued his lies by describing how he and Anna had exchanged marriage vows just before she died. With Elsa in the dungeon, he just needed to do one more thing to become Arendelle's ruler....

"I charge Queen Elsa with treason and sentence her to death," he declared.

Down in the castle dungeon, Queen Elsa knew nothing of what was going on upstairs – of what was happening to her kingdom and her sister. She thought the only way to protect everyone from her powers was to get away from Arendelle. She became so upset that she froze the whole dungeon.

Hans went down to the dungeons to give Elsa her sentence. But when he reached her cell he found that she had escaped!

Meanwhile, Kristoff was heading back up the mountain, but his reindeer, Sven, forced him to stop. He had watched Kristoff and Anna together and knew that Kristoff was Anna's real true love.

As they turned back, Kristoff saw a violent storm forming over Arendelle. He and Sven ran back towards the kingdom. He knew he had to help Anna, but he didn't realize just how much trouble she was in.

Shivering on the library floor, with little hope of survival, Anna was giving up hope.

What no one knew, however, was that a little snowman, Anna's friend, had sneaked into the castle and was heading to the library....

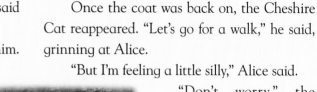

Sillying the Blues Away

"Oh, me, oh, my!" the White Rabbit said as he rushed past Alice.

"Wait! Excuse me!" Alice called to him. But he was gone.

Alice sat down. "I'm never going to get out of here," she said worriedly.

"What's the matter?" a voice asked. "You seem blue."

Alice looked all around, but she didn't see anyone. "Where are you?" she asked.

"Is that better?" the Cheshire Cat said as he suddenly appeared out of nowhere.

"Why, yes," Alice replied.

"Would you like some help?" the Cheshire Cat asked.

"You'll help me?" Alice cried.

"Absolutely!" the Cheshire Cat said with a grin. "But you have to do exactly as I say."

"Okay," Alice agreed.

"First," the Cheshire Cat told her, "you have to put on this winter coat."

"But it's spring," Alice protested.

"You promised to do as I say," the Cheshire Cat reminded her.

"Okay." Alice started putting it on.

"Backwards!" the Cheshire Cat ordered.

"But ..." Alice began. The Cheshire Cat started to disappear. "Wait, don't go!" she pleaded. "Here, I'm putting it on."

Once the coat was back on, the Cheshire Cat reappeared. "Let's go for a walk," he said, grinning at Alice.

"But I'm feeling a little silly," Alice said.

"Don't worry," the Cheshire Cat told her. "No one's looking."

But the truth was, Alice could have sworn she heard the bread-and-butterflies laughing at her.

"Now, drink this cup of apple sauce," the Cheshire Cat said.

"Don't you mean apple juice?" Alice asked.

"No, I mean apple sauce," the Cheshire Cat said. "Drink it while walking around in a circle – three times."

Alice hesitated. "Are you sure about this?"

"It's always worked for the bread-and-butterflies," the Cheshire Cat told her.

"All right, then," Alice said. But, by the time she started her second circle, her doubts grew stronger. "I think you're playing a trick on me," she said. "You're having me do all these things to make me look silly."

"True," the Cheshire Cat agreed. "But it's awfully hard to feel blue when you look this silly!" His smile hung in the air a moment before he entirely disappeared.

Alice thought for a second, and she had to agree. She was still lost, but now she didn't feel quite so sad about it!

Goodbye, Friendship

With Joy and Sadness lost in Long Term Memory with the core memory spheres, Anger, Fear and Disgust had been trying to take care of Riley on their own. But, after Riley's argument with her parents, all they could do was watch as Goofball Island collapsed inside Riley's mind.

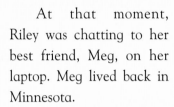

To get back to Headquarters, Joy realized that she and Sadness would first have to weave through the endless maze of shelves full of memory spheres in Long Term Memory. They had to get Riley's core memories back to Headquarters before more Islands of Personality collapsed!

Sadness did not like Joy's plan. She thought they would get lost.

"Think positive," said Joy.

"I'm too sad to walk." Sadness moaned from the floor. "Just give me a few … hours."

Joy didn't have a minute to lose, so she picked up one of Sadness's legs and dragged her along.

They met a couple of Mind Workers, called Forgetters. It was their job to dispose of memories Riley didn't need anymore. They vacuumed old memories from the shelves and sent them down to the Memory Dump below, where the old memories would fade away into mist. Joy watched the Forgetters with a great deal of concern. She and Sadness had to get back to HQ before Riley stopped caring about everything and the core memories were lost forever!

At that moment, Riley was chatting to her best friend, Meg, on her laptop. Meg lived back in Minnesota.

"Do you like it there?" asked Meg.

But before Riley could reply, Meg started telling her about a brilliant new girl on their hockey team.

"We can pass the puck to each other without even looking!" said Meg.

Riley missed playing with her old team, so hearing about this made her feel angry.

In HQ, Anger took charge of the console.

"Hey, hey," said Disgust. "We do NOT want to lose any more islands!" But Anger had already pushed a button.

"I gotta go," Riley said and slammed her laptop shut. It sounded like her old friends didn't miss her at all.

In Riley's Mind World, Joy and Sadness heard a horrible groaning sound. They both watched, helplessly, as Friendship Island toppled and fell into the dark dump below.

"Ohh, not Friendship!" Joy exclaimed.

"Goodbye friendship," Sadness sighed. "Hello loneliness."

Winnie the Pooh

Pooh's Neighbourhood

"I say, it's a splendid day in the neighbourhood!" cried Owl.

"Which neighbour wood are we talking about?" asked Pooh.

"Neighbour*hood*," said Owl. "The place where we live and where all our neighbours live and are neighbourly."

"Oh," said Pooh, "it is a splendid day in it, isn't it?"

"Now I'm off for an owl's-eye view!" said Owl. He flew up and circled once around Pooh's house. "I can see the Hundred-Acre Wood spread out below me, and it's a fine place indeed."

As Owl flew off, Pooh began to think about what it means to live in a neighbourhood, and he thought perhaps he would bring a neighbourly present to his closest neighbour, Piglet. Pooh went inside his house and took a honeypot out of his cupboard. He tied a nice blue ribbon round it.

When he reached his Thoughtful Spot, Pooh suddenly had a thought: I could take the path straight to Piglet's house. Or – I could go up the path and around the whole neighbourhood. And sooner or later the path would take me to Piglet's house, anyway. So that's what he did.

As he walked the long way to Piglet's house, Pooh came across each of his neighbours in turn. He joined Kanga and Roo for a snack at the picnic spot, and collected some carrots from Rabbit. After lunch and a longish snooze at Christopher Robin's house, he soon reached Eeyore's Gloomy Place, which was where Eeyore lived.

Eeyore was feeling sad, so Pooh offered him a nice lick of honey. Pooh put the jar down, and Eeyore peered in. The honey pot was empty! Pooh walked away glumly and, before long, Owl flew over.

"I've seen our whole neighbourhood today," Pooh told him. "But now I have no neighbourly present left for Piglet."

"The bees have been quite busy at the old bee tree lately," said Owl. "Perhaps you can get a fill-up there."

So they walked together until they came to the old bee tree. Up, up, up Pooh climbed. Owl had a thought, and told Pooh to go to the very top of the tree and look around.

"Our neighbourhood!" cried Pooh. "Our beautiful home!" The Hundred-Acre Wood was spread out below him.

"That's the owl's-eye view," said Owl grandly.

Then, Pooh filled the honeypot once more, and he and Owl went to Piglet's house for supper.

Tink Causes Trouble

The fairies were on the mainland to bring the season of summer. Tinker Bell had found herself with no work to do, because all of her inventions were working perfectly. She had nothing to fix, so she had entertained herself by flying after a car! She had followed it all the way to a house where a little girl called Lizzy lived with her father.

Vidia had tried to teach Tink a lesson, trapping her inside a tiny fairy house that Lizzy had made. But then, the little girl discovered Tinker Bell. Vidia panicked. She hadn't meant to put Tink in danger. She flew back to the fairy camp to get help.

But Vidia didn't realize that Tinker Bell had become friends with Lizzy. She had chosen to stay and help Lizzy and her father, Dr Griffiths. The scientist didn't believe in fairies and he was often too busy to spend time with his daughter. When Lizzy tried to show him her special fairy journal, he said he had no time – he had to fix some leaks in the roof.

So, Tinker Bell decided she would fix the leaks herself. She flew up into the attic and, in no time at all, she rigged up a system to take the water back outside. Then she flew back inside and couldn't help but notice a butterfly fluttering in a jar on Dr Griffith's desk. The scientist had caught it earlier to study. Tink felt terrible seeing the poor creature trapped, so she set it free.

The next morning, Dr Griffiths came by to check on his daughter.

"All the leaks have stopped," he said. "It's as if they mended themselves."

After he had gone, Tinker Bell tried to tell Lizzy to go and show her father the fairy field journal. "I would like to show him this," Lizzy said. "He has so much to learn about fairies."

But when Lizzy got downstairs, her father was very upset. "The butterfly is gone," he announced. "I was going to present it at the museum tonight. I didn't let it go, and since there is no one else in this house, it must have been you."

"I didn't," replied Lizzy. "It must have been...." Tinker Bell headed towards the office, but Lizzy waved her away.

"It must have been who?" he asked.

"I could tell you, father," Lizzy declared, "but you wouldn't believe me."

"Very well," Dr Griffiths said, "off to your room. I'm very disappointed in you."

Tinker Bell felt very bad for getting Lizzy into trouble. She wanted to show herself to Dr Griffiths, but Lizzy wouldn't let her new friend put herself in danger.

123

Faith, Trust and Pixie Dust

The fairies were bringing summer to the mainland and Tinker Bell was very excited to be there. She was curious about the human world. Her curiosity had led her to a little fairy house, made by a girl named Lizzy.

Vidia felt cross that Tink was putting them in danger and wanted to teach her a lesson. She slammed the door of the fairy house shut, but the door got stuck and Tink was found by the little girl! Vidia panicked and quickly flew to get help.

A storm had broken out, so Vidia and the other fairies had built a boat to reach Tinker Bell. They had sailed through the flooded meadow, survived a crash and saved Vidia from being stuck in the mud. Now, they were trudging quietly through the rain.

"I was just thinking if Tink were here," said Silvermist, "how not quiet it would be right now. I really miss her."

"Tinker Bell getting trapped is all my fault," Vidia admitted. "I'm so sorry."

To Vidia's surprise, the other fairies weren't upset with her.

"Tinker Bell can get into plenty of trouble by herself," Rosetta declared.

They gathered around and chanted the fairy motto: "Faith, trust and pixie dust!"

They vowed to work together to save Tinker Bell.

Vidia loved feeling part of the group. She usually liked to be by herself and was sometimes even mean to the other fairies. But she was finally beginning to understand the importance of friendship.

Back in Lizzy's room, Tinker Bell was apologizing to Lizzy. She had got the little girl in trouble with her father, who didn't believe that fairies existed. Lizzy understood.

"I wish I were a fairy just like you," Lizzy told Tink. "Then I could fly around with the other fairies all the time."

Tink knew how to make Lizzy's wish come true: pixie dust!

She told Lizzy to close her eyes and spread out her arms. Then Tink hovered above Lizzy's head and showered her with pixie dust. It was time for some flying lessons!

Lizzy was so happy to have a friend like Tinker Bell. She knew her father loved her and wanted to spend more time with her, but, being a grown-up, he found it hard to believe in magic and especially in fairies.

Lizzy hoped that, one day, her father would believe in magic and that they could spend lots of time together.

A Deal is a Deal

Tiana had just had a big shock! She had kissed a talking frog, who was once Prince Naveen, in order to turn him back into a prince. But it hadn't worked. Instead, she had turned into a frog too!

"What did you do to me? I ... I'm green and I'm ... slimy!" Tiana hurled herself at Prince Naveen, mad with rage. As they were tussling with each other, they landed in the middle of Charlotte's masked ball. The appearance of the two frogs obviously caused great panic amongst the guests. Fortunately, Naveen managed to grab a bunch of balloons, and with Tiana clinging to his neck they made an airborne escape. Now they were drifting through the darkness above the bayous, the swamps of Louisiana, which were filled with all manner of dangers.

"Who was the fake Prince Naveen dancing with Charlotte?" asked Tiana.

"My valet! He is hoping to make his fortune by obeying the sorcerer!" he replied.

"Voodoo? You mean to tell me all this happened because you were messing with the Shadow Man? It serves me right for wishing on stars. The ONLY way to get what you want in this world is through hard work," she muttered.

"Hard work?" retorted Naveen, surprised. "A princess doesn't work!"

"I'm not a princess. I'm a waitress."

At these words, Naveen uttered a cry. "Well, no wonder the kiss didn't work," said Naveen indignantly. "You lied to me! You were wearing a crown!"

"It was a costume party!" Tiana shouted.

Realizing his mistake, Naveen decided to get revenge on Tiana.

"Well, the egg is on your face, because I don't have any riches! I am completely broke!" He started to laugh.

At that moment, the balloons burst on the branches of a tree, and the frogs tumbled into the mud.

"And you call *me* a liar?" fumed Tiana.

"I didn't really lie," protested Naveen. "I intend to be rich again! Once I marry Miss Charlotte La Bouff, if she will have me!"

Suddenly, hungry alligators surrounded them! Quickly, Tiana took refuge in a hollow log by the water's edge. Naveen begged her to save him.

"A deal is a deal," replied Tiana. "Tell me you'll keep your promise or I won't save you!"

"It's a deal," relented the Prince. "But you have to keep your side of the deal – to turn me back into a prince."

Tiana sighed. She had just been caught in her own trap!

101 DALMATIANS

Patch and the Panther

One dark night, 15 Dalmatian puppies sat huddled around a black-and-white television set. They watched as Thunderbolt, the canine hero, crept through a deep, dark jungle.

Suddenly Thunderbolt pricked up his ears. The puppies held their breath. Two yellow eyes peered out of the bushes. It was a panther!

"Thunderbolt, look out behind you!" Penny barked at the television.

"How will Thunderbolt escape the hungry panther?" the TV announcer asked. "Don't miss next week's exciting episode!"

"Aww!" the puppies groaned, disappointed that their favourite show was over.

"I'll bet Thunderbolt tears that ol' panther to pieces," said Patch.

"I'd be scared to fight a panther," said his brother Lucky.

"Not me!" cried Patch.

"All right, kids. Time for bed," Pongo said, shutting off the television with his nose. He watched as the puppies padded upstairs and settled down in their baskets.

"Good night, pups," Pongo said.

"Good night, Dad," the puppies replied.

Pongo switched off the light. Moments later, the sound of soft snores filled the room. The puppies were fast asleep.

All except for one. Patch was wide awake.

He was still thinking about Thunderbolt and the panther.

"I wish some ol' panther would come around here," Patch said to himself. "I'd teach him a thing or two."

Just then a floorboard creaked. Patch pricked up his ears. Then he crawled out of his basket to investigate.

The floorboard creaked again. What if it's a panther? Patch thought with a shiver. But I'm not scared of any ol' panther, he reminded himself.

Suddenly Patch saw a shadow flicker across the doorway. The shadow had a long tail. Panthers have long tails. Just then two yellow eyes peered out of the darkness.

"Aroooo!" Patch yelped. He turned to run, but he tripped on the rug. In a flash, the panther was on top of him. Patch could feel its hot breath on his neck. He shut his eyes....

"Patch, what are you doing out of bed?" the panther asked.

Patch opened his eyes. It was Pongo!

"I – I was just keeping an eye out for panthers," Patch explained.

Pongo smiled. "Why don't you get some sleep now," he suggested. "I can keep an eye out for panthers for a while."

"Okay, Dad," Patch said with a yawn.

Pongo carried Patch back to his basket. And in no time at all, the puppy was fast asleep.

A Scientific Discovery

Tinker Bell was a very curious fairy. She loved exploring new places. This is why, while the fairies were bringing summer to the mainland, Tink flew off after a car. Vidia had followed and tried to get Tink to come back, but Tink had ignored her.

Tink ended up being discovered by a little girl. The girl's name was Lizzy and her father, Dr Griffiths, was a scientist. He didn't believe in fairies and found it hard to find time to spend with his daughter, because he was so busy.

Tink decided to help Lizzy and her father. She fixed the leaks in the roof of their house, so that Dr Griffiths wouldn't have to – he would be able to spend time with Lizzy instead!

But Tinker Bell got Lizzy in trouble by freeing a butterfly that her father had caught. To make it up to Lizzy, Tink sprinkled her with pixie dust so that she could fly around her room!

Meanwhile, Vidia and the other fairies had been travelling from fairy camp to rescue Tinker Bell. They thought she was in danger. They had just arrived at Lizzy's house. "Okay," began Vidia. "Tinker Bell is upstairs."

But before they could move, Mr Twitches, the family cat, appeared! The fairies couldn't fly because their wings were wet from the rain.

But Vidia had an idea. She shot some pixie dust at a plate, which began to hover in the air. The others joined in, sprinkling the dust on more plates. Then the fairies jumped on the crockery to reach the stairs. But Mr Twitches was right behind them!

"You know where Tink is," Rosetta told Vidia. "Go, we'll take care of the cat."

Meanwhile, Dr Griffiths could hear strange noises coming from Lizzy's room. "What's going on in here?" he demanded. "Look at this room! How did you get footprints on the ceiling? The truth this time."

"Well, I ..." began Lizzy. "I was flying. My fairy showed me how."

"You've got to stop this nonsense!" insisted Dr Griffiths. Just then, Vidia sneaked into the room, but he didn't see her. "You will never convince me that fairies exist!" he added.

Tinker Bell couldn't stand it any longer. She flew out of hiding and hovered directly in front of his face! "It can't be!" Lizzy's father cried. He stared at Tink in wonder. "This is going to be the discovery of the century!"

Vidia saw him raise a jar. "Watch out!" she warned. Now that her wings were dry, she was able to fly over and knock Tink out of the way. *SLAM!* The jar caught Vidia instead. Now it was Vidia that needed rescuing!

WRECK-IT RALPH

Bad Guys Don't Win Medals

Wreck-It Ralph worked in the *Fix-It Felix, Jr* video game. Every time someone played the game, Ralph would come on-screen and yell, "I'M GONNA WRECK IT!"

Then Fix-It Felix, the Good Guy, would arrive with his magic hammer and fix everything. All the Nicelanders cheered for Felix and gave him pie and a medal. But Ralph? They threw him off the building and into the mud.

The *Fix-It Felix, Jr* game had been in Litwak's Family Fun Centre for thirty years now. It was one of the arcade's original 8-bit games, and kids had been helping Felix fix up the Nicelanders' building for a very long time.

Inside the game, Felix and the Nicelanders were happy. Felix enjoyed his work, and the Nicelanders were glad to reward him ... game after game, year after year.

Ralph, however, was getting tired of that mud puddle. It didn't feel fair. He was just doing his job. Why did Felix always get to be the Good Guy, while he ended up covered in mud?

On the game's anniversary, Ralph travelled through the power cord to a support group for video game Bad Guys. He told the group that he wished he could be the Good Guy, just once.

"We can't change who we are," the others said. Then they all recited the Bad Guy Affirmation: "I am Bad. And that's good. I will never be Good. And that's not bad. There's no one I'd rather be than me."

Ralph headed home through Game Central Station, the hub for all the games in the arcade. As usual, Surge Protector stopped him for questioning. Ralph knew it was just because he was a Bad Guy.

Then Ralph dropped off treats for the homeless video game characters living in the station. Their games had been unplugged, so they had nowhere to live.

That evening, the Nicelanders held a big anniversary party in their apartment building. Ralph couldn't believe that he hadn't been invited. "I am going to that party!" Ralph declared.

At the party, Ralph tried to be polite. Then he noticed the cake, with a Felix figurine on top, wearing a medal. Ralph wanted his own figurine to wear a medal, too. But Nicelander Gene said, "Bad Guys don't win medals!"

Ralph was so upset that he accidentally wrecked the cake!

Ralph sighed. Would he ever be able to have his very own medal...?

Mickey & Friends

Prize-winning Pooch

One day, Minnie was walking her dog, Fifi, when she saw a poster.

"Look, Fifi," she said. "A dog show – with prizes! You should enter!"

Minnie and Fifi went straight home to practise.

"Fifi, sit!" said Minnie. Fifi sat.

"Shake. Good girl!" said Minnie, shaking the paw Fifi held up. "Roll over."

Fifi sat up. "Arf!"

"No," said Minnie. "You're supposed to bark when I say 'speak'."

Fifi rolled over.

"We've still got work to do!" said Minnie.

On the morning of the show, Minnie gave Fifi a bath and dressed her in a red polka-dot bow.

Fifi pulled at the lead as they walked towards the town square. She'd seen a squirrel!

Minnie held on tight, but Fifi slipped from her collar. Minnie watched the squirrel disappear round a corner – followed by a red polka-dot bow!

"Fifi!" cried Minnie. "Come back!"

Minnie raced after Fifi but when she turned the corner her dog was gone. Minnie searched and searched, then she called Daisy.

"I'll be right there!" announced Daisy. "And I'll bring Mickey!"

"Don't worry, Minnie," said Mickey when he and Daisy arrived, "we'll help you find her."

Minnie and her friends made posters that read: *Missing! Tan and cream dog. Name of Fifi. If found, please call 555-5736.*

Then they went all around town, calling for Fifi and putting up the posters.

"Now let's go back to your house, Minnie," suggested Daisy. "Fifi may have found her way home."

But there was no little dog at Minnie's house.

"I'm sending a message to my friends: *Lost: little tan and cream dog with a red polka-dot bow. If you see her, please send a message!*" said Daisy.

Within minutes, Daisy started getting messages and a picture came up on her phone. It was of a dog with a red polka-dot bow – and a big blue rosette!

Daisy sent back: *That's Fifi! Where is she?*

The answer came. "She's at the dog show!" Daisy said.

The three friends raced to the park.

Fifi barked when she saw Minnie.

"Fifi, I was so worried!" said Minnie. "How did you win a blue rosette?"

"Your dog is so well behaved," one of the judges explained. "When we said 'sit', your dog sat. When we said 'shake', your dog held up her paw. We just had to give her the prize."

Minnie smiled. "You're lucky none of the judges said 'roll over'."

Fifi sat up. "Arf!"

Disney PRINCESS
THE LITTLE
MERMAID

A History Lesson

"Ariel, what am I going to do with you?" King Triton asked with a sigh. He looked wearily at his daughter. "You know you're not allowed to visit the surface. None of us are – it's just too dangerous!"

Ariel hung her head. She had been caught going to visit the surface – again – to visit her seagull friend, Scuttle. King Triton couldn't understand Ariel's interest in the human world. It made him sad that most of his conversations with his favourite daughter involved him yelling and her storming off. Suddenly, the King had an idea.

"You know, Ariel," he said thoughtfully, "you're so interested in learning more about the human world, but I bet you don't know that much about the world you live in!"

Ariel looked up. "What do you mean, Daddy?" she asked, looking confused. "What's there to know?"

"Well," said Triton, "for starters, do you know about the first Queen of the Merfolk?"

"I guess not," Ariel replied.

Ten minutes later, Ariel and her father were swimming slowly through the Royal Merseum (that's a merfolk museum, you know), and Ariel was discovering that merfolk history was much more exciting than she had ever imagined.

"This is a portrait of Queen Fluidia, the first Queen of the Merfolk. She was my Great-great-great-great-great-great-great-great-great-great-great-great-grandmother," said King Triton. He gestured at a sandpainting of a regal mermaid holding a pearl sceptre. "That would make her your Great-great-great – well, you get the idea. Anyway, Fluidia united all the merfolk into one kingdom many years ago, to fight an invasion of sharks. The Shark Army was the greatest, fiercest army the ocean had ever seen, but Fluidia was more than a match for them! She used that pearl sceptre as a club – she was so strong that she could start whirlpools just by swinging it around."

"Wow," said Ariel. "She sounds fierce."

"She was. She drove those sharks off almost single-handedly, and in gratitude the merfolk made her Queen," King Triton said.

"You know, you come from a pretty interesting family," he continued. "And you remind me a lot of Fluidia, Ariel. You have her strength of will. I think you'll do great things – even if we won't always agree on *how* you'll do them."

"Thank you, Daddy," said Ariel. She decided not to mention to her father how much his trident looked like a dinglehopper. Maybe she would tell him some other time!

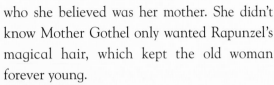

Tangled
Leaving the Tower

Thief Flynn Rider wanted his satchel back – the crown he had stolen was inside! But Rapunzel refused to give it to him unless he took her to see the floating lanterns. She had been kept hidden in a tall tower her whole life, and she wanted to know why there were floating lights in the sky every year on her birthday.

"Are you coming, blondie?" Flynn slipped down the wall using his arrows as steps.

Leaning from her window, Rapunzel hesitated ... but with one glance back at her painting of the floating lights, Rapunzel overcame her fear.

With Pascal on her shoulder, and clasping on to her long hair, she made her way down the outside of the tower. She was so quick that she soon overtook Flynn, who stopped in astonishment. Once at the bottom, she put one foot on the soft grass, then the other.

"Oooh! The grass is exactly as I imagined it would be! It's wonderful! I can run, dance and jump without stopping! I'm free!"

Overcome with excitement, Rapunzel began to roll around on the ground.

"I can't believe I did this! I can't believe I did this!" she shouted.

Rapunzel began to explore. But she also felt guilty for betraying Mother Gothel, who she believed was her mother. She didn't know Mother Gothel only wanted Rapunzel's magical hair, which kept the old woman forever young.

One moment Rapunzel was jumping excitedly, and the next she was sobbing facedown in a field of flowers. "I am a despicable human being," she cried.

Flynn saw the chance to get hold of his satchel without fulfilling his part of the bargain. He murmured, "Don't worry too much about your mother. When we grow up, we always argue with our parents – it's normal. Your mother will be broken-hearted. Her heart will be in so many tiny pieces that it can never be mended. But she'll get over it."

"Do you think so? Her heart is broken?"

"In smithereens!"

Rapunzel looked sad. Flynn accompanied her back to the tower, adding, "I'm letting you out of the deal, let's go back to the tower. I get back my satchel, and you get back a mother-daughter relationship."

Rapunzel suddenly froze.

"I'm seeing those lanterns," she insisted, and she turned around and stormed away from the tower.

Flynn was amazed at Rapunzel's strength. He couldn't help but give in.

Paradise Falls

Carl had wanted to be an explorer ever since he was a child. So had his friend and wife, Ellie. He had promised Ellie that he'd take her to see Paradise Falls in South America one day.

But they were never able to save enough money to go. When they grew older, Ellie sadly passed away, and Carl was told he had to move out of his house.

But Carl decided he had to keep his promise to Ellie. He tied thousands of balloons to their little house and slowly it lifted into the sky.

Carl steered the flying house using ropes attached to the weather vane. He checked his compass and map, and set a course to Paradise Falls in South America.

"We're on our way, Ellie," he said happily.

Suddenly, there was a knock at the door. Carl was shocked. He was thousands of feet up in the air! Who could be at his door?

It was Russell! A Junior Wilderness Explorer who had knocked on his door a few days before. Carl had told him to find a Snipe – a bird that didn't really exist – just to get rid of him. Russell had been under Carl's porch, looking for the snipe, when the house lifted off.

"Please let me in!" Russell begged.

What choice did Carl have? He let Russell come inside.

Carl hated to stop, but he knew he had to land and send Russell home. He started to cut some of the balloons free.

Meanwhile, Russell was watching the clouds out of the window. "There's a big storm coming," he said. But Carl didn't hear him.

A flash of lightning lit up the room. Carl quickly tried to steer the house away from the storm, but it was too late. The little house tossed in the wind. Carl ran this way and that, trying to save Ellie's belongings. Finally, exhausted, he fell asleep.

When Carl woke up, the storm was over. "I steered us down," Russell told him proudly. "We're in South America."

As Carl and Russell stepped out onto the porch, the house crash-landed and sent them both flying. "My house!" Carl cried as it started to drift away from them. Grabbing hold of the garden hose, he and Russell managed to pull the house back down. Just then, the fog cleared. There, a short distance ahead, was Paradise Falls! It looked just like Ellie's picture!

"We made it!" Carl shouted. "We could float right over there!"

Carl was amazed. He had finally made the trip he and Ellie had always dreamt about.

Disney · PIXAR
FINDING
NEMO

Finding Ne-who?

"The coral reef is falling down, falling down, falling down."

Nemo was home, brushing up against the anemone, when the most awful singing he ever heard in his life made him cringe. He swam deeper into the anemone, but it didn't help. The song went on.

"My fair octopus."

And there was something familiar about it.... Still cringing, Nemo poked his head out of the golden tentacles to see who was making the awful racket.

"Dory!" Nemo should have known. How could he have forgotten that voice? Nemo swam as fast as he could toward the regal blue tang fish. "Dory! Where have you been?" It seemed like a whale's age since Nemo had seen the fish that helped his dad rescue him from the dentist's fish tank. And he couldn't wait to give her a big hug!

When Nemo got closer Dory stopped singing. That was good. But when she looked at him her face was blank. That wasn't so good.

"Did you say something, kid?" she asked.

"Dory, it's me. Nemo," he replied.

"Ne-*who*?" She looked at Nemo blankly. "Sorry, kid, don't know you. I was just swimming by, minding my own business, singing a song. Hey, why was I singing? Am I famous? Maybe that's how you know me."

"Dory! We're friends, remember?" Nemo had been missing Dory a lot. She just *had* to remember who he was.

"Friends? I just made friends with a hermit crab ... I think." Dory swam in a circle looking for the crab, but got distracted and started chasing her tail.

"Please try to remember, Dory," Nemo asked again. "You helped save me. You helped me find my dad. You know my dad. Big orange guy? Three white stripes? Looks kind of like me?"

"My dad? Looks like you? Sorry, kid, you don't look anything like my dad." Dory looked at Nemo like he was crazy and began to swim away.

Nemo swam after her. "Just think about it for a second," he pleaded. She *had* to remember something. "I'm Nemo!"

Dory did not turn around but she slowed down. Swimming in a wide circle, she came back. She looked at Nemo sideways, and then started laughing so hard bubbles came out of her nose.

"Had you going, huh?" Dory gave Nemo a big hug and smiled at him slyly. "That was just my little joke. You know I could never forget you!"

Nemo giggled and swam circles around his friend. "Good one, Dory!" He grinned.

Dory smiled back. "Good one, *who*?"

Nemo groaned. That Dory!

Simba's Thank-you Present

Simba lounged in the jungle, feeling happier than he'd felt in ages. After the terrible stampede near Pride Rock, he didn't think he'd ever be happy again. But his new friends Timon and Pumbaa had helped him feel better.

"I should do something to thank them," Simba told himself as he watched his friends in the river nearby. "Something really special!"

He decided to make them a present. When he saw a piece of bark lying on the ground, he had an idea.

"Ta-da!" he exclaimed a while later, leading his friends to the gift.

Pumbaa blinked. "Thanks," he said. "Er, what is it?"

"A scratching spot," Simba said, flexing his claws. He'd used vines to attach it to a thick tree trunk at shoulder height.

"Gee," Timon said. "Nice thought and all, Simba. But it's a little high for me." He stretched to his full height but could barely reach it.

Pumbaa nodded. "And I don't scratch." He held up one foot. "Hooves, you know."

"Oh." Simba hadn't thought of that.

"Thanks anyway, kid," Pumbaa said.

Simba decided to try again by building them a nice, soft bed to sleep in. He dug a cosy hole in the ground, then filled it with soft things – feathers, sand and bits of fur.

"Ta-da!" he cried when he showed his friends.

Timon sighed. "What are you trying to do, kill us? Prey animals here, remember? If we sleep on the ground, we become somebody's midnight snack!"

Simba sighed as they left again. Why couldn't he think of a present they would like?

"I would've loved that scratching spot," he mumbled. "The bed, too."

Suddenly he sat up straight, realizing what he'd just said. All this time he'd been thinking of presents HE would like – but the presents weren't for him.

"I've got to think like they think," he whispered. Slowly, a smile spread across his face....

A little while later he called them over. "I've got something for you." He pointed to a pile of palm fronds. "I think you're really going to like it. Ta-da!"

He pulled back the leaves. Underneath was a mass of wriggling, squirming, creeping, crawling creatures – bugs and grubs and worms of every shape and size ... and flavour.

Timon and Pumbaa gasped with delight. "Simba!" Timon cried. "You're a prince! It's just what we always wanted!"

"Yeah, thanks," Pumbaa mumbled through a mouthful of grubs. "You're a real pal!"

Simba smiled. "No," he said. "Thank *you*. Both of you. *Hakuna matata!*"

A Birthday Surprise

"Get up, Jaq! Get up!" Gus cried.

"Go away, Gus," Jaq mumbled sleepily and rolled over.

"No, no, Jaq. Get up. It's a special day." Gus pulled on his tail. "It's Cinderelly's birthday."

Jaq sat up. "Today?" he asked, wide-eyed. "Today is her birthday?"

Gus smiled and nodded vigorously.

"Well, come on! We haven't got much time!" Jaq cried. "We have a lot to do if we're throwing a surprise party!"

Soon the birds and mice were gathered on the windowsill for a meeting.

"We can make a cake!" Suzy and Perla volunteered.

"Watch out for L-L-Lucifer," Gus stuttered. Baking would mean stealing eggs and butter from the kitchen!

"We'll take care of that cat," Mert and Bert said, crossing their arms.

The birds whistled that they would decorate the room.

"But we still need a present," Jaq said.

"Something pretty!" Gus cried.

"I've got it!" Jaq sat up straight. "I saw some slippers in the garbage last night when I was looking for food. There's a hole in one toe, but the bottoms were okay."

"We can fix them," the mice chorused.

"And I have a bit of ribbon I've been saving. We can use it on the slippers to pretty them up." Jaq pulled a rose-coloured silk ribbon from his small bag. "Now, let's get to work. We have lots to do!"

It took the mice all day to get ready, but everything turned out beautifully. The sun was setting when the mice and birds heard Cinderella's soft steps coming up the stairs.

"Here she comes!" Gus whispered.

Jaq took a match and lit the candle stump that was stuck in the iced cake. Beside it the slippers were mended and wrapped. The ribbon was twirled into two pink roses, one at each ankle.

The door opened slowly.

"Surprise!" the mice squeaked. The birds twittered and dropped confetti.

"Oh, my!" Cinderella gasped. "This *is* a surprise!"

"Happy birthday," Gus said shyly.

"It's all so lovely," Cinderella said. "But I'm afraid it's not my birthday."

"It's not?" Jaq's smile vanished. The rest of the mice and birds were silent.

"I'm afraid not, but that's what makes this such a special surprise." Cinderella beamed. The animals laughed and they all sat down to share the delicious cake together.

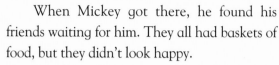

A Perfect Picnic

Mickey and his friends were planning a picnic!

"We can all make our favourite foods and then swap baskets!" Mickey suggested.

"Sharing our lunches sounds like fun. I can't wait!" said Minnie.

The friends raced home and each began to pack a lunch.

Donald made a sandwich. He chose his favourite drink and a piece of fruit. But as Donald looked at the food, he realized he didn't want to share them!

Over at Minnie's house, things were not going well either. Minnie had packed all her favourite foods. But she started to wonder if she would like the lunches her friends had packed.

Daisy was excited about sharing her lunch. She hummed to herself as she packed her basket. But when Daisy picked up a banana, she thought about someone else eating it and began to frown. Maybe she didn't want to share her lunch after all….

Meanwhile, Goofy was making lemonade to take to the picnic. Covered in lemon juice, Goofy tasted his lemonade. It was delicious and he wanted to drink it all himself!

Mickey didn't know that his friends had changed their minds. As he walked to the park, he grew more excited about the picnic.

When Mickey got there, he found his friends waiting for him. They all had baskets of food, but they didn't look happy.

"What's wrong?" Mickey asked his friends.

Donald explained that everyone wanted to eat their own food.

"Oh," Mickey said, disappointed. "I guess we don't have to share…."

Minnie looked at Mickey. He looked so sad. She didn't want to be the reason he was upset!

Minnie handed Mickey her basket. "I'll trade lunches with you, Mickey," she said.

"Really? Thanks, Minnie!" Mickey said.

Mickey's friends saw how happy Minnie had made Mickey and swapped baskets, too.

Mickey laid out a blanket, sat down and opened his picnic basket. When he saw what was inside, he started to laugh.

"What's so funny?" Minnie asked. She looked in her basket and started to laugh, too.

Everyone had packed peanut butter sandwiches and lemonade! The only difference in the baskets was the fruit. There was an orange, a banana, an apple, grapes and a pineapple!

"I have an idea," said Mickey. While his friends ate, Mickey made a big fruit salad!

As Mickey's friends ate their dessert, they realized that Mickey had been right. Sharing was fun, after all!

A Frog's Appetite

Tiana and Naveen, now transformed into frogs, found themselves lost in the bayou. They had to get back to New Orleans quickly, so they could find out how to undo Dr Facilier's evil curse. Tiana, working hard as usual, had just finished building a raft to cross the swamp. As for Naveen, he was happy to sing while she manoeuvred their makeshift boat.

"I could do with a little help!" she grumbled.

"I'll sing louder then!" replied Naveen without moving.

Suddenly, an enormous alligator emerged from the muddy waters! The frogs froze in terror. But he wasn't dangerous. This was Louis, who was mad about music! He loved the jazz pieces that Naveen was singing.

"I am Naveen, Prince of Maldonia, and she is Tiana, the waitress," introduced Naveen. Then he leaned closer to Louis. "Do not kiss her."

"Delighted to make your acquaintance, Louis," Tiana intervened, ignoring Naveen. "And thank you for not eating us ... but we're in a hurry!"

"Where are you going?" asked Louis.

"To find someone who will be able to turn us back into humans," explained Naveen. "An evil sorcerer changed us into frogs!"

"We'll have to ask Mama Odie!"

exclaimed Louis. "Queen of the bayou! She's a real voodoo priestess ... but one who does good magic!"

Louis was frightened about going to find Mama Odie, who lived in one of the most remote and dangerous swamps. But in the end he agreed to guide Tiana and Naveen, his new friends.

They sang and entertained themselves along the way, until Naveen started to get hungry. Very hungry. So hungry that his frog's tongue suddenly shot out all by itself – *doing!* – into the path of a cloud of mosquitoes! Then, a big firefly landed on a nearby dandelion ... and this time, Tiana's tongue shot out without warning!

"Oh no, no, no!" she panicked as she slapped a leg over her mouth. "There is no way I'm kissing a frog and eating a bug in the same day!"

But Tiana couldn't fight it. Her tongue shot out in the direction of the chubby firefly at the same time as Naveen's. And *splosh!* they missed the firefly, but got their tongues tangled up!

"What an embarrassing situation!" laughed the firefly, fluttering around them. "I've always said: there is nothing worse in the whole bayou than a frog's appetite!"

The Perfect Pearl

Belle and Chip were in the library. "My library is your library," the Beast had told her. "Read and enjoy any book you find." Belle took him at his word. She spent hours there, reading book after book. To her, books were priceless treasures, and she looked after them.

One morning, Belle noticed the Beast had left the only book he ever read lying open on the arm of his chair.

She picked it up and turned it over. Although the leather cover was worn, it was a beautiful volume with a decorative brass clasp containing three pearls.

"Chip, look!" she said to the enchanted cup, pointing at the clasp. There was an empty hole where a fourth pearl should have been.

They looked around on the floor nearby, in case it had fallen out.

"I found something!" called Chip. There by the library door was a single, perfect pearl.

"Let's see if it fits!" Belle suggested.

She dropped the pearl into the empty hole in the clasp.

"Just right!" said Chip.

"I have an idea," Belle said. "As this book is your master's favourite, I'll fix it up for him."

"Then you can surprise him!" Chip cried.

Belle nodded. She was happy to do something nice for the Beast.

She borrowed some polish from Mrs Potts to clean the leather cover. Then she put the book back on the Beast's chair so that he wouldn't miss it. But when the Beast came into the library, he didn't pick it up. He seemed to be looking for something.

"Can I help?" Belle asked.

"NO!" he bellowed. "I mean, no. Excuse me." And without another word, he left the room.

That afternoon, Belle smoothed out the crumpled pages and polished the brass clasp.

That evening, she passed the Beast in the hall. Belle smiled at him but he simply snapped "Goodnight!" and hurried on by.

The next morning, Belle was about to add the pearl to the clasp when the Beast burst through the door.

"You?" he cried. "I've been looking for that pearl!"

"Well, why didn't you say so!" Belle shouted, tossing the pearl onto the table. "I've been fixing up your book as a surprise."

The Beast looked at the book. Then he picked up the pearl and began to laugh.

"I've been working on something for you, too," he said, holding up an antique pin. "I wanted you to have it, but first, I had something to add."

He placed the pearl on the pin and it fitted perfectly.

"I removed the pearl but dropped it ... I'm sorry I blamed you," said the Beast.

Now it was Belle's turn to laugh. They still had so much to learn about one another!

Lady and the TRAMP

Howling at the Moon

Lady had been having a really bad day. First, she'd had a run-in with two nasty cats. Then, she'd been put in a horrible muzzle. But, because of Tramp, everything had changed.

"It's amazing how a day can start off terribly but end wonderfully," Lady told Tramp as they trotted through the moonlit park. "Thank you for helping me escape that terrible muzzle – and for dinner at Tony's."

"Aw, shucks, don't mention it!" said Tramp. "Hey, you wanna have some real fun?"

"I don't know," Lady said cautiously.

While she was very fond of Tramp, she also knew they were very different dogs. Tramp was used to life on the streets. So his idea of 'fun' might be very different from hers.

"Don't worry," Tramp teased. "This is something I think you'll enjoy."

"What is it?" asked Lady.

"Well, for starters, you have to look up," said Tramp.

Lady did. The sky was filled with stars and a big, bright moon.

"What am I looking for?" she asked.

"The moon, of course!" cried Tramp. "Haven't you ever howled at the moon?"

Lady laughed at Tramp's suggestion.

"What's so funny?" asked Tramp.

"I'm a practical dog," explained Lady. "I bark politely when the situation calls for it, but I don't see any point in howling at the moon."

"Why not?" asked Tramp.

"Well," said Lady, "what's the use of it?"

"You know, Lady," said Tramp, "a thing doesn't have to be useful to be fun. You like to chase a ball, right?"

"Right," said Lady.

"So, there you go," said Tramp. "Sometimes it's good to chase a ball. And sometimes it's good to just let go and howl at the moon, even for no reason."

Lady thought it over. "Okay," she said. "What do I do?"

"First, sit up real straight," said Tramp. "Then, look up at the moon, take a deep breath, and just let all the troubles of your day disappear in one gigantic howl!" He demonstrated: "Ow-ow-OWWWWWWW!"

Lady joined Tramp and howled as loudly as she could.

"You're right!" she cried. "It does feel good to howl at the moon!"

"Stick with me, kid," said Tramp. "I know what's what."

Lady suspected Tramp did know what was what, but there was an even better reason for her to stick with him. He'd become the very best friend she'd ever had.

Peter Pan

The Lost Boys Get Lost

The Lost Boys were walking single file through the woods of Never Land, on their way home after an afternoon of adventure-seeking, when Slightly, who led the way, stopped in his tracks on the bank of Mermaid Lagoon.

The others – Rabbit, the Raccoon Twins, Cubby and Tootles – came to an abrupt halt behind him.

"Wait a minute," said Slightly. "We already passed Mermaid Lagoon. What are we doing here again?"

Behind a bush, Tinker Bell giggled as she watched the Lost Boys looking around in confusion.

Tink had spotted them on their march and had not been able to resist playing a joke. So, she had flown ahead of them and used her fairy magic to enchant various landmarks on their route home. She had made Bald Rock look like Spiky Rock, causing the Lost Boys to make a right turn where they should have turned left. Then she had enlisted the help of the sparrows, convincing them to move from their usual perch in the Sparrow Bird Grove to another group of trees, thus tricking the Lost Boys into making another right turn too soon. And finally, she had enchanted the Towering Elm Tree to look exactly like the Weeping Willow, and the Lost Boys had made yet another wrong turn, thinking they were nearly home.

But now, here they were, walking past Mermaid Lagoon, when Slightly remembered passing the same spot a good while back.

"I think we're walking in circles!" Slightly proclaimed. "Lost Boys, I think we're ... lost!"

Tinker Bell overheard and tried desperately to stifle her laughter. But, before she could contain it, one giggle exploded into a full-fledged laugh and –

"Hey!" said Cubby. "Did you hear that?"

He darted over to a bush growing alongside the path and moved a branch to one side. There was Tinker Bell, hovering in mid-air, holding her stomach and shaking with laughter.

"Tinker Bell!" cried Tootles.

It didn't take them long to work out that Tinker Bell was laughing at *them* – and that she was the cause of their confusion.

Still laughing, Tinker Bell flitted away, taking her normal route home to the fairy glade: left at the Weeping Willow Tree, right just before Sparrow Bird Grove, right again at Spiky Rock, and on towards the Sparkling Stream, which led to Moon Falls and the fairy glade entrance.

But – wait a minute! After turning right at Spiky Rock, Tinker Bell saw no sign of the Sparkling Stream anywhere. Where was she? She had got completely lost.

Do you know how?

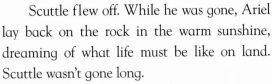

Dinglehoppers and Jibbermutts

Ariel sat on a rock, talking with her friends, Scuttle the seagull and Flounder the fish. She loved visiting the surface, although she knew it was dangerous for mermaids to venture there. Her father would definitely not approve, but then, these days, he seemed to disapprove of so much of what she liked to do.

"What's it like on land, Scuttle?" she asked.

"Land?" echoed Scuttle. "Oh! Land! Yeah, well, it's great on land. I know all about humans."

"Like what?" Ariel asked eagerly.

"Well! For instance ... you know all about the dinglehoppers they use to comb their hair, right? And the snarfblatts that they make music with?"

"Yes," said Ariel.

"Well, did you know that they also have these strange rectangular objects with sheets of paper inside? They're called jibbermutts. Humans like to throw them to one another," Scuttle explained.

"Oh, Scuttle," said Ariel breathlessly. "Would you fly up to Eric's window and come back and tell me what you have seen?" Eric was the young prince whom Ariel had rescued after he was shipwrecked during a terrible storm. Even though she had seen him only once, she had fallen head over fin in love with him.

Scuttle flew off. While he was gone, Ariel lay back on the rock in the warm sunshine, dreaming of what life must be like on land. Scuttle wasn't gone long.

"Did you see him?" asked Ariel eagerly. "What was he doing?"

"Yep, I saw him!" Scuttle replied importantly. "He was trying to eat with a dinglehopper! And he had a jibbermutt, but it almost looked like he was trying to read it, instead of throwing it like he's supposed to. Ariel, I don't think your prince is too bright...."

Ariel sighed dreamily, imagining her handsome love. She did wonder why he would try to use a dinglehopper to eat, though. Maybe he was so distracted by thoughts of her, he didn't know what he was doing, the Little Mermaid thought hopefully.

"Don't suppose you'd want his dinglehopper for your treasure chest, would you?" asked Scuttle with a mischievous glint in his eye.

"Oh, Scuttle! You didn't!" shouted Ariel.

"Yup. Just as soon as he set it down, I flew in through the window and grabbed it. Boy, was he surprised!"

Ariel clutched the dinglehopper to her chest. "I'll probably never know what it's like to live on land, but no matter what happens, Scuttle, I will treasure this forever!"

Baloo's Secret Weapon

Mowgli and his pal Baloo were taking a lazy afternoon stroll through the jungle. Suddenly, Mowgli stopped in his tracks. "Did you hear that?" he asked.

"Hear what, little buddy?" Baloo asked.

"It sounded like twigs snapping," Mowgli said. "I think somebody might be following us!"

"That was just your old Papa Bear's stomach growling," Baloo told him. "It's time for some lunch."

"And I know just where to get it," announced Mowgli. He shimmied up a tree, plucked a bunch of bananas and tossed them down to the bear.

"That's my boy!" Baloo cried proudly.

But, as he was scrambling back down, Mowgli spotted a flash of orange and black.

"Shere Khan!" Mowgli whispered to Baloo. "We've got to get out of here!" The tiger had been after Mowgli ever since the boy had first set foot in the jungle.

The two friends didn't know which way to turn. Now that Shere Khan had their scent, it would be almost impossible to lose him. Then they both heard a lively beat drumming its way through the jungle.

"Oh, no," said Mowgli. "King Louie and his crazy band of monkeys. That's all we need!"

Baloo's eyes suddenly lit up. "That's *exactly* what we need, Little Britches!"

Still clutching the bananas, Baloo and Mowgli ran towards King Louie's compound. When they arrived, Baloo disguised himself as a monkey. The orang-utans were so busy dancing and singing they didn't notice his disguise. Then the bear quickly found a huge empty barrel, and filled it with the bananas.

"Look!" cried Baloo, peering into the barrel. "Lunch!" The monkeys ran over and jumped right into the barrel! They greedily ate the feast, tossing peels out as they made their way through the bunch.

Baloo signalled to Mowgli, who came out of hiding. "Come and get me, Shere Khan!" the Man-cub taunted.

Within seconds, the tiger appeared in the clearing, a fierce gleam in his eye. "Hello, Stripes," Baloo greeted him cheerfully. Then the bear picked up the barrel, heaved it, and sent King Louie's troop flying at Shere Khan. The orangutans landed on the tiger's back, where they frantically jumped up and down, pulling on his tail and ears. Mowgli and Baloo watched as Shere Khan raced back into the jungle, trying to free himself from his shrieking passengers.

"Like I always say," Baloo declared as he grinned at Mowgli, "there's nothing more fun than a barrel of monkeys!"

A Sister's Love

Anna was shivering on the library floor of Arendelle's castle. Ice was creeping over her body and it wouldn't be long before she was completely frozen. Prince Hans had locked her in there as part of his plan to become ruler of Arendelle.

To her great relief she lifted her head to see her friend Olaf. The snowman lit a fire to warm her up, even though Anna worried that he might melt.

"Some people are worth melting for," he said. Then, as he looked out of the window, he saw Kristoff.

Just like Sven the reindeer, Olaf had realized that Kristoff was the true love who could save Anna. He helped Anna outside and she spotted Kristoff across the frozen fjord. If she could reach Kristoff in time, she would be saved! But then she saw something else: Hans was about to strike her sister Elsa with his sword!

With her remaining strength Anna threw herself in front of Elsa. Hans's sword came down just as Anna's body froze to solid ice. With a loud CLANK, the blade shattered.

Elsa wrapped her arms round her frozen sister. "Oh, Anna," she sobbed.

Then something amazing happened: Anna began to thaw! "You sacrificed yourself for me?" Elsa asked in disbelief.

"I love you," replied Anna weakly.

"An act of true love will thaw a frozen heart," Olaf said, echoing the old troll's words.

That's when Elsa realized that love could bring back summer. She raised her arms and the snow melted away. The people of Arendelle cheered. They had seen everything.

But Olaf was melting, too! Elsa quickly made him his own little snow cloud to keep him safe.

Hans was astonished to see Anna alive. "But, Anna," he said, "Elsa froze your heart!"

"The only frozen heart around here is yours!" Anna said, and sent him reeling with one punch.

With summer restored, the visiting ships sailed away, and Arendelle returned to normal – except now the castle gates were open for good!

Anna replaced Kristoff's sled and his supplies. But he wasn't anxious to leave – especially when Anna surprised him with a kiss.

Elsa created an ice-skating rink in the castle and welcomed everyone in the kingdom. Everyone had a wonderful time skating with Queen Elsa and Princess Anna, and the kingdom of Arendelle was a happy place once more.

Snow White
and the Seven Dwarfs

Good Housekeeping

Snow White and the Prince were going to be married. Her dear friends, the Seven Dwarfs, were filled with joy to see Snow White so happy. But they knew they were going to miss her – not to mention her wonderful cooking and how she kept their cottage so clean and tidy.

Snow White was also worried about how the little men were going to get along without her. She decided it was time they learned how to cook and clean for themselves.

"First, let's see you sweep out the cottage," she said. "Remember to push the dirt out of the door and not just move it around the floor." The men all grabbed brooms and set to work.

"*Ah-chooooo!*" boomed Sneezy as a huge cloud of dust rose into the air.

"Don't forget to open the door *first*," Snow White added. She moved on to the next task. "Now we'll wash the dishes. First you dunk the plate, then you scrub it, then you rinse and dry it," she said, demonstrating as she went.

Doc stood, holding a dirty plate. "Let's see," he mumbled. "Scrub, dunk, dry, rinse? Or is it dunk, rinse, dry, scrub? Or ... oh, dear!"

Snow White chuckled good-naturedly. "Never mind," she said. "On to the laundry! First you heat the water over the fire, then you scrub the clothes with a bar of soap, rinse them and then hang them on the line to dry."

Dopey was first in line. He jumped into the tub and rubbed the bar of soap all over the clothes he was wearing.

"Dopey," said Snow White, "it's easier if you wash the clothes *after* you've taken them off."

A bit later, the Dwarfs trooped into the kitchen for a cooking lesson.

"Today we're going to make stew," said Snow White. "You take a little of everything you have on hand, throw it into a pot, and let it simmer for a long time."

As Snow White was leaving, Doc said, "Don't worry, Snow White. We're going to be fust jine ... I mean, just fine."

The next night, the Dwarfs made dinner. When their guests arrived, Dopey led Snow White and the Prince over to the large pot simmering over the fire and grandly lifted the lid. An old boot, some socks, a bunch of flowers and a cake of soap were floating on the top. "We made it with a little of everything we had on hand, just like you said," Sleepy said.

"Perhaps we should go over that recipe again," Snow White said gently. Then she brought out four gooseberry pies from her basket. Ordinarily, Snow White didn't believe in eating dessert before dinner, but this time she would make an exception!

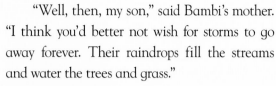

Rain, Rain, Go Away

Rrrrumble, rrrrumble, BOOM! The loud clap of thunder startled Bambi and his friends.

"I hate thunderstorms!" cried Thumper, looking a little scared.

"I don't like them either!" exclaimed Flower.

"Bambi!" called his mother as the clouds grew dark and the rain began to fall. Bambi followed his mother out of the open meadow and into the woods. From their warm, dry thicket, Bambi watched sheets of rain pour down.

"I hate thunderstorms," he told his mother, echoing Thumper's words. "I wish the storm would go away and never come back again."

"Oh, my," said his mother. "Do you mean you never again want to drink the cool, fresh water from the forest stream?"

"Well, no," said Bambi.

"Then, do you want the big trees to go thirsty? Their leaves to wither and branches to become brittle?" asked his mother.

"No! Of course not!" cried Bambi. "The trees give us shelter, and their branches give the birds a place to make their nests."

"Then, do you want the sweet grass to turn brown?" asked his mother.

"No," said Bambi. "We eat the grass. We'd go hungry if that happened!"

"Well, then, my son," said Bambi's mother. "I think you'd better not wish for storms to go away forever. Their raindrops fill the streams and water the trees and grass."

"But storms are so scary," Bambi said.

Just then, the rain began to let up, and Bambi's friends scampered through the underbrush and into Bambi's thicket.

"Look at the pond!" cried Flower.

Bambi peered through the thicket. The pond was alive with activity. The frogs were leaping and playing. And a family of ducks were shaking their feathers and waddling into the water.

"Uh-oh," said Thumper. "That old bullfrog's gonna get a surprise."

Bambi watched the lily pad with the big bullfrog drift closer and closer to the line of ducklings. The last duckling wasn't paying attention. The sudden collision sent the frog toppling off its lily pad with a startled *croak!* and surprised the duckling so much it did an underwater somersault!

Bambi, Thumper and Flower laughed.

"I guess I like thunderstorms after all," Bambi told his mother.

"You didn't like thunderstorms?" said Thumper. "That's silly! Why would you ever say a thing like that?"

Just Believe

The fairies from Pixie Hollow had been bringing summer to the mainland when they had heard a car pass by on a nearby road. Curious Tinker Bell had followed the car and been discovered by a girl called Lizzy.

The fairies thought it was very dangerous for humans to see them, but Lizzy and Tinker Bell had become friends. Tink tried to help Lizzy spend more time with her hard-working father, Dr Griffiths, but so far her plan hadn't worked.

Meanwhile, Tink's friends had come to rescue her – they thought she was in danger. But just as Vidia arrived upstairs, Tink had shown herself to Dr Griffiths! Tink wanted to prove to him that fairies did exist. He too often scolded Lizzy for believing in them.

Dr Griffiths was about to capture Tink in a glass jar, when Vidia pushed her out of the way. Now Vidia was trapped!

"I must get this to the museum right away!" declared Dr Griffiths.

"Father, you can't do this!" cried Lizzy – but it was no use. Dr Griffiths ran out of the house, jumped into his car and drove off.

When the other fairies arrived upstairs, Tink told them that Vidia was in danger.

It was still raining, though. The fairies wouldn't be able to fly.

"We can't fly," said Tink, "but I think I know somebody who can...."

The fairies swirled around Lizzy and showered her with pixie dust. "All aboard!" cried Tink.

The fairies tucked themselves into Lizzy's coat and off she flew down the road that led to the city. Shortly after nightfall, the twinkling lights of London came into view.

"There he is!" cried Lizzy as she spotted her father's car.

Tinker Bell flew down and bravely darted into the engine. After some quick tinkering, she stopped the car. Dr Griffiths jumped out and raced off towards the museum on foot. Tinker Bell – and Lizzy – were right behind him. "Father!" Lizzy called.

Dr Griffiths turned to see his daughter flying towards him. "Lizzy ... you're ... flying!"

"But I don't understand," he continued.

"You don't have to understand," Lizzy told her father. Dr Griffiths looked at all the tiny magical fairies hovering around him. His eyes filled with wonder.

"I just need to believe," he said. He handed the jar to Lizzy. Seconds later, Vidia was reunited with her relieved and grateful friends. And Dr Griffiths hugged his daughter, realizing she had been right all along....

DUMBO

The Best Gift Ever

Apart from Dumbo's mother, Mrs Jumbo, all the elephants at the circus made Dumbo feel like a nobody. They laughed at Dumbo's large ears and said that he would never amount to anything.

But Timothy Q. Mouse was different. Since the day he and Dumbo had met, Timothy had encouraged Dumbo. Dumbo was so happy to have a friend like Timothy. He wanted to do something nice for him.

So, one afternoon, Dumbo decided to give Timothy a gift. At feeding time, Dumbo put aside a bale of hay. Then he lugged the hay behind the Big Top and looked around for Timothy. Dumbo found him lounging in the shadow of the lion cage and plopped the hay bale down.

"Hiya, Dumbo!" said Timothy. "What's with the hay?"

Using his trunk, Dumbo nudged the hay bale closer to Timothy.

"For me?" Timothy said. "Wow. Uh ... thanks. I, uh, wonder what I'll do with it all."

Dumbo's heart sank as he realized that mice didn't eat hay. And he wanted to give Timothy something he'd really like.

The next day, Dumbo came upon a patch of flowers growing just outside the elephants' tent. He picked a nice big bouquet and took it behind the Big Top to Timothy.

"Shucks, Dumbo," said Timothy. "You shouldn't have." Tiny Timothy took the flowers from Dumbo's outstretched trunk and promptly fell over, dropping the flowers everywhere. "Oh dear, look what I did," said Timothy.

But Dumbo thought *he* was the one who should feel bad. The bouquet was too heavy for Timothy to enjoy.

The next day, under the Big Top, Dumbo spotted a bunch of balloons tied to a seat, left behind by one of the children. Balloons! thought Dumbo. Why, those wouldn't be too heavy for Timothy. They stayed up all by themselves. So Dumbo untied them and brought them to Timothy.

But, when Timothy took hold of the balloon strings, the helium-filled balloons lifted him right off the ground! Quickly, Dumbo reached out with his trunk, grasped Timothy around his waist, and placed him gently on the ground.

Then, with a disappointed sigh, Dumbo took the balloons back. Would he ever find a good gift for Timothy? he wondered.

"Dumbo," Timothy said, "I wanted to thank you for giving me the best gift ever."

Dumbo's eyes widened in surprise. What could Timothy mean? Every gift he had tried to give him had been all wrong.

"You're my best friend," Timothy said. "And that's the best gift I could ever ask for."

A Happy Ending

Lizzy, a little girl, loved fairies. And one day she had discovered a curious little fairy called Tinker Bell!

Tink had been on the mainland with the other fairies from Pixie Hollow, helping to bring the season of summer.

But Tink had been bored because she couldn't find anything to fix, so she had flown off to explore a human house instead!

Luckily, Tinker Bell and Lizzy became friends and Tink realized that the little girl was sad because her father was always so busy. He was a scientist called Dr Griffiths and he didn't believe in fairies. Tink had proved him wrong by showing herself to him! Dr Griffiths tried to catch Tink, but caught Vidia instead and raced off to the museum with her.

Lizzy and the fairies managed to catch up with Dr Griffiths and, finally, convinced him to just *believe* in the magic of fairies.

Vidia was reunited with her fairy friends and then everyone – including Dr Griffiths – received a generous sprinkling of pixie dust to fly back home!

The next day, everyone enjoyed a picnic.

"Isn't this pleasant, father?" asked Lizzy.

"I can't imagine anything better," he answered.

"Although flying over London Bridge is a close second!" he added

Tink and Vidia sat together, sipping their tea. Before this adventure, Vidia had been a bit of a loner. She was sometimes rude to the other fairies and thought she was better than them. But now, Vidia realized the importance of friendship. It was only by working as a team that she and the fairies had managed to rescue her from being a museum exhibit!

Not only did Vidia and Tink know each other better now – but they had actually become good friends!

A little while later, everyone settled in to hear Dr Griffiths read from Lizzy's fairy field journal. Tinker Bell had helped the little girl to fill the journal with facts about fairies – where they lived, what they liked to eat and much more! It made magical reading.

Just then, Terence – Tinker Bell's very good fairy friend – arrived. He had been delivering pixie dust to all the fairies who were busy working on the mainland.

"Well," Terence said to Tinker Bell, "you found something to fix after all!"

Tink looked at Lizzy snuggled close to her father. "I guess I did," she replied with a smile.

Disney
**Sleeping
Beauty**

How Rose Dozed

The moon hung high in the sky, and the stars twinkled around it. It was late at night, and Briar Rose was supposed to be sleeping. But, with all those owls hooting and the frogs in a nearby pond croaking, who could sleep? So, after tossing and turning for hours on end, Briar Rose woke up her three trusted aunties, Flora, Fauna and Merryweather, to see if they could help.

"I've got the solution!" Fauna exclaimed. "You need to count sheep."

"Lie down now, dear," Flora joined in, "and picture a fence. Then imagine sheep jumping over it one by one, and don't lose count!"

Briar Rose lay back and did as they said. But, when she got to sheep 544, she knew it wasn't working. Briar Rose went back to her aunts. "No luck," she said.

"Oh, dear," said Flora. "We'll have to think of something else instead."

"Sleep, schmeep!" Merryweather chimed in. "The night has its own brightness, twinkle and shine. It's such a shame to sleep through it all of the time!"

"You really think so?" Briar Rose asked.

"Absolutely!" Merryweather exclaimed. "Look at the stars burning bright and the moon sending down its own special light."

"That's all well and fine," Flora interrupted.

"But if Briar Rose doesn't sleep at night, she'll be tired during the day."

"Good point," Briar Rose agreed.

"Well, then, try reading a book! Reading always puts me to sleep," Merryweather said with a yawn.

"But I *like* reading," Briar Rose protested. "I'll never fall asleep."

There was a pause, as each of the aunts thought and thought about how to help Briar Rose.

"I know a way to help you sleep!" Fauna said suddenly. "All you have to do," she explained, "is think good thoughts about the day that's passed, and hope for the happy things that tomorrow may bring."

"Is that true?" Briar Rose asked.

"Absolutely!" Flora agreed.

"Now, close your eyes," Merryweather instructed, "and we'll see you in your dreams."

Briar Rose wasn't sure at first, but Flora, Fauna and Merryweather had never let her down before. So she lay back down and closed her eyes. She remembered her favourite things from that very day, then thought about the wonder tomorrow would bring. Just as she was drifting off, she thought, I hope that never happens to me again. I need my beauty sleep! And wouldn't you know, pretty soon, she was lost in her dreams.

Disney
ALICE
in
WONDERLAND

"R U Slee-P?"

As Alice wandered around Wonderland, she encountered a blue Caterpillar sitting on a mushroom. He was smoking an exotic-looking pipe, and every puff of smoke formed a different letter.

"R U slee-P?" asked the Caterpillar's smoke.

"Am I sleepy?" Alice scratched her head. "I hadn't thought about it – I'm so worried about getting home, it's hard to think about anything else. I don't know, I suppose."

"U kn-O," said the Caterpillar, puffing out a U and an O in red-and-orange smoke.

"I do?" asked Alice.

"Ye-S, U do," said the Caterpillar. "For instance, have U O-pened your mouth without speaking?"

"Oh! You mean a *yawn?*" asked Alice. "No, I haven't yawned."

Then the Caterpillar yawned himself and asked, "Have U felt your I-lids gr-O-ing heav-E?"

"My eyelids growing *heavy?*" repeated Alice. She blinked, trying to determine if her eyelids had gained any weight since the morning.

"No," she told the Caterpillar, "my eyelids are no heavier than usual."

"I C," said the Caterpillar, puffing out a yellow *I* and a lime green *C.* Then his own eyelids began to flutter, and his head began to nod.

"Perhaps *you're* the one who's sleepy," Alice observed, watching the Caterpillar.

"Y?" asked the Caterpillar.

"You yawned, then your eyelids drooped and you began nodding off," Alice explained.

"I cannot B slee-P," the Caterpillar replied, "because n-O one has sung m-E a lul-lab-I."

"I can sing you a lullaby if you like," said Alice.

"Pro-C-d," said the Caterpillar.

"Hmm ... let's see...." murmured Alice. Ever since she'd entered the world of Wonderland, none of the poems and songs she knew came out quite right.

"I'll just try an easy one," she said with a shrug. Then she sang:

"Tow, tow, tow your rope
Slowly up the wall.
Merrily, merrily, merrily, merrily,
Life is a round ball....

"Blow, blow, blow your soap
Bubbles in the tub.
Merrily, merrily, merrily, merrily,
Rub-a-dub-a-dub...."

After she finished, Alice asked the Caterpillar, "How did you like it?"

"Come back l-A-ter," said the Caterpillar. "U may B right. I am the slee-P one."

And, with that, the Caterpillar fell fast asleep.

DISNEY
POCAHONTAS

Chief Mischief-maker

Like all raccoons, Meeko was curious – and that often got him into trouble. And though Pocahontas had a lot of patience when it came to her small furry friend, other members of the tribe were not as understanding.

"Pocahontas, you must teach that animal how to behave!" Chief Powhatan exclaimed when he caught Meeko playing with the tribe's peace pipe.

"Not him again!" cried the women when Meeko upset the baskets of grain they had spent the morning collecting.

"Don't worry," Pocahontas told her friend. "They can't stay mad at you for long. Tomorrow is your birthday, after all!"

Meeko chattered excitedly. He loved birthdays – especially opening presents!

"Now stay out of trouble," Pocahontas warned. "I'll be back soon."

Meeko sat outside the hut Pocahontas shared with her father. He wondered what gift his friend had chosen for him this year. Soon, unable to resist temptation any longer, he slipped inside and spied a parcel. He wasted no time unwrapping it and discovered ... a feather headdress just his size!

Meeko couldn't wait to try it on. He didn't want to be discovered, so he grabbed his gift and scampered off towards the river. There, he put on the headdress and gazed at his reflection. As he was admiring himself, the headdress fell into the water.

The raccoon fished it out, dragging it through the mud as he pulled it ashore. Meeko's heart was pounding. He rinsed the feathers as best he could and headed back to the village. On the way, the headdress caught on the bushes. By the time he reached the village, all the feathers except one had fallen out.

Meeko knew what he had to do. He found Pocahontas and showed her what was left of the present. Pocahontas looked at Meeko sternly, but after a moment her face softened. "Meeko, I am proud of you. You had the courage to admit what you have done," she said. "But you must try to do better. No more getting into places where you shouldn't!"

All day on his birthday, Meeko behaved perfectly. That night, Pocahontas presented him with a gift. It was the headdress, but now it had two feathers instead of one. "For every day that you are able to stay out of other people's belongings, we will add another feather," she said.

Meeko was grateful to Pocahontas for being so understanding, and he was determined to make her proud. He would do his best to fill the headdress – but he knew it would probably take him until his *next* birthday!

THE JUNGLE BOOK

A Bear-y Tale

It was time for Mowgli, Bagheera and Baloo to go to bed.

"Good night, Man-cub," purred Bagheera.

"But I'm not sleepy yet," protested Mowgli. "I need a bedtime story."

"Bedtime story?" said Bagheera. "At this hour?"

Mowgli turned to the big bear. "Please, Baloo?"

"A bedtime story, huh...." said Baloo. "Now, how do those things begin?"

"Once upon a time...." purred Bagheera.

"Oh, right ... Once upon a time ... in a house not far from this very jungle, there lived a clan of men," Baloo began.

"Real men?" asked Mowgli.

"Yep," said Baloo. "A father and a mother, and a little cub, just like you. Well, now, this clan, they cooked their food, and one day, don't you know, they made a mighty tasty stew ... only thing was, when they sat down to eat, it was just too hot. So the mother got an idea. They'd go for a walk in the jungle and, by the time they got back, their stew would be nice and cool. But do you know what happened next?"

"No," Mowgli said.

"Well, that family had barely been gone a minute, when an old bear came wandering up, and stuck his nose into the Man-house."

"He did?" gasped Mowgli.

"Well, now, can you blame him? That stew just smelled so awfully good. And the next thing you know, he was tastin' it – startin' with the biggest bowl, but that was still too hot. So next he tried the middle bowl, but that was too cold. So – he tried the littlest bowl, and, don't you know, it was just right! That old bear didn't mean to, but he ate the whole thing right up!"

"What happened next?" said Mowgli.

"Oh, well, after that, this bear, he started to get tired. Real tired. And, don't you know, Little Britches, that right there in that house, looking so soft and comfortable, were three cushy-lookin' pads ... I think men call them 'beds'. Anyway, that bear, he had to try them, too. Naturally, he laid down on the biggest one first. But it was too hard. So he tried the middle one, but that was much, much too soft. So, he tried the littlest one, and, son, let me tell you, that thing was so comfortable, he fell asleep right then and there! And he would have slept clear through the next full moon ... if only that family hadn't returned and ..."

"And what?" Mowgli asked breathlessly.

"And startled that bear so much, he ran back into the jungle ... full belly and all."

Mowgli smiled and tried to cover a big yawn. "Is that a true story, Baloo?"

The bear grinned. "Would I ever tell you a tall tale, Little Britches?"

A Three-Star Pub

Rapunzel had finally left the tower where she had lived her whole life. But there was no point in trying to hide it – being outside was terrifying. Mother Gothel – an old woman that Rapunzel thought was her mother – had told Rapunzel terrible stories about the outside world! Rapunzel didn't know Mother Gothel was just trying to keep her hidden.

Rapunzel had made a deal with a thief called Flynn Rider. She would give him back his satchel – which contained a stolen royal crown – as long as he took her to see the lights that appeared in the sky every year on her birthday.

Suddenly, there was a noise in the bushes and Rapunzel jumped, terrified. "Is it ruffians? Have they come for me?"

Just then a little rabbit hopped out from the bushes. Rapunzel blushed. If she carried on like this, Flynn would guess that she had never been out of her tower before!

But Flynn had realized why Rapunzel was scared, and that gave him an idea. He decided that a little pub called the Snuggly Duckling was the perfect place to take her for lunch. "I know a pub, in the forest. Shall we go there?" he suggested.

"Oh, yes please!" Rapunzel agreed quickly.

Meanwhile, Mother Gothel was returning to the tower and saw Maximus, a horse that had been chasing Flynn. She thought the guards might have come for Rapunzel – who was actually the Princess.

Mother Gothel ran to the tower. "Rapunzel!" she called. But there was no reply. She raced into a secret entrance and soon realized the awful truth: Rapunzel was gone. But then she saw something glimmering beneath the staircase. It was the crown in Flynn's satchel! She found Flynn's WANTED poster, too. Now she knew who had taken Rapunzel – and nothing would stop her from finding him!

Meanwhile, Flynn and Rapunzel had arrived at the pub. Rapunzel was horrified! The place was full of ruffians and they were loud and scary – one of them even touched her long, golden hair!

"You look very pale, blondie," said Flynn, delighted at his idea of bringing the delicate Rapunzel to the disgusting pub, so she would want to go back to the tower. "Don't you like it here then?"

Flynn escorted her to the door, thinking it was about time one of his plans had finally worked! But, little did he know, he wasn't going to trick Rapunzel that easily! She was stronger than he thought....

Disney·PIXAR

BRAVE
Elinor-Bear

Merida was a princess who lived in the ancient Scottish Highlands, in a kingdom called DunBroch. Her mother, Queen Elinor, wanted Merida to marry a son from a neighbouring kingdom, in order to keep peace in the land. Merida, however, wasn't ready to marry. She wanted to have her own adventures!

Merida and her mother couldn't understand each other's point of view. They argued and Merida angrily slashed the family tapestry. She rode into the woods and met a witch, who gave her

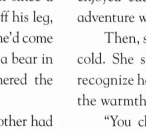

a magic cake. Merida thought the spell would change her mother's mind about the marriage, but instead it turned her into a bear!

Merida and Elinor-Bear were upstairs in the castle. Downstairs, King Fergus – Merida's father – suddenly smelled a bear. Ever since a huge bear called Mor'du had bitten off his leg, the king had hunted down every bear he'd come across. And now it seemed there was a bear in his castle! King Fergus quickly gathered the clans for a hunt.

Merida knew that she and her mother had to get out of the castle and find the Witch. While Merida's three little brothers distracted King Fergus and the clan lords, Merida and Elinor-Bear sneaked out through the kitchen.

"I'll be back soon," Merida told the triplets.

In the forest, Merida and Elinor-Bear found the Witch's cottage – with a message she'd left behind: "Fate be changed, look inside, mend the bond torn by pride."

Suddenly, a cloud surrounded them. When it cleared, the cottage was in ruins. They searched for something to turn Elinor into a human again – but they found nothing.

They spent the night in the ruins of the Witch's cottage. In the morning, they were hungry. Merida caught a fish for breakfast. Acting like a queen, Elinor-Bear refused to eat it until it was cooked.

Before long, though, Elinor-Bear was catching fish on her own. Soon Merida and her mother were playing together in the stream. For the first time in a long while, they enjoyed each other's company. This strange adventure was bringing them closer together.

Then, suddenly, Elinor-Bear's eyes turned cold. She sniffed at Merida as if she didn't recognize her. Merida screamed, but just then, the warmth returned to the bear's eyes.

"You changed," Merida told Elinor-Bear. "Like you were a bear on the inside, too."

Merida and Elinor-Bear were worried. What if Elinor turned into a bear for good? Suddenly, their argument didn't seem to matter as much as it did before.

A Big Imagination

Desperate to get Riley's core memories back to Headquarters, Joy led Sadness through the maze of Long Term Memory in Riley's mind. They had already lost two Islands of Personality – Goofball and Friendship – they couldn't afford to lose any more or Riley would forget everything about herself!

Soon, they ran into a funny-looking creature. It appeared to be made from candyfloss, but was shaped like an elephant crossed with a cat and a dolphin! Joy recognized the creature immediately. "You're Bing Bong!" she said. "Riley's imaginary friend!"

When Riley was little, she and Bing Bong used to play together. They put on concerts where they banged pots and pans, and they had a rocket wagon which would take them to the moon when they sang a special song! But, over the years, Riley had forgotten her imaginary friend.

Bing Bong's dream was to rocket to the moon with Riley, so Joy suggested he come to Headquarters with them.

"Ha ha!" Bing Bong cried, dancing around.

Bing Bong offered Joy a satchel so she could carry the core memories.

"Thanks!" she said. "This'll make it a lot easier to walk back to Headquarters."

"Walk?" asked Bing Bong. "We're not walkin'! We're taking the Train of Thought!"

He pointed to a train speeding towards Headquarters. Joy couldn't believe she hadn't thought of that.

"There's a station in Imagination Land," Bing Bong explained. "Come on, this way!"

Imagination Land was full of crazy places that Riley had imagined. Joy and Sadness were amazed by what they saw. They passed through French Fry Forest, where Bing Bong stopped every now and again to munch another chip. Then there was Trophy Town, filled with medals, ribbons and certificates, followed by Cloud Town! Joy leaped on to a small chunk of cloud and floated into the air. "Ha ha!" she cried. "It's so soft!"

Suddenly, a handsome teenage boy rolled towards them on a conveyor belt. A Mind Worker explained that the boy was an Imaginary Boyfriend who Riley had created in her mind.

"I would die for Riley," the Boyfriend said.

"Oh, gaa!" Joy said. She was not impressed.

"Anyway," said Bing Bong, as they walked past the Boyfriend, "This way, through Preschool World! We're nearly to the train!"

"Riley, here we come!" Joy said, happily.

They didn't have time for any more distractions. They had to get the core memories back to Headquarters – and fast!

The Winter Woods

Seasons come and seasons go – at least that's how it is in the human world. But in a magical place called Pixie Hollow, spring, summer, autumn and winter exist side by side. The warm fairies live in spring, summer and autumn. The winter fairies live in the snowy Winter Woods. No matter where they live, though, fairies always help each other....

In Tinkers' Nook, tinker fairies were making snowflake baskets for the fairies of winter while Fairy Mary supervised.

"I can't believe we make the baskets, but we don't get to take them to the winter fairies," Tinker Bell said to her friends Bobble and Clank.

"You'd get pounced on by a glacier!" Clank joked.

Just then, a group of snowy owls arrived and began to pick up the baskets. One owl brought Fairy Mary a note written on ice.

"They need twenty more baskets for tomorrow's pick-up!" she announced.

Tink watched as the majestic birds headed off towards the Winter Woods. How she wished she could go with them!

A few minutes later, Tink ran into her friend Fawn, who was chasing a bunny through the tinkers' workshop.

"Look out!" Fawn cried.

As one of the animal fairies, it was Fawn's job to round up the animals for their trip across the border to the Winter Woods. Tink helped Fawn catch the bunny.

"You're taking the animals today?" she asked. "How about if I help?"

Fawn happily agreed.

At last, this was Tinker Bell's chance to see the place where the winter fairies lived!

Soon the two fairies were escorting the animals to the border that separated autumn from winter. Fawn told Tink that only the animals were allowed to cross the border.

"No warm fairies are allowed in the Winter Woods, just like winter fairies aren't allowed over here."

But Fawn was having trouble getting one of the animals to cross into winter. He was already asleep! "Oh, no, no hibernating yet," she said. "You do that in winter."

As Fawn was talking to the animal, Tinker Bell moved closer to the border. She felt the freezing winter air, but it didn't stop her curiosity. She was desperate to see the snow-covered landscape and meet the winter fairies. She gathered her courage, took a deep breath – and jumped! Was winter really the white wonderland she imagined...?

BRAVE

Disney · PIXAR

Mend the Bond Torn by Pride

Princess Merida was an adventurous teenager, who lived in the Scottish Highlands with her family. Her father, King Fergus, was missing a leg – he had lost it when he fought a huge bear called Mor'du.

Merida's mother, Queen Elinor, wanted her to marry in order to keep peace in the land. But Merida wasn't ready to give up her freedom. Elinor told Merida about an ancient prince who had broken tradition and split from his three brothers. Their kingdom had then fallen to ruin.

Feeling angry with her mother, Merida slashed the family tapestry with her sword. Soon afterwards, Merida stumbled upon a witch. She asked for a spell that would change her mother.

The Witch told Merida about a prince who, long ago, had asked for the strength of ten men. She showed Merida the ring the prince had given her. Two crossed axes were carved into it. Merida would get a similar spell.

The spell had changed Queen Elinor ... into a bear! Now Elinor-Bear and Merida were searching for something to break the spell. But all they had found was a riddle: "Fate be changed, look inside, mend the bond torn by pride."

Soon, they came upon an old stone arch with crossed axes carved on it – just like the Witch's ring. It led to an ancient ruin.

As they explored, Merida fell through a hole. She was in the throne room of a ruined castle. Merida saw a stone engraved with the pictures of four princes. The stone had been split in two – the fourth prince was broken off from the rest. "Split," Merida said. "Like the tapestry."

Suddenly, Merida realized that the Witch's prince had lived here – and he was the same prince of her mother's legend. "The strength of ten men," she said, seeing that the room was covered in claw marks. "The prince became ... Mor'du!"

At that moment, Mor'du appeared. The demon bear lunged at Merida, but Elinor-Bear pulled her to safety just in time. They raced away from the ruins. Mother and daughter ran until they came to the Ring of Stones.

"I know what to do now," Merida said. She had to find the family tapestry that she had slashed and "mend the bond torn by pride".

The Witch's spell had shown Merida that she must learn to understand her mother's wishes, and fix what had broken between them.

The Power of Dreams

Rapunzel had finally managed to leave the tower she'd been kept in her whole life, and now Flynn had taken her to a pub full of horrible ruffians!

Mother Gothel was right, she thought, the world was too dangerous. Rapunzel didn't realize that Mother Gothel had just been trying to scare her into never daring to leave the tower.

Rapunzel had made a deal with Flynn – she had hidden his satchel of stolen goods and demanded he take her to see the floating lights that she saw from her tower every year on her birthday.

She was just about to give up on her dream when a huge thug slammed the door shut, blocking their way out. He was holding a WANTED sign. Rapunzel was confused but Flynn knew there was a reward for anyone who could find him. He swallowed nervously – his plan had backfired.

"Run and tell the guard!" the thug told his sidekick. "This reward will come in handy: I could do with some money right now!"

"Me too," the landlord shouted, grabbing hold of Flynn.

"Calm down, my friends. I'm sure we can come to some sort of arrangement!" said Flynn.

Rapunzel, terrified, stammered, "Um,

excuse me? Ruffians?" She took a deep breath and carried on. "Is it possible to get my guide back? I need him to show me the way...."

The thugs just ignored her and continued to hold Flynn.

Suddenly, Rapunzel forgot she was afraid.

CLANG! Rapunzel stood fiercely on top of the bar and hit her pan against a giant pot.

"Put him down!" she shouted. The thugs stopped.

Rapunzel explained that she needed Flynn to take her to see the lights.

"Have some humanity. Haven't you ever had a dream?!" she asked

Everyone was stunned. Who would have believed that such a delicate young girl could get so angry? What's more, she was right!

"I've always wanted to play the piano," one good-for-nothing admitted, moved to tears. "I know I may not seem like it, but I'm really a sensitive soul!"

"Me too!" another thug continued. "I've always dreamed of falling in love...."

And little by little, everyone in the pub began to describe their hidden hopes and dreams. Flynn couldn't believe his ears, or eyes! The girl had managed to win over a room full of the meanest, toughest-looking men in the kingdom!

Lucky's Last Laugh

It was getting quite late at Pongo and Perdita's house, but their darling little puppies were still not asleep. Not that they didn't want to go to sleep. At least most of them. No, the problem was that one of them wouldn't let them go to sleep – Lucky!

"And then, don't you remember, you guys, the part at the very beginning, when Thunderbolt jumped across that canyon? Whoosh! Like a rocket! Clear to the other side!" Lucky said.

"Yes, Lucky, we remember," his sister Penny said with a groan. "How could we forget? You've reminded us 101 times!"

"Yeah! It was so great! And then there was that part when – "

"Lucky!" wailed Rolly. "We all watched the same episode of Thunderbolt tonight. You don't have to tell us about it."

"Yeah, I know, but I just wanted to tell you about the part when Thunderbolt found the little girl, then ran back to tell the sheriff – "

"Lucky! It's late! We want to go to sleep!" barked Patch.

Lucky laid his head on his paws. "Okay," he said. "I'll be quiet."

All the puppies closed their eyes.

"Oh! But what about the part when the sheriff told Thunderbolt to climb up that cliff, and he got to the top, and he grabbed that rope with his teeth, and he pulled up the little girl – "

"Lucky!" yelped Pepper. "We don't care about Thunderbolt. We want to go to bed!"

"Right." Lucky sighed, lying down once again. "Wait a sec!" He sat up. "Don't care about Thunderbolt? How could you not care that he carried that little girl across that broken bridge and through those raging rapids?"

"We mean," said Freckles, "we want you to be quiet so we can go to sleep!"

"You mean," said Lucky, "you don't want me to tell you about the last part where Thunderbolt ran back to the mountains and into that cave, and found that amazing thing?"

"Yes!" Lucky's brothers and sisters shouted together.

"Why didn't you say so?" said Lucky. "Good night."

And with that, Lucky closed his eyes. For a minute, everyone enjoyed the silence. Then Penny sat up.

"Hey, wait a minute," she said. "What thing did he find?"

"Yeah," said Patch. "I missed that part."

"Me, too," said Rolly. "What was it exactly that he found, Lucky? Tell us."

But there was no answer. Lucky was fast asleep. And now the *other* Dalmatian puppies were wide awake!

Sparkling Wings

Pixie Hollow is a magical place where the four seasons exist side by side. Warm fairies live in spring, summer and autumn. Winter fairies live in the snowy Winter Woods. The animals of Pixie Hollow can come and go through the seasons, but only winter fairies are allowed in the Winter Woods.

But Tinker Bell is a curious little fairy. On a trip to the border with her friend Fawn, Tink couldn't resist jumping into winter to see what it was like!

And it was amazing! Tink looked around in wonder at the wintry landscape, admiring the sparkling snowflakes that drifted down from the sky.

Then suddenly, Tink's wings lit up in a burst of colourful light! Then she heard the faint sound of a baby's laugh....

At that moment, Fawn looped a lasso around Tink and pulled her back into autumn.

"I told you we're not allowed to cross!" Fawn scolded. Then she realized that Tink's wings were very cold. "We'd better get you to a healing-talent fairy!"

Fawn took Tink straight to a healing-talent fairy, who warmed Tinker Bell's wings under a special lamp. Soon, Tink's friends Silvermist, Iridessa, Rosetta and Vidia arrived. They were so worried about her!

"Your wings appear to be fine," the healing-talent fairy reported. Tinker Bell's friends were relieved, but Tink wanted to know what had caused her wings to sparkle in the Winter Woods.

"It must have been the light reflecting off the snow," the healing-talent fairy said.

But Tink wasn't convinced. She went to Book Nook to do some research and spotted a wing-shaped book on one of the shelves. She felt certain it held the answer. She eagerly reached for the book but it flew away! She chased after it.

"Gotcha!" she cried, but as she turned the pages, she discovered that a bookworm had eaten through the pages! The words that were left didn't make any sense. Tink asked a nearby fairy for help.

"Do you know anything about sparkling wings?" she asked.

"No, but the Keeper does," he replied. "He is the Keeper of All Fairy Knowledge. But he's a winter fairy. In order to talk to him, you have to go to the Winter Woods."

So the next morning, Tink tucked her wings under a warm coat and loaded the heavy book into her satchel. She had decided to go to the Winter Woods! She knew it was dangerous, but she had to find out the truth.

Disney · PIXAR

WALL·E

A Robot Kiss

When WALL•E met EVE, he had fallen in love. He had latched onto the spaceship that came to take her away from Earth. Now, the spaceship was docking inside an enormous ship called the Axiom. This was where all the humans from Earth now lived.

The Captain's robot assistant, Gopher, wrapped EVE in energy bands and drove her away. WALL•E raced after her. And M-O, a cleaner-bot, chased WALL•E. (M-O was programmed to clean, clean, clean. WALL•E, the little trash-compacting robot from Earth, was his biggest challenge ever.)

As WALL•E chased EVE, he accidentally disabled a human passenger's electronic system. The human blinked and looked around. She saw the world around her, instead of viewing it digitally over her holo-screen. She liked it!

Meanwhile, EVE was finally ready to give the plant she had found among WALL•E's treasures to the Captain. By doing so, she would prove that Earth was clean enough that a plant could now grow there. That meant everyone could return to the planet.

But EVE's compartment was empty. The plant had disappeared!

Disappointed, the Captain sent EVE to the repair ward, along with WALL•E. When they got there, WALL•E thought some orderlies were hurting EVE. So he helped her escape, along with all the reject-bots from the repair ward.

But there was a problem. Once they ran, they looked like convicts. A warning broadcast their escape throughout the Axiom. The ship's stewards tried to catch them.

To avoid being captured, EVE took WALL•E to an escape pod. She would send him to Earth where he would be safe, and then she could find the plant. Instead, Gopher appeared. He had the plant! He put it in the escape pod, and WALL•E and the plant were launched into space – not towards Earth, but far into outer space! WALL•E panicked and pushed a lot of buttons.

WALL•E pushed the wrong button. The pod exploded! WALL•E managed to escape, and EVE went to try to help him. *Whoosh!* WALL•E zoomed up to EVE and showed her that he had saved the plant. Delighted, she leaned in towards him, and an arc of electricity passed between their foreheads – a robot kiss.

Soon they were floating in space, dancing and giggling, excited about taking the Earth plant back to the Captain.

DUMBO

'Ears a Job for You, Dumbo!

It had been a hard day for little Dumbo. It was bad enough that everyone made fun of his ears except his mother, but then they had put his mother in a cage, so Dumbo couldn't even be with the one person who loved him and treated him decently.

What made things even worse was that Dumbo didn't have anything to do. It seemed that he was the only creature in the circus who didn't have a job. Everyone had a purpose except Dumbo. All he could do was feel sad and be laughed at.

Dumbo heaved a sigh and went for a walk through the circus tents. Soon, he found himself among the refreshment stands. Everyone here had a job too. Some were squeezing lemons to make lemonade. Others were popping popcorn or roasting peanuts. Wonderful smells filled the air.

Finally, Dumbo came to a little candyfloss wagon. The puffy cloud of sugar looked tempting, and Dumbo wanted a taste, but there were so many customers he couldn't get close enough.

Suddenly Dumbo heard a loud buzzing. Then all the customers waved their hands over their heads and ran away.

The smell of sugar had attracted a swarm of nasty flies!

"Scat!" cried the candyfloss man. "Go away before you scare off my customers."

Dumbo reached out his trunk to smell the delicious candyfloss.

"Not you, Dumbo!" the candyfloss man cried. "It's bad enough chasing flies. Do I have to chase elephants too?"

Poor Dumbo was startled. With a snort, he sucked candyfloss right up his nose.

Ahhh-choo! When he sneezed, Dumbo's ears flapped, and something amazing happened.

"Remarkable!" the candyfloss man cried. "All the flies are gone. They think your ears are giant fly swatters!"

The candyfloss man patted Dumbo's head. "How would you like a job?"

Dumbo nodded enthusiastically and set to waving his ears. Soon, the candyfloss stand was the most popular refreshment stand in the circus – and had the least flies. But, best of all, Dumbo now had something to do to take his mind off his troubles. He was still sad, but things didn't seem quite so bad. And, who knows, perhaps soon he'd have his mother back.

"I wonder what other amazing things those big ears can do?" said the candyfloss man, giving Dumbo a friendly smile. "I'll bet they carry you far...."

Disney · PIXAR
FINDING
NEMO

Hide, Dude!

"Come on, Squirt!" Nemo cried happily. "Race you to the coral shelf!"

Nemo took off, pumping his mismatched fins as hard as he could. His young sea turtle friend laughed and swam after him.

Squirt was visiting Nemo at his home on the reef. "This way, dude!" Squirt yelled, flinging himself through the water. "I'm catching some rad current over here!"

Nemo hesitated for just a second, watching as his friend tumbled along past some stinging coral. Squirt was so brave! Even after all that Nemo had been through – being captured by a scuba diver, then escaping from a tank to find his way home again – he still got scared sometimes.

With a deep breath, he threw himself into the current. He tumbled after Squirt, fins flying as the water carried him along. Finally, he came out the other end of the current, landing in the still ocean beside Squirt.

He giggled. "Hey, that was fun!" he cried. "Let's do it again! Squirt? Squirt, what's wrong?"

The sea turtle was staring into the distance, his eyes wide. "Hide, dude!" Squirt cried.

Before Nemo could respond, Squirt's head and legs popped into his shell and he landed on the sea floor with a flop.

Nemo started trembling. What had scared Squirt so much?

Nemo looked around, expecting to see a shark. But all he could see nearby were a few pieces of coral with a lone Spanish dancer floating along above them. He swam down and tapped on Squirt's shell. "Hey," he said. "What is it? There's nothing scary here."

"Whew!" Squirt's head popped out. He looked around, then gasped and hid again. When he spoke, his voice was muffled. "It's totally still there!"

Nemo blinked and looked around again. Again, all he saw were the coral and the Spanish dancer.

"Hey, wait a minute," he said, suddenly realizing something. "Haven't you ever seen a Spanish dancer before?"

"A – a Spanish wha-huh?" Squirt asked, still muffled.

Nemo knocked on his friend's shell again. "It's a kind of sea slug," he explained. "Don't worry, Spanish dancers are nice – you don't have to be scared. I promise."

Finally Squirt's head popped out again. He smiled sheepishly at Nemo.

"Sorry, dude," he said. "I never saw one of those before. It totally freaked me out."

"It's okay." Nemo smiled back. He already knew that new things could be scary – and now he knew he wasn't the only one who thought so. "Come on, let's go play," he said.

The Best Fisherman of All

Simba and his friends Timon and Pumbaa were hungry. They wandered through the forest until they came to an old, rotten tree. Timon knocked on the trunk.

"What's it sound like, Timon?" Pumbaa asked.

"Like our breakfast!" Timon replied.

He yanked at the bark and hundreds of grubs slithered out.

Timon handed Simba a grub.

"No, thanks." Simba sighed. "I'm tired of grubs."

"Well, the ants are tasty," said Timon. "They come in two flavours. Red and black."

Simba shook his head. "Don't you eat anything but bugs?"

"Fish!" Pumbaa declared.

"I love fish!" Simba exclaimed.

"Why didn't you say so?" said Timon. "There's a pond at the end of this trail." The three friends started off down the trail.

"What now?" asked Simba when they arrived at the pond.

"That's the problem!" said Timon. "We're not the best fishermen in the world."

"I'll teach you!" Simba said.

The lion climbed up a tree and crawled onto a branch that hung over the water. Then he snatched a fish out of the water.

"See!" Simba said, jumping to the ground nimbly. "Not a problem. Fishing's easy."

"Not for me!" Timon cried. He dangled from the branch, but his arms weren't long enough to reach the fish.

Simba laughed. "Better let Pumbaa try."

"What a joke!" cried Timon. "Pumbaa can't even climb this tree."

"Want to bet?" asked Pumbaa.

"Stay there," Timon warned. "I don't think this branch is strong enough for both of us."

With a hop, Pumbaa landed on the branch next to Timon. The limb started to bend.

"Yikes!" Timon cried as he leaped to another tree.

Crack! The branch broke under Pumbaa. With a squeal, he landed in the pond. The splash was enormous!

Simba, sitting on the bank, was soaked. Timon was nearly blasted from his perch. Pond water fell like rain all around them.

Simba opened his eyes and started to laugh. So did Timon.

Pumbaa was sitting in a pool of mud where the pond had been. He'd splashed so much of the water out that dozens of fish squirmed on the ground, just waiting to be gobbled up.

"Wow!" Timon cried. "I think Pumbaa is the very best fisherman of all!"

Cinderella

Dressed to Scare

Cinderella worked from morning until night doing the bidding of her stepmother and stepsisters. In return, they treated her unkindly and dressed her in tattered old clothes. It wasn't a very fair deal.

Luckily, Cinderella had the friendship of the animals in the manor, including two mice named Jaq and Mary.

"Poor Cinderelly," said Jaq as he and Mary watched their dear friend scrubbing the floor. "She needs a present."

"Hmm," Mary replied. She led Jaq out to the barnyard so that Cinderella wouldn't hear them planning. "Let's make a new dress!" she suggested.

"Good idea!" Jaq replied. But he wondered what they could use for cloth. Jaq looked around, then scurried over to a sack of feed and gnawed it open with his teeth.

"Jaq, no!" Mary scolded. "You can eat later."

"No-no," Jaq explained. "This cloth is for Cinderelly's new dress. See?" He gestured towards the sack.

The other mice joined to help. They cut out the dress in no time, sewing it together with some thread they had borrowed from Cinderella's sewing kit. They stepped back to admire their work. "Too plain!" Gus announced.

"Yes," Jaq agreed in a disappointed voice. "What should we do to fix it?"

The birds in the barn twittered excitedly. They had just the thing! In no time, they strung berries and kernels of corn, then helped the mice stitch them along the hem, sleeves and neck of the dress.

"There!" said Perla. "Much better!"

With the birds' help, the mice hung the dress on a post in the garden where Cinderella kept her straw hat. "Cinderelly's gonna love it!" Jaq proclaimed.

The mice went inside, got Cinderella, then told her to close her eyes as she walked out into the garden.

"Open your eyes now, Cinderelly!" Jaq instructed.

"Surprise!" the mice shouted.

Cinderella gazed at the sackcloth dress on the post with her hat perched on top. "Oh, thank you!" she exclaimed. "I've been needing a scarecrow for the garden!"

Jaq opened his mouth wide to explain, but Mary clamped her paw over it.

"You're welcome, Cinderelly," Mary said.

After Cinderella had gone, Jaq frowned. "We sewed a bad dress."

"But we made a good scarecrow," Mary told him, trying to look on the bright side.

"Yes! And Cinderelly's happy!" Jaq agreed. And to the mice, that was the most important thing of all.

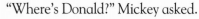
Goodbye, Hiccups!

Mickey sighed. No matter what he did, he couldn't stop hiccuping.

"What's wrong, Mickey?" Minnie asked, peering over the fence.

"Oh, hi – hic – Minnie," Mickey said. "It's these hiccups. They won't – hic – go away."

"Maybe Daisy and I can help," said Minnie.

"Help with what?" asked Daisy, walking up.

"Mickey has the hiccups!" said Minnie.

Leading Mickey into the kitchen, Minnie poured him a glass of water.

"Take a tiny sip," she said. "Then another." Mickey did as Minnie said.

"I think it worked!" he said. "Thank– hic!"

"Hmmm," said Minnie. "I think we need another idea!"

"It sounds like you need my tried-and-tested hiccup cure!" said Daisy. "This may seem silly, but just do what I do."

Daisy did two high kicks, a little tap dance, then spun around once and took a bow.

Mickey started to do the same, but halfway through – "Hic!"

"Maybe Donald knows a cure for the hiccups," said Minnie.

They went to find Donald, but Minnie and Daisy raced ahead. When Mickey arrived at Donald's house, they were waiting by the door.

"Where's Donald?" Mickey asked.

"BOO!" Donald jumped out at Mickey.

"Aaah!" Mickey cried.

"Sorry," Donald said. "I thought I could scare your hiccups away. Did it work?"

But poor Mickey just hiccuped again.

Mickey tried everything he could think of to get rid of his hiccups.

He stood on his head while saying the alphabet backwards. "Hic!"

He held his nose and whistled a tune. "Hic!"

"It's no use," he told his friends. "I think they're – hic – here to stay."

Minnie led Daisy and Donald to the side of the garden. "I have one last idea," she told them.

The friends whispered to one another. Then Donald went inside and returned with a big sack.

Minnie pulled out some blocks. She balanced three of them on her nose.

Daisy and Donald pulled out two rings. They hung one on each of Minnie's arms and she began to twirl them.

"Your turn, Mickey!" Minnie said.

All Mickey could do was laugh. "I'm sorry, Minnie," he giggled. "You just look so … silly!"

When Mickey finally stopped laughing, he realized his hiccups were gone!

"You cured me," said Mickey. "I guess laughter really is the best medicine!"

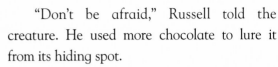

Strange Animals

Carl Fredricksen and a Junior Wilderness Explorer named Russell had just arrived in South America! Carl had dreamed of seeing Paradise Falls his whole life. He had promised his wife, Ellie, that he'd take her there one day. Sadly, Ellie had died before they could take the trip.

When Carl was told he had to move out of their home, he decided it was time to keep his promise to Ellie. He tied thousands of balloons to their house, and it lifted up into the air!

But Carl hadn't planned on taking a companion along – a boy called Russell had been on Carl's porch when the house took off!

They had hit a storm and crash landed very near Paradise Falls. There was just one problem: the crash had sent them flying out of the house, and now they couldn't get back in – it was hovering too high off the ground.

Russell had an idea: they could walk the house to the Falls. They made a harness out of the garden hose and pulled the house along.

"This is fun already, isn't it?" Russell said as they trudged along. "Don't you worry. I'm gonna assist you every step of the way."

After a while, they stopped to take a break. As Russell nibbled a chocolate bar, a beak poked out of the bushes and began to nibble it too!

"Don't be afraid," Russell told the creature. He used more chocolate to lure it from its hiding spot.

When the creature emerged, Russell gasped. It was the biggest bird he had ever seen! The bird liked chocolate. It liked Russell, too. Russell named the bird Kevin. He couldn't wait to show his new friend to Carl! But Carl yelled with fright when he saw the bird.

"Can we keep him?" Russell asked.

"No," said Carl.

Carl and Russell set off again. But Russell didn't want to leave Kevin behind, so he dropped a trail of chocolate for the bird to follow.

They hadn't gone far when they met a dog. "Hi there," said the dog. "My name is Dug." A talking dog? Carl and Russell were stunned! "My master made me this collar so that I may talk," Dug explained. "My pack sent me on a special mission. Have you seen a bird? I want to find one. I have been on the scent."

Suddenly, Kevin flew out of the bushes and tackled Dug. "Hey, that is the bird! May I take your bird back to camp as my prisoner?" Dug asked Carl.

"Yes! Yes! Take it!" Carl told him. He didn't want to deal with all these strange animals – he just wanted to reach Paradise Falls. But would he ever get there?

The Frog Hunt

Deep in the bayou, the frogs Tiana and Naveen faced countless dangers. But of all the predators, the most frightening were the hunters – even the alligators were wary of them. Fortunately, Tiana and Naveen could count on the help of the friends they met along the way....

"My name's Raymond, but everybody calls me Ray!" announced the large firefly that had just joined them. Tiana and Naveen had got their tongues tangled after becoming hungry. The firefly helped Tiana and Naveen untangle themselves.

Tiana explained to Ray that Louis was guiding them to the home of Mama Odie, so that she could change them back into humans.

"Mama Odie?! Well you folks is goin' in the wrong direction! First rule of the bayou: don't take directions from a 'gator!"

And Ray whistled into the night, summoning his family of fireflies to the rescue. Shortly afterwards, Naveen, Tiana and Louis were following a long string of firefly lights across the bayou. In the romantic glow of the evening, Ray told Tiana about his true love, Evangeline. "She is the prettiest firefly that ever did glow."

"Just do not settle down too quickly," Naveen advised.

Tiana rolled her eyes and took to land. She blazed a trail through the bushes while Louis followed her, trying to escape the pricker bushes. Suddenly – *WHOOSH!* – a net swooped down and scooped up Naveen. Three frog hunters – Reggie, Darnell and Two Fingers – were out to capture the two frogs!

"Oh no!" panicked Ray. "Have courage, my fellow, a bug's got to do what a bug's got to do!" he cried as he shot straight up Reggie's nose.

Quickly, Naveen escaped while Ray was blown out of the hunter's nose. Meanwhile, Darnell and Two Fingers had captured Tiana! Naveen leapt in to save her.

While Naveen diverted the men's attention, Tiana jumped out of her cage. Naveen and Tiana jumped all over the place, and try as they might, the hunters only succeeded in knocking each other out.

"Those aren't like any frogs I've seen! They're smart!" Reggie marvelled.

"And we talk too!" called Tiana to him.

The hunters opened their eyes wide, speechless. Then they screamed in terror and ran off!

Now that's a frog hunt that they won't easily forget – probably the last hunt of their lives!

Hockey Trials

A lot had happened since Riley and her family moved to San Francisco. Inside Riley's mind, two of her Emotions, Joy and Sadness, had accidentally got lost in Long Term Memory with Riley's vital core memory spheres. Now they were travelling through the Mind World, trying to make their way back to Headquarters.

Meanwhile, Riley was at the trials for her new hockey team, and she was feeling more nervous than ever before.

In Headquarters, Riley's other Emotions were trying to hold things together. Fear had recalled every hockey memory Riley had to try to replace the missing hockey core memory, but he could see through the window of Headquarters that Hockey Island was struggling to light up. Two Islands of Personality – which made Riley who she was – had already crumbled into the Memory Dump after Riley had argued with her parents and best friend.

Out on the ice, Riley tried to hit the puck, but missed and fell over.

Hockey Island began to shake. Anger pushed Fear aside and took over the console. Riley immediately threw down her hockey stick and stormed off the ice. Riley's mum stood up, concerned, as Riley joined her in the stands.

"Let's go," said Riley, tugging off her skates.

"Are you sure?" asked Mum.

But Riley was already heading for the exit.

Inside Riley's mind, Hockey Island crumbled into the Dump.

Joy was shocked. "No, she loves hockey," said Joy. "She can't give up hockey." But there was nothing Joy or Sadness could do, except press on with Riley's old imaginary friend, Bing Bong. They were on their way to catch the Train of Thought back to Headquarters.

They had almost made it when a Mind Worker accidentally pushed Bing Bong's magical rocket wagon over a cliff and down to the Memory Dump.

"No!" said Bing Bong, starting to cry. Instead of tears, sweets sprang from Bing Bong's eyes – something Riley had dreamed up as a little girl. Joy tried to cheer him up, but nothing worked.

Sadness sat beside Bing Bong. "I'm sorry they took your rocket," she said.

"It's all I had left of Riley," Bing Bong replied, still crying. The pair talked for a bit longer, then Bing Bong stood up and said, "I feel okay now."

Joy was surprised. Sadness had actually made Bing Bong feel better! If only Sadness could make Riley feel better…. Suddenly, Joy heard the train in the distance – they had to hurry!

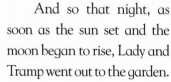

Lady and the **TRAMP**

In the Doghouse

"Good morning, Tramp," said Lady, with a yawn and a stretch. She rolled over on her silk cushion. "Wasn't that just the most wonderful night's sleep?"

But Tramp's night's sleep had been far from wonderful. In fact, he hadn't had much sleep at all. The past night had been Tramp's first sleeping in Lady's house ... or in any house, come to think of it.

"How do you do it?" he grumbled. "That bed is so soft, I feel like I'm sinking in a feather pool. And between Jim Dear's snoring and the baby's crying, I could barely hear the crickets chirping."

"Oh, dear," Lady said, feeling truly sorry for her mate. "I know!" she exclaimed. "Jim Dear and Darling love you so – I'm sure they'd let you sleep up on their bed tonight. There's nothing in the world better than that!"

But Tramp shook his head. "I'm afraid it's the outdoors I need," he explained. "I mean, I know you grew up this way and all ... but it's just so much fun to sleep under the stars. And the moon, too. There's nothing to howl at in this bedroom."

"You can see the moon out of the window," Lady told him.

But Tramp shook his head. "It's not the same. You know," he went on, "we've still got that fine doghouse in the yard. What do you say we go back out there tonight? It'll be like a honeymoon!"

"Well ..." Lady looked at Tramp's tired eyes. "Okay."

And so that night, as soon as the sun set and the moon began to rise, Lady and Tramp went out to the garden.

Happy at last, Tramp turned three times and then plopped down. "Oh, how I love the feel of cool dirt on my belly!" he said with a dreamy smile ... while Lady gingerly peeked into the dark and slightly damp kennel. The stars were not even out, and already she missed the comforts of Jim Dear's and Darling's room.

Tramp watched as Lady stretched out on the kennel floor, then got up and moved outside, then back in once again. It was plain to see: try as she might, Lady just could not relax on the cold, hard ground.

"Don't worry," Tramp announced, "I have an idea."

And with that, he ran into the house ... and in seconds reappeared with Lady's cushion in his teeth. Carefully, he swept the kennel with his tail, and laid the cushion down just the way Lady liked it.

Lady smiled and lay down. And, do you know what? That night, they both had the sweetest dreams either one had ever had.

A 'Snappy' New Ship

"My ship, my beautiful ship!" Captain Hook moaned. It had not been a good day for the pirate. Peter Pan and the Darling children had stolen his ship. And now, Hook was stranded on an island with Smee and the other pirates, their rowing boat having been chomped to bits by the crocodile.

"It's a nice island, Captain," offered Smee, trying to cheer up his boss. "And you could use a vacation. Why, look at those dark circles under your eyes."

Captain Hook turned to Smee with a furious look on his face. "Pirates don't take vacations!" Hook boomed. "Pirates seek revenge! Which is precisely what we are going to do, as soon as we have a new ship to sail in."

Smee looked around. "Where are we going to find a ship around here, Sir?" he asked.

"*We* aren't going to find one," Captain Hook answered. "You and the rest of this mangy crew are going to *build* one! And I don't mean a little one either. I mean a big, menacing, fit-for-a-magnificent-pirate-like-me one!"

For weeks, the pirates chopped trees and cut them into planks for the ship. They whittled thousands of pegs to use for nails, and crushed countless berries to use for paint. "You're not moving fast enough!" Hook complained as he sat in the shade, sipping juice out of a pineapple.

Finally, an exhausted Smee fetched Hook as he awoke from his afternoon nap.

"It's ready, Captain!" he announced.

Even Hook had to admit the ship was magnificent. Shaped like a gigantic crocodile, it was painted a reptilian shade of green. "No one will dare come near this ship. Not even that pesky crocodile. He won't want to tussle with anything this terrifying," Smee assured him.

Captain Hook was delighted. "We set sail tomorrow!" he crowed.

That night, Smee couldn't resist putting one more finishing touch on the ship. He painted a row of eyelashes on the crocodile's eyelids.

The next morning, Captain Hook and the crew climbed aboard and pushed off. The ticking crocodile soon appeared.

"Smee!" yelled a terrified Captain Hook. "I thought you said he wouldn't come near us!"

"But look how calm he is," said Smee, puzzled. "He's even smiling!"

Smee leaned over the side of the railing. "You know, it might be those eyelashes I painted. Maybe the croc thinks the ship is its mother."

Hook lunged at the roly-poly pirate. "You made my ship look like a *mother* crocodile? This vessel is supposed to be terrifying!"

"Mothers *can* be terrifying, sir," said Smee. "You should have seen mine when I told her I was going to become a pirate!"

Jasmine and the Star of Persia

Princess Jasmine loved stories about the stars. Every night, she and Aladdin would gaze up at the sky.

"What's that star?" Jasmine asked one evening.

"The Star of Persia," said Aladdin. "It belonged to a kind and beautiful queen. When she died, they hid the jewel away in a tower, sure that no-one would be worthy of its beauty again."

Jasmine's eyes shone. "Is that story true?"

Aladdin shrugged. "I don't know. But there is one way to find out."

The next morning, Jasmine and Aladdin set off on the Magic Carpet. Before long, a tall tower rose from a square in a tiny kingdom.

"Let's fly down and see if there's a way in," Aladdin said.

But they discovered that the tower was locked. Without a key there was little chance of getting in.

All of a sudden, a guard spoke up. "What do you want?" he demanded.

"We've heard about the Star of Persia," Jasmine explained, "and we've come to see the jewel."

"That's impossible," the guard said. "No one can see the jewel except a queen as lovely and worthy as our own."

"Well," said Aladdin, "this is Princess Jasmine. She's not a queen, but she will be."

"I'm very fair," Jasmine assured him.

The guard's eyes searched the square. "Fair enough to solve the argument happening over there?" he asked.

Jasmine made her way across the square and solved the argument.

"You did well," said the guard. "But the answer is still no. For our queen was also kind."

Jasmine turned to Aladdin. "Let's not bother him," she said. "I'll go and get him a drink from the fountain, then we'll leave."

Jasmine found the fountain dry. However, as she held a jar under it, a stream of water came out. Everyone in the square stared.

"The fountain!" blurted the guard. "It hasn't had water since our queen was alive!"

The people bowed and the guard unlocked the tower door. He led Jasmine to the highest room where the gleaming Star of Persia sat. The guard offered the jewel to Jasmine.

"You have proved you are worthy enough to keep it. But promise to come and visit us whenever you can."

"Oh, I will!" exclaimed Jasmine.

And because she was not only fair and kind, but also honest, she most certainly did.

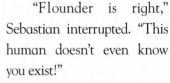

Love Letters

"**A**hhh," Ariel sighed dreamily. "Oh, no," Sebastian fretted. "A sigh like that can only mean one thing."

"What?" said Flounder.

"She's obviously writing love poetry for that human she's so obsessed with," Sebastian said.

"Oh," said Flounder.

Ariel was hard at work writing in her seaweed notebook. "How do I love thee...." she said out loud.

"Oh, yuck!" Flounder exclaimed.

"You're telling me," Sebastian agreed. "Terribly trite and overused."

"What would you write?" Ariel asked.

"Me? Well, this is just off the top of my head." Sebastian ceremoniously cleared his throat. "But I would write something like, 'Oh, crabby crab, Oh, crab of my heart, My crabbiest crab, May our claws never part!'"

"Double yuck!" Flounder exclaimed again.

"What do *you* know?" Sebastian snapped.

"But he's a total stranger!" Flounder cried, turning back to Ariel.

"What's that supposed to mean?" Now Ariel was offended.

"How can you be in love with someone you don't even know?" Sebastian said, joining in.

"I know him," Ariel protested. "Besides, haven't you ever heard of love at first sight?"

"Oh, please!" Flounder moaned.

"You're such a guppy!" cried Ariel.

"Hey! Who's being a guppy?" Flounder said defensively.

"Flounder is right," Sebastian interrupted. "This human doesn't even know you exist!"

"You don't know that!" Ariel cried, and went back to work on her poem. She wrote and wrote....

Finally, when she had finished, she cleared her throat dramatically.

"How's this sound?" she asked Sebastian and Flounder, and began reading:

"I'm always thinking of you,
It sets my heart a-twitter.
But I'm also easily distracted – ooh!
By things that shine and glitter.
Do you remember me?
Of me have you thunk?
Sorry, I've just got to go see
This boat that has just sunk.
(Now I'm back)
I love you more than anything,
Even more than my snarfblatt.
I wish this was a song to sing.
I'm really much better at that."

"Wow – " Sebastian exclaimed.

" – that's pretty bad!" Flounder finished.

"True love, indeed!" Sebastian concluded.

101 DALMATIANS

The Twilight Bark

Rolly, Patch, Lucky and the rest of the puppies were watching the end of *The Thunderbolt Adventure Hour*. As the credits began to roll, Pongo turned off the TV.

"Aw, come on, Dad!" Patch complained.

"We let you stay up late to watch the whole show," Pongo said.

Lucky sat staring at the blank television screen, hoping it would magically turn itself back on.

Perdy licked his face encouragingly. "Sit down, children," she said. "Your father and I need to speak with you."

"Uh-oh," Penny said worriedly.

"Oh, it's nothing like that," Pongo assured her. "We just think it's time to tell you about the legend of the Twilight Bark."

"Sounds cool!" Pepper cheered.

"What's the Twilight Bark?" Freckles asked.

"Legend has it," Perdy began, "that there's a special way that dogs can send each other messages. It stretches from the farthest side of the city all the way to the countryside."

"Wow!" Penny gasped. "Why would you need to do that?"

"Sometimes," Pongo began, "you need to communicate information from one place to another quickly, and you don't have time to go to the other place yourself."

"I don't need any Twilight Bark!" Patch said. "I can take care of myself."

"Fat chance!" Lucky said under his breath.

"What do you know?" Patch barked.

"If you ever get into any trouble," Perdy told the pups, "just go to the top of the highest hill you can find and bark out your message, and the members of the Twilight Bark will pass it along until someone can come and help you."

"That sounds like a bunch of baloney," Patch told his parents.

"Patch!" Pongo scolded his son. "That isn't very nice."

Just then, Lucky started howling at the top of his lungs.

"What's got into you?" Perdy asked.

"I'm trying out the Twilight Bark," Lucky said. "To get us rescued from Patch."

"Lucky," Perdy scolded him, "apologize to your brother."

"That's okay," Patch said. "I don't need his apology. I was right anyway. All that howling and no word from the Twilight Bark."

Just then, the doorbell rang. All of the puppies gasped and turned to look at Patch.

Perdy and Pongo smiled at each other, knowing it was actually Roger returning from the shop with milk for tomorrow's breakfast.

Back to the Winter Woods

For Tinker Bell, today was a great day for an adventure! She lived in a magical place called Pixie Hollow, where all four seasons existed side by side. Warm fairies like Tink were only allowed in the warm seasons, but Tink had sneaked into winter to see what it was like.

Tink loved the snowy landscape, but she was even more amazed when her wings started to sparkle strangely. She discovered that the only person who could explain why this had happened was the Keeper of All Fairy Knowledge – and he was a winter fairy. Tink just had to go back to the Winter Woods!

She wrapped up in a warm winter coat and hid inside one of the snowflake baskets that the warm fairies made for the winter fairies every year. She would be carried into the Winter Woods by the snowy owls. It was a clever plan, but dangerous. Tink's friends Bobble and Clank tried to talk her out of it, but she was determined to find out why her wings had sparkled so magically.

Soon a snowy owl swooped down and grabbed Tinker Bell's basket. He rose into the sky and flew off into the distance. Tink felt an icy blast of air as the owl crossed over into winter. "Wow!" Tink marvelled as they crossed a magnificent winter valley. "I made it!"

A few minutes later, a winter animal fairy named Sled appeared. "You ready for the drop off?" he asked the owl. The owl hooted nervously and then let go of the basket. Tink started falling!

"Look out!" cried the snowflake fairies below.

Tink's basket crashed and scattered snowflakes everywhere. The book that Tink had brought with her flew out of her grasp and onto the ice. She crept towards it, but a giant shadow fell over her. It was Lord Milori, the Lord of Winter!

"That's odd," he remarked, picking up the book. "Return this to the Keeper," he said to Sled, the animal fairy. "He can send it back to the warm side with his next delivery."

Ah-ha! thought Tink. *I just need to follow Sled and he'll take me straight to the Keeper.*

She trailed close behind Sled until he came to the Hall of Winter. Tink slipped inside the icy hall and ran right into a snowy lynx! Tinker Bell jumped back in surprise, but the lynx just looked at her and yawned.

Tink saw the Keeper sitting behind an easel. Then she noticed the shadow of another fairy – with sparkling wings! And Tink's wings began to sparkle, too! There was something very special happening, and Tink couldn't wait to find out what it was.

175

A Beastly Makeover

One evening, the Beast was heading towards the dining room when Lumiere suddenly stopped him.

"You can't go to dinner looking like *that*!" Lumiere said.

"Why not?" the Beast demanded. "I'm wearing my best outfit!"

"Clothes aren't enough," Cogsworth chimed in. "You have to make a good impression."

"You always told me looks don't matter, anyway," the Beast said.

"There's a difference between looks and style," Lumiere told him.

"And you may have no control over your looks," Cogsworth added, "but you certainly can do something about your style!"

"What's wrong with my style?" the Beast said, looking a bit hurt.

"Okay," Cogsworth began, "let's talk about your hair."

"What's wrong with my hair?" the Beast cried, offended.

"Women like hair long, but neat – not straggly," Cogsworth explained. "When was the last time you combed it?"

"I –" the Beast began.

"You've got it all wrong," Lumiere interrupted. "Women like hair short, closely cropped." He brandished a pair of scissors.

"I don't *want* a haircut!" the Beast said.

"We could always try ringlets," Cogsworth offered, nodding wisely.

"Or braids," Lumiere suggested. At this, the Beast climbed onto a bookcase that swayed under his weight.

"How about a French twist?" Cogsworth said.

A low growl began in the Beast's throat. Just then, Belle hurried into the room, and this is what she saw: the candelabra and mantel clock brandishing combs and ribbons at the snarling, cornered Beast – who was scrabbling to stay on top of the bookcase. Belle burst into laughter.

"What's going on?" she asked.

"We were just trying to fix his hair," said Lumiere. "It's a dreadful mess!"

"Actually," Belle said, "I happen to like it just the way it is. Beast, are you going to stay up there all night?"

And at that, the Beast leaped off the bookcase and strode towards her. "Do you really like my hair?" he asked.

"It looks just fine," Belle reassured him. "Now, would you escort me to dinner?"

"I would be honoured," the Beast replied.

Cogsworth and Lumiere looked baffled as the two headed off to the dining room.

"Kids these days!" Cogsworth said.

A Dance with Snow White

No one could remember a more wonderful day. The sun was shining, the sky was blue, and the Prince was holding a glorious ball for his true love, Snow White. Nearly everyone in the land had come to join in the fun, including seven rather short men who loved Snow White very much. They had never been to a royal ball before!

After a great banquet, the guests entered the ballroom, and each was announced. "Doc, Happy, Sneezy, Bashful, Grumpy, Dopey and Sleepy!" the announcer cried into the great room as the Seven Dwarfs tripped over one another, dazzled by the splendour.

"Gawrsh," Bashful said, hiding behind Doc, amazed by the marble and chandeliers.

Then, as the orchestra began to play, the Prince took Snow White in his arms and they waltzed across the dance floor.

The Dwarfs sighed. They could not take their eyes off Snow White.

"Wouldn't it be wonderful to dance with Snow White?" Happy asked. That gave Doc an idea. He led the other Dwarfs into the cloakroom and borrowed a few things.

"Sneezy, stand here. Bashful, you stand on his shoulders. Dopey, do you think you can make it to the top?"

When Dopey was balanced on Bashful's shoulders, Doc wrapped a cloak around the tower of Dwarfs and buttoned it around Dopey's neck.

Wobbling, the Dwarf prince tottered towards the dance floor and Snow White.

"May we have this dance?" Bashful asked from within the cloak.

"Of course!" Snow White giggled when she saw the familiar faces peeking up at her from beneath the cloak.

As the song began, Snow White and the Dwarf prince lurched and swayed precariously into the middle of the room.

"Yikes!" Sneezy squeaked. "This cloak is tickling my nose!"

Above them all, Dopey was having the time of his life, when suddenly the Dwarfs heard a sound that made their blood go cold.

"Ah ... ah ... ah ..."

"Hang on, men!" Doc shouted.

"... CHOOO!"

The cloak billowed. The Dwarf prince was knocked off balance!

"I got you!" The Prince caught the Dwarfs just before they all came toppling down. After steadying them, he turned to Snow White and held out his hand.

"May I cut in?" he asked.

Bambi

Sweeter than Clover

"Hi, Bambi," said a soft voice.

Bambi looked up from the grass he was eating, and his friend Flower stopped searching for berries. Standing there was the pretty young fawn Bambi had met that spring.

"Hi, Faline," Bambi said. "It's nice to see you!"

"It's nice to see you too," Faline said shyly.

"Faline!" a young male deer called across the meadow. "Come over and play with me!"

Bambi's eyes narrowed. He didn't like the idea of Faline going off to play with someone else.

Faline blinked in confusion. "Do you want me to go?" she asked Bambi.

"No, don't go," said Bambi. But what could he say to make her stay? he wondered. Suddenly, Bambi had an idea.

"I want to show you something special," he told her.

"Something special?" asked Faline.

"I know where to find the sweetest clover you'll ever taste," Bambi bragged. Thumper had shown him exactly where to find it.

"Where?" asked Faline.

"Just follow me!" exclaimed Bambi.

He led Faline across the meadow to the babbling brook. Then he followed the brook all the way up a steep grassy hill.

Finally they came to a big waterfall.

"The sweet clover is right here by this weeping willow tree," said Bambi.

Bambi couldn't wait to share it with Faline. But, when he got to the tree, there wasn't one single clover blossom left.

"Oh, that Thumper!" complained Bambi.

"What's the matter?" asked Faline.

Bambi shook his head. He felt very silly. He'd brought Faline all this way, and now he had nothing special to share with her! But, just then, Bambi looked up.

"Look," he whispered. "Up in the sky."

Faline looked up and gasped.

Shimmering bands of colour had formed an arch over the waterfall.

"It's so beautiful," whispered Faline. "I've never seen anything like it."

"Neither have I," said Bambi. "But I remember hearing my mother talk about it. I think it's called a rain ... bow."

"It's wonderful!" cried Faline.

"I'm glad you think so," said Bambi, a little relieved. "But I'm sorry you came all this way for no clover."

"Oh, Bambi," said Faline. "I came because I wanted to be with you. And, besides, a rainbow is a much sweeter surprise than some silly old clover, anyway!"

A Magical Discovery

The fairies of Pixie Hollow lived in a divided land. The warm fairies lived in spring, summer and autumn. The winter fairies lived in the winter. Only the animals could cross from one season to another. But curious little Tinker Bell hid away in a snowflake basket so a snowy owl would carry her into the Winter Woods!

It wasn't the first time she had visited winter. She had jumped over the border once before and her wings sparkled strangely. She was determined to find out why, and the only fairy with the answer was the Keeper of All Fairy Knowledge.

When Tinker Bell found the Keeper, he was with a winter fairy whose name was Periwinkle. As soon as Tinker Bell and Periwinkle were near one another, their wings began to sparkle. They flew around each other in surprise. What was happening?

The Keeper, whose name was Dewey, couldn't believe his eyes. "In all my years...." he marvelled. Then he said, "Follow me."

Dewey guided them onto a giant snowflake. It lit up, and when Tink and Peri put their wings into the light, the chamber filled with pictures! The fairies saw the journey of a baby's first laugh – a laugh that split in two! One half of the laugh travelled to the Pixie Dust Tree on the warm side of

Pixie Hollow – and Tinker Bell was born. The other half blew into the Winter Woods, and Periwinkle was born.

Tinker Bell and Periwinkle gasped. What did this mean? Dewey had the answer – they were born of the same laugh.

"That is why your wings sparkle," said Dewey. "They're identical!"

"We're sisters!" Tinker Bell and Peri cried.

Suddenly, they heard Lord Milori's voice. Dewey told Tink and Peri to hide.

"Keeper? Are you here?" Lord Milori asked. He wanted to talk to Dewey about a strange book that he had found. He was worried that a warm fairy might have brought it to winter. And he was right. It was Tink's book! She had dropped it when she'd landed.

"Crossing the border is forbidden," Lord Milori reminded Dewey. "If a warm fairy comes here, you will send them back."

"Of course," Dewey replied.

After Lord Milori had gone, Dewey told the girls they could spend a little time together before Tink had to go home. The sisters talked non-stop, trying to learn all about each other. They quickly discovered that they had a lot in common – Periwinkle even liked to collect things, just like Tinker Bell! The sisters were thrilled to have found each other.

Tangled

The End of the Tunnel

Flynn the thief was cunning. To frighten Rapunzel, he had taken her to a horrible pub full of thugs. It was the worst ruffians' hangout in the kingdom! He thought this would make her want to return to her tower straight away and give up on the idea of seeing the floating lanterns.

If Rapunzel hadn't kept his satchel with the golden crown inside, he would never have agreed to guide her through the forest in the first place!

Rapunzel is going to go home like a good girl and give me back my satchel, he thought to himself as they entered the pub. But in his plan, Flynn hadn't reckoned on the young girl bringing all these thugs to their knees in a matter of moments! They were even describing their life's dreams to her one by one ... it really was an unbelievable sight!

While Rapunzel befriended the thugs, Mother Gothel arrived at the pub. She could not believe what she was seeing either. She mumbled, "At last I've found Rapunzel, but she seems to be managing perfectly well without me ... I'm going to have to come up with a really clever trick to make her come back to the tower!" She was still thinking this when a thug arrived at the pub with the royal guards.

"Where's Rider? Where is he?" demanded the Captain.

The Stabbington brothers entered the pub in shackles, followed by Maximus. The horse was still hot on Flynn's trail.

Luckily, Flynn and Rapunzel had time to slip behind the counter before anyone saw them!

Suddenly, the landlord leaned towards Flynn and grabbed him by the arm! The young thief was panic-stricken. The landlord was bound to hand him over to the guards to get the reward! But, instead, he lifted up a heavy trap door hidden behind the bar, and whispered, "Go, live your dream."

"I will," Flynn replied.

"Your dream stinks. I was talking to her!" The thug nodded towards Rapunzel.

"Oh, thank you!" said Rapunzel.

Flynn slipped into the dark tunnel first. Rapunzel was nervous about following him. Perched on her shoulder, Pascal, her chameleon, gave her a little sign that she should go. Rapunzel took a deep breath and plunged into the dark tunnel behind Flynn. The landlord closed the trap door.

Rapunzel shuddered.

"Don't worry," said Flynn as he tried to reassure her. "There's always light at the end of the tunnel."

Rabbit's Frightful Garden

Rabbit woke up bright and early. He had a lot of work to do in his garden. There were weeds to be pulled up. There were vines to be trimmed. And there were lots of delicious, ripe vegetables just waiting to be picked. The only problem was that Rabbit had lent all his tools to his friends – and they hadn't returned them.

In the meantime, Pooh and Piglet were enjoying breakfast at Kanga's and Roo's house when Roo bounced in with a bunch of wildflowers for his mother.

"Thank you, Roo!" Kanga exclaimed, giving him a kiss. "Let me just trim these and put them in some water." She rummaged around in a kitchen drawer, where she came across Rabbit's gardening shears. "Oh, no," Kanga said. "I never returned these to Rabbit after I borrowed them."

"That reminds me," said Piglet. "I still have Rabbit's rake. And, Pooh, I'll bet you still have Rabbit's shovel."

The friends decided the neighbourly thing to do would be to return Rabbit's tools right away. When they arrived at Rabbit's house, though, their friend was not at home. He was on his way to *their* houses to get his tools back.

"Rabbit's garden could use some work," Kanga said. "Why don't we take care of it for him as a way of saying that we're sorry for keeping his tools for so long?"

Everyone agreed that this was a splendid plan. Pooh set about weeding while Piglet raked. Kanga snipped ripe tomatoes, peppers and cucumbers off the vines. Roo gathered them into big baskets.

When they'd finished, they spotted some birds hungrily eyeing the harvest.

"This garden needs a scarecrow!" cried Roo.

The work crew sprang into action, and soon a towering scarecrow was planted right in the middle of the garden. They propped the tools against the scarecrow, placed the baskets of food in front of it and started for home. "Won't Rabbit be surprised!" Piglet said proudly.

When Rabbit returned home a few minutes later, he couldn't quite believe his eyes. First he looked at the vegetables, all neatly picked. Then he looked at his garden tools, which had mysteriously reappeared. Finally, he looked at the strange scarecrow, which seemed to be looking right back at him! "D-d-d-did you do this?" he stammered to the straw man. Just then, a gust of wind knocked over the rake resting on the scarecrow's arm.

Convinced his garden was haunted, Rabbit turned and ran for his life. "Ahhhhhhhhh!" he screamed as he rushed past his friends.

"I *told* you he'd be surprised," said Piglet.

Olaf Loves Summer!

Summer had finally arrived in Arendelle and everyone was enjoying the long sunny days after a very cold winter.

Today was going to be the hottest day of the year so far and Olaf could hardly wait to get outside!

Olaf ran into Anna's room. "Anna, guess what today is? It's a perfect summery day! Let's go outside and play!"

Anna groaned, sitting up in bed. "It's so hot and sticky, Olaf." But she smiled when she saw Olaf's hopeful face.

Together, they went to look for Elsa.

"There you are, Elsa!" Olaf cried. "Today is the best day for warm hugs because it's sunny and hot. Please can we go and play in the sunshine?"

Elsa laughed. "Sounds like fun!"

"It's so hot outside. Couldn't you cool things down a bit?" Anna looked hopefully at her sister.

"Olaf's always wanted to experience heat. Shouldn't we give him a special day?" Elsa said.

"You're right," agreed Anna. "How about a picnic by the fjord?"

Olaf clasped his hands. "Ooh, I love picnics!"

Anna, Elsa and Olaf trooped to the royal kitchens for picnic supplies. They found Gerda with her head in the icebox, trying to keep cool.

Olaf giggled. "Did you bake cookies today?"

"Too hot for baking," Gerda called.

Elsa didn't want to disappoint Olaf. "Ice-cold lemonade?" she suggested.

Olaf was thrilled. "Ooh, I love lemonade!"

So Olaf, Anna and Elsa set off for their picnic.

At the docks, they chose a beautiful sailing boat and when they reached the shore, Anna set up the picnic.

"I love the feeling of sand on my snow!" Olaf squealed. "Let's make sand angels!"

Anna stuck a toe in the sand. "Oh, that is … uh … warm!" she squeaked, running to the fjord's edge. "Ah," she said, as water washed over her feet.

Anna, Elsa and Olaf spent the whole afternoon playing. They built sandcastles, chased waves and danced with seagulls. Finally, they had a picnic on the shores of the fjord.

"This is the best day of my life," said Olaf.

Back at the docks, Kristoff and Sven were waiting. They'd spent the afternoon harvesting mountain lakes and their sledge was full of ice.

Jumping out of the boat, Anna flung herself on the cold blocks. "Oh, I'm glad to see you!"

Olaf told Kristoff and Sven all about their adventures. "I wish it was always summer!" he said.

"Summer is wonderful," Elsa agreed, smiling at Anna. "But tomorrow, I predict a chance of snow."

DISNEP·PIXAR

BRAVE
Choose Your Own Fate

"Mend the bond torn by pride." That was what Princess Merida needed to do.

Merida's mother, Queen Elinor, had wanted her daughter to marry a son of a local lord in order to keep peace in their Scottish kingdom. The clans had all come to the castle and the sons had taken part in an archery competition to win the princess' hand.

But Merida wasn't ready to marry.

Determined to choose her own fate, Merida had picked up her bow and beat all three of the sons in the competition!

Queen Elinor was upset with Merida, and Merida was angry with her mother. She slashed the family tapestry with her sword.

Upset, Merida rode her horse into the forest and came upon a witch. She asked for a spell to change her mother's mind. But, instead, the spell had changed her mother into a bear!

Merida and Elinor-Bear needed to break the spell, and the only clue they had was a riddle from the Witch: "Fate be changed, look inside, mend the bond torn by pride."

Merida now realized what this meant – she needed to mend the tapestry. She took her mother, the bear, back to their castle.

Inside the Great Hall, they found Merida's father, King Fergus, and the other clans locked in battle – all because Merida refused to marry one of the sons!

Merida looked to her mother for help. But there was nothing Elinor-Bear could do. It was up to Merida to stop the fight.

Merida marched into the centre of the room. She was just about to agree to marry one of the lords' sons, when, from the shadows, her mother stopped her.

Elinor-Bear mimed what she wanted Merida to say. "The queen feels ... that we should ... find love in our own time," Merida translated.

"A grand idea!" Young Macintosh exclaimed happily.

The other lords' sons agreed. They all wanted to be able to choose their own fates. Everyone cheered.

"That settles it," Lord MacGuffin said. "Let these lads try to win her heart before they win her hand."

Elinor-Bear felt very proud of her daughter, and Merida realized the importance of what her mother had wanted her to do. It had taken a spell that turned Queen Elinor into a bear ... but they finally understood each other.

Now, surely, the spell would be broken?

A Salty Surprise

Briar Rose picked up a large basket and stepped out of the door. It was a beautiful afternoon, and she couldn't help but sing a little song as she headed into the forest.

Rose had spent many afternoons in the forest and knew exactly where the cherry trees grew. She put her basket down by her favourite tree and began to fill it with juicy cherries. A pair of bluebirds came and landed on her shoulder while she picked. Soon the basket was heavy with fruit.

"That should be more than enough for a pie," she told the bluebirds. She was going to bake her aunts a surprise pudding. Still humming to herself, Rose carried the cherries back to the cottage.

Rose put down the basket and looked around the cosy kitchen. She felt nervous. She had never baked a pie by herself! She wasn't even sure where to find all the ingredients.

"It can't be that hard to find the butter, flour and sugar," she assured herself.

Taking a deep breath, Rose searched the cupboards. Then she set to work cutting the butter into the flour for the crust. After adding cold water, she gently patted the dough into a ball.

"And now for the tricky part," she said to the bluebirds, who had followed her home.

Rose put the dough on the worktop and began to roll it out. Soon it was a large, flat circle.

"Here we go," Rose said as she folded it in half and lifted it into the pie tin. After unfolding it, she crimped the edges. It looked perfect.

"And now for the filling," Rose said. She washed the cherries and pitted them. Then she mixed in some spice and sprinkled on spoonfuls of the coarse, white sugar.

The pie was just coming out of the oven when her aunts tumbled through the door.

"What is that delicious smell, dear?" Flora asked as she took off her pointed hat.

Rose beamed. "It's a cherry pie," she said. "I baked it myself!"

Fauna clapped her hands together. "How wonderful!"

After dinner, Rose cut four nice-sized pieces of pie. Smiling, everyone dug in. But their smiles soon turned to severe puckers.

Then Rose burst into tears. "Salt!" she cried. "I used salt instead of sugar!"

"There, there, dear," Flora consoled her. "I once made the same mistake with an entire batch of fruitcake – 20 cakes! – and it took a while before anyone would touch my cooking again! But they got over it eventually."

Rose wiped her tears as Merryweather began to giggle. "I remember that!" she said.

Rose smiled, then giggled too. After all, she had ruined only *one* pie!

How Does Your Garden Grow?

Everything around Alice was gigantic. Flowers looked as tall as lampposts.

"The Caterpillar said one side of this mushroom will make me bigger and the other will make me smaller," Alice told a nearby dandelion, holding up two pieces of mushroom. "But I don't know which piece will do which."

"Which do you want?" asked the dandelion. "To grow bigger or smaller?"

"Bigger!" cried Alice.

"Put your roots in the ground and turn your leaves to the sun," said the dandelion. "You'll grow bigger in no time!"

"But I'm not a flower," said Alice.

"Of course she's not," said a daffodil. "She's a bug!"

Suddenly, Alice heard another voice. "Little buuuug ..." it sang. "I can give you what you want. Just step into my petals, buglet."

Alice placed the mushroom pieces in her pocket and approached the plant. Its flower buds looked very strange – like split green kidney beans with fine hairs around the edges.

"Get in," said the plant eagerly.

Alice climbed inside one of the strange buds. Immediately, she felt the bud begin to close up tight, trapping her inside!

"What kind of plant are you?" cried Alice.

"A Venus flytrap," said the plant.

"But I'm not a fly," Alice protested.

"Doesn't matter," said the flytrap. "I eat other bugs."

"I'm not any kind of bug!" cried Alice, banging on the springy green walls. "Let me out."

The flytrap just laughed. "I can tell you're going to be a tasty treat, little bug," it mumbled.

"You know," said Alice angrily, "it's not polite to talk with your mouth full, especially when your mouth is full of me! Why, if I were my normal size, I'd – "

Normal size? she thought and suddenly remembered the pieces of mushroom in her pocket. She pulled out the two pieces. Taking a chance, she bit into one.

Alice got bigger and bigger and burst out of the flytrap and onto the ground.

Still angry, she peered down at the flytrap. It looked completely harmless now, no higher than her ankle. She gave it a glare, and then went on her way.

The flowers watched her go. "That was the biggest bug I ever saw," said the violet, in a quaking voice.

"I can't believe I let it go," the Venus flytrap said wistfully. "That bug would have been breakfast, lunch and dinner for the next 50 years!"

Lady and the TRAMP

Lost and Found

Lady stretched and rolled over. It was so cosy up on the window seat. Sunlight shone through the glass and glinted on her diamond-shaped name tag. Lady sighed contentedly. The tag was her most prized possession. Besides her owners, of course.

Jim Dear and Darling were very good to her. Just last night, they had given her and Tramp steak bones to munch on. There were so many, they had not been able to eat them all.

The bones! Lady had almost forgotten them. Leaping off the window seat, she hurried to the kitchen. Luckily, they were still right next to her food bowl.

Lady began to carry the bones into the garden. It took three trips, but soon the bones were lying in a heap on the grass. Then she got to work.

Dig, dig, dig. The soil piled up behind her as Lady dug yet another hole. She carefully nosed the last bone into the hole and covered it with soil. After prancing delicately on top to pat down the soil, she collapsed in an exhausted heap. Burying bones was hard work!

Rolling over, Lady let the sun warm her belly. The garden was the perfect place for a late-afternoon nap. She was just dozing off when, suddenly, her neck itched.

Sitting up, Lady gave it a scratch. But something was missing.

Lady stopped scratching and gingerly felt her neck. Her collar! It was gone! Panicked, Lady searched the garden for the collar. It was nowhere to be found.

I must have buried it with one of my bones! Lady realized with a jolt. She looked at all the freshly dug holes. It would take her all night to dig up the bones. But she just had to find her collar!

Tramp will help, Lady thought. She ran inside to get him. He was playing with the puppies, but ran outside as soon as he heard what was wrong. Soon the two dogs were busy undoing all of Lady's hard work.

"I see something shiny!" Tramp called. Lady was by his side in an instant, but it wasn't the collar. It was just an old bottle cap. Lady dropped her head sadly.

Lady and Tramp got right back to digging. And, just as dusk was falling, Tramp found a thick blue band with a golden tag. Lady's collar!

Lady let out a happy bark. Then she carried the collar into the house and sat down at Jim Dear's feet.

"Your collar came off, Lady?" Jim asked as he fastened the collar around Lady's neck. "It's a good thing you didn't accidentally bury it with your bones!"

The Bravest Dog

Minnie was in her garden when she saw Mickey run to his car. "Where are you going?" she asked.

"A circus train was going through town and some animals got lost!" Mickey replied. "The sheriff asked me to help find them."

Pluto tried to follow, but Mickey stopped him. "You stay here with Minnie," he said and drove away.

Soon, Pluto began to tug at Minnie's skirt.

Minnie knew he wanted to go for a walk. "Okay," she said. "We're not likely to run into any of the animals."

So Minnie followed Pluto down the path to the river. Suddenly, they heard a hissing sound coming from behind a log.

"Snakes!" Minnie cried. "They must have escaped from the circus train!"

But Pluto wasn't afraid. He pounced into the grass … and found a small cat and her kittens.

Minnie giggled. "Come on, Pluto, let's not disturb them."

Minnie stayed close to Pluto. If there were snakes around, she didn't want to run into them.

"It would be fun to find a seal," said Minnie.

Just then, they heard a splashing sound coming from the river. Pluto dashed down a hill and plunged into the water.

But it was not a seal splashing around in the water. It was a puppy!

"It's okay, Pluto," Minnie laughed as they started home. "I love you even if you never capture anything wilder than a cat and a puppy!"

When Minnie and Pluto walked into Mickey's kitchen, they found that milk had been spilled, dishes had been broken and one of the windows was open!

"Oh, Pluto!" Minnie cried. "Someone has been in here! What if it was one of the circus animals?"

Pluto sniffed around. Finally, he leaped through the open window and raced across the garden to the shed.

"Be careful!" Minnie called. "Whatever it is may be dangerous!"

Just then, Mickey pulled up.

"Oh, Mickey," Minnie said, "something broke into your kitchen! Pluto is tracking it!"

Minnie pointed to the shed, where Pluto had disappeared inside. What would Pluto find?

The shed door opened and Pluto came out – and he was not alone. On his back was a monkey dressed in a little hat and waistcoat.

"The last missing animal!" Mickey said.

The monkey jumped into Mickey's arms. "This little guy isn't so wild," he said, "but it took a lot of courage to go into the shed."

"Pluto's been brave all day," Minnie said.

Pluto and Mickey returned the monkey.

"Thanks, Pluto," the circus ringmaster said. "The show couldn't have gone on without you!"

WRECK-IT RALPH
Hero's Duty

Wreck-It Ralph worked in the *Fix-It Felix, Jr* video game, and he was sick and tired of always being the Bad Guy. At the end of every game, he got thrown in the mud by the other characters, and he was fed up with it. He wanted a medal to prove that he could be a Good Guy, just like Fix-It Felix.

So, Ralph did something that no character had done before – he decided to leave his game. He was searching for a medal in another game when a dazed-looking soldier staggered in.

The poor fellow was so confused, he couldn't stop walking into the wall. The soldier's name was Markowski, and he muttered that he'd just come from a new game called *Hero's Duty*, where he'd been battling swarms of cy-bugs. The goal of the game, the soldier explained, was to climb a tower and find the Medal of Heroes.

Suddenly a tiny beetle scuttled across the table, and Markowski fainted. That gave Ralph an idea. Maybe HE could take the soldier's place in the game – and win that medal! Finally he could prove to everyone that he could be a good guy for a change!

Ralph borrowed Markowski's armour and sneaked into *Hero's Duty*.

As Ralph waited with the other soldiers and the first-person shooter – the robot that handled the game player's actions – it looked as though Ralph's plan might work!

But once the game started, huge, hungry cy-bugs attacked! They gobbled up characters, vehicles and weapons. Then they turned into freakish versions of whatever they ate! Ralph was TERRIFIED!

Ralph grabbed the first-person shooter game player and begged for help. But before the girl could wonder why a game character was talking so strangely, a cy-bug chomped her avatar. A loud voice boomed: "GAME OVER!"

Inside *Hero's Duty* the game began to reset. Characters went back to their places and a beacon appeared on top of the huge tower in the centre of the game. The cy-bugs flew into the light, which zapped them all.

The soldier's leader, Sergeant Calhoun, was furious! "Never interfere with the first-person shooter!" she yelled at Ralph.

But he wasn't listening. He wanted the Medal of Heroes, up in that tower. This was his chance to prove he could be a Good Guy!

Ralph headed towards the tower. He was determined to get his medal and prove himself, no matter what he had to do.

Across the Border

Tinker Bell and Periwinkle were sisters. Both lived in Pixie Hollow, but they had never met! Periwinkle was a winter fairy who lived in the Winter Woods and Tink lived in the warm seasons.

Warm fairies weren't allowed to cross the border into winter, because the cold was dangerous. But one day, Tink had jumped across and her wings had sparkled strangely! She was determined to find out why, so she sneaked further into winter. She had no idea she was about to discover her long-lost sister, whose wings sparkled too when Tink was nearby!

It didn't take the sisters long to discover that they had lots in common. Peri showed Tink a bundle of items she had collected.

"You collect Lost Things, too?" Tink asked, amazed.

Periwinkle laughed. "I call them 'Found Things'," she said.

Peri spent the rest of the afternoon showing Tinker Bell around the Winter Woods. Then they went to the Frost Forest, where Tink met Peri's friends, Gliss and Spike. They all went ice sliding, which was like sledging down an icy rollercoaster. Tink had a lovely time!

That night, Tink built a fire to stay warm while she and Periwinkle stayed up late chatting. She told Peri all about the beautiful things in the warm seasons of Pixie Hollow. How Periwinkle wished she could go there! But it wasn't allowed, because the warmth might damage Peri's wings.

Suddenly, the snowy floor of Peri's home crumbled beneath them. It was melting from the fire!

At that moment, the Keeper of All Fairy Knowledge, Dewey, arrived with his snow lynx. He rescued Tink and Peri!

"Lord Milori was right," said Dewey. "Crossing the border is too dangerous. We have to take Tinker Bell home."

The three fairies went to the border. Tinker Bell and Peri sadly gave each other a hug goodbye. As the Keeper turned away, Tink whispered to Peri, "Okay, here's the plan. Meet me here tomorrow. There's something I need you to bring."

Tink had a plan that meant they could meet again. Both fairies knew that they might get into a lot of trouble, but now that they knew about each other, nothing would keep them apart.

Back across the border, Tink went to her friends Clank and Bobble. She needed their help. "It's kind of a secret," she told them.

Clank and Bobble loved secrets! So Tink told them all about her long-lost sister.

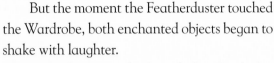

Castle Cleaning

I t was a particularly warm and sunny April morning, and Belle and Chip the teacup were gazing out of a castle window at the blue sky and the budding trees and plants.

"Well, Chip," Belle said, "it is definitely spring at last. And you know what that means, don't you?"

Chip hopped up and down in excitement. "It means we get to play outside?" he asked.

Belle laughed. "Well, yes, that too," she replied. "But first it's time to do some spring cleaning."

So Belle got together a few cleaning supplies. "I think I'll start in the dining room," she said. Belle pulled the silverware out of the silver cabinet and began polishing a fork.

"Ooh!" exclaimed the enchanted fork. "Careful! Ouch! Not so hard around the tines!"

"Oh, dear!" said Belle. "I'm sorry." She gently polished the rest of the utensils.

Next, Belle gathered all the dishes. But when she dipped the first enchanted dish into the soapy water in the sink, it cried out, "Ahh! Too cold! Too cold!"

Belle gasped ... and hurried to add more warm water to the sink.

After finishing the dishes, Belle moved to her bedroom, where she began dusting the Wardrobe with the Featherduster.

But the moment the Featherduster touched the Wardrobe, both enchanted objects began to shake with laughter.

"Hee, hee! Ha, ha!" said the Wardrobe. "That tickles!"

"You've got that right!" the Featherduster said.

Belle went to the library to take a break from her cleaning. Chip hopped in. "Oh, Chip," she said wearily, "spring cleaning in this castle is a challenge. I'm not used to cleaning enchanted objects!"

Chip giggled. "And I guess we're not used to it either. We always just clean ourselves!"

"Clean yourselves?" said Belle.

That gave her an idea. If the enchanted objects could clean themselves, they could clean other objects too!

Belle called the enchanted objects together. "I wonder if I could ask your help with a little project," Belle began.

Soon Belle had a small army of enchanted objects cleaning everything else in the castle. In a few short hours, the entire castle had been cleaned, and Belle and Chip were relaxing in the library.

"Well," Belle said as she sank into a comfortable chair, "you know what they say: 'Many hands make light work.' And a little enchantment never hurt either!"

A Bad Dream

Inside Riley's mind, two of her Emotions – Joy and Sadness – were trying to make it back to Headquarters with Riley's core memory spheres. These spheres held memories of the things that mattered most to Riley and kept her Islands of Personality running.

Joy, Sadness and Riley's old imaginary friend, Bing Bong, made it on to the Train of Thought, the fastest way to travel through the Mind World to get to Headquarters. But they hadn't been on the train long when it came to an abrupt halt. Riley had gone to sleep, and when Riley was asleep, the train went nowhere.

But Sadness had an idea. She spied Dream Productions off in the distance. All of Riley's dreams were made there, and Sadness thought they could wake Riley up with a dream.

Joy, Sadness and Bing Bong walked on to the set of Riley's dream for the night. It was teeming with actors in costume and staff wheeling set pieces around, and the camera operator was talking with the dream director. A special filter was used on the camera to make everything look completey real to Riley.

Sadness thought that a scary dream would wake Riley up best, but Joy wanted to wake Riley up with a happy dream.

"That's never happened before," said Sadness. But Joy was certain it would work. She and Sadness put on a cute dog costume and ran on to the stage, while Bing Bong looked after the all-important core memories.

Back at Headquarters, Fear was at the console. He watched on the screen as the dog ran around. Then, suddenly, the dog split in half! Fear's mug flew from his hand, spilling tea everywhere!

At Dream Productions, the dog costume had come apart when Joy had run faster and Sadness hadn't kept up. Now Sadness was chasing Joy around the set. Through the reality filter, it looked pretty scary!

As Riley began to stir in her sleep, the Dream Production guards realized what Joy and Sadness were up to.

"They are not part of this dream!" the director yelled at the security guards. "Get them!"

Joy and Sadness hid offstage, but the guards spotted Bing Bong and he was arrested.

The guards took Bing Bong down into Riley's Subconscious, which contained her deepest fears. Joy and Sadness followed to attempt a rescue. Down there, they met a huge scary clown called Jangles. This gave them an idea. Before long, Jangles was stomping through the set of Dream Productions and Riley sat bolt upright in her bed, wide awake and terrified. Sadness's idea had worked! The Train of Thought would be moving again in no time!

An Extraordinary Secret

Flynn and Rapunzel fled through the pub's secret passage – this was no time to hang around!

When she had made Flynn guide her to the floating lanterns, Rapunzel had never imagined for a moment she would find herself in a filthy tunnel hiding from the Royal Guards!

In the Snuggly Duckling, Maximus led the guards straight to the secret passageway. The horse and the guards all charged into the tunnel.

Meanwhile, Mother Gothel had watched the scene unfold and approached a ruffian at the pub door.

"Where does the tunnel let out?" Mother Gothel demanded. She threatened the ruffian until he told her.

Flynn and Rapunzel ran along the tunnel, the guards hot on their heels.

"Run!" Flynn cried.

They raced out of the tunnel and skidded to a stop at the edge of an enormous cavern.

Rapunzel lassoed her hair around a rock, swung through the air and landed on a stone column. Flynn spun around and fought off Maximus and the guards with Rapunzel's frying pan!

Then Rapunzel threw Flynn her hair and held on as he leaped off the cliff.

Flynn swung right over the heads of the Stabbington brothers!

But Rapunzel and Flynn weren't safe yet. Maximus had a different plan – with one kick of his hoof he brought down the dam! Water quickly came flooding into the cavern.

The guards and the Stabbingtons were swept away by the raging flood!

Flynn and Rapunzel ducked into a cave, just as a stone column crashed to the ground, closing off the entrance. They were trapped!

Water quickly began to fill the cave. Flynn cut his hand trying to dislodge the large rocks surrounding them, but the boulders wouldn't budge. There was no way out.

"It's all my fault!" sobbed Rapunzel. "I'm so sorry, Flynn!"

"Eugene. My real name's Eugene Fitzherbert," Flynn admitted. "Someone might as well know."

"Eugene?" Rapunzel exclaimed. "Well, since we're telling secrets," she continued, "I have magic hair that glows when I sing...."

The thief stared hard at her, in shock.

Then suddenly, Rapunzel realized that her hair may actually be able to save them! Maybe they would be okay, after all.

One Lucky Pup

"Where are we going?" Penny asked. "Why do we have to get in the car? We're going to miss 'Thunderbolt'!" Pepper pouted. The puppies all hated to miss their favourite dog hero TV show. They groaned in disappointment.

"This will be even more fun," Perdy said soothingly as she coaxed the puppies into the car. "I promise."

Roger and Anita got into the front seat. It didn't take long to leave the city. Soon the car was winding down a country lane. The puppies smelled all kinds of good things. They smelled flowers and hay. Then they smelled something sweet – peaches!

"Here we are!" Anita opened the car door.

"Where's here?" Freckles asked Lucky.

"It looks like an orchard!" Lucky yipped. He loved to eat fruit.

Roger stretched. "You dogs run and play," he said. "We'll call you when it's time for our picnic."

"Don't eat too many peaches," Pongo barked, but the puppies were already running off.

All morning, the puppies romped and played in the green grass until Pongo and Perdy came to call them. "Time for lunch!" Pongo barked.

"I'm not hungry," Rolly said, rolling over in the grass.

"I hope you didn't eat too much," Perdy said.

The big dogs herded their puppies up the hill towards the spot where Roger and Anita were laying out a picnic.

Perdy scanned the group. "Wait a minute," she said to Pongo. "Where's Lucky?"

The black-and-white pack stopped in its tracks. Pongo counted them. Lucky was definitely missing!

Perdy sighed and began to whimper.

"Don't worry, Mother," Pepper said sweetly. "I have an idea." He turned to his brothers and sisters. "Hey, everyone. Let's play 'Thunderbolt'!" he barked. "We have to find Lucky!"

All of the puppies yipped excitedly and tumbled over one another to find Lucky's trail. Soon every nose was sniffing the ground.

Penny sniffed around a tree and behind a patch of tall grass. She'd caught the scent! "Here he is!" Penny barked.

The rest of the dogs gathered around to see the puppy asleep in the grass.

Lucky's ears covered his eyes, but there was no mistaking the horseshoe of spots on his back, or the pile of peach stones by his nose!

"Lucky is lucky we found him," Perdita said with a relieved sigh.

"And," Pepper joked, "he'll be *really* lucky if he doesn't wake up with a tummy ache!"

FAIRIES
Tinker Bell
and the
SECRET
of the
WINGS

Periwinkle's Trip

Tinker Bell lived in Pixie Hollow. Her sister Periwinkle also lived there, but they had only just met! You see, Tink was a warm fairy who lived in the parts of Pixie Hollow where it was always spring, summer and autumn. Her sister Peri was a winter fairy who lived in the Winter Woods – and no fairy was permitted to cross the border.

So how did they meet? Well, Tink is a curious fairy. No rule was going to stop her taking a sneaky glimpse at the Winter Woods! And that's when she discovered she had a long-lost sister! But the Lord of Winter, Lord Milori, suspected there was a warm fairy in the Winter Woods so Tink had to go home. Before she left, the sisters came up with a plan for Peri to visit the warm side. They just needed their friends' help.

The next day, Periwinkle arrived at the border with her frost-fairy friends and a glacier fairy. They had a huge block of ice with them.

Tink arrived with her tinker friends, Clank and Bobble, and the strangest-looking contraption the winter fairies had ever seen. It was a snowmaker!

Clank and Bobble loaded the ice into the snowmaker, which grated it and turned it into snow.

"You did it!" cried Peri.

Peri flew across the border and into a cascade of snow pouring out of the snowmaker. She loved it! It meant that she could stay cold while she visited the warm seasons.

The tour of the warm seasons soon began. It was time for Peri to meet the rest of Tink's friends.

"This is Periwinkle, my sister!" Tink announced.

Tink's friends surprised Peri with a rainbow and a field of blooming flowers!

Rosetta gave Peri a flower. "It's called a periwinkle," she told her.

"Thank you!" Peri exclaimed. "I'll keep it forever." She held up the little purple flower and covered it with frost. The others gasped as the flower glistened in the sunlight.

A few moments later, Peri felt very weak. Her wings were wilting! Clank and Bobble noticed that the snowmaker was running out of ice. There wasn't enough snow to keep Peri cold. They had to get her back to the border!

As Tinker Bell and Vidia carried Periwinkle into winter, Lord Milori appeared. Tink pleaded with him to help Peri as Vidia gently pulled Tink back to the warm side. Tink was in just as much danger as Peri if she didn't leave.

Tink was sad. Would she ever be able to spend time with her sister again?

DUMBO

Pass It On!

"Did you hear the news, my dear?" one of the circus elephants said to another.

"What is it?" the second elephant asked.

The first elephant looked around carefully to make sure that no one was listening. "Well," she whispered in the second elephant's ear. "You know Mrs Jumbo's son, Dumbo, right?"

"Of course," the second elephant said. "The small fellow with the big ears. The one who became a ..." she shuddered with distaste, "... a clown."

"That's right," the first elephant said. "Well, a little bird told me that the first show was a hit! Everyone loved the 'Building on Fire' act. Dumbo leaped off a platform 20 feet high. And they're going to raise it up much higher next time!"

"Oh, my!" the second elephant said.

"But don't tell a soul!" the first elephant warned.

But, as soon as the first elephant turned away, the second elephant turned to another of her friends. "Listen, dear," she said. "You'll never believe what I just heard!"

"What is it, dear?" the third elephant asked.

The second elephant lowered her voice to a whisper. "Oh, you'll never believe it!" she began. "It's Dumbo – 20 clowns had to hit him with a tyre to get him to leap off a platform!"

"Oh, my!" the third elephant gasped. "That is big news!"

"But don't breathe a word to anyone!" the second elephant exclaimed.

"Certainly not!"

Soon, the third elephant was whispering to another friend. The fourth elephant gasped with amazement as she listened.

"... and so Dumbo set the platform on fire, and it took 20 clowns to put out the flames," the third elephant confided.

The fourth elephant told a fifth, and a fifth told a sixth. Soon, the whole circus was buzzing with the news of Dumbo's first clown show.

A little bird was flying over the Big Top when he saw a pair of elephants chattering below.

He flew down to see what was going on, landing on one elephant's trunk. "Good day, ladies," he said. "What's the word around the circus this evening?"

"It's about Dumbo," one elephant said excitedly. "It seems he fell off a platform in the last show, and hit 20 clowns. Now they're talking about setting him on fire next time!"

The little bird didn't stick around to hear the end of the discussion. "I can't wait to spread this news!" he squawked, fluttering back up into the sky. "Wait until everyone hears – they'll never believe it's true!"

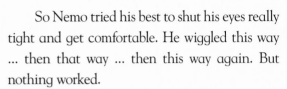

Sleep Tight, Nemo

It was late at night at the bottom of the sea – but little Nemo was wide awake.

"Nemo," said Marlin, poking his head into the anemone, "you should be asleep!"

"But I can't sleep," said Nemo. "I need another story."

"No more stories," said Marlin. "I told you five already."

"Then maybe another snack?" said Nemo.

But Marlin rolled his eyes. "No, Nemo. You just had a plankton snack five minutes ago. What you should do now, young clownfish, is go to sleep!"

"Okay, Dad," said Nemo. Then he did as his dad told him and closed his eyes. But, seconds later, they popped open again.

"Dad!" Nemo called out. "Daaaad!"

"Nemo!" Marlin groaned. "I'm beginning to lose my patience!"

"But, Dad," said Nemo, "I ... I ... I heard a noise."

"What kind of noise?" Marlin asked.

"Um ... a ... a spooky noise," answered Nemo.

"Hmph." Nemo could tell Marlin did not like this reason for being awake either. But still, Marlin stopped and listened ... and listened ... and listened.

"I don't hear anything, Nemo," he said after a moment.

So Nemo tried his best to shut his eyes really tight and get comfortable. He wiggled this way ... then that way ... then this way again. But nothing worked.

"Daaaaaaaaaaad!" he called out.

"Nemo," Marlin said. "For the last time, it's time to go to sleep. If you call for me again, it had better be a good one or ... or ... or else. Good night!"

Now, Nemo knew his father well, and he knew when Marlin was just a teeny, tiny, itsy, bitsy bit angry with him. But Nemo also knew that when you can't go to sleep, you can't go to sleep. And no matter how many moonfish or angelfish or sea stars you count; no matter how tightly you close your eyes; no matter how mad your dad gets – you'll never go to sleep until you're absolutely, positively, no-doubt-about-it ready. And Nemo wasn't. But why not?

Suddenly, Nemo bolted up. "Dad!" he shouted. "Dad! Oh, Daaaaad!"

"All right. That's it, Nemo!" Marlin said.

"But, Dad," Nemo said. "There's one more thing I really, really, truly need. Then I promise, I'll go to sleep."

And with that, he snuggled into Marlin's fins for a great big good-night hug.

"I love you, Dad," he said. "See you in the morning."

Meeting a Hero

Carl and a young boy called Russell were in South America. They had flown there in Carl's house with thousands of balloons tied to it! Carl had been married to a woman called Ellie for many years. They had always dreamed of becoming explorers and visiting Paradise Falls in South America. Sadly, they were never able to save enough money to take their trip, and Ellie had passed away. But Carl still wanted to make their dream come true.

Since arriving in South America, Carl and Russell had met a strange, huge bird – Russell named him Kevin – and a talking dog called Dug! Dug was on a mission to find Kevin and wanted to take the bird prisoner.

They were walking to Paradise Falls, holding onto the house with the garden hose. That night, they stopped to rest. "Dug says he wants to take Kevin prisoner. We have to protect him!" Russell told Carl while the others slept. Carl agreed that Kevin could come with them to the Falls.

"Promise you won't leave Kevin? Cross your heart?" Russell asked Carl.

Carl thought for a moment. The last time he'd crossed his heart was when he'd promised Ellie he would take her to Paradise Falls.

"Cross my heart," he finally told Russell.

The next morning, they found Kevin perched on the roof of the house. The bird was calling towards the distant rocks. "The bird is calling to her babies," Dug explained.

"Kevin's a girl?" Russell asked in surprise.

Soon Kevin set off for her home. Russell wanted to go with her. But Carl was in a hurry to get to the Falls. "She can take care of herself," he told Russell.

Suddenly, three fierce dogs burst from the bushes. They surrounded Carl, Russell and Dug, and demanded they hand over the bird. The dogs were part of Dug's pack. When they realized that Dug had lost the bird, they wanted to take the travellers to their master.

The dogs led Carl and Russell to a huge cave. An old man stood in the entrance, surrounded by more dogs. When the man saw Carl's house, he laughed. He had thought that Carl and Russell were explorers – but real explorers wouldn't come in a floating house! "My dogs made a mistake," he told Carl.

Carl thought the man looked familiar. "Wait," he said. "Are you ... Charles Muntz?"

Carl couldn't believe it – Muntz was his and Ellie's childhood hero! "My wife and I, we're your biggest fans!" he said, shaking Muntz's hand. Carl wished that Ellie was there – he knew she would have been thrilled.

Runaway Hippo!

One morning Simba, Timon and Pumbaa were eating breakfast.

"Mmm, crispy, crunchy bugs," said Pumbaa.

"Try the big red ones," said Timon. "They have lots of legs. They come with their own toothpicks!"

Suddenly, they heard a sad cry from the jungle.

"Sounds like somebody is in trouble," said Simba.

"The sound is coming from over here," said Pumbaa. He led them to a muddy pond full of thick vines. In the middle of the swamp was a baby hippo. He was tangled up in vines and half buried in mud.

"Help!" the hippo cried as he struggled against the vines. The more the hippo squirmed, the more tangled he became, and the deeper he sank into the mud.

When the little hippo saw Simba, he became very frightened. "Oh, no, a lion! He's going to eat me!" he cried.

"Take it easy," Simba replied. "These guys have got me on an all-bug diet."

Timon grabbed a vine and swung over to the hippo. He began digging the little hippo out of the mud.

Meanwhile Simba jumped onto the hippo's back and began tearing at the thick vines with his teeth.

That made the hippo even more afraid!

"You *are* trying to eat me!" he shouted.

Finally, Simba and Timon got the hippo unstuck. Free at last, the hippo started to cry. "P-p-please don't eat me," he said to Simba.

"I'm not going to eat you, I promise," said Simba. "I just want to know how you got stuck in the mud."

"I was angry at my little brother and I bit his tail and made him cry. I was afraid my parents would be upset so I ran away from home," said the little hippo.

"I'll bet your parents *are* upset," said Simba. "Because you're gone and they're worried about you."

"They won't care," the hippo said.

"Come on," said Simba. He led the little hippo to the edge of the river. When they got there, they could hear the other hippos calling.

"Oyo! Oyo! Oyo!"

"Listen," said the hippo. "Oyo's my name. They're calling me! They miss me!"

"Sure," said Simba. "You can't just run away without being missed. When you're part of a family, no matter what you do, you'll always belong."

"What about *your* family, Simba?" Timon asked as they watched the little hippo rejoin his family. "Do you think they miss you?"

"I didn't use to think so," Simba replied thoughtfully, "but now I wonder...."

Disney PRINCESS

Cinderella

Fit for a Princess

Cinderella hummed to herself as she slipped the silver needle through the colourful fabric. She had been working hard on her new quilt for weeks, and it was finally almost finished!

Though it was made of scraps of fabric from her stepsisters' old gowns and other rags, Cinderella knew the quilt would be fit for a princess. The worn fabrics were colourful and soft, and with the cotton wadding she'd found in the attic, the quilt would be wonderfully cosy. No more shivering under her threadbare blanket!

Gus agreed. He couldn't help but climb between the sewn-together quilt fabric and snuggle into the cotton filling.

"This is very cosy, Cinderelly," he called from deep inside the quilt. "I think I'd better see how it is for sleeping...."

Suzy and Perla, the mice who were helping Cinderella with the sewing, giggled.

"Go and get us some more thread, sleepyhead," they called. But Gus was already dozing off. The sound of his snores drifted out from between the layers of quilt.

"Gus!" Jaq called. But the snores only got louder. "That mouse hasn't helped with this quilt one bit!" Jaq sighed and went to get the spools of thread himself.

Cinderella, the mice and the birds worked all evening. They were just sewing together the last edge when loud footsteps echoed on the attic stairs.

"Cinderella!" called an angry voice. It was Anastasia, her stepsister. A moment later she stormed into the room, carrying a fancy blue gown. "My dress was not ironed properly!" she shouted. "Can't you do anything right?" Then she spotted the quilt.

"It's beautiful!" she cried. "And it will look wonderful on my bed!"

Cinderella looked at Anastasia in shock. Would her stepsister really steal her quilt? Cinderella knew Anastasia and Drizella could be mean, but that would be very cruel!

Suddenly the quilt began to move. A moment later Gus's quivering nose poked out from between the unsewn pieces of fabric.

"A rodent!" Anastasia screamed. She dropped her dress in fright and leaped onto a small wooden chair. "Why, that quilt isn't fit for use in the stable!" she cried.

Cinderella tried not to laugh as her stepsister leaped off the chair and fled down the stairs. Yawning, Gus climbed the rest of the way out of the quilt.

"Well, Gus," Jaq said admiringly, "I guess you did end up helping with the quilt, after all!"

A Royal Visit

Snow White was very happy. She had married her true love and she lived in a beautiful castle. But she missed her good friends from the forest, the Seven Dwarfs, very much.

"Well, why don't we go for a visit?" the Prince said.

"That would be lovely!" Snow White cried.

Snow White wrote a note to tell her friends that she was coming, and asked a bluebird to deliver it.

At the Dwarfs' cottage, Doc read the note then ran downstairs to tell the others. "Hooray!" Happy cheered. "Snow White is coming!" But the other six Dwarfs looked around their messy cottage. "We have a lot to do, men!"

"She'll want lunch." Grumpy huffed. "Someone's gonna have to cook!"

"Why don't you and Happy fix somethin' suitable for Snow White to eat?" Doc suggested. The Dwarfs started to work on their chores right away. It didn't go very well. Sleepy got tired and lay down. Sneezy kept sneezing as he dusted. And Dopey knocked furniture over as he swept. Meanwhile, Happy and Grumpy couldn't agree on what kind of sandwiches to make.

"Snow White likes peanut butter and jelly, I know," Happy declared.

"She likes ham and cheese," Grumpy grumbled. "Everyone knows that."

By the time Doc finally got them to agree on something, the clock struck twelve and there was a soft rap on the door. Their beloved princess was here! They smiled as Snow White hugged each of them and kissed their foreheads. "How I've missed you all!" she cried.

"Please forgive the mess, Princess," Bashful whispered to her. "We didn't quite get it cleaned up."

"Oh, please," Snow White said with a laugh, "forgive me for giving you such short notice! Besides, I've come to see you – not your cottage."

"Would you care for a ham-and-jelly sandwich?" Doc offered, holding up a platter. "Or peanut butter and cheese?"

"Oh, how sweet," Snow White kindly replied. "If I had known you'd go to all this trouble, I wouldn't have brought a picnic with me."

"Picnic?!" the Dwarfs exclaimed.

"Well, yes. I remembered how much you liked it when I cooked, so I brought some of your favourites. But let's eat your sandwiches first."

The Dwarfs looked at one another and Doc cleared his throat.

"We can have ham and jelly any time," he said. "Let's enjoy your picnic and have a great visit." And that's exactly what they did.

Disney · PIXAR
BRAVE
Mending the Bond

Deep in the ancient Scottish Highlands, in a kingdom called DunBroch, Princess Merida lived with her family.

Merida's mother, Queen Elinor, wanted her daughter to marry in order to keep peace in the kingdom. But Merida was an adventurous teenager – she wasn't ready to marry.

The bond between Merida and her mother had broken, because they couldn't understand each other's points of view.

Merida asked a witch for a spell that would change her mother's mind. But the spell cake changed Elinor into a bear!

Now, Merida was trying to break the spell. She knew she had to mend the family tapestry, which she had slashed in anger.

But King Fergus had found Merida and Elinor-Bear in the castle. Fergus didn't like bears because, long ago, a huge one named Mor'du had taken his leg!

Fergus slashed at Elinor-Bear, not realizing it was actually his beloved wife. And Elinor-Bear was starting to act more like a real bear! She struck back, knocking Fergus to the ground. The noise drew the lords and the rest of the clans, who were visiting the castle.

"Mum, run!" Merida cried.

Elinor ran, with the men in pursuit. Merida tried to explain to her father what had happened, but he didn't believe her. He locked her in the tapestry room for her own safety, and gave the key to the nursemaid. Then he set off to hunt the bear.

Merida was desperate to get out. Through the window in the door, she spotted three little bear cubs. They were her little brothers, the triplets! They'd eaten the rest of the spell cake and turned into bears, too! Merida told the triplets to get the key.

Meanwhile, a terrified Elinor-Bear was running from the hunters. Fergus and the lords were closing in on her....

Freed by the triplets, Merida grabbed the tapestry. She climbed onto her horse and raced into the forest to save her mother. As she rode, Merida mended the tapestry.

Merida finally caught up with the hunters. She saw the king raise his sword to kill the bear. Merida stepped in front of him.

"Are you out of your mind, lass?" Fergus exclaimed.

Gathering all of her strength, Merida swung her sword and chopped off Fergus' wooden leg! King Fergus couldn't understand why his daughter would do such a thing. But Merida was willing to risk everything to save her mother. The bond between them was finally beginning to mend.

A Little Help

"This is bad," fretted Cogsworth the clock, pacing at the bottom of the castle's staircase. "Bad, bad, bad!"

"What is wrong, my friend?" asked Lumiere the candelabra.

"The Beast hurt Belle's feelings," said Cogsworth. "Then Belle hurt the Beast's feelings. Now they're sulking in their rooms."

"Ah, that *is* bad," said Lumiere. "We will never be human again unless the spell on the Beast is broken. And the spell won't break until Belle falls in love with him."

"Well, there's no chance of that happening now!" cried Cogsworth.

"Nonsense," said Lumiere. "Sometimes love just needs a little help."

After Lumiere told Cogsworth his plan, they got to work. When everything was ready, Lumiere knocked on Belle's bedroom door.

"*Mademoiselle*," he called sweetly. "I am here to tell you that the Beast is very sorry about what happened."

"He is?" asked Belle.

"Oh, yes," said Lumiere. "Now do you wish to see your surprise?"

The door slowly opened. "My surprise?" asked Belle.

"*Oui, mademoiselle*," said Lumiere. "Just follow me."

At that very moment, Cogsworth was standing outside the Beast's bedroom door, his gears quaking with fear. "Darn that Lumiere," muttered Cogsworth. "Why do *I* get the Beast?"

Gathering his courage, Cogsworth finally knocked.

"Go away!" roared the Beast.

Cogsworth wanted to! But, instead, he called, "Master, I am only here to tell you that Belle is very sorry about what happened!"

After a long pause, the Beast said, "She is?"

"Oh, yes indeed," said Cogsworth. "Now follow me to see your surprise."

The door slowly opened. "My surprise?" asked the Beast.

"Yes, Master," said Cogsworth.

Both Belle and the Beast were led into the large drawing room. The room had been filled with fresh flowers from the greenhouse. And there stood Plucky the golden harp.

"Ohhhhh," said Belle and the Beast when they heard the beautiful harp music.

"You're sorry?" asked Belle.

"I am," the Beast admitted.

"I am too," said Belle.

They smiled at each other.

Lumiere and Cogsworth sighed. "You see, my friend," whispered Lumiere, "in their hearts, each really was sorry. They just needed a little help to admit it!"

Elsa's Royal Tour

"There's our ship, Elsa!" Anna cried.

Elsa had been planning a royal tour of nearby kingdoms for months. She was excited!

As the sisters climbed aboard, the captain scurried over. "Your Majesty," he said to Elsa. "With waters this still I don't think we'll make it to the first stop on time."

"I'll give us a little nudge," Elsa said. She created a light snow flurry, pushing the ship along.

Soon they arrived at the kingdom of Zaria.

"Welcome!" King Stebor and Queen Renalia called.

First, Anna and Elsa went on a tour of Zaria's gardens, then there was a grand festival.

"We've heard about your talents," Queen Renalia said to Elsa. "Won't you show us?"

Suddenly, Elsa felt shy. She gave an icy flourish, then looked down.

"Shall we join the dancing?" Anna asked, changing the subject.

Next stop was Chatho, where the sisters met Queen Colisa.

She took the sisters through the kingdom's rainforest and then to a gallery. Chatho was known for its art.

"Would you like to carve a sculpture?" Queen Colisa asked Elsa.

Elsa saw a block of ice. Again, she felt shy.

Anna jumped in. "That's my speciality!"

Later, Anna asked Elsa why she didn't want to show her powers.

"I got nervous," Elsa confessed.

Anna smiled. "You do wonderful things."

Elsa hugged her sister. "Thanks, Anna. You're …"

"… the Duke of Weselton!" At the next port the sisters saw a familiar face. This duke had been unkind to Elsa once.

"What are you doing here, Duke?" Anna asked. Their last stop was Mandonia – they'd avoided Weselton.

"Visiting my mother's cousin's wife's nephew. You should turn the ship round," the duke replied. "Mandonia's summer is the hottest in years!"

He led the sisters into the hot, sticky village. The Maldonians were sweaty and tired.

Elsa didn't feel shy. She had to help these people cool down! Elsa conjured snow clouds….

"Thank you!" people cheered.

Mandonia became a frozen wonderland. People slid down snowy piles on wooden planks.

"I guess a thank you is in order," the duke said.

"Grab a plank," Elsa suggested.

"A duke would never … It isn't…."

"We'll show you how," Anna called, racing up the hill.

Later, it was time to return to Arendelle.

"Did you have a good trip?" Anna asked.

"The best royal tour ever!" Elsa replied.

Beauty and the Beast

The Mysterious Book

"What are you looking at, Belle?" Chip asked. Belle smiled at the little teacup. "Oh, you caught me daydreaming, Chip," she said. "I was just looking up there."

She pointed to the highest shelf in the Beast's library. The only thing on the shelf was a single book.

Belle had wondered about that book almost since the day the Beast had first shown her the library. The trouble was, none of the ladders quite reached the shelf. So the book had remained a mystery.

Belle's curiosity had grown until she could hardly stop thinking about the book. What could it be about? Surely it had to be the most magical, unusual, wonderful book in the world!

She explained the problem to Chip. He went straight to his mother, Mrs Potts.

Mrs Potts called a meeting of all the enchanted objects. As soon as she told them about the book, they wanted to help Belle.

"What we need is a plan," Cogsworth said.

"Yes!" Lumiere cried. "And I've got one!"

That evening the enchanted objects gathered in the library. First the Wardrobe stood at the base of the shelves. The Stove climbed on top of her, then the Coatrack climbed up next. Soon a whole tower of enchanted objects stretched almost to the top shelf.

Finally Lumiere started to climb. When he reached the top, the book was still a few inches away. He stretched as far as he could....

"What are you doing?" Belle exclaimed from the doorway.

"Oh, *mademoiselle!*" Lumiere cried. "You're just in time – *voilà!*"

With that, he finally managed to reach the book, knocking it off the shelf into Belle's hands.

A moment later, the tower collapsed in a heap.

As soon as Belle made certain that everyone was all right, she opened the book. She couldn't wait to see what new wonders lay within its covers....

"Oh!" she said when she saw the first page.

"What is it?" Chip asked breathlessly.

Belle smiled sheepishly. "I can't believe it! I've already read this one."

The enchanted objects sighed. Had their plan been for nothing?

"But thank you anyway!" Belle said quickly. "It's so nice of you to get it for me." She hugged the book to her. "Even though I've read it before, it's one of my favourites – it's full of far-off places, magic spells ... well, let me show you...."

Soon all the enchanted objects were gathered around as Belle read the book to them. And, wouldn't you know, it became one of their favourite books too!

Lady and the TRAMP
A Tramp Tale

It was a warm evening, just about the time that the first star comes out to shine, and *long* past the time for Lady's and Tramp's puppies to go to sleep.

"Just one more story, Dad," begged Scamp.

Tramp rolled his eyes.

"Well ..." he said, "okay, but just one."

Happily, the puppies snuggled down onto their cushion. Tramp stretched out beside them.

"Did I ever tell you kids about the time I stole my very first sausage?" he asked.

"*Tramp!*" Lady warned him from her seat across the parlour. "That hardly sounds like a proper story for the children."

"Oh, tell it, Dad!" Scamp urged him.

"Well, maybe 'stole' isn't exactly the right word," Tramp reassured his wife. "And besides, it's got a great moral!" And with that, he began his tale:

"Now this all happened way back when I was just a little pup, already living on my own in the big city. I hope you puppies know just how good you have it living here in this nice house, with Junior and Jim Dear and Darling. Your old dad, though, was not so lucky. Oh, I had a lot of friends. And I had a lot of fun. But I'd be lying if I said I wasn't hungry – just a little – nearly every day.

"Well, one day I was especially hungry, and my nose was picking up all sorts of savoury scents. If there was bacon frying a mile away, I could have told you how many strips. So you can imagine the interest I developed in a certain, spicy smell coming from the butcher shop. Well, I followed my trusty nose, which has still never let me down and, sure enough, there was a heaping tray of steaming sausages. Can you believe it?"

"So you jumped up and gobbled them all up! Right?" Scamp broke in.

"That's my boy!" Tramp laughed. "But no. Don't forget, I was just a little guy. Couldn't reach the tray. All I could do was think about how to get that sausage ... when up walked a lady with a kid in a carriage. Well, at first I was irate. Competition! But then I noticed the crumbs all over the carriage. Hey! I thought to myself. This might be the ticket – this kid obviously can't hang on to anything. Sure enough, when the lady handed the kid a piece of sausage, the kid dropped it, and down it fell into my waiting mouth! Delicious!

"See, Lady," Tramp added with a grin, "no stealing!"

"And what exactly is the moral of that story?" Lady asked.

Tramp laughed. "Why, good things come to those who wait, of course!"

Disney
THE
PRINCESS
AND THE
FROG

Dining Under the Stars

It didn't take the two frogs, Tiana and Naveen, long to arrive at the home of Mama Odie. The voodoo priestess would restore them to normal and finally it would all be over!

Tiana thought that the time had come to enjoy a rest.

"Let's take a break!" she shouted to Louis the alligator, Ray the firefly and Naveen. "Is anyone feeling hungry?"

"I'm dying of hunger!" admitted Louis.

"How about swamp gumbo?" suggested Tiana. "It's my speciality!"

"That'll do!" said Naveen, leaning against a tree, his legs on a mushroom.

He placed a leaf on his knees as a napkin, and added, "Sounds delicious! I'll start with a free dinner cocktail and something to nibble on while I wait, thanks."

"Oh no, no, no, Your Royal Highness!" protested Tiana immediately, with a hint of irony in her voice. "That's not how I go about things! Your job is to slice the mushrooms!"

"But I don't know how to slice," Naveen complained, slowly and carefully cutting a slice of mushroom.

Tiana chuckled, amused. "At that rate, we'll still be here tomorrow!"

So, standing behind Naveen, she guided his hand. Tiana was chopping very fast! Naveen winced.

"Yes, OK, OK, I'm not really used to doing this. Most of the time I had servants do everything for me: dress me, brush my teeth, even help me get out of bed!"

"Aw, you poor baby." Tiana said mockingly.

However, Naveen sliced the mushrooms and soon the swamp gumbo was ready.

Suddenly, Ray raised his eyes to the sky, seeing the Evening Star.

"There she is. The sweetest firefly in all creation ... Evangeline!" he sighed. "So far above me, yet I know her heart belongs to me!"

Of course, no one wanted to spoil his happiness by telling him he was wrong and that he was actually talking to a star.

He began to sing softly, romantically, and Naveen invited Tiana to dance.

"Impossible!" she refused. "I don't know how to dance."

"If I can chop, you can dance," he retorted. Tiana gave in, and Naveen led her in a gentle waltz.

He guided her steps, then he said, "You see? Dancing, chopping, what's the difference? The main thing is to give it a try!"

Peter Pan

A Feather in His Cap

Peter Pan and Tinker Bell were off on an adventure and the Lost Boys were bored.

"Never Land is a dull place without Peter Pan," Slightly complained.

Then Rabbit spoke up. "We can play Pirates! That's always fun."

"Can't," said Slightly. "I lost the feather off my pirate hat."

"We could find another feather," Tootles suggested.

"An extraordinary feather," Cubby said. "Like Captain Hook's."

"That's it!" Slightly cried. "I'll steal Captain Hook's feather!"

A short time later, the Lost Boys were sneaking aboard Hook's pirate ship. Luckily for them, the pirates were taking a nap!

There, hanging from a peg on the mast, was Captain Hook's hat.

"There it is," whispered Tootles. "Get it!"

"M-m-m-me?" stammered Slightly.

Smee, Hook's first mate, awoke with a start. He thought someone had said his name. "Smee you say! That be me. But who be calling Smee?"

He opened his eyes and spied the Lost Boys. "Ahoy!" he cried, waking up the others. Quick as a flash, the Lost Boys were caught.

Captain Hook burst from his cabin. "Lash them to the mast!" he commanded. "We'll catch Peter Pan when he comes to save his friends."

Floating high on a cloud, Peter Pan and Tinker Bell saw their friends being captured.

They flew down to Pirates' Cove and landed on the ship's mast. Peter cupped his hands around his mouth and made a most peculiar sound.

"Tick tock," Peter went. "Tick tock!"

Down on deck, Captain Hook became very frightened. "It's that crocodile!" he cried. "The one that ate my clock and my hand! Now he's come back to eat me!"

"Tick tock ... tick tock," went Peter.

"Man the cannons!" Hook cried. "Shoot that crocodile!"

The Lost Boys, tied to the mast, were forgotten. As the pirates ran in circles, Tinker Bell began to flap her wings. Fairy dust sprinkled down onto the Lost Boys. Soon they floated right out of the ropes and up into the clouds. On the way, Slightly snatched the feather from Hook's hat and stuck it in his own.

Peter Pan, Tinker Bell and the Lost Boys met on a drifting cloud.

"Thanks for saving us!" exclaimed Tootles.

"You helped me scare old Hook!" Peter Pan cried. "That's a feather in all your caps."

"But the best feather of them all is in mine," Slightly said, as he showed off Captain Hook's prized feather!

Disney
THE LITTLE
MERMAID

A Hair-raising Experience

Ariel looked at her hair in the mirror and sighed. *Ugh*! It was so straight ... and red ... and boring! Ordinarily, it wasn't such a big deal. She'd run a dinglehopper through it, and that would be that. She had more important things to think about, you know. But today, for some reason, she felt like a change.

Ariel was still staring in the mirror when her six mermaid sisters arrived.

"Hi, Ariel, what are you doing?" the oldest, Aquata, asked.

"Oh, nothing," said Ariel. "Just trying to figure out something new to do with my hair."

"Just parting it on the other side can make a big difference," said Aquata. "Shall I try?"

"Sure!" said Ariel.

But, when Aquata had done it, Ariel's sister Andrina shook her head. "Not enough," she declared. "What you need, Ariel, are some curls."

"Okay." Ariel shrugged. She sat patiently as Andrina rolled her hair in curlers and took them out half an hour later.

"Oh, my," said Ariel, gazing into the mirror.

"Still not enough," said another sister, Arista. "Imagine how great your hair would look if we coloured it black with squid ink!" And, just to prove her point, that's exactly what she did.

"Well it certainly is different," said Ariel, looking at her new inky-black hair.

"Different, yes," said her sister Attina, "but if you want *better*, you should really put your hair up. You know, a ponytail or two ... no! I know, three!"

And soon Ariel's new hair was in not one, not two, but three curly black ponytails – all sticking straight up from her head.

"You know what you need?" said her sister Adella, looking at the finished product. "Plaits! Definitely plaits! Girls, come and help me."

And, before she knew it, Ariel's ponytails had been divided into 99 tight, twisty plaits.

Ariel looked in the mirror ... and then looked away twice as fast!

"What if we just cut it all off?" said her sister Alana.

"Hold it!" said Ariel, suddenly jumping up. "You're *not* cutting off my hair! I wanted a change – not a total reconstruction!" She reached up and began to unbraid her hair.

"Suit yourself," said her sisters. They helped her undo their hard work. Soon Ariel was back to normal, to her great relief. Still, she thought, it had been an interesting experiment. Changing her hair hadn't worked out so well, but what about changing something else? She shook her head and sighed. She was a redheaded mermaid princess, and that was that.

A Bouncy Babysitter

"Roo, I have to go out tomorrow evening," said Kanga. "So you'll need a babysitter. Who would you like?"

"Tigger!" shouted Roo.

Kanga was not surprised. Tigger was the only animal she knew who liked to bounce more than a baby kangaroo!

The next day, Tigger came over to Kanga's house.

"Now, Tigger, I know you and Roo like to bounce," said Kanga. "But a good babysitter must know when to put the bouncer to bed."

"Don't worry, Kanga!" said Tigger.

For hours, Tigger and Roo had a fine old time bouncing around. Then Tigger looked at the clock and said, "Time for bed!"

Roo hopped right into his room.

"That was easy," Tigger said to himself. "Now I'll just tuck you in and – hey! I said bounce *into* bed. Not *on* it!" cried Tigger. But Roo wouldn't stop. So Tigger gave up and started bouncing too.

Then Tigger remembered Kanga. "Wait a minute! I'm the babysitter!" said Tigger. "I'm supposed to be tucking you in!"

"I don't want to be tucked in!" said Roo.

"What if I read you a story?" asked Tigger.

"No," said Roo. "I'm not even sleepy. I could bounce all the way to Pooh's house!"

"But it's time for *bed*, not bouncing," said Tigger. "I'll get you some milk. That will make you sleepy."

But when Tigger came back to Roo's bedroom, Roo was gone!

"Uh-oh!" said Tigger. He rushed to Pooh's house.

"I'm sorry, Tigger," said Pooh, "but Roo isn't here."

Then Tigger rushed to Piglet's house. But Roo wasn't there either.

And he wasn't at Owl's or Rabbit's.

Finally, Tigger returned to Kanga's house. Where could Roo be? Just then, Tigger passed Roo's room – and saw Roo in his bed!

"Where were you, Tigger?" asked Roo.

"Where was I?" said Tigger. "Where were *you*?"

Roo explained that when Tigger had gone to get the milk, Roo had decided he did want to hear a story. But his favourite book was under the bed.

"You were *under* the bed?" cried Tigger.

"I'm home!" called Kanga at the front door. Tigger sighed with relief.

"How did it go?" she asked Tigger.

"Kanga," said Tigger, "the wonderful thing about Tiggers is bouncing – and from now on I'm sticking with that. Babysitting just has too many ups and downs!"

The Reason for the Rule

Tinker Bell and her sister Periwinkle both lived in Pixie Hollow, but they had only just met. There was a fairy rule that warm fairies like Tink lived in the spring, summer and autumn. Winter fairies like Peri lived in the Winter Woods. Neither could cross the border, but Tink had sneaked to the Winter Woods. Then, Peri had returned the visit, thanks to a brilliant snowmaking machine built by Tink's friends, Clank and Bobble. But when the snowmaker ran out of ice, Periwinkle's wings started to wilt. They had to get her back to winter and, as they did so, Lord Milori, the Lord of Winter, appeared.

He told Peri to lift her wings and let the cold air surround them. Soon, her wings were back to normal.

"This is why we do not cross the border," Lord Milori said. "The rule is there to protect you."

"Your rule will not keep us apart!" Tink cried.

"This is not Lord Milori's rule," said Queen Clarion, appearing behind her. "It's mine. I'm sorry."

Tink and Peri were so sad. They gave each other one last hug before they parted. Lord Milori flew off on his owl, knocking the snowmaker into the stream as he went.

But instead of going over the waterfall, it got caught on a ledge, creating a small snowstorm out of the ice that flowed into it!

Meanwhile, on the warm side, Queen Clarion tried to explain the importance of the rule to Tink. Lord Milori did the same with Periwinkle.

They told the girls that long ago, two fairies fell in love. One of the fairies was from the warm seasons, while the other was from winter. Every day at sunset, the couple met at the border. One day, one of the fairies crossed the border and ended up breaking a wing, for which there was no cure. After that, Queen Clarion made the rule to keep all fairies safe.

As Tink listened to the tale, she gazed out of the window. It was snowing! Queen Clarion and Tink raced outside and towards the snow. It was coming from the snowmaker!

The Queen stopped at the edge of the stream. Clank and Bobble were desperately trying to free the snowmaker – but snow still filled the air. It began to get colder.

"The seasons have been thrown out of balance," Queen Clarion said worriedly. The snow was freezing the warm side of Pixie Hollow. And if the Pixie Dust Tree froze, there would be no more pixie dust! Tink knew she had to think of a plan, and quickly!

Minnie's Summer Day

It was a hot summer day and Minnie and her friends were relaxing in her living room. The friends were just deciding what to do with their day when POP! Minnie's air-conditioning broke!

"Let's all go outside. Maybe there will be a breeze," said Minnie.

But there was no breeze at all.

"What are we going to do now?" asked Daisy.

Minnie looked around. "Maybe we could make fans. Or we could try sitting in the shade under a tree...." she said.

"Those sprinklers look nice and cool!" said Goofy, pointing at Minnie's lawn.

Donald nodded. "But there isn't enough water coming out of them to keep us cool!" he said.

Minnie had an idea. "I've got it!" she shouted. "Let's go to the lake! There's always a breeze there and there's so much to do!"

"It is the perfect day for a swim," Daisy added.

Minnie's friends were so excited! They quickly raced to the lake.

"What should we do first?" Minnie asked.

Everyone had a different idea. Daisy wanted to play basketball. Mickey and Pluto wanted to play fetch. And Donald wanted to go fishing!

Before anyone could stop him, Donald raced off towards a little boat.

Donald was about to hop into it when Minnie called out to him. "Donald, I don't think we can all fit in the boat. Let's do something together! Why don't we go for a swim?" suggested Minnie. "We can all do that!"

Donald wanted to go fishing, but finally he agreed.

The friends jumped into the water....

"Aah," said Donald. "You were right, Minnie. This was a good idea!"

Minnie smiled. She was glad she and her friends had found a way to cool off.

"I could stay in this water all day!" Daisy said. And that is just what they did.

As the sun set and the day started to get cooler, Minnie and her friends got out of the water and Minnie had one last surprise for her friends ... marshmallows!

"Minnie, you really do know how to plan the perfect day!" said Mickey as they roasted marshmallows over a campfire.

Finally, it really was time to leave.

"That was so much fun!" said Donald as they drove home. "Let's do it all again tomorrow!"

Snow White
and the Seven Dwarfs

A Relaxing Picnic

"What a lovely day for a picnic!" Snow White cried as she arrived at the Dwarfs' cottage for a visit one morning.

"We can't have a picnic," Grumpy said. "We have to work."

"But we've been working so hard in the diamond mine." Sleepy yawned. "Can't we take a day off?"

The other Dwarfs cheered – all except for Grumpy. He just folded his arms and frowned.

"Please don't worry, Grumpy," said Snow White. "A relaxing picnic will cheer you up."

"I doubt it," he grumbled.

"Now, what shall we rake – I mean take – on our picnic?" Doc asked.

"How about some porridge?" suggested Sleepy with a yawn.

"That is not a very good picnic food," said Snow White. "It's much more fun to pack food you can eat without spoons or forks."

"Gosh, like s-s-sandwiches?" stammered Bashful shyly.

"Exactly!" cried Snow White.

"How about fruit?" asked Doc.

"And cookies!" suggested Happy.

"And hard-boiled eggs," added Sneezy.

"Wonderful!" exclaimed Snow White. The Dwarfs helped Snow White pack.

"After lunch, we'll want to play," said Snow White. "So you should pack up some things to play with."

They did, and then they were off, hiking through the forest. When they came to a clearing with a babbling brook, Snow White spread a blanket on the grass, and they all sat down to eat.

After lunch, Doc and Happy played draughts, Bashful and Sneezy tossed a ball back and forth, Sleepy took a nap and Dopey launched an enormous blue kite.

Snow White watched Dopey as he ran through the meadow. She clapped when the wind took the kite up in the air. Then the kite lifted Dopey off the ground too!

"Oh, my!" cried Snow White. "Someone help! Dopey is flying away!"

Grumpy, who had been pouting by the brook, jumped to his feet. He raced after Dopey. Huffing and puffing, he followed the kite up one hill and down another.

Finally, Grumpy climbed all the way up a tall oak tree and grabbed Dopey as he flew by. Snow White cheered.

Still huffing and puffing, Grumpy collapsed on the blanket.

"Jiminy Cricket!" he cried. "I can't wait to get back to the diamond mine tomorrow. Relaxing picnics are way too much work!"

Tinker Bell's Plan

Tink and her sister Periwinkle had only just met. They were separated at birth, with Periwinkle living in the Winter Woods and Tink living in the warm seasons.

There was a strict rule in Pixie Hollow that no fairy could cross the border between the seasons. But Tink and Peri had broken it in order to visit each other. Tink and her friends had made a snowmaker so Peri could visit the warm side. But now it was making so much snow that the seasons were out of balance. If the Pixie Dust Tree froze, there would be no more pixie dust!

While some of the warm fairies covered the tree with blankets of moss, others helped animals find shelter. Then, Tink discovered that a frost-covered flower, given to her by Peri, was blooming again. She wondered why, and she knew who could tell her!

Tink flew into winter, but her wings iced over and she fell. Peri and her friends rushed to help her. Tink showed them the flower. A frost fairy explained that frost tucks warm air inside it like a blanket. That gave Tink an idea – maybe they could save all the flowers, and the Pixie Dust Tree, by covering them with a layer of frost!

Lord Milori, the Lord of Winter, and all of the frost fairies flew to the warm seasons.

"Start at the freeze line and spread out across the seasons," ordered Lord Milori. "The rest of you – cover the tree!"

Then he draped his cloak around a shivering Queen Clarion. It broke her heart to see his damaged wing. Many years ago, the two had been in love. They used to meet where spring touches winter, but one day Lord Milori had crossed over the border and broken his wing. That was when Queen Clarion made the rule that no fairies could cross over.

Time passed, and sunbeams began to stream through the frozen Pixie Dust Tree's branches. Everyone waited.

As the frost melted, the pixie dust started to flow again! The plan had worked!

But then, Tink admitted that she too had broken her wing. Peri was heartbroken, but she had to head back to the Winter Woods before it became too warm. The sisters touched wings to say goodbye.

Just then, there was an explosion of sparkling energy. The magic between the sisters healed Tink's broken wing!

From that day on, warm fairies visited winter fairies whenever they liked, with a coating of frost to protect their wings. New friendships formed – and long-lost loved ones were reunited at last!

Disney Bambi
A Manner of Speaking

Bambi and his mother were out for a summer's walk. As always, they stopped by the rabbit den where Thumper lived.

"And how are you today, Thumper?" asked Bambi's mother.

"I'd be better if my mum didn't just give me a dumb old bath," he said.

"Thumper! Mind your manners!" his mother scolded him.

"I'm sorry, Mama," Thumper said. He looked back at the doe. "I'm fine, thank you," he replied.

Bambi and Thumper were given permission to play, so they headed off into the woods.

"So, what do you want to play?" Bambi asked Thumper.

"How about hide-and-seek?" Thumper suggested. "I'll hide first, okay?"

Bambi turned his back to Thumper, closed his eyes, and started to count. "One ... two ... three ... four ... five ..."

"Save me! Help! Bambi, save me!" Thumper cried. Bambi whirled around to see Thumper hopping towards him with a terrified look on his face. A moment later, a mother bear emerged from a nearby cave with three small cubs toddling behind her.

Though he was terrified, Thumper *still* managed to make a rude comment. "That's the meanest-looking creature I ever saw!"

"I beg your pardon?" the mother bear said. "First, you come into my home and disturb my children while they're sleeping. And then you have the nerve to call me mean? I think you owe me an apology!"

"Do it!" whispered Bambi. "Apologize."

"I'm s-s-sorry you're mean," Thumper stammered.

"Thumper!" Bambi cried. "That isn't funny."

Thumper looked confused. "I wasn't trying to be funny," he said.

"Try again!" the mother bear boomed.

"Um," Thumper tried again. "I'm, um, sorry I disturbed your cubs ... and, um, you look just like a bear mum should look ... which is big. And nice. Yup, you sure look nice."

Before the mother bear let Thumper and Bambi go, she said, "Like I always tell my children: manners are important!"

Bambi and Thumper ran home as quickly as they could. When they arrived at Thumper's, his mother said, "Just in time for a nice lunch of greens." Thumper was about to tell his mum how awful he thought the greens tasted, then changed his mind. "Thank you, Mama. That sounds wonderful," he said.

Thumper's mother beamed. "What lovely manners! I guess you have been listening to me, after all!" she said, as pleased as could be.

Tangled

Incredible Tales

Flynn and Rapunzel were trapped in a cave. The water was rising and it had already reached as high as their chins!

Flynn tried diving under the water to find a way out, but it was so dark that he couldn't see a thing. He cut his hand trying to dislodge the large rocks surrounding them, but the boulders wouldn't budge. It wasn't easy feeling his way along the walls.

"My hair glows in the dark!" Rapunzel suddenly remembered.

Flynn gave her a strange look, convinced that she'd gone crazy.

"I promise you. If I sing, my hair will glow!" Rapunzel insisted.

Flynn was still in shock when Rapunzel broke into a beautiful song and then dived underwater. He quickly joined her and was stunned to see her hair glowing so brightly it lit up the entire cave!

Flynn spotted an opening in the rocks and swam towards it, pulling Rapunzel along with him. They soon emerged into the open air and found themselves on the riverbank.

"We made it! We're alive!" exclaimed Rapunzel, as she helped revive Pascal.

She looked over at Flynn who was in a state of shock – but not because they had just nearly drowned.

"Her hair glows," he murmured. Then he turned to Pascal. "I didn't see that coming. Why does her hair glow?"

Rapunzel pulled her hair from the river and began wringing the water out of it. "It doesn't just glow," she said calmly.

They started walking to find somewhere to dry off. Flynn gathered some wood to light a campfire.

"Just don't freak out," Rapunzel told Flynn once the fire was lit, and she wrapped her hair around his hand, which he had wounded getting out of the cave. As Rapunzel began to sing, her hair once again glowed brightly. Within moments Flynn's hand was healed.

"Your hair really is magic," he muttered in bewilderment. "It's incredible! How long has your hair been like that?"

"Always. That's why my mother kept me in the tower, because people might steal it. How long ago did you change your name?"

Flynn blushed with embarrassment.

"Flynn was my favourite storybook hero when I was young, at the orphanage. I always wanted to be a swashbuckling hero like him!"

Rapunzel burst out laughing.

"One thing's certain, Eugene, each of us, in our own way, has an incredible tale to tell!"

Woodland Washing

"La, la, la, la, la," Briar Rose sang as she hung the sheets on the washing line. She could feel the sunshine on her back and it felt good. It had been raining for days, and the change in the weather was a welcome surprise. She could catch up on the washing and spend some time outdoors.

"Doesn't the sunshine make you want to sing?" she asked a bluebird who was chirping along with her. The bird chirped a new song in response, and Briar Rose laughed as she pulled her Aunt Flora's red dress out of the basket of clean laundry. Once she was finished, she could take a nice walk through the forest.

Aunt Merryweather's blue dress was next. Briar Rose was just pegging the shoulder to the washing line when suddenly a pair of cheeky chipmunks leaped onto the line from a tree branch and raced down the length of it, covering the dresses and the sheets with muddy footprints.

"Look what you've done, you naughty chipmunks!" Briar Rose scolded, shaking a finger at the wayward creatures. "It took me two hours to get those dresses and sheets clean!"

The chipmunks leaped up to a tree branch and twittered guiltily at her in response. Then they turned and scampered off into the forest, their striped tails waggling.

Sighing with frustration, Briar Rose unpegged the sheets from the line and pulled a fresh bucket of water up from the well. Then, taking the washboard and the bar of laundry soap, she began to scrub out the muddy prints. It looked as if she wouldn't get a walk in today after all.

Suddenly, a chattering noise caught her attention. Looking up, she saw the chipmunks hurrying out of the forest with several other forest animals at their heels! There were two rabbits, four chipmunks, three bluebirds, a deer, a skunk and an owl.

Briar Rose laughed. "Why, you've brought all your friends!"

The chipmunks chattered excitedly while everyone got to work. The bluebirds lifted the sheet into the air so the edges wouldn't get dirty while Briar Rose scrubbed. The deer, the skunk and the rabbits brought fresh water from the well. And the chipmunks scampered across the laundry soap to get their feet all soapy, then walked across the muddy parts of the sheets until they were clean. Then everyone helped hang the newly washed laundry on the line for a second time.

Briar Rose smiled at her animal friends and gave the chipmunks a little pat. "Finished at last," she said. "Now we can all take a walk in the forest ... together!"

Disney

ALICE
in
WONDERLAND

Alice's Mad Manners

"Clean cup! Clean cup! Move down!" The Mad Hatter shoved Alice aside, nearly spilling her tea. Poor Alice had been at the tea party for some time and had not even had a sip. It was a most unusual tea party.

Alice took a new spot and waited patiently while the Hatter and the March Hare poured a fresh round of tea. Folding her hands in her lap, Alice tried to recall what her mother and sister usually did at tea parties. It seemed to her that they just sat around and chatted. Perhaps, thought Alice, that is what I ought to do too.

"Pardon me," Alice addressed the March Hare because the Mad Hatter seemed quite busy buttering his saucer. "Our neighbours got a new dog. He's a – "

"A dog? A dog?" the March Hare shouted. "Where?" He hopped up onto the table, upsetting a plate of toast.

"Oh, I'm terribly sorry." Alice stood and tried to calm the poor hare. "I should have known you wouldn't like dogs. Dinah hates them too, you know." The March Hare was hopping all around the table and Alice had to jog in circles beside him to keep up the conversation. "When Dinah sees a dog, she practically climbs the curtains."

"Very sensible!" the Hatter said, waving his butter knife. "Just who is this clever 'Dinah'?"

"Oh, she's my – " Alice stopped herself. She had got into trouble for mentioning her cat before. The Dormouse had run off in a panic, and the Hatter and March Hare had given chase. She would not make that mistake again. She whispered in the Hatter's ear. "She's my kitten."

"But that's a baby cat!" the Hatter cried.

Just as Alice feared, the Dormouse bolted. The March Hare started hopping about just as soon as the word 'cat' was out of the Hatter's mouth. The Hatter chased the Dormouse round and round the garden. Finally, the Hatter threw his hat over the little creature. Alice caught him in the teapot and closed the lid.

"Really, my dear. It is most rude to threaten us on our unbirthdays!" the Hatter cried.

"I'm really very sorry," Alice sighed, sinking back into a chair. She was only trying to be polite. Perhaps, Alice thought to herself, in this place it is better to say what you think you oughtn't instead of what you think you ought.

Turning to the Hatter, she said, "This party isn't very fun, and you aren't very nice!"

The Hatter grinned. "Thank you ever so much, my dear young lady. Tea?" he asked.

"Thank you ever so much," said Alice. She was beginning to get the hang of this!

Running Away

After Joy and Sadness had created a scary dream to wake Riley up, the Train of Thought started moving again, and the two Emotions were finally on their way back to Headquarters with Riley's core memory spheres.

Butthingsweren'tgoing so well for the Emotions in Headquarters. Anger, Fear and Disgust were finding it hard to keep Riley happy without Joy around. Riley had already cried in front of her new classmates, and had argued with her parents and best friend. Three Islands of Personality had collapsed into the Memory Dump and Riley was starting to forget who she was. After everything that had happened, Anger decided the best thing for Riley to do was run away – back to Minnesota. After all, Riley's happy core memories were made in Minnesota. If she went back, she could just make more.

"Who's with me?" Anger asked.

Fear and Disgust agreed, so Anger plugged an idea bulb in the console.

The idea entered Riley's head just as she awoke from her scary dream. She climbed out of bed and fetched her computer.

"She took it," said Anger, after Riley accepted the idea. "There's no turning back."

Clicking through to a bus website, Riley looked at a map and selected her route.

At that moment, Joy and Sadness were on the Train of Thought moving towards Headquarters.

Joy turned to Sadness. "Hey, that was a good idea. About scaring Riley awake," she said.

"Really?" said Sadness. She was glad to know she'd been helpful. Then the pair found a memory on the train and discovered that it was both of their favourites. Sadness remembered it as the day that Riley's hockey team had lost the play-offs when she missed the winning shot. But Joy loved the memory because the whole team had come to cheer Riley up.

Meanwhile, Riley had secretly taken her mum's credit card to buy a one-way bus ticket. Usually, Riley would never lie to her parents – in fact she would normally tell them everything.

Back in the Mind World, the tracks beneath the Train of Thought suddenly began to crumble. Some Mind Workers helped Joy, Sadness and Bing Bong, escape before the train plummeted over the cliff edge. Joy looked up to see a huge space where Honesty Island used to be – it was gone!

"That was our way home!" Joy cried. "We lost another island … what is happening?"

"Haven't you heard?" replied a Mind Worker. "Riley is running away!"

Out of Order

Inside the *Hero's Duty* computer game, Sergeant Calhoun, the leader of the soldiers, was yelling at Wreck-It Ralph.

"Never interfere with a first-person shooter!" she cried. Ralph belonged in his own game, *Fix-It Felix, Jr*, but he wanted to get the Medal of Heroes from *Hero's Duty* to prove he could be a Good Guy. He was fed up of always being the Bad Guy in his game.

Meanwhile, a girl who was playing in Litwak's Arcade moved to play on *Fix-It Felix, Jr*. She put in the coins to play, but there was a problem ... Ralph wasn't there to wreck anything!

"Mr Litwak!" the girl called out. "This game's busted!"

Mr Litwak taped an 'Out of Order' sign to the screen. The characters in the game were stunned! What if their game was unplugged? Luckily, someone had seen Ralph enter *Hero's Duty*. Felix decided to bring Ralph back. "I can fix this!" he told everyone.

Over in *Hero's Duty*, Ralph had just climbed the tower which contained the Medal of Heroes. By this time, the arcade was closed for the night, so no game-players could see him. The tower contained loads of cy-bug eggs. Every time the game started, the eggs hatched, and the soldiers had to battle hundreds of dangerous cy-bugs! Ralph tip-toed past the eggs ... and he made it! The Medal of Heroes was his!

But, just then, Ralph knocked over an egg. It cracked open and a baby cy-bug hurled itself onto Ralph's face. Ralph fell backwards into an escape pod. Instantly, the escape pod launched into the sky – with the cy-bug still attached to Ralph's face!

At that same moment, Felix stepped into *Hero's Duty*. "Have you seen my colleague, Ralph?" he asked Calhoun. Suddenly, the escape pod zoomed past. They could see Ralph – and the cy-bug – inside! The ship whooshed down the tunnel to Game Central Station.

Ralph's escape pod ricocheted through the station and finally landed in a world made entirely of sweets. Ralph was ejected from the ship, and the cy-bug disappeared in a lake of toffee.

Ralph realized he was in a racing game called *Sugar Rush*. His medal had landed in a peppermint tree!

Suddenly, a little girl called Vanellope showed up. She thought the medal was a gold coin. "Race you for it!" she yelled.

Poor Ralph lost the race – and his medal! How would Ralph ever prove he was a Good Guy now?

Beauty and the Beast

Belle and the Castle Puppy

Belle was strolling through the castle garden one day when she saw a puppy huddled outside the castle gates. He looked cold and dirty.

"Oh, you poor thing!" Belle cried. "Let's get you warmed up and fed!"

Once inside, Belle gave the puppy a bath. When he was clean and dry, the puppy ate a bowl of warm stew.

"I hope we can keep him!" Chip exclaimed.

All the enchanted objects were happy to have a guest. But the Ottoman remembered when he had been a real dog. What if Belle liked this dog more?

"Do you want to play?" Belle asked, letting the puppy outside. As Belle and the others followed, the Ottoman slinked out behind them.

A while later, the Beast walked up to Belle. "Someone has dug up my roses!" he exclaimed. Then the Beast saw the puppy. "Get rid of him – NOW!" the Beast roared as he stomped away.

Just then, the Ottoman ran past Belle and chased after the Beast – his legs were muddy. Belle suddenly understood.

"The Ottoman dug up the roses! He just wanted some attention, too!" Belle realized.

The puppy raced after the Ottoman, barking playfully. "What if they get lost?"

Belle worried. "I have to bring them back safely."

"I'll come and light your way," Lumiere called to Belle.

Belle, carrying Lumiere, walked along a dark path. "Puppy! Ottoman!" she called.

Suddenly, Belle heard barking and followed the sound to a clearing where she saw the Ottoman and puppy – who was barking loudly. Belle gasped. A large wolf was sitting nearby.

"Look at that, the puppy is protecting the Ottoman!" Lumiere exclaimed.

Quickly, Belle put Lumiere on the ground and lit a large stick she'd found.

"Get away! Get away!" she shouted, swinging it towards the wolf.

Just then, the Beast showed up, roaring loudly. The wolf yelped with fear and ran away.

Later that night, everyone settled by the fireplace. Belle watched the Beast stroke the Ottoman and feed biscuits to the puppy.

"May the puppy stay until I can find him a home?" she asked.

The Beast cleared his throat. "His home is here – with us," he answered gruffly.

Belle smiled. She loved the Beast's gentle, caring side that he was starting to show.

DISNEY · PIXAR
BRAVE
Together Again

Merida was a free-spirited princess who lived in the ancient Scottish Highlands. Merida's mother, Queen Elinor, had wanted Merida to be a 'proper' princess and marry in order to keep peace in the kingdom. The clans had come to compete for Merida's hand, but Merida had refused to choose a suitor. She had argued with her mother and slashed the family tapestry.

Soon after, a witch gave Merida a spell, which turned Queen Elinor into a bear! Now, Merida just wanted her mother back. A riddle from the Witch had told her to "mend the bond torn by pride". So, Merida had sewn the tapestry back together.

But her father, King Fergus, and the other clansmen had chased Elinor-Bear into the forest, not realizing it was really the queen.

The men were about to hurt Elinor-Bear when, suddenly, another bear appeared.

"Mor'du!" Merida said with a gasp. It was the bear that had taken her father's leg.

The lords ran forward to attack the giant bear, but Mor'du swatted them away easily. Then he grabbed Fergus and tossed him aside.

Mor'du closed in on Merida. Bravely, Merida raised her bow and arrow. Then, with a deafening roar, Elinor-Bear charged at Mor'du and shoved the demon bear away from Merida.

After a vicious battle, Elinor-Bear pushed Mor'du against a huge stone. The stone fell, crushing Mor'du beneath it.

In the silence that followed, Merida draped the mended tapestry over her mother. But nothing happened. Merida watched as Elinor-Bear's eyes turned cold and more bear-like.

"I want you back! I just want you back, Mum," Merida said. "I love you!"

Then, Merida felt a hand brush her hair. She looked up and saw her mother smiling down at her. When their bond was repaired, the spell had been broken. Elinor had changed back into the queen!

The triplets, too, had turned back into boys. The whole family was together again.

Back at the castle, Merida and Elinor began a new tapestry, one that would forever record the story of the challenge they had faced – and conquered – together.

Later, they watched as the clans sailed for home. Queen Elinor would never again doubt that Merida's strong, free spirit was that of a proper princess, and the future Queen of DunBroch.

As for Merida, she had finally come to appreciate her mother's strength and courage. She knew now that she wouldn't change a thing about her.

The Curious Fairy

It was another busy day for the fairies of Pixie Hollow. An enthusiastic fairy named Zarina was strolling towards the Pixie Dust Depot – the spot where all the pixie dust came from. Tinker Bell and her friends thought it was strange that Zarina was walking and not flying. But Zarina usually walked wherever she went, even though she was a dust-keeper fairy and it was her job to package up the golden pixie dust that helped all fairies fly.

Zarina took her place on the assembly line at the depot. All of Pixie Hollow relied on the golden pixie dust that they packaged. Most fairies used it to fly, but Zarina was completely fascinated by the stuff!

She had just sprinkled some on her hair to see what it would do when the head dust-keeper, Fairy Gary, and Terence appeared. Fairy Gary announced that Zarina would be on Blue Dust Duty that day.

As Zarina excitedly followed Fairy Gary to the Blue Pixie Dust Vault, he reminded her that she was not allowed to touch the Blue Dust directly. Inside the vault, he instructed her how to gather the dust. "Exactly twenty-six specks," he said as he eyed her closely.

"But why?" she asked.

"Zarina, you are the most inquisitive fairy I've ever known. Correction: it's a tie. Let's just say you are the Tinker Bell of dust-keepers." Zarina didn't see this as a bad thing.

When the Blue Dust was ready Zarina and Fairy Gary flew up to the boughs of the Pixie Dust Tree. Fairy Gary poured the Blue Dust into a special container.

Instantly, the golden pixie dust the tree produced flowed faster and grew brighter than before. "Takes the golden dust from a trickle to a roar," Fairy Gary said.

"If there's Blue Dust," Zarina pondered aloud, "why can't there be other colours? What if there's pink dust? What if we make it?"

"We do not tamper with pixie dust," a concerned Fairy Gary declared. "It is far too powerful."

But Zarina's curiosity got the better of her and she dipped her bracelet into the golden dust. Coated in pixie dust, the bracelet rose into the air, met a speck of Blue Dust and flew all over the room!

The bracelet hit Fairy Gary in the face – SMACK! Zarina was sorry. She could see he was disappointed with her.

"Let me be absolutely clear, Zarina," Fairy Gary declared. "Dust-keepers are forbidden to tamper with pixie dust."

Pluto's Surprise

One sunny morning, Mickey looked out of the window. "This is perfect building weather!" he cried.

"What are you going to build?" asked Morty and Ferdie.

"A tree house!" he said.

"Can we help?" the boys asked.

"You would be great helpers," Mickey replied, "but there will be lots of tools and it might not be very safe. Why don't you take Pluto to the park?"

"Sure!" they replied.

Mickey called his friends and soon Minnie, Donald, Daisy and Goofy arrived to help.

"It's a big job. Let's split up the work," Mickey said. "Why don't you saw the boards, Goofy? Then Donald and I can hammer them together."

"I have an idea," Minnie said. She showed Mickey a drawing she had made.

"Good thinking, Minnie!" Mickey replied. "That'll be one of the most important jobs of all."

Goofy dumped his toolbox in the garden and began sawing the boards.

"Goofy, I was wondering if you would cut some boards for me, too?" Minnie asked him.

"Sure!" Goofy said. "What do you need?"

Goofy looked at Minnie's drawing then started cutting.

Donald and Mickey worked together to make a rope ladder, then Mickey attached it to the thickest tree branch.

"Once we finish building, we can use this ladder to climb into the tree house," Mickey said.

Goofy brought them a stack of boards. "I still have to saw boards for the roof, but you can use these for the floor and walls," he said.

"Thanks, Goofy!" Mickey said.

Mickey and Donald pulled the boards into the tree and started building.

Minnie hurried over. "Do you have any extra nails?" she called up.

"Here," Donald said, passing them down.

On the way back across the garden, Minnie stopped to watch Daisy mixing up some paint.

"Wow," Minnie said. "That's a lot of paint!"

"Too much!" Daisy giggled. "Need any?"

"Great, thanks, Daisy," Minnie said.

Mickey's garden was a very busy place!

When Morty, Ferdie and Pluto came home they couldn't believe their eyes. "Wow!" the boys cried as they scrambled up the rope ladder.

But Pluto couldn't climb it like the others.

"Come round here!" Minnie called.

Pluto trotted round to the other side of the tree and found a set of stairs that was just right for him!

"Minnie made them for you," Mickey explained. "Come on up and join the fun!"

Pluto thought it was the best tree house ever!

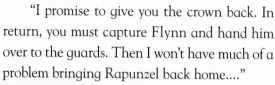

Tangled

A Professional Thief

Mother Gothel was angry. Rapunzel – the girl she had kidnapped and kept hidden her whole life – had dared to leave the tower! Even though Mother Gothel had warned the girl about the dangers of the world outside, Rapunzel had still followed that thief Flynn into the forest!

"She can manage perfectly well without me!" Mother Gothel realized with irritation.

Mother Gothel followed Rapunzel's trail to the pub where Rapunzel had befriended a group of ruffians. They had helped Rapunzel to escape with Flynn when the guards came to arrest him for stealing the royal crown.

"How can I persuade Rapunzel to return to the tower now?" wondered Mother Gothel. "She will never believe my stories about monsters any more!"

Mother Gothel went on thinking and soon she had hatched a plan. Spying on the ruffians at the pub, she had discovered that the Stabbington brothers had been Flynn's partners in crime. But Flynn had tricked them by keeping the crown for himself, so now the Stabbingtons wanted revenge. Since Mother Gothel had found the crown hidden in the tower, she had an offer for the two brothers.

"I promise to give you the crown back. In return, you must capture Flynn and hand him over to the guards. Then I won't have much of a problem bringing Rapunzel back home...."

The Stabbingtons immediately agreed. Mother Gothel then headed off to find Flynn and Rapunzel.

Flynn had just gone to gather firewood and Mother Gothel surprised Rapunzel, jumping out angrily from behind a tree.

"Oh, Mother! How did you find me?"

"I followed the trail of lies and treachery," Mother Gothel replied scornfully. "Come with me, we're going back to the tower."

"But I'm not in any danger here!" the girl protested. "Flynn really likes me and...."

"He's making fun of you, you silly little girl: he's a professional thief! As soon as you give him back the crown he will forget you completely! Here's the crown. Give it back to him and you'll see how quickly he abandons you!"

Then Mother Gothel ran off before Flynn returned.

Rapunzel sighed. Her mother really was so mistaken! Flynn was indeed a professional thief, but he had not needed to steal her heart – she had given it to him freely. She knew she would prove Mother Gothel wrong.

Peter Pan
Tiger Lily

It was a hot summer night in Never Land – so hot, in fact, that the poor Lost Boys couldn't sleep. And so it was decided that instead of trying to stay in their hideout in Hangman's Tree, Peter Pan and the Lost Boys would camp out for the night in the wild wilderness.

Certainly, they thought, the woods would be cool and shady, and the trees would catch any breeze kind enough to blow through. But little did they know how mysterious – and spooky – a forest could be once the sun went down.

"It's dark out here," said Cubby.

"And awful quiet," said Tootles.

"Won't you tell us a story, please, Peter?" asked Slightly, who was shivering in his fox suit despite the sticky heat.

"Very well," agreed Peter. "If it will make you all be quiet! I will tell you the story of the very first time I ever camped out in the wilderness – which, by the way, was the first time I met Tiger Lily...."

"I had made myself a fire, a great big one, 'cause it was autumn and the nights were getting cool. I'd just laid my head down on a patch of nice, soft moss, when all of a sudden I heard a rustling in the shadows."

"*Indians?*" the Lost Boys gasped.

But Peter shook his head.

"Not Indians," he told them. "That's what I thought at first too. No, this was something bigger. It was a *bear*! It jumped out of the trees, growling and waving its big paws in the air like Captain Hook swattin' blue flies. I've never seen such a mean, angry beast, before or since!"

"So wha-wha-what did you do?" asked the Lost Boys.

"Told him to get lost, of course. To *scram*! Apparently, he didn't understand English, however, 'cause he just kept charging.

"Well, I'm not going to lie to you; I started to get nervous. And then, there she was – Tiger Lily – as quiet as a mouse. Without a 'hi' or 'how do you do', she grabbed a stick from my fire and waved it at the bear. The next thing I knew, the bear had turned around and was running off crying! I suppose Tiger Lily saved my life that night," said Peter. "And it wasn't the last time either. The end."

"Um ... Peter," said Cubby, peering out into the darkness, "do you know what ever happened to that bear?"

Peter thought for a moment. "Nope," he said and shrugged. "Probably still out there, wandering around, I guess." He yawned a big, mischievous yawn. "Now stop yer yammerin' and close your eyes and go to sleep!"

Zarina's Experiments

After her busy day at the Pixie Dust Depot, Zarina returned to her cottage and emptied her daily allowance of pixie dust into a large jar. She was saving all her dust for experiments – that's why she walked everywhere.

So far, her attempts to make pixie dust with different powers had failed. With a sigh, she shut her experiment journal and laid her head on top of it. Out of the corner of her eye she saw something blue and glowing fall from her hair. It was a speck of Blue Dust! It must have stuck to her hair while she was working in the Blue Dust Vault!

Simply looking at the Blue Pixie Dust inspired Zarina.

With the help of a magnifying glass and a sharp blade she delicately cut slivers from the speck. Then, she tried her last failed experiment again – mixing in a sliver of Blue Dust.

Suddenly, the dust turned orange. With her hand coated in the dust, Zarina found she could bend a moonbeam. "I knew it!" Zarina exclaimed.

She couldn't wait to show her curious friend Tinker Bell her discovery! Tink was always making new discoveries of her own, so Zarina knew Tink would appreciate her exciting news.

Tink was amazed when she saw the orange dust that Zarina had created.

"I'm doing more!" declared Zarina. She put a rattled Tink to work stirring another recipe. This time the dust was purple and with it, Zarina created a fast-flying whirlwind!

But Tinker Bell was concerned that Zarina hadn't told Fairy Gary about her experiments. "Zarina, I really think you should stop!" she said firmly.

Surprised by Tink's words, Zarina bumped into a table and spilled all the pink dust she had just created on to a potted sapling. Suddenly, thick vines sprouted and tore through the cottage. They twisted and turned, spreading across Pixie Hollow and destroying everything in their path – including the Dust Depot!

Queen Clarion was relieved to discover that no one had been hurt in the accident, but when Fairy Gary saw the pink dust, he looked pointedly at Zarina. He told her she could no longer be a dust-keeper.

Zarina's eyes filled with tears. She loved pixie dust and being a dust-keeper. She fled home to pack her stockpile of dust, and a few of her belongings. Then, after one last look at Pixie Hollow, she sprinkled dust on her wings and flew towards the shores of Never Land.

Mama Odie to the Rescue

The evil sorcerer, Dr Facilier was worried. With the help of his magic talisman, he had made Lawrence, a valet, look like Prince Naveen, so that he could marry Charlotte. This way, the sorcerer hoped to get his hands on the girl's fortune!

But the talisman was losing its power. So he had to find Naveen and restore its magic with a few drops of his blood....

"Come to me, Shadows!" he invoked. "Bring me the Frog Prince without delay!"

The clawed beasts flew out of the window and soon found Naveen's tracks in the bayou. He and Tiana were on their way to the home of Mama Odie, the good voodoo priestess. They were going to ask her how they could become human again.

But suddenly, the Shadows grasped Naveen and carried him away. "Help!" he shouted.

Tiana, Louis the alligator and Ray the firefly tried to hold on to him. But no one could fight against the forces of darkness ... except a powerful voodoo priestess! And whoosh! Mama Odie made the evil Shadows disappear!

"Not bad for a 197-year-old blind lady, hey?" she laughed.

Mama Odie and her snake Juju lived in

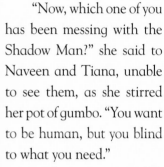

a swamp boat that was wedged between the branches of a tree. The wise woman was a little eccentric. However, with all her knowledge, they couldn't help but respect her.

"Now, which one of you has been messing with the Shadow Man?" she said to Naveen and Tiana, unable to see them, as she stirred her pot of gumbo. "You want to be human, but you blind to what you need."

"What we want, what we need, it's all the same thing, yes?" Naveen insisted.

"No, you listen to your Mama now. The only thing important is what's under the skin ... you got to dig a little deeper." Still, Mama Odie knew that the frogs would have to learn that the hard way.

"Gumbo, gumbo, in the pot! We need a princess. What you got?!" Mama Odie conjured an image of Charlotte and her father in the tub of gumbo.

"Charlotte is not a princess!" said Naveen.

"But of course she is!" countered Tiana. "Her father was crowned king of Mardi Gras. So she is still a princess until midnight!"

"A Mardi Gras princess is better than no princess at all, isn't it?" Mama Odie pointed out in a mischievous tone.

Naveen blushed. Yes, a kiss from Charlotte would suit him very well!

A Nice Day for a Sail

One lovely summer day, Mickey Mouse asked Minnie if she'd like to go for a boat ride.

"I would love to," Minnie said with a smile.

Mickey and Minnie were preparing to set sail when Goofy came running by on the shore.

"Hiya," he said. "What a great day for sailing!"

But Goofy didn't see a squirrel in front of him and he accidentally stepped on its tail. The squirrel squealed, then leaped up and landed in the boat! Mickey and Minnie were so startled that they jumped, making the boat rock.

Mickey tried to stop the rocking, but the boat tipped over, and Minnie shrieked as she and Mickey fell into the water.

Donald Duck came up in his speedboat and helped Mickey and Minnie into his boat. "Why don't you ride with me?" he suggested.

Relieved, Mickey and Minnie sat back and started to relax. But moments later, the boat's engine suddenly stopped.

"What do we do now?" Minnie asked.

"I have an idea," Donald said. He took off his hat and started to paddle with it. Mickey and Minnie did the same. Huffing and puffing, they made their way back to shore.

"How about lunch while we dry off?" Mickey said. So they ate hot dogs in the sun.

As they were enjoying their lunch, Pluto came running by. When he saw the hot dogs, he decided he wanted one, too. He jumped into Mickey's lap and tried to grab the food.

"No, boy!" cried Mickey.

But it was too late. Pluto knocked Mickey and Minnie into the water again!

Mickey and Minnie swam to shore and climbed out of the lake. Coughing and spluttering and really fed up, they settled on the grass to dry off yet again.

Not long after, Huey, Dewey and Louie came by in their sailing boat.

"Would you like to borrow our boat?" called Dewey. "There's a good wind today."

"Yes, please!" said Mickey. He and Minnie hopped into the boys' sailing boat and took off.

"Aah, this is the life," Mickey said.

Just then, the wind stopped blowing.

"Oh, no!" Mickey groaned. "Not again!"

Mickey and Minnie tried to paddle with their hands, but it was no use. The boat just kept going round in circles. As they huffed and puffed, Mickey saw Goofy and Donald coming towards them in rowing boats.

"We thought you might need some help," said Donald.

As Donald and Goofy towed the sailing boat, Mickey and Minnie sat back and relaxed. They had finally got their nice, easy boat ride!

MULAN

Looks Can Be Deceiving

Yao, Ling and Chien-Po missed Mulan. They had become friends in the army – even though, when they had first met her, Mulan was disguised as a young man. They forgave her for tricking them, because Mulan went on to bravely save China from Shan-Yu and the rest of the Huns. Mulan was famous; even the Emperor himself had bowed to her!

Now, her three friends decided they would go to her village and follow Mulan in whatever adventure she might embark on next.

"But what if Shan-Yu is seeking revenge?" Ling said. "He might be looking for us. After all, we did help Mulan defeat him."

Yao thought they should disguise themselves. So the friends donned kimonos, wigs and makeup, and set out for Mulan's village, looking like a trio of women.

When they arrived, the Matchmaker instantly approached them. "And who would you lovely ladies be?" she asked. The Matchmaker was desperate. There weren't many single women in the village, and she had a list of bachelors a mile long to marry off!

"Visitors from far away," said Chien-Po, speaking in a high voice.

"And are you unmarried ladies?" the Matchmaker asked.

Ling said, "We're unmarried, all right!"

"Well, let me be the first to welcome you to our village," the Matchmaker said, ushering them into her house. "Would you like some tea?"

The three men were hungry and thirsty after their long journey. They didn't realize the Matchmaker wanted to see if they would make suitable wives.

"Perhaps you would like to pour?" she asked Yao. He tried to remember the way his mother served tea at home. Yao set out the cups and poured as daintily as he could.

"Cookie?" the pleased Matchmaker asked Chien-Po, holding out a plate.

Chien-Po resisted the urge to grab a fistful of cookies. Instead, he chose one, stuck out his little finger and took small bites.

Perfect! The Matchmaker was delighted.

Next she asked Ling what his favourite pastime was. "Wrestling," he answered.

Then, seeing the shocked look on the Matchmaker's face, he added quickly, "Yes, I find that *resting* keeps my complexion lovely." He batted his eyelashes.

The Matchmaker led the three back outside, just as Mulan was riding into the village. "Stop! You can't marry them off!" Mulan cried, seeing her friends with the woman.

"I certainly can," said the Matchmaker. "Unlike you, Mulan, these three are real ladies!"

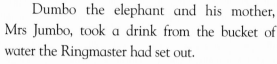

Lend Me Your Ears

"I think I can, I think I can, I think I can," chugged Casey Jr, the circus train. The train moved slowly around a bend. "I think I can. I think I ... *Ah-choo*!" he sneezed.

Suddenly, he came to a halt. "I know I can't," he admitted finally. The animals and the performers poked their heads out, wondering what was wrong.

"Well?" asked the Ringmaster.

"Casey Jr here has a cold," the engineer replied. "He's going to need some rest before he can take us any further."

The Ringmaster frowned. "But we're due at the fairground in a few hours. What will we do? After all, the show must go on!"

The engineer just shrugged and turned his attention back to the sneezing, coughing and spluttering little engine.

The Ringmaster went down the train, swinging open the doors to all the cages and cars. "Come on, everyone," he said. "Might as well stretch your legs."

The animals lumbered, scampered and pranced onto the wide open field. Next, the clowns and acrobats and animal trainers sauntered out. Some set up crates in the grass and played cards, others rehearsed and a few pulled out packed lunches and sprawled on the ground.

Dumbo the elephant and his mother, Mrs Jumbo, took a drink from the bucket of water the Ringmaster had set out.

Mrs Jumbo gazed around. "Looks like we're in the middle of nowhere," she said. "I do hope poor Casey Jr is feeling better soon."

"Me too," Dumbo's friend Timothy Q. Mouse said hopefully.

Just then there was a clap of thunder. Rain began to fall from the sky. The animals and performers ran for the shelter of the circus wagons. Dumbo held on to his mother's tail, but just then, the wind picked up. The gust caught Dumbo's huge ears and sent him flying backwards.

"That's it!" yelled the Ringmaster over the howling wind. "Dumbo, come with me!" He led Dumbo over to the train, climbed onto the front wagon, and motioned for the little elephant to join him.

"Now spread out those great ears of yours!" the Ringmaster said. Dumbo's ears billowed out, catching the wind like giant sails and pushing Casey Jr along the tracks. "The show will go on!" the Ringmaster shouted happily.

"I know I can. I know I can. I know I can," chanted Casey Jr. And then he added, "Thanks to Dumbo!"

Disney · PIXAR

FINDING NEMO

Nemo's Best Shot

"Come on, Dad! We're going to be late!" cried Nemo. Nemo and Marlin were hurrying through the busy swimming lanes of the colourful Great Barrier Reef.

"Are you sure you want to play pearl volleyball?" Marlin asked nervously. "There are lots of other things you can do. Sponge jumping, for example. Or maybe reef dancing."

"Reef dancing!" cried Nemo, horrified. "No way! That's for babies! I want to play pearl volleyball!"

At Sea Urchin Stadium, Mr Ray made the opening announcements. "Hello and welcome, everyone! Before we get started, let's give a big thank you to Ms Esther Clam for donating today's ball."

Everyone applauded as Esther opened her shell and spat out the pearl.

"Let's play pearl volleyball!" cried Mr Ray.

"Good luck, son," said Marlin. "Just remember what I told you – "

"I know! I know!" said Nemo, rolling his eyes. "When you give it your best shot, even if you lose, you win."

The players lined up on either side of the sea fan net. Ray's Raiders were on one side, and Nemo's team, the Fighting Planktons, were on the other.

Marlin watched anxiously. He was sure that Nemo wouldn't be able to play as well as the other fish because of his small fin. And Marlin wasn't the only one who had doubts.

Turbot Trout came up to Nemo on the court.

"Coach may be letting you play today," Turbot snapped, "but you better not mess up the Planktons' winning streak."

Turbot didn't know Nemo had spent hours smacking around pebbles in a dentist's fishtank.

"Just watch and learn," murmured Nemo.

Suddenly, the pearl came right to Nemo. *Smack*! Using his good left fin, Nemo sent the pearl flying right over the net. The pearl flew so fast, the other team couldn't return it. Nemo scored his first point for the Planktons!

Nemo played like a pro. He scored again with his good fin, then with his tail. And, just to show his father and Turbot Trout, he scored the winning point with his little fin.

"Go, short fin!" cried Turbot Trout. "With a player like you, we're going to go all the way to the Lobster Bowl Clam-pionship!"

"Wow, Nemo," said Marlin after the game. "That was amazing."

"Thanks, Dad," said Nemo. "I gave it my best shot, like you said. And we actually won too!"

Disney
THE
LION KING

The Hic-hic-hiccups

"What a day!" Pumbaa said as he led Simba and Timon through the forest.

"What a day, indeed," Timon agreed.

"Hic!" said Simba.

"What was that?" Timon cried.

"Don't be scared. It's just that I have the – *hic*! I have the hiccups," Simba explained.

"I'll tell you what to do," Timon said. "Forget about it! They'll go away – eventually."

"Forget about it? *Hic*! But I can't roar," Simba explained. And to demonstrate, he opened his mouth really wide. But, just as he was about to roar, he hiccupped!

"See?" he said sadly.

"Have you tried licking tree bark?" Pumbaa asked.

"Licking tree bark?" said Simba.

"It always works for me," Pumbaa explained. "That or closing your eyes, holding your nose and jumping on one foot while saying your name five times fast – backwards."

Timon watched Simba hop around on one foot, holding his nose with his eyes closed. "Abmis, Abmis, Abmis – *hic*! It's not working!" Simba cried.

"Maybe there's something caught in his throat," Timon offered.

"There's nothing caught in his throat," Pumbaa said.

"How do you know?" Timon asked.

"I just know about these things," Pumbaa answered.

Suddenly, right on cue, Simba interrupted their argument with the biggest hiccup of all.

"HIC!"

And, wouldn't you know, just then the biggest fly you've ever seen came soaring out of Simba's mouth. It flew right into a tree and crashed to the ground.

The fly stood up groggily and shook itself off.

"It's about time, buddy!" the fly said to Simba.

Simba was about to reply, but he was interrupted by two voices, shouting in unison –

"DINNER!"

The fly gave a frightened squeak and flew off, as Timon and Pumbaa both pounced on the spot where it had been just a moment earlier.

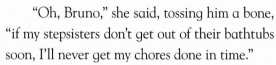

Cinderella

Lucifer's Bath

Cinderella's stepsisters didn't like the idea of Cinderella going to the Prince's ball.

"But Stepmother told me I could," said Cinderella.

"*Only* if you finish your chores," pointed out Drizella. "Which includes giving our cat, Lucifer, his bath."

"And that reminds me," said Anastasia. "I'll be needing a bath myself."

"Me, too," said Drizella.

"You heard my girls, Cinderella," her stepmother said. "Get their baths ready at once!"

Cinderella already had far too many jobs to do. But she didn't argue.

Once Anastasia and Drizella were soaking in their bubble baths, all Cinderella had to do was mend their clothes, clean the house, wash the curtains and give Lucifer his bath – then she could get ready for the ball.

Unfortunately, her stepsisters wouldn't leave her alone.

"Cinderella! Bring my face cream!" cried Drizella.

"Cinderella! My bath salts!" cried Anastasia.

Each time her stepsisters called, Cinderella had to stop whatever she was doing and take care of them.

When Drizella called for tea, Cinderella went down to the kitchen and put the kettle on. Then she let Bruno the dog in for a snack.

"Oh, Bruno," she said, tossing him a bone, "if my stepsisters don't get out of their bathtubs soon, I'll never get my chores done in time."

Bruno narrowed his eyes. Those stepsisters were the most selfish, lazy, nasty girls he'd ever known – and their cat was just like them. He wanted to help Cinderella. So, when the tea was ready, Bruno followed her up the stairs and down the long hallway.

Just as Cinderella walked up to Drizella's bathroom door, Bruno saw Lucifer sleeping nearby.

"Woof, woof!" Bruno barked loudly. "Woof, woof!"

With a screeching yowl, Lucifer ran into Drizella's bathroom.

Splash! Bruno chased the cat right into Drizella's tub! Then Bruno jumped in himself!

Drizella screamed. Lucifer jumped out. And Bruno chased the cat down the hall and into Anastasia's bathroom.

Splash! Lucifer was now in Anastasia's tub. And Bruno jumped right in after him!

"Get out of your tubs this instant!" Cinderella's stepmother cried. "You don't want to smell like that dog, do you?"

Cinderella sighed in relief. Although she still had many jobs to finish before the ball, at least one job was now done. Thanks to Bruno, Lucifer had had his bath!

Winnie the Pooh

Tigger's Moving Day

After breakfast, Tigger likes to bounce. Sproing! Sproing! Sproing! He likes to bounce all day long, but he is always bumping into things. Thump!

"Tigger, you don't have enough bouncing room in this little house," said Rabbit. "We've got to find you a bigger house. That's all there is to it!"

By evening, everyone was excited about the big new house they had found.

"It IS a bouncy house," said Tigger. "The kind of house tiggers like best!" He bounced, and he didn't bump into anything. "But," he said, sighing, "I won't live next door to little Roo anymore."

"I know you'll miss being neighbours with Kanga and Roo," said Christopher Robin, "but now you'll live much closer to me. We can have fun being neighbours."

Kanga told Tigger she would bring Roo to visit. Tigger felt better and invited everyone to stay awhile. Rabbit put his paws on his hips. "We aren't finished yet. We need to move all your things from your old house to this house," he explained. Rabbit told everyone to bring all the boxes they could find to Tigger's house. Then he told Eeyore to get his donkey cart.

"Wow! Boxes are fun!" cried Roo as he and Tigger bounced in and out of the boxes everyone brought.

"There'll be time for fun later," grumbled Rabbit.

Tigger packed all his games and his stuffed animals in a box. He took his favourite lion out and hugged him. Rabbit packed Tigger's dishes. Kanga packed Tigger's hats and scarves. Pooh and Piglet packed Tigger's food. Soon Eeyore arrived with his donkey cart. Christopher Robin and Owl hoisted Tigger's bed and table and chairs onto the cart.

"Now my new home will be perfect," Tigger said, as they unloaded the cart and carried everything inside. "Thanks for your help, everyone!"

After his friends had gone, Tigger put all his things just where he wanted them. When he was finished, he sat down to rest. Hmmm. Seems like an awfully quiet house, he thought. He tried out a few bounces, but decided he wasn't in such a bouncy mood, after all. But just then, Tigger heard a little voice.

"Hallooo!"

"Roo!" cried Tigger. "Kanga! Come on in!"

"Hallooo!" Tigger soon heard all his friends calling outside his new door. Everyone had brought housewarming presents!

"Our work's all done," said Rabbit. "Now it's time for fun!"

Together is Better

The Beast paced up and down his castle's long hallway. *Click, click, click* went his claws against the marble floor.

"It's been hours," he grumbled. "What do you suppose she's doing in there?" the Beast asked Lumiere.

"Reading," Lumiere replied. "After all, *monsieur*, it *is* the library."

"I know it's the library!" bellowed the Beast. "I know my own castle!"

Suddenly, the library doors burst open. Belle stormed out. She looked around the hallway.

"What is going on?" she asked. "There's a terrible ruckus out here."

"It's the servants," complained the Beast. "They make too much noise."

"Don't blame them," said Belle. "*You're* the one who's been clicking your claws for hours."

"I have not," said the Beast, embarrassed.

"You have so!" insisted Belle. "It's been driving me crazy!"

"You were hearing things," said the Beast.

"And then you started bellowing," said Belle.

"So what if I was?" roared the Beast. "It's my castle!"

Suddenly, Mrs Potts rolled up on a serving cart. "Anyone care for tea?" she asked.

"Not me," huffed Belle.

"Me, neither," huffed the Beast.

"Oh, come now. Just a spot?" asked Mrs Potts, pouring two cups anyway. Humming merrily, she rolled her cart into the library.

Belle and the Beast followed her in and sat down.

"So why were you so angry?" asked Belle, sipping her tea.

"I was bored," said the Beast. "I guess I ... missed you."

"Why didn't you just say so?" Belle wondered.

"Because ... I didn't think you missed me," said the Beast.

"I've been reading," said Belle. "I just love to read."

"I know," said the Beast.

Belle thought for a moment. "I have an idea," she said. "How about we read together?"

Belle picked out a book about a princess and a dragon. First Belle read aloud to the Beast. And then the Beast read aloud to Belle.

"That was fun," said the Beast.

"Yes," said Belle. "Let's do it again tomorrow night."

"Tomorrow," he said, "and every night after."

In the hallway, Lumiere sighed with relief.

"Maybe now we'll get some peace!" he said to himself.

The Missing Vegetables

Of all the things Belle loved about the Beast's castle, the thing she loved the best was the garden at the back. She had read every one of the Beast's books about gardening, and every season she experimented with something new. This summer, she'd decided to try growing vegetables. And now they were ready to be picked.

"Don't tell the Beast," she whispered to Mrs Potts, "but today for lunch I'm going to make him a salad."

"Oh, really," said Mrs Potts.

"Mmm-hmm." Belle nodded proudly. "Yesterday, I saw so many things ready to be harvested. Lettuce, carrots, cucumbers, peas ... even tomatoes! Can you believe it? The Beast is going to be so surprised!"

"Indeed," Mrs Potts smiled. "Lunch is definitely going to be a surprise."

Belle slipped on her gardening gloves and her sun hat, grabbed her biggest basket and happily skipped out into the garden.

"First," she said out loud, to no one in particular, "let's get some lettuce!"

But, when she bent down where the lettuce should have been, she found a bed of empty soil.

"My lettuce!" she cried. "Where did it go?"

Rabbits? Deer? Bewildered, Belle moved on to where her tender, sweet, young carrots had been growing.

"Oh, dear!" she cried. "There's nothing here now either!"

There wasn't a single pea to be found. "I don't understand," she said.

But facts were facts. The garden was empty and there was nothing she could do ... but go back to the castle and look for a book about building fences for next summer's garden!

As she walked back inside, empty-handed and disappointed, Belle passed Mrs Potts and Chip.

"What's the matter?" asked Mrs Potts.

"Oh, everything!" Belle sighed. "My whole garden has been robbed." Then she shrugged. "So much for my salad idea."

"Don't feel sad, Belle," Chip said. "Come and have some lunch."

"I'm not hungry," Belle replied, smiling sadly.

"Oh, I don't know," said Mrs Potts, steering her into the dining room. "You might be ..."

"SURPRISE!" called the Beast.

"What?" Belle gasped. There, laid out upon the table, was what looked like every possible vegetable from her garden, washed and sliced and arranged, just so, on fancy dishes.

"You've worked so hard in the garden," the Beast explained, "I thought it would be nice if I did something for you. I hope you like it."

Belle smiled. What a treat!

Winnie
the
Pooh

Eeyore Beats the Heat

One day, when it seemed the sun was shining even more sunnily than ever over the Hundred-Acre Wood, Eeyore sighed and wished that autumn – if it wouldn't be too much trouble – would hurry itself up and get there.

"Something the matter, Eeyore?" asked Roo.

"Oh, it's just that it's so terribly hot," replied Eeyore. "If I weren't stuffed with sawdust, I think I would melt."

"Well, come with me!" squeaked Roo. "I'm going to the swimming hole to cool off."

But Eeyore shook his head. "Can't do, Roo," he said. "Not with my sawdust and all ... I'd probably just sink. And that's if I'm lucky."

And so Roo, who felt sorry for Eeyore, but who was also eager to swim, continued on his way.

Soon, another friend came along. And this friend was Winnie the Pooh.

"You're looking a little warmish, Eeyore," Pooh said.

"Same to you," said Eeyore with a sigh. "Same to you."

"Ah," said Pooh, "but I am off to catch a breeze – and pay a call on some bees – with my trusty balloon here. Care to join me?"

"No, thanks, Pooh," said Eeyore. "I never did like feeling like the ground was missing. And ... I expect that with my luck, the balloon would probably pop."

"Well, Eeyore, I understand completely. Wish me luck, then, won't you?" Pooh replied.

"Good luck, Pooh," said Eeyore. "As if anything I ever wish comes true...."

The next friend to come upon Eeyore was little Piglet.

"Hello, there, Eeyore," said Piglet. "Whoo! Are you as uncomfortably hot as I am?"

"Oh, no," said Eeyore. "I'm sweltering. Parched. Smouldering. Torrid. Yes – 'uncomfortably hot' would be an understatement."

"Poor Eeyore," said Piglet. "Why don't you come play in the cool mud with me?"

But once again, Eeyore shook his head. "Afraid mud is not an option, Piglet," he said. "Once I get dirty, I'll never get clean. No. Go enjoy yourself on this hot day like everyone else. All except me. As usual. I'll just suffer."

And suffer poor Eeyore did ... until not too terribly much later when his friends all returned with something sure to cool even Eeyore off on this sultry day.

"Guess what we've brought you, Eeyore!" Roo squealed with delight.

"It's ice cream," whispered Pooh.

"Ice cream, huh?" Eeyore sighed. "I suppose I'll have to eat it all before it melts."

And do you know what? He did!

Disney PRINCESS

BRAVE
The Missing Gem

"**O**ch!" Merida complained. "I spent all month working on a brooch for Mum's birthday tomorrow but it's still not right!"

Maudie clucked in sympathy, but as cook and nursemaid at Castle DunBroch, she was more worried about her muffins.

"Mm! Who are those for?" asked Merida.

"For the DunBroch Brownie, the wee elf that lives outside the gate," Maudie replied.

"Have you ever seen him?" quizzed Merida.

"Brownies don't like to be seen by humans," explained Maudie. "But every day I leave him muffins, milk – and thistles for good luck. If the Brownie isn't happy, who knows what mischief he could make? Especially with the Queen's birthday tomorrow."

Merida sighed again, thinking about the brooch. It had started as a good idea. She had chosen a beautiful smoky quartz, her mother's favourite gem, but she couldn't get the setting right.

Merida went to take another look at the gem ... but it was gone!

Then Merida saw her mischievous little brothers with a glint in their eyes.

"What did you do this time?" Merida asked them.

She quickly found out what had happened. Her brothers had 'borrowed' the brooch because it had looked so royal on their capes, but they had dropped it somewhere when they were playing.

Merida looked more closely at Hubert's shirt. "Is this a thistle?" she asked. Then she looked at the others. "Are those crumbs on your shoes, and milk on your face?"

Suddenly, Merida knew where the triplets had been playing that morning. She led the boys to the large flat rock under the bridge.

"Just as I thought," Merida said. "You ate Maudie's treats for the DunBroch Brownie!"

They looked all around the clearing ... but they couldn't find the brooch. "What if the Brownie took it because you ate his treats?" said Merida. "Maudie said he makes mischief if he isn't taken care of."

They ran to get more muffins, more milk and more thistles and set up the tray again.

They waited but nothing happened.

Then Merida remembered that Brownies don't like humans to see them. So they closed their eyes and Merida whispered into the air, "We're sorry," she said, "but we've tried to fix everything. Could you help us in return?"

There was silence.

But when they finally opened their eyes, Harris spotted something shiny in the crook of a tree. It was the brooch! Had it been there the whole time?

When Merida examined it she saw that the gem was now set in a beautiful silver thistle! The Queen was delighted and Merida knew that everything was set right. In fact, everything was perfect.

Lady *and the* TRAMP

Trusting Trusty

"Tramp!" cried Lady one morning. "One of our puppies is missing!"

"Don't worry," said Tramp with a yawn. "Scamp is always getting into mischief."

"It's not Scamp," said Lady. "It's little Fluffy! She never gets into trouble. Tramp, what should we do?"

"You look inside. I'll look outside," said Tramp worriedly. He searched their back garden. Then he went to the next garden, and the next.

From a neighbour's porch, Trusty the bloodhound called, "Howdy! Whatcha looking for?"

"My daughter, Fluffy! She's missing," said Tramp.

Trusty's long floppy ears pricked up. "A missing puppy – now that's serious! And I should know. I used to help my grandpa track down missing persons through the swamps!"

"I know," said Tramp. He'd heard Trusty tell that story 100 times.

"Have you found a trail yet?" asked Trusty.

Tramp shook his head.

"Well, let me at it!" Trusty loped back to Tramp's garden. He put his big nose to the ground. *Sniff, sniff, sniff....*

"Tramp, have you found Fluffy?" Lady called from the dog door.

Tramp ran over. "No," he replied. "But Trusty offered his ... uh ... services."

"He can't smell any more," Lady whispered. "I know he tracked that dogcatcher's wagon and saved you – but he hasn't tracked anything since."

"He helped us once," said Tramp. "I think we should trust him again."

Just then, Trusty shouted, "Look at this!"

He had spotted a bluebird's feather below a window. "That's the window the puppies look out," said Lady.

"Look! A bit of puppy fur," said Trusty. "And footprints!" Trusty followed the trail of footprints to the back of a shed.

And that's where Trusty found the missing puppy! Fluffy was fast asleep under a big tree.

"Fluffy! What happened?" Lady cried.

"I woke up and saw a bluebird," said Fluffy with a yawn. "And I didn't want Scamp to bark and scare it away, like he always does. So I didn't wake anyone. I followed the bird all the way to this tree. Then I guess I got sleepy."

Lady walked over and gave Trusty a kiss.

"Thank you," she told the bloodhound.

"Aw, shucks," said Trusty, blushing. "It weren't nothin'."

As the bloodhound trotted home, Tramp turned to Lady. "See that," he said with a grin, "I told you we should trust Trusty!"

Tangled
The Horse Charmer

Flynn and Rapunzel were camping in the woods. The royal guards were hot on the thief's heels, but he was escorting the young girl to the town all the same. To begin with, he had just wanted to get back the crown that she had taken from him. Now he genuinely wanted to help her make her dream come true: to see the floating lanterns being launched.

"Good night blondie!" he said, lying down by the fire.

"Good night Eugene!" Rapunzel said, using his real name.

They soon fell peacefully asleep. But at dawn Flynn awoke with a start, feeling what he thought was rain. *Plip*! A drop of water splashed on his forehead. *Plop*! Another fell on his cheek.

The thief opened his eyes ... and found himself face to face with Maximus, the captain of the guard's horse! Maximus was soaking wet because he had just come out of the flooded tunnel where he had been chasing Flynn the evening before.

"Well I never! The proud steed of the head guard!" said Flynn mockingly. "I hope you've come to apologize for your shocking behaviour yesterday!"

But of course, Maximus had really come to arrest him and Flynn was well aware of it!

The two enemies immediately started fighting. The noise of their struggle soon woke Rapunzel from her sleep and, seeing Maximus dragging Flynn towards the path, she leapt to her friend's aid. The horse was holding Flynn by the foot. Rapunzel took hold of Flynn's arm and, stuck in the middle, Flynn had the feeling that he would end up being torn in half!

Then, *pop*! Maximus accidentally pulled off Flynn's boot. The thief was free and quickly ran off. Maximus rushed after him, but Rapunzel stood on the path and blocked his way. "There now. Calm down, my beauty. Nice horse! Sit!" she said.

Maximus was enchanted by the pretty young girl and, as Flynn looked on, the horse began to obey her like a well-behaved dog!

"There, there!" Rapunzel continued. "You've had enough of running after this naughty Eugene, haven't you? You're a good horse. You know, it's my birthday today. It would make me really happy if you'd leave Eugene in peace until tomorrow. What do you say?"

Maximus stretched out his hoof as a gesture of peace. The thief agreed to shake his hoof, wide-eyed in disbelief – he had heard stories about snake charmers, but never about a horse charmer!

A New Reindeer Friend

Anna and Elsa were preparing for the kingdom's first ball since Elsa's powers had been revealed. The people of Arendelle had accepted Elsa – and her magic – and the sisters wanted to thank them.

"There you are, Elsa!" Anna cried. "I haven't seen you all week!"

"Do you like the decorations?" Elsa said. "This ball must be perfect!"

"Oh," said Anna. "Just having a ball is special!"

Gerda, the kindly servant, looked around. "Crocuses would be nice for the centrepieces," she said.

"True. Let's gather them ourselves, Elsa," said Anna. "Then we can spend time together."

Olaf waved as the sisters ran outside. "Hi! Where are you going?"

"To look for crocuses!" called Anna.

"Ooh! I love crocuses!" Olaf cried.

So, they hiked into the mountains together.

"Maybe our party should be a fancy-dress ball?" Anna suggested, spotting Wandering Oaken's Trading Post and Sauna. She ran inside, pulling Elsa behind her.

"Hello! Do you have anything special for a ball?" asked Anna.

"Half-price snowshoes! Or karts for sliding down mountains!" Oaken exclaimed.

Minutes later, the girls were back outside and Anna was dragging a sledge full of shopping. "We already did the winter in summer thing," Elsa said, looking at her sister.

Anna grinned. "But how could I say no?"

They set out again and finally they found the crocuses. As the girls collected flowers, Olaf suddenly cried, "Look at that!" A young reindeer was trapped on a ledge below.

"How did you get there?" Anna asked, peering over the cliff edge. "And how will we get you back up?"

Elsa created an ice ramp but it was too slippery for the reindeer to climb out!

"Now what?" asked Elsa.

"I know!" said Anna. She grabbed her shopping, jumped on to the ramp and slid down.

Anna fitted the snowshoes on the reindeer, before tying a rope round him. Throwing the rope to Elsa, Anna shouted, "Pull!"

Soon, everyone was safe at the top!

"Can we invite the reindeer to the ball?" asked Olaf.

"The ball!" Anna and Elsa shouted, climbing into the kart. Elsa created snow slides to help them speed down the mountain.

When the group arrived at the palace, they slid through the halls and landed in the ballroom. Crocuses rained down on the guests, who were delighted at the grand entrance.

"Nobody has ever seen a ball like this!" said Anna. "And best of all, we're together!"

THE LITTLE
MERMAID

A Working Holiday

Sebastian the crab loved his busy job as court composer to King Triton. He wrote songs, ran rehearsals, consulted with the King – and he even watched out for Ariel to make sure she stayed out of trouble.

One day, King Triton burst into the rehearsal hall and announced, "Sebastian! You need a vacation! I want you to relax and forget about work for a few days. And that's an order."

"Yes, sire," said Sebastian without any enthusiasm. Sebastian wasn't very good at relaxing.

After Sebastian had gone, King Triton assembled his daughters and the court musicians. "Sebastian has been my court composer for many years," he announced, "and I've been wanting to honour him with a grand concert. Now that he's away, we can finally prepare a wonderful surprise for him." Triton smiled. "I can't wait to see the look on Sebastian's face when the big night arrives!"

Meanwhile, Sebastian was at the Coral Reef Resort. "Well, here I am at the most beautiful spot in the sea," he said to himself. "But I am bored out of my mind!"

When he couldn't sit still any longer, Sebastian decided that he would sneak back to the palace for a few minutes just to see how everything was going. He wandered into the concert hall, where he found the orchestra and Triton's daughters about to rehearse. "Sebastian!" cried Ariel. "What are you doing here?"

"Oh, nothing," he said. "I forgot my conducting baton. I never go on a vacation without it." He looked at Ariel. "And what are *you* doing here?"

Thinking quickly, Ariel told Sebastian that they were preparing a last-minute concert for her father. It was all Sebastian had to hear! He immediately set to work rehearsing the musicians.

He worked harder than he had in weeks. And he loved every minute of it.

After the three days were up, Sebastian made a big show of returning to the palace. "I feel so refreshed!" he announced to the King. "Thank you, sire, that was just what I needed."

"That's grand, Sebastian!" replied the King. "Now follow me."

Triton led Sebastian to the concert hall, where the King gave a glowing speech about the crab's many contributions throughout the years. Then the elaborate programme of music began. The orchestra played beautifully, Ariel and her sisters sang exquisitely, and the King beamed proudly.

"What do you think?" Triton asked.

"It's perfect!" said Sebastian. "I couldn't have done a better job myself!"

Zarina Returns

A year had passed in Pixie Hollow without a word from Zarina. She had left after her experiment with Blue Pixie Dust had destroyed the Dust Depot and Fairy Gary had told her she could no longer be a dust-keeper fairy.

It was the day of the annual Four Seasons Festival and the stadium was filled with an excited crowd – including Clank and Bobble. Every fairy talent from every season would be on display!

Tink was hard at work backstage, fiddling with the latch on an elaborate music box. She and her friends would be performing in the grand finale.

"It's starting!" cried Clank as the lights went down. He thought he'd better nip to the little boys' room – and quickly!

Everyone was enchanted as the winter fairies gave a spectacular show on the ice.

"That's my sister!" said Tink proudly as Periwinkle skated by, frosting flowers in front of the crowd. But while everyone was watching the show, Zarina emerged from the shadows and sprinkled pink dust behind the crowd. Soon poppies began to sprout around the stadium.

"Wait, is that … Zarina?" Tink asked.

Garden-fairy Rosetta knew the pollen from the flowers would put everyone to sleep.

"Guys! We gotta hide! Now!" Rosetta cried, leading her friends into Tink's music box.

When Clank returned to the stadium, he was shocked to find that every last spectator – including Bobble – was asleep. Then he heard cries for help from backstage – it was the fairies in the music box!

After Clank had freed them, the fairies looked out at the snoozing audience. "Why would Zarina do this?" asked Vidia.

"Clank, did you see her?" asked Tinker Bell.

Clank told Tink that he had seen Zarina flying towards the Dust Depot.

The fairies made a beeline for the Depot, but they were too late! The Blue Pixie Dust was gone!

The girls knew they had to find Zarina and get back the Blue Dust. Their supply of golden pixie dust, and the well-being of all of Pixie Hollow, depended on it.

"Clank, stay here and watch over everyone," said Tinker Bell, "especially the winter fairies. Make sure they get a steady stream of snow."

Clank promised he would take care of everything. Tinker Bell and her friends took as much golden pixie dust as they dared, before zooming off in search of Zarina and the Blue Pixie Dust.

Switching Talents

Tinker Bell and her friends from Pixie Hollow had almost caught up with Zarina and the stolen Blue Dust. "There!" Iridessa cried, spotting a blue glow up ahead. It had to be Zarina!

As the girls struggled to reach Zarina, a heavy fog rolled in from the sea. The fairies flew higher and spotted a pirate ship in the distance. "The pirates must have captured her and forced her to take the dust," said Tink.

Sure enough, a small rowing boat carrying three pirates was making its way towards the ship. The girls flew down to the boat and peered into a knothole. Tink saw a blue glow coming from the keel!

Inside the boat, Zarina was holding up the Blue Pixie Dust triumphantly. "Let me just say your plan worked perfectly ... Captain," said James, the cabin boy.

The other pirates, Port and Starboard, bowed to their tiny leader. The fairies couldn't believe it – Zarina was now a pirate!

"Let's just get the dust and get out of here," ordered Tink. The fairies sprang into action. Rosetta grew seaweed that grabbed the oars and held them in place, Iridessa reflected a moonbeam into James's eyes and Silvermist rocked the boat with a wave. James was tossed off his feet and his arm pinned Zarina against the side of the boat. Vidia snatched the Blue Dust from Zarina and threw it to Tink.

The fairies headed for the shore, but Zarina soon caught up with them and demanded that they return the dust. She promised to show the fairies mercy if they did as she asked.

Tink refused. "This dust belongs to Pixie Hollow," she said.

Zarina responded by hurling a fistful of multi-coloured pixie dust at her former friends. The strange dust knocked the fairies out, allowing Zarina to grab the Blue Dust and escape.

When Tink and the others woke up they soon discovered that the colourful dust had switched their outfits and their talents! Tink was now a water fairy! She tried to part a nearby waterfall, but Silvermist – now a fast-flying fairy – accidentally hit her as she passed by, causing the water to push the fairies down a long, winding leaf. The friends ended up on a beach, where Rosetta landed on a crocodile egg! The baby croc hatched and hugged an alarmed Rosetta tightly.

"It's okay!" Fawn reassured her. "They imprint on the first thing they see."

The croc thought Rosetta was its mother. She had changed from a garden fairy into an animal fairy!

The Good Old Summertime

The Seven Dwarfs were on their way back home after a long day at the diamond mine. Each swung a shovel in one hand and a bucket in the other.

As they marched through the forest, Happy enjoyed the sounds of the birds singing and the warmth of the summer sun on his face. "Summer is such a wonderful time of year!" he exclaimed.

"Oh, yeah?" snapped Grumpy. "What's so wonderful about it?"

"Well ... the days are longer," said Happy.

"The days are hotter," complained Grumpy.

Doc spoke up. "I like the summertime too. It's a very healthy season."

"Healthy?" said Grumpy. "This heat?"

"Look at all the fresh vegetables and fruit you can eat all summer long," said Doc.

"Like what?" asked Grumpy.

"Like peaches," Sleepy said with a yawn. "I like them with cream before I go to bed."

"And just look at the melons on those vines," said Doc. "They're as big as Dopey's head!"

Dopey grinned and nodded.

Grumpy rolled his eyes and said, "Dopey's a melon head, all right!"

"Don't be such a grump!" scolded Doc.

"Yes, cheer up! Summer's a great season," Happy said with a grin.

"It's too hot, I say," Grumpy insisted. "And all those blooming plants make Sneezy sneeze even more!"

"Yes," said Sneezy. "Sorry, but ... *Ah-choo*! I think Grumpy's right."

"No, he's not," said Happy. "Summer's the very best time of year."

"It's too hot, I say!" repeated Grumpy.

By this time, the Seven Dwarfs had reached a small bridge running over a brook.

"Well, if it's too hot for you, Grumpy, then I have a special warm-weather remedy," said Doc, stopping in the middle of the bridge.

"Yeah?" snapped Grumpy. "What is it?"

Doc motioned for the other Dwarfs to gather around him. They blocked Doc from Grumpy's view as he leaned over and filled his bucket with cool water from the stream.

"Well?" said Grumpy. "Are you going to give me your special remedy?"

"Of course," said Doc.

With a big "Heave-ho!" Doc dumped his bucket of water over Grumpy's head.

Splash!

"That should cool you off," said Happy.

Grumpy sputtered with surprise. But he had to admit, the soaking actually did cool him off!

Flower's Power

It was a warm summer afternoon in the forest, and a shy little skunk named Flower was playing a game of hide-and-seek, searching for his friend Thumper. He had been looking for quite a while.

"Come out, come out, wherever you are!" Flower called. "I give up."

"*Surprise!*" shouted Thumper, bursting out of a thicket. "Here I am! *Ugh!*" Thumper wrinkled his nose. "What's that *smell?*"

Flower blushed bright pink. "Sorry," he said miserably. "I sprayed. It happens when I get scared."

"*Whew!*" Thumper waved his paw in front of his face. "You should warn us before you let out that kind of stink!"

"Well *you* should warn *me* before you jump out like that," Flower said. "Anyway, it'll go away ... in a day or two."

But a day or two was too long for his friends to wait. The smell was just too strong!

"Sorry," Bambi told Flower. "I, uh, think my mother's calling me," he said.

"Me, uh, too," Faline gasped. "See you later, Flower ... in a day or two."

"Or three!" Thumper added, giggling.

And the next thing he knew, Flower was all alone.

Poor Flower. If only he weren't a skunk, he thought. If only he didn't *stink* so much

whenever he got scared. What was the point? It only drove his friends away. But now it seemed he couldn't even play hide-and-seek!

No matter what his mother and father said, being a skunk stunk!

And that's why Flower wouldn't have been very surprised if, two days later, his friends had still stayed away. But, to his bashful pleasure, there, bright and early, were Bambi and Faline – with Thumper hopping close behind.

"Want to play?" Bambi asked Flower cheerfully.

"Anything but hide-and-seek!" said Flower.

"How about tag?" said Thumper. "Ready or not, you're It!"

But before the game could begin, a soft *crunch, crunch* of leaves made the friends turn.

"Wha-wha-what's that?" Bambi said, staring straight into a hungry-looking, red face.

"That's a fox!" said Thumper.

"A fox?" shrieked Flower. "Oh no!" He spun around and lifted his tail and buried his head in fear ... and the next thing the friends knew, the hungry fox was running away, whimpering and rubbing his nose.

"Sorry," Flower sighed, blushing.

"Don't be!" said Bambi and Thumper.

And do you know what? Flower wasn't!

Patch's Plan

"Whoa!" Patch said. "Look at all these other puppies!"

His brothers and sisters were still whimpering with fear. They had just been dognapped, and after a long, bumpy ride in a car, they had arrived at a big, draughty house. But Patch was already trying to work out a way to get back home. He looked around the large, shabby room. "Hey," he asked the closest stranger. "Where are we?"

The spotted puppy smiled at him. "Oh, you must be new!" he said. "Which pet shop did you come from?"

Patch scowled at the strange new puppy. "We're not from a pet shop – we were stolen from our house."

Several other puppies heard him and moved closer. "Stolen? Really?" they exclaimed.

The first puppy shrugged. "Well, bought or stolen, we're all stuck here now."

"Maybe *you're* stuck here," Patch said boldly. "Our parents and their human pets will be here soon to rescue us, just see if they don't!"

"I hope so," Patch's sister, Pepper, said. "I wonder why someone would want to steal us, anyway?"

Patch didn't know. But he was sure that their parents would find them soon. In the meantime, he wanted to make sure he and his siblings stayed well away from all the pet-shop puppies, so there wasn't any confusion.

"We don't know why there are so many of us," the strange puppy told Pepper. "I guess Cruella just really likes puppies."

Patch gasped aloud. "Cruella?" he cried. "Do you mean Cruella De Vil?"

His brothers and sisters shuddered. Their parents had told them scary stories about that nasty woman. Could it be true?

"Yes, she's the one who bought us," several of the other puppies spoke up, while others nodded their heads.

This changed everything! "We have to get away," Patch declared.

Rolly sighed. "We know," he said. "Mum and Dad will be here soon. I just hope we get home in time for breakfast...."

"No, you don't understand!" Patch shook his head. "Cruella is bad news – that's what Dad always says. We have to get away from her now – all of us!" He gestured to the entire group of puppies, bought and stolen. It didn't matter where they'd come from. What mattered was they were in this mess together. "We have to work as a team."

The first puppy smiled at him. "I'm with you!" he exclaimed. "When we're done with her, Cruella will be seeing spots!"

Disney · PIXAR
FINDING NEMO

First Day of School

It was the first day of a brand-new school year for Nemo and his friends.

"Hey, Tad! Hey, Pearl!" called Nemo as he swam into the playground. "Isn't it great to be back at school?"

"Well," said Tad, "I wouldn't go *that* far."

"What do you mean?" asked Nemo. "It's gonna be awesome! I heard this year we get to learn how to subtract and speak Prawn."

"Sure," said Tad, "but did you also hear who's gonna be teaching us all that?"

"No," said Nemo. "Who?"

Just then, up swam Sheldon, Jimmy and Jib.

"Hey, Sheldon," Tad called out. "Why don't you tell Nemo here about our new teacher, Mrs Lobster?"

"Mrs Lobster?" said Nemo.

"Yeah," said Sheldon. "Ooooh, they say she's the worst!"

"Who says she's the worst?" asked Nemo.

"Well, Sandy Plankton, for one. He says his cousin, Krill, had her last year – and that she was so mean, he'll never go to school again!"

"And you know what I heard from Sandy," said Tad. "I heard she has these great big claws, and that she uses them to grab students real hard when they give the wrong answer!"

"Oh!" said Pearl. "Don't say that. You're going to make me ink!"

"Yeah," said Nemo. "That sounds awful!"

"I know," said Jimmy. "Sandy says Mrs Lobster never goes on field trips like Mr Ray did. And she sends you home with tons of homework, and makes you stay after school if you forget to bring it in the next day!"

Oh, no! Nemo shuddered. All summer long he'd been looking forward to this day. And now school hadn't even started yet and already he wished it would end!

"Don't look now," Sheldon whispered, "but I think she's coming!"

"I'm gonna ink!" whimpered Pearl.

Nemo shut his eyes and wished with all his might for his dad to come and take him back home....

"Hello there," said a warm voice. "You must be my new pupils! I'm Mrs Lobster."

Huh? thought Nemo. Surely this wasn't the Mrs Lobster the kids had been talking about. And yet, when he opened his eyes, there she was, taking the register.

"Jib, Jimmy, Nemo, Pearl, Sheldon, Tad ... my, what a smart-looking class. I do hope you kids are ready to have fun."

Nemo sighed. That silly Sandy Plankton – they should know by now not to believe everything he said. Because Nemo was pretty sure: this was going to be a great year, after all!

Ask Nicely

"Steady, Samson," Prince Phillip said absentmindedly, tightening the horse's reins. "No need to hurry. We'll get there soon enough – and I need some time to think."

Phillip had a lot to think about. He was riding through the forest towards the castle of King Stefan and Queen Leah. Phillip's father, King Hubert, would be meeting him there. So would the girl Phillip was destined to marry ... Princess Aurora.

Phillip had heard her name since her birth 16 years earlier. Their parents had long planned their marriage. But Aurora had been cursed by the evil Maleficent at birth, and had been forced to go into hiding until her 16th birthday, when the curse would end.

That meant Phillip had never set eyes on his bride-to-be, nor spoken with her. He had always wondered what she might be like.

"I hope I like her," he murmured to his horse. Then another thought occurred to him. "I hope she likes me!" he added. "I'd better make sure I impress her." But how? he wondered.

"I know!" he exclaimed. "I'll make a dramatic entrance. We'll gallop in and slide to a stop right in front of her. That will impress her for sure!" He whistled and gave Samson a little kick. "Come on, Samson! We've got to practise."

The startled horse snorted and gave Phillip a dirty look. He planted his hooves and stood stock-still.

Phillip frowned impatiently. "Come on!" he urged his horse. "Go, Samson!"

But Samson refused to budge.

"It's like you don't even *want* to help me," he muttered. Suddenly, Phillip blinked. "Wait a minute," he said. "Why should you want to help me when all I do is yell at you?" He patted the horse's shoulder. "Sorry, old boy."

He reached into his pocket for a carrot. He fed it to the horse, still patting him.

Samson finished the carrot and snorted. Suddenly, he galloped forward, then leaped up and kicked out his heels. Phillip hung on tightly, gasping with surprise as the horse skidded to a halt.

Phillip laughed. "Wow!" he exclaimed. "Thanks, Samson. That was perfect – I guess all I had to do was ask you nicely! Now if we can just repeat that for the princess...."

Suddenly, he stopped short. He heard the faint sound of beautiful singing. He listened carefully. Who would be out in the forest singing like that?

"Come on, Samson," he said. "Let's go see – if you don't mind, of course!"

Disney
THE
PRINCESS
AND THE
FROG

True Love

Time was running out for Tiana and Naveen to return to the town. They had to find Charlotte and get her to kiss Naveen while she was still the Mardi Gras princess – and that was only until midnight. After that, her kiss wouldn't lift the evil spell, and Tiana and Naveen would be frogs forever!

"But surely we aren't going to swim across the bayou?" worried Tiana.

"I've got an idea!" declared their friend Louis, the alligator.

He led them to the steamer that was coming down river, taking costume-clad revellers to the New Orleans carnival. Tiana, Naveen, Louis and Ray the firefly climbed onboard. Luckily, a jazz band thought Louis was a trumpet player in disguise and invited him to play with them! The alligator's dream had come true at last!

Naveen sighed. He would like to have his dream come true too! And Mama Odie had helped Naveen realize something important. He had finally discovered what mattered more than anything else to him – Tiana.

"She is the love of my life, Ray!" he confided to his friend. "She's the one I want to marry, not Charlotte! I will ask her to marry me tonight!"

Of course, Naveen was giving up Charlotte's fortune, but with Tiana he would be rich in love!

"And then I will help Tiana to buy her restaurant anyway," he resolved as he prepared a candlelit dinner on the roof of the boat. "I will work hard, and I will earn all the money she needs."

Full of good intentions, he ran in search of Tiana.

"Oh, Naveen!" she enthused when she saw the pretty table. "What are we celebrating?"

"Errm ... our last hours as frogs!" he replied with embarrassment.

He was seeking the courage to make his declaration when Tiana cried, "We're arriving at the port, Naveen, and there's the building that I'm going to buy for my restaurant! Thanks to your marriage to Charlotte, I will be able to pay the estate agent! It's my last chance – if I don't settle the amount tomorrow, the sugar mill will go to the other buyer!"

On hearing these words, Naveen quickly changed his mind. He would rather sacrifice himself and marry Charlotte; otherwise Tiana would be so unhappy at losing her restaurant – her only dream.

I really love Tiana, he thought. *All I want is her happiness.*

Yes, he was sure now. She was definitely his true love!

Tangled
From Dream to Reality

Rapunzel had been locked away in a tower her entire life, but now her dream of seeing the floating lanterns up close was about to come true, with the help of a thief called Flynn.

When they finally reached the town, Rapunzel couldn't believe her eyes. There was a castle standing high above the kingdom, as if keeping watch over the people below – and what a lot of people there were!

One group of girls were amazed by Rapunzel's hair as she passed by. But people kept treading on it. "We can help you braid it!" the girls shouted.

Laughing, Rapunzel accepted their offer and was soon able to admire her new hairstyle: a magnificent braid studded with fresh flowers. And now no one could tread on it!

Being careful to stay hidden from the guards, Flynn went with Rapunzel to a stage, where an entertainer was inviting people to dance in honour of their lost princess. Rapunzel was enjoying herself so Flynn offered to show her around the town. He took her to the dressmaker where she tried on a wonderful dress. Then they treated themselves to some delicious cakes. At the bookshop, Rapunzel admired the hundreds of books. The day went happily by and, when evening fell, Flynn took Rapunzel on a boat trip.

"Where are we going?" she asked him.

"Out by the castle. We'll see the lanterns better from there. It's time for your dream to come true – soon we'll see the lanterns float up into the sky!"

Suddenly, the young girl seemed terrified. If her greatest dream came true, what would she dream about then?

But already, the King and the Queen were launching the first lantern from their balcony. As soon as Rapunzel saw it, she forgot her fears. It was even more beautiful than she had imagined! Soon the sky was filled with hundreds of lanterns. Rapunzel stared into Flynn's eyes and smiled.

I wish this moment would never end! she thought. *I could stay here forever!*

Flynn handed her a lantern so they could launch it together into the sky. "You know what?" said Rapunzel. "I'm going to give you back your crown. I should have done it sooner but I was afraid that you might leave. Now I know I can trust you. Do you understand?"

"I understand perfectly," Flynn replied, and he placed the crown in the bottom of the boat. He no longer cared about getting rich. Now his only dream was to be with Rapunzel, and this amazing dream seemed to be about to come true.

Disney·PIXAR
FROM THE MOVIE **INSIDE OUT**

Down in the Dump

Since leaving Minnesota, nothing had gone right for Riley. She hadn't made any friends and she had failed to get on the ice hockey team. Worse still, she'd argued with her parents and best friend back in Minnesota. So Anger had decided the best thing Riley could do was run away.

Riley had taken her mum's credit card, without permission, to buy a bus ticket but because of this, Honesty Island had crashed into the Memory Dump inside Riley's mind!

When Honesty Island crumbled, the Train of Thought had fallen with it. Joy and Sadness had been riding the train, trying to get back to Headquarters with Riley's core memories before everything that made Riley who she was was lost forever. Joy, Sadness and Riley's old imaginary friend, Bing Bong, had managed to leap from the train just before it fell.

After the crash, Joy and Sadness realized they could get back to Headquarters through one of the Recall tubes used to bring memory spheres back from Long Term Memory. Joy and Sadness stepped into the tube, but the tube was narrow and Sadness accidentally touched the core memory spheres. The spheres started to turn blue!

"Sadness, stop!" Joy cried, pushing Sadness out of the tube. "I'm sorry, but Riley needs to be happy." Joy began travelling up the tube alone, but the ground underneath was breaking apart. Riley was running away and Family Island was crumbling! Bing Bong stepped forward to help, but the tube broke, and Bing Bong and Joy fell into the Memory Dump.

"Joy!" Sadness cried. She was left all alone on a cliff overlooking the Dump.

At that moment, Riley was walking to the bus station and she felt nothing.

In the Dump, Joy felt hopeless for the first time ever. She checked the bag for the core memories – they were all still there. Then Joy took out her and Sadness' favourite memory of Riley's afternoon by the twisty tree. One of Joy's tears fell on to the sphere and the memory rewound and turned blue. Joy saw that Riley had been sitting, sad and alone, before the happy part of the memory. She suddenly realized that Sadness was important.

"The team …" she mumbled, "… they came to help because of Sadness!"

Joy slid the memory sphere back into the bag and began to scrabble up the nearest hill of memory spheres. The forgotten memories slid beneath her feet, making it impossible to grip.

Bing Bong saw what Joy was doing, but he knew it was no good trying to climb out of the Dump and told Joy to stop.

"Don't you get it, Joy?" he said. "We're stuck down here!"

A Deal with Vanellope

Wreck-It Ralph was in a racing game called *Sugar Rush*. He had just lost a race to a little girl called Vanellope, and she won his Heroes Medal from him! Ralph had left his own game and got the medal from a game called *Hero's Duty*, to try to prove that he was a Good Guy. In his own game, he was the Bad Guy ... and he was fed up of it.

Inside Game Control, the Good Guy from Ralph's game – *Fix-It Felix, Jr* – was trying to find Ralph. He was with Sergeant Calhoun, the leader of the soldiers from *Hero's Duty*. Felix and Calhoun followed Ralph's trail of destruction into the tunnel leading to *Sugar Rush*.

Felix needed to bring Ralph home so that their game wouldn't be unplugged. Calhoun needed to capture the cy-bug that had escaped from *Hero's Duty* with Ralph – even one loose bug could endanger the entire arcade!

At the Sugar Rush Stadium, the Random Roster Race was about to begin! King Candy explained that each racer needed a coin to enter. The top finishers would appear as game characters in the arcade the next day. Vanellope stepped out of the shadows, and tossed Ralph's medal into the pot. She held her breath.

Vanellope's name appeared on the list of racers! The crowd gasped in shock. To them, Vanellope was a 'glitch', a fault in the game's programming. No one wanted Vanellope and her rickety little kart to race. Quickly, King Candy ordered the Doughnut Police to take her away.

Just then, Ralph burst onto the track, desperate to find his medal. "Thief!" he cried at Vanellope. He chased after her, accidentally wrecking everything in his path.

Vanellope escaped, but Ralph was taken to King Candy's castle. The King told Ralph that the medal would belong to the winner of the Random Roster Race, to be held later that night, once the racetrack was fixed. Then he ordered Ralph to leave *Sugar Rush*. But Ralph had other plans....

Ralph tracked Vanellope through the Lollistix Forest. But just as he was about to confront her, a group of other racers arrived. They demanded that Vanellope drop out of the race. Then they smashed her kart and tossed her in the mud! That made Ralph mad! He chased the mean racers away.

Afterwards, Vanellope promised that if she won the race, she'd give Ralph back his medal. But to win, she would need a new kart. Reluctantly, Ralph agreed to help ... would he finally get his medal back...?

Playing School

Now, it just so happened that when the wind changed ever so slightly, and the leaves began to turn scarlet or golden, depending on their preference, and the days grew ever so much more eager to be over and done, this was also the time that Christopher Robin returned to school, as well as the time, not so surprisingly, when his friends in the Wood felt as if they should really do the same.

But *playing* school, as you might suspect, is not as similar to real school as perhaps it should be. First of all, there's no teacher to tell you what to do. And, after sitting at their desks for what seemed like a good three and a quarter hours (but was really just five or so minutes), Winnie the Pooh and his friends came to the conclusion that something rather important in their game of school was missing.

"Perhaps it's time we had a snack," suggested Pooh.

"I don't think that's it, Pooh," said Piglet.

"Our problem," announced Owl, "is that we do not have a teacher. No classroom is complete – and this is a well-known fact – without a teacher. Which is why I'm quite happy to offer my considerable expertise."

"Just a minute, Owl," Rabbit broke in. "And why is it, exactly, that we should let you be the teacher? Some might say – myself included –

that I'm better suited to the job."

"You?" Owl scowled.

"Perhaps we should have a vote," said Piglet. "I'd like to nominate Pooh."

"Me?" Pooh said. "Why, thank you, Piglet. I gladly accept. Now ... what's a 'teacher' again?"

"Really!" said Owl, with no small amount of scorn. "A 'teacher', my dear Pooh, is the someone who stands before the class."

"To give out snacks?" asked Pooh, hopefully.

"No," said Owl. "To give out knowledge."

"Oh," said Pooh. "I don't think I'd enjoy that nearly so much."

"Well, if it's all the same to you, and if anyone cares, I'll be the teacher," Eeyore said glumly. "I probably wouldn't have made a good student anyway."

"That will never do!" exclaimed Rabbit.

"Hi-ho!" said Christopher Robin, returning from a thoroughly enjoyable, and very well taught, day at school. "Whatever are you up to?"

"Playing school ... I think," said Pooh.

"Only we don't have a teacher," Piglet explained.

"I could teach you. I learned ever so many things today," said Christopher Robin.

"Hooray!" cheered Roo. "Let's start right away!"

Zarina's New Friends

Tinker Bell and her friends were still on the beach, struggling to cope with their switched talents. They had to get back the Blue Dust from Zarina and the pirates, but the pirate ship had disappeared!

Vidia, who to her dismay was now a tinker fairy, took charge. She made a boat out of the crocodile egg and the girls climbed in. Silvermist, who was now a fast-flying fairy, pulled them along the water.

Soon a giant wave carried the fairies straight on to the pirate ship and they landed inside one of the cannons.

"Twenty-one gun salute to the captain!" announced a pirate named Yang.

"Out, out, out!" Tink ordered her friends. BOOM!

The fairies escaped just in time to see the pirates toasting Zarina. It appeared that she was now their captain because she had promised to make them fly!

The pirates couldn't wait. They imagined travelling the skies, dropping down wherever they pleased. It was going to be so easy to rob the world of its great treasures. After all, no one would be able to catch a flying ship!

Tink and the other fairies flew up to the crow's nest. Suddenly, they were gripped by fear. The pirate ship was sailing straight for the dreaded Skull Rock! The dark and scary cave was the last place they wanted to go.

When the ship passed through the rock's open mouth, the girls were shocked to see a Pixie Dust Tree inside. "Zarina must have grown it!" exclaimed Silvermist.

"So that's how they're going to fly. She's going to make pixie dust!" Tink concluded.

The ship docked inside the cave and the fairies followed Zarina to her cabin. When James brought her some food, Tink, Vidia and Silvermist slipped in behind him while the others listened at the door.

"You're quite the little genius," James said as he watched Zarina sift the Blue Dust. "Hard to believe the other fairies didn't appreciate your talent."

Zarina jingled with happiness as she poured the Blue Dust into a bottle. James was the only pirate who could understand what she said – he had become her most trusted friend.

When Zarina and James turned away, the fairies flew up to hide in a desk drawer. Vidia tried to hook the precious bottle with a fishing line she had tinkered.

But Zarina came back, grabbed the bottle of Blue Dust and left with James. The fairies had missed their chance.

Enchanted Stew

Belle hummed to herself as she strolled through the castle. She had been living in the castle for a few months now and was finally beginning to feel at home. The enchanted inhabitants were truly good to her, and even the Beast seemed to be softening a bit.

Finishing her song, she stepped into the kitchen for a chat with Mrs Potts and the Stove. They were always pleased to see her, and Belle enjoyed talking to them while learning new recipes.

"Well, hello dear!" Mrs Potts and the Stove called out together as Belle stepped into the large kitchen. The smell of roasting meat and vegetables greeted Belle as well, and her mouth watered. Dinner would be delicious, as usual.

"Hello," Belle replied.

"You're just in time for a spot of tea," Mrs Potts said.

Belle smiled as Chip hopped across the counter, stopping right in front of her. "I'll be your teacup," he said. "And no bubble tricks, I promise," he added seriously.

"All right then," Belle agreed. Mrs Potts filled Chip with steamy tea and dropped in a sugar cube.

"How was your morning in the library, dear?" Mrs Potts asked.

"It was wonderful!" Belle exclaimed. "I finished my book about knights in shining armour and started one about a prince who's disguised as a frog."

"A frog!" the Stove exclaimed. "Oh, my!"

Suddenly, black smoke began to billow out of the sides of the oven door.

"Oh, my!" the Stove said again, throwing open the door. Smoke poured into the room. When it finally cleared, Belle spied a scorched roast and crispy black vegetables inside.

"Oh, my!" the Stove exclaimed again.

"What are we going to feed the Beast for supper?" Mrs Potts fretted.

The kitchen door opened, and Lumiere rushed into the room. "What is that awful smell?" he asked. A moment later, he spied the roast. "It's absolutely scorched!" he shouted. "We can't possibly feed that to the Beast! What will we do?"

Belle got to her feet. "Enchanted Stew," she said calmly. Taking down a large stew pot and a few vegetables, she began to chop and simmer. The last ingredient was the scorched roast.

"It adds the perfect smoky flavour," she explained. Just then the Beast came into the kitchen. "What smells so delicious?" he asked.

"Supper," Belle replied with a smile and a wink at the Stove and Mrs Potts. "It's called Enchanted Stew, and we cooked it together!"

The Real Captain

On the pirate ship, Tinker Bell, Vidia and Silvermist joined back up with the other fairies, and they followed Zarina to the Pixie Dust Tree she had grown inside Skull Rock.

Unfortunately, Iridessa – now a garden fairy – accidentally touched a branch as she shooed away a bee, which made the branch grow so violently that it pushed them out of their hiding place and straight into Zarina!

Zarina whistled and the pirates swooped in. They captured Tink and the others in a net.

"Don't do this," pleaded Tinker Bell. "Come back home. You don't belong here."

Zarina refused. "This is exactly where I belong," she declared.

"We appreciate what she can do," James chimed in. "Treasure it, actually."

Zarina ordered Oppenheimer, the cook, to take the fairies away. He put them in a crab cage in his galley and locked it tight. "Welcome to your new cabin," he said.

Just then his favourite alarm clock went off.

"Oh, my stock is ready!" Oppenheimer cried delightedly.

Meanwhile, Zarina was plugging the bottle of Blue Dust into the top of the tree.

Everyone held their breath and waited. The tree glowed and shook, and then … produced a tiny bit of golden pixie dust!

"We're going to fly!" James cried.

Zarina beamed at him with happiness.

In the galley of the ship Tink and her friends had lifted their crab-cage prison off the ground and stuck their legs between the slats to try to escape.

"No, no, no, not today, my darlings," said Oppenheimer, and he weighed the crate down with a sack of potatoes.

Back at the new Pixie Dust Tree, the pirates were still celebrating. The golden pixie dust was now flowing steadily. Zarina sprinkled some on James and taught him how to fly.

"As long as we have the Blue Dust, we'll never run out of pixie dust, right Zarina?" he asked, once they had landed.

"Yes," Zarina replied.

"Well, then, we won't need you any more," James announced with an evil grin. He grabbed the stunned Zarina and shut her inside a lantern!

"Once we're past the second star … the world will be my oyster!" James said.

The pirates hailed James – he had been the real captain of their ship all along!

Thanks to the Croc

Trapped in the galley of the pirate ship, Tinker Bell and her friends were delighted to see Rosetta's crocodile had hopped through a cannon hole.

With a little bit of encouragement from Rosetta, the baby croc pulled down the crate holding the fairies. He wanted his mama!

Oppenheimer, the ship's cook, tried to catch his escaping prisoners with a saucepan and lid, but the croc bit the cook on his backside! The fairies didn't have to worry about him anymore.

Out on deck, while the pirates were preparing the ship to sail, an odd-looking pirate emerged from the galley – it was Tink and the other fairies in disguise! When the time was right they zipped out of the pirate clothes and snatched the bottle of Blue Dust from the Pixie Dust Tree.

"Return that Blue Dust!" commanded James. He dangled the lantern holding Zarina above the water. "Or your friend is done for!"

The fairies didn't want Zarina to get hurt so Tink solemnly flew back to the tree and replaced the Blue Dust. Golden pixie dust soon flowed from the tree once again.

James pulled a lever and the golden dust was directed over the ship. As the entire vessel rose up in the air, he grabbed the bottle of Blue Dust.

"Bon voyage, little captain," he sneered at Zarina. Then he picked up the lantern and tossed it into the sea without a second thought!

The fairies rushed to pull the lantern to the surface, but Zarina was still in trouble! Water was pouring into the lamp! The girls struggled with the latch and it sprang open just in time. The fairies flew Zarina to the safety of the rocks to dry off.

Zarina was grateful to the other fairies – and sorry for her betrayal. She was determined to make things right again.

"We have to get the Blue Dust back before they reach the second star, or we'll never find them," she said.

The others gladly joined her as she soared out of the cave.

The girls caught up to the flying ship in no time, but the second star was just ahead! They needed a plan and they needed one quickly!

They slipped into the Captain's cabin undetected – and reappeared looking like pint-sized swashbucklers, ready to fight! The real pirates couldn't believe their eyes.

Invincible Mushu

After helping Mulan defeat the Huns and restore the Fa family honour, Mushu had been given back his old job as family guardian. He was supposed to help guard the temple of the Fa ancestors.

One day Mushu was sunning himself on the temple roof, when a big lizard waddled up. He seemed to be staring right at Mushu.

Mushu frowned. "Who you lookin' at?" he said to the lizard.

The lizard flicked out his tongue.

Mushu was offended. "Oh, yeah?" he said. "Stick your tongue out at me, will you? Well, get a load of this!" Puffing out his tiny chest, Mushu spat out a miniature burst of fire, no bigger than the flame of a match.

The lizard just blinked.

"Not good enough for you, eh?" Mushu said. "All right, tough guy. Try this on for size!" Mushu cleared his throat dramatically. Taking a deep breath, he opened his mouth and spat a bigger flame at the lizard.

The lizard crouched, lowering his chest to the ground. Then he straightened his legs. Then he crouched again. The lizard was doing push-ups, as lizards will do.

"Oh-ho!" Mushu shouted. "Think you're tough, do you? Well, Scales for Brains, I didn't spend time in the Imperial Army for nothing!"

And with that, Mushu crouched down on all four legs and began to do push-ups, too.

"... Ninety-eight ... ninety-nine ... one hundred!" Mushu counted, panting. He leaped to his feet and began to run circles around the lizard. "Just ask anyone," he told the lizard. "I'm the dragon that defeated hundreds of Huns. I could eat you for lunch, small fry."

The lizard just sat there.

Huffing and puffing, Mushu stopped in front of the motionless reptile. He began to box at the air, bouncing around on his hind feet. "Think you can take me on, do you? Well, watch out. I'm a three-time champion in the featherweight division. 'Float like a dragonfly, sting like a bee,' that's me all ri – "

Suddenly – *snap!* – the lizard snatched up a fly that landed on Mushu's nose.

"Ahhhh!" Mushu screamed. He was so startled, he leaped backwards ... and fell off the roof. He landed on the ground in a puff of dust.

"Ha-ha-ha-ha-ha-ha-ha!" The air filled with the sound of roaring laughter. The ancestors had seen everything.

"Cheer up, Mushu," one ancestor said. "It looks like you have a new friend."

Sure enough, the lizard had followed Mushu down from the roof. "Well," Mushu said, "I always did want a pet."

259

101
DALMATIANS

Cruella Sees Spots

Cruella looked around the living room of the old De Vil mansion and rubbed her hands together. The room was full of Dalmatian puppies. Everywhere Cruella looked she saw spots, spots, spots! At last, her dream was coming true! Cackling with glee, Cruella thought back to the day this had all started....

It had begun as a perfectly miserable day. Cruella had been shopping for fur coats all morning and she hadn't found a single thing she liked.

"Too long! Too short! Too black! Too white!" she screeched, knocking an armload of coats out of the shop assistant's hands. "I want something unusual! I want a coat that has never been seen before!"

Cruella stormed out of the shop, slamming the door so hard that the glass cracked. She needed something to cheer her up. Just then she remembered that her old school friend, Anita, lived nearby.

Soon Cruella stood at the door, ringing the buzzer impatiently. She could hear cheerful piano music coming from an open window.

Just then, a pretty brown-haired woman answered the door. Her eyes opened wide when she saw the skinny woman, covered in fur, standing on her doorstep. "Oh, Cruella!" she cried. "What a surprise!"

"Hello, Anita, darling," Cruella said, walking into the sitting room. At that moment, a tall, thin man strolled down the stairs, smoking a pipe. But, when he caught sight of Cruella, he leaped back in fright!

"Ah, prince charming," Cruella said, smirking at Anita's new husband. Roger scowled. Suddenly something else caught Cruella's eye. Two black-and-white spotted dogs were sitting in the corner of the room.

"And what have we here?" Cruella asked.

"Oh, that's Pongo and Perdita," Anita explained. "They're wonderful pets." But Cruella wasn't looking at the dogs. She was looking at their coats. Their glossy fur wasn't too long or too short. It wasn't too black or too white. Cruella had never seen anything like it before. It was perfect.

"And soon we'll be even happier," Anita went on. "Perdita is going to have puppies!"

"Puppies!" Cruella shrieked. Suddenly she had an idea that made her smile an evil smile.

"Oh, Anita, you have positively made my day. Now, you must call me just as soon as the puppies arrive. I think they are *just* what I have been looking for."

Pongo snarled, but Cruella didn't notice.

"What a perfectly *marvellous* day," Cruella said to herself as she strode out of the door.

... And *that* was how it all started.

The Monster of Paradise Falls

Carl Fredricksen had dreamed of becoming an explorer since he was a boy. He had met a girl called Ellie who shared his dream, and they grew up and got married.

Carl had promised Ellie he'd take her to Paradise Falls one day. But they never managed to save enough money to go. When Ellie passed away, Carl missed her very much. One day, when he was being forced to move out of their home, he tied thousands of balloons to the house and flew to South America – to Paradise Falls. And he accidentally took a young boy called Russell along with him.

Carl and Russell had met a large, strange bird – Russell had named it Kevin, but then discovered it was a girl! They also met a talking dog called Dug. He had been sent by his pack to capture Kevin. More dogs had appeared and taken Carl and Russell to their leader. Much to Carl's surprise, their leader was Charles Muntz – a famous explorer who had been his and Ellie's childhood hero!

Muntz invited Carl and Russell into his giant airship – the *Spirit of Adventure*! When Dug tried to follow, the other dogs blocked his way. "He has lost the bird," declared Alpha, the leader of the pack. Dug was left outside.

Onboard the airship, the dogs served dinner while Muntz told Carl and Russell about the Monster of Paradise Falls.

"I've spent a lifetime tracking this creature," Muntz said.

"Hey, that looks like Kevin!" said Russell, noticing a bird skeleton.

"Kevin?" Muntz asked.

"That's my new giant bird pet," Russell explained. "I trained it to follow us."

Muntz became very angry. He thought Carl and Russell were trying to steal the bird from him.

At that moment, they heard a wail outside. Kevin had followed Carl and Russell into the cave! All the dogs began to bark. In the confusion, Carl and Russell slipped away.

"Get them!" Muntz roared at his dogs.

Carl and Russell untied the house and started to run. The snarling dog pack came racing after them. Kevin scooped Russell and Carl onto her back and raced for the cave opening, with the house still floating behind.

But Kevin wasn't fast enough to stay ahead of the pack. The dogs were closing in. Suddenly, an avalanche of rocks tumbled down and blocked the dog pack. "Go on, Master. I will stop the dogs!" someone cried.

It was Dug! He had come to rescue Carl and Russell. But would Carl, Russell and Kevin be able to escape…?

BRAVE
Merida's Wild Ride

Merida sat in the stables reading from an old book of Highland tales. She and her horse Angus wanted to go for a ride, but it was a wet afternoon.

"Look, right there," Merida said to Angus, pointing to a picture in her book. "Magical horses. That one there is called a kelpie. It's a water horse."

Angus snorted, shaking his head. It was clear that he wanted nothing to do with magic.

The raindrops slowed and the clouds scattered. When the sun finally came out, Merida said, "Come, lad. Let's go for a ride."

They galloped across the bridge and down the hill to the woods. Suddenly a flash of grey caught Merida's eye.

"What was that?" she gasped. "Come on, let's follow it."

But Angus didn't want to follow it – whatever it was.

"Don't be a ninny," Merida teased him. "I'm sure it's not a bear."

She guided a reluctant Angus to a clearing and there stood a magnificent grey horse. Its coat shimmered and its mane was like fine black silk.

The horse lowered its head as Merida approached, but Angus blocked her path.

"Don't be jealous, lad!" she said. "This horse must be lost. We need to help him."

Merida talked to the grey horse and it responded with a soft whinny, so she swung on to its back. She didn't have a bridle, but she thought she could guide him by his mane.

Even though the horse bolted, Merida wasn't frightened. She had been around horses all her life. But as she tried to calm the horse, she realized her hands were stuck to the horse's mane.

When the horse brushed against some tree branches, rainwater fell on her hand and it miraculously came free. She tried to grab a bridle that was hanging from another tree, but it was just beyond her fingertips.

"Angus, help!" she called. She and the grey horse were racing towards a cliff's edge!

Merida tugged and pulled on the horse's mane but nothing worked. Suddenly, Angus galloped up next to them and tossed a bridle at Merida. She caught it and slipped it over the horse's head. With the reins in her hand, she was able to guide the horse to safety.

When they reached a loch the horse finally stopped. Merida jumped off and looked into the horse's eyes. Something made her remove the bridle, and the horse nodded before galloping down to the misty shoreline. Was he really racing into the water, or was it the fog playing tricks on Merida's eyes?

Back at the stable Merida read more about the legend of the kelpie. "Once a bridle is put on the water horse will do your bidding," she read. She looked up at Angus. Had she really been riding a kelpie?

What a Crab!

Nemo was having trouble at school – and its name was Ruddy. The big crab was mean to Nemo and the other kids whenever he got the chance. The trouble was, he was crafty and he never did it when the teachers were looking.

One day, he shoved Nemo into a tide pool and made him late for their coral lesson. Another time, he taunted Nemo by saying, "My dad's bigger and stronger than your dad!"

"Ignore him," Marlin told his son. "And just so you know, his dad *may* be bigger and stronger than I am, but he's certainly not as smart or good-looking."

"My friends and I have tried everything," Nemo complained to his shark friends, Bruce, Chum and Anchor. "But he won't leave us alone. What do *you* think we should do?"

"Just leave it to us!" said Bruce. "We're experts in behaviour modification."

The next day, three huge shadows fell over Nemo's classmates as they played in the school playground.

"Hello," Bruce said, putting a fin around the crab. "You must be Nemo's new little friend."

While Ruddy trembled, Bruce snarled, "We just wanted you to know that any friend of Nemo's is a friend of ours. You are a *friend* of Nemo's, aren't you?"

Everyone looked at Ruddy. "Oh, yeah!" he managed to splutter, throwing a claw around Nemo. "You bet! Nemo and I are buddies. Yessiree!"

"Good!" Anchor said. "Because you don't want to know what happens to anyone who's not nice to our little pal here."

Chum cleaned a piece of seaweed from between his razor-sharp teeth with a spiny urchin. "You should stop by for lunch sometime," he said to Ruddy with a wink.

When Mrs Lobster arrived to pick up the class, the sharks said goodbye and swam away.

Ruddy sidled up to Nemo. "You're friends with three sharks?" he said. "Wow! That's pretty cool! I wish I had friends like that. In fact, I wish I had any friends at all."

"How do you expect to have friends when you're so, well, *crabby* all the time?" Nemo said.

Ruddy admitted that he hated being the new kid. He had decided to pick on everyone else before they had a chance to pick on him.

"If you promise to stop acting mean, I promise to be your friend," Nemo said.

"Deal," Ruddy agreed. "Besides, I guess I'd better be your friend if I don't want your shark pals to eat me."

Nemo didn't say a word. Bruce, Chum and Anchor were vegetarians, but Ruddy didn't need to know that – at least not today!

Snow White's Special Day

And with one kiss, Snow White awoke. The Prince lifted her onto his horse, and together they rode towards his castle. As they neared his castle, the Prince helped Snow White from the saddle.

"There's something I must ask before we go through those gates," he said. "Will you do me the honour of marrying me?"

Of course, Snow White said yes!

Just then, the gates to the castle opened wide. It seemed all of the kingdom's people had gathered to meet them!

Soon the Prince's staff was bustling around Snow White, making preparations for the wedding. She glanced at the Prince nervously, but his smile put her at ease. She knew he would always be there to help her.

Soon Snow White was at the royal dressmaker's, trying to choose a style for her wedding dress. It was a difficult task.

Later that evening, Snow White went to her room. It seemed very large – and quite lonely! She missed her friends. Just then, there was a knock at her door....

"Hello, my dear," the Prince said, "I'm not sure about you, but I'm having some trouble planning this wedding – especially finding the perfect ring for you. So I thought I should bring in the best helpers I know...."

The Prince opened the doors to the balcony outside of the room. There stood the Seven Dwarfs, along with all of Snow White's animal friends from the forest! She was so happy to see everyone!

The next day, as Sneezy, Doc and Sleepy helped Snow White with the dressmaker, Dopey and Happy helped the Prince find his own diamond in the mine for Snow White!

When the wedding day arrived, Snow White's friends helped her to get dressed in her wedding gown. The royal dressmaker couldn't help but smile – the little animals' special touches did complete his work perfectly.

As she stood ready to walk down the aisle, Snow White looked at her seven dear friends. "You know," she said, "I do need to be walked down the aisle. Would you do that?"

The Seven Dwarfs were overjoyed! They walked their beloved Snow White down the aisle to her prince. Dopey even stood on top of Sneezy so that they could be a bit taller.

Thanks to a little help from her friends, Snow White had the most wonderful wedding day. And as day turned into night, the royal couple rode off in a carriage decorated with flowers. Everyone knew that Snow White and the Prince would live happily ever after.

Disney
Sleeping Beauty

The Gift Horse

"I can hardly wait to see her!" Prince Phillip told his horse, Samson. He had just met the woman of his dreams singing in the forest. And she had invited him to her cottage that very evening.

Suddenly, the Prince pulled his horse's reins up short. Samson jerked to a stop and chuffed angrily.

"Sorry, boy," said the Prince. "But I just realized that I should bring her a gift tonight – something to show her how much I love her. Let's go to the village."

Samson shook his mane and refused to move a hoof. Shopping wasn't his idea of fun. He was tired and wanted to go back to the castle for some oats!

"C'mon, boy," pleaded the Prince. "I'll give you some nice crisp apples."

Apples! Samson's eyes widened. Suddenly, he wasn't so tired any more! With a whinny, he kicked up his hooves and took off.

When they reached the village square, the Prince scratched his head in thought. There were so many shops.

"What sort of gift do you think she will like?" he asked.

As a horse, Samson didn't care all that much. Yet he did his best to answer.

"Red roses?" asked the Prince, passing a flower shop.

Samson shook his head.

"Yes, you're right," said the Prince. "She lives in the forest. She must see flowers every day."

They passed a dress shop and the prince peered in at the window.

"How about a new dress?" he asked Samson.

Samson shook his mane in irritation.

"No, huh?" said the Prince. "Girls like to choose their own dresses, don't they?"

They passed more shops: a bakery, a hat shop and a blacksmith's.

Samson sighed. If he didn't help the Prince find a gift soon, they could be here all day! With a whinny, Samson took off down the street.

The Prince yelped in surprise. By the time he'd taken back control of the reins, Samson had stopped in front of a jewellery shop.

"Samson, you're a genius!" the Prince cried at the sight of the gems glittering in the window. "That sapphire ring sparkles as beautifully as her blue eyes."

The Prince bought the ring, slipped it in his pocket, then mounted Samson again.

"To the castle!" said the Prince. "I've got to tell my father I've found the girl of my dreams."

Samson whinnied and took off at a gallop. He didn't know what the King would say to the Prince, but one thing he was sure of – he had certainly earned those apples!

Timon and Pumbaa Tell It All

It was a very hot day on the savannah. Simba, Timon and Pumbaa were lying in the shade, barely moving. It was too hot for the three friends to do anything except talk. Pumbaa had just finished telling a story about the biggest insect he had ever eaten (to hear him tell it, it was the size of an ostrich) and a silence fell over the little group.

"I know," said Simba. "Hey, Timon, why don't you tell me the story of how you and Pumbaa met each other?"

Timon looked at Pumbaa. "Do you think he's ready for it?" he asked.

"Knock him dead," said Pumbaa.

"It all started in a little meerkat village far, far away," began Timon.

"No," interrupted Pumbaa. "You've got it all wrong. It all started near a little warthog watering hole far, far away."

"If I recall correctly, Simba asked *me* to tell the story," said Timon. "And this is the story as told from *my* point of view."

"All right," said Pumbaa sulkily.

"And in that little meerkat village there was one meerkat who didn't fit in with the rest. All the others were content to dig, dig, dig all day long," said Timon. "*I* was that isolated meerkat. How I hated to dig! I knew I needed to go elsewhere, to find a home of my own, a place where I fitted in. So I left. Along the way I ran into a wise old baboon who told me what I was seeking – *hakuna matata* – and pointed me in the direction of Pride Rock. So I boldly set off towards this rock of which he spoke. And on my way there, I ..."

"Met me!" Pumbaa interrupted.

Timon gave him a dirty look and continued. "I heard a strange rustling in the bushes. I was scared. What could it be? A hyena? A lion? And then I found myself face to face with a big, ugly warthog!"

"Hey!" said Pumbaa, looking insulted.

"We soon realized we had a lot in common – our love for bugs, our search for a home to call our own. So we set out for Pride Rock together. A lot of bad things happened along the way – hyenas, stampedes, you name it. But before long we managed to find the perfect place to live. And then we met you, Simba!"

"That's a nice story," Simba said with a yawn. "Now I think I'm going to take a nap...."

Pumbaa cleared his throat. "It all started near a little warthog watering hole far, far away," he began.

"You always have to get the last word, don't you?" said Timon.

"Not always," said Pumbaa. And then he continued with *his* side of the story.

Disney PRINCESS

Cinderella

The Prince's Dream

The Grand Duke was a little worried about Prince Charming. At tonight's ball, the Prince had finally met the girl of his dreams. But, at the stroke of midnight, she'd run away. And now it was impossible to reason with the Prince.

"You must bring her back!" the Prince told the Grand Duke.

"Of course, Your Highness!" said the Duke. "I've already sent the royal guards after her carriage ... as I told you four times already!" he added under his breath.

But the guards had no luck. The captain bowed to the Prince. "I'm very sorry, Your Highness," he said. "I don't understand what happened. I could see her carriage ahead of us – and an extraordinary carriage it was. It actually seemed to shimmer."

The Prince remembered how the girl's gown and tiara had shimmered too. The Duke sighed as he watched Prince Charming's eyes glaze over. The Prince would clearly be distracted until they found this mystery girl.

"Then what happened?" asked the Duke.

"We turned a corner and the carriage simply ... vanished," said the captain.

"I don't even know her name," said the Prince, in a daze.

"Well, for now, you must try to focus on your duties as the host of the ball," the Duke advised the Prince. "The ballroom is still filled with eligible maidens."

The Prince shook his head. "There is no other maiden. Not for me. If only she had left some clue!" he cried despairingly. "Some token to remember her by!"

The Duke rolled his eyes. "Your Highness might try investigating your right jacket pocket, then."

Startled, the Prince stuck his hand into his pocket and withdrew a glass slipper! He had been so distracted by his newfound love for the mystery girl that he had completely forgotten about the tiny glass slipper she had left behind on the stairs. He looked at the slipper, then at the Duke.

"I ... I ..." the Prince stammered.

"I suggest you allow me to see to the arrangements," the Duke said kindly, taking the slipper. "We'll find your mystery lass, Your Highness."

The Prince nodded gratefully, then turned towards the window and gazed out into the night. Somewhere out there, his princess was waiting for him. "Dreams can come true," he murmured. "After tonight, I'm sure of it."

Little did he know that on the other side of his kingdom, Cinderella was standing by her own window, holding the other glass slipper – and saying the very same thing!

Disney
Tangled
Tricked

Flynn Rider had realized that he was in love with Rapunzel. Now, nothing mattered to him except being with her. So he decided to put his life as a thief behind him. Farewell crown, farewell wealth, farewell gold coins! At last he had found his true treasure. From now on he would take care of his precious Rapunzel with all of his heart.

As they floated along in their boat, watching the lanterns, Flynn was getting up the courage to finally kiss Rapunzel, when he suddenly spotted his old partners in crime, the Stabbington brothers, on the shore. The villains wanted to get hold of the crown he had refused to share with them, and Flynn knew they would do anything to get their revenge. He needed to give them back the crown straight away. Flynn turned away from Rapunzel.

"What's the matter?" she said in surprise, disappointed to have not had her first kiss.

"Oh, nothing important. Just a small matter I have to attend to. I'll be back!" And Flynn headed to the shore before running off with the satchel containing the crown. Pascal, Rapunzel's pet chameleon, was worried. What if Flynn didn't come back, as Mother Gothel had predicted?

"He will come back," Rapunzel said.

But Rapunzel didn't know that the Stabbington brothers were in fact following Mother Gothel's orders. When Flynn showed them the gold crown and explained that he was giving them his share, they refused to take it!

"We know that you have found treasure a thousand times more valuable than this. This Rapunzel has magic hair that cures illnesses. It's her we want!" The Stabbingtons knocked Flynn out, tied him in a boat and pushed it out. Then they rushed to capture Rapunzel!

Rapunzel dodged the Stabbingtons and ran into the forest. She didn't get far, though, before her hair got tangled on a tree branch! As she tried to free herself, she heard a scuffle and then Mother Gothel's voice. "Rapunzel!"

"Mother?" Rapunzel ran back and found Mother Gothel standing over the brothers. They lay unconscious at her feet. Rapunzel still thought Mother Gothel was her real mother, but in fact the wicked woman only wanted Rapunzel's magical hair to keep her young.

"You were right, Mother," said Rapunzel.

"I know, darling, I know," said Mother Gothel, as she led Rapunzel back towards the tower where she'd been hidden her whole life.

Disney
Beauty and the Beast

Lessons at Hide-and-seek

"Belle," Mrs Potts called. "Oh, Belle!" Belle was sitting in the library, surrounded by a pile of books.

"There you are!" Mrs Potts cried.

"Hi, Belle," Mrs Potts' son, Chip, chimed in.

"Hello to both of you. Were you looking for me?" Belle asked Mrs Potts.

"As a matter of fact, I was," Mrs Potts told her. "I was just stopping by to enquire as to whether or not you would like some tea."

"Thank you," Belle said. "I would love some."

Mrs Potts poured Belle a piping hot cup of tea. Belle drank it, and thanked her.

"You're welcome, Belle," Mrs Potts said. "Come along now," she called to Chip.

"But Mama," Chip whined. "I want to stay here with Belle!"

"Belle is busy," Mrs Potts explained. "You'll just get in the way."

"That's all right," Belle said. "I was just about done for today. I'd love to spend some time with Chip."

"All right," Mrs Potts said. "But Chip, you come right back to the kitchen when Belle tells you to."

"Okay, I promise," Chip said.

"So," Belle began when Mrs Potts had left, "how about a game of hide-and-seek?"

"How do you play that?" Chip asked.

"It's simple," Belle said. "One person hides and the other person tries to find him."

"I can do that!" Chip said.

"Of course you can," Belle told him. "So, do you want to be the hider or the seeker?"

"I want to be the hider," Chip told her.

"Okay," Belle said. "I'll close my eyes and count to ten. One, two, three...."

Chip took off, darting behind the curtains just as Belle called, "Ten! Ready or not, here I come! Hmm, now where could he be?" she wondered aloud.

Belle looked under the table. "He isn't there," she said. Then she looked in the corner. "He isn't there, either," Belle continued. She looked high and low. But she just couldn't seem to find Chip anywhere. "I give up," Belle said. "Come out, come out, wherever you are!"

Chip silently giggled from behind the curtain, but he was careful not to make too much noise. He was having fun!

"It seems that Chip doesn't want to come out from his hiding place," Belle said. "I guess that means I'll have to eat a slice of Mrs Potts' chocolate cake all by myself."

And, upon hearing that, Chip jumped out from his hiding place and called after Belle, "Here I am! Wait for me!"

DISNEY
THE LITTLE
MERMAID

Stackblackbadminton

After dinner at Prince Eric's castle, Ariel, Eric and Grimsby went into the drawing room to relax.

"My dear, do you play?" Grimsby asked Ariel. He pointed to a table. On it sat a red-and-black chequered board.

Of course, Ariel could not answer because she had exchanged her voice for legs. But she nodded eagerly.

"I'll take the first move," Eric said, and slid a black disc from one square to another.

That seems simple enough, thought Ariel. The game seemed similar to a merpeople game called 'Conch'. She reached over and pushed the same black disc to a third square.

Eric laughed. "No, no. I'm black. And you're red. *You* move the *red*. Understand?"

Ariel gazed at Eric and sighed.

"Perhaps I should show the young lady?" suggested Grimsby.

He took Ariel's seat, and the two men moved the discs all over the chequered board. But Ariel still didn't understand what they were doing – this game wasn't like Conch at all!

Suddenly, she heard a flapping sound on the windowsill. It was Scuttle!

Ariel pointed at the men and mouthed, *What are they doing?*

"They're playing Stackblackbadminton, a popular human game," said Scuttle.

Ariel's eyes widened. That sounded like something she had better learn if she wanted to fit into Eric's world.

"You see those discs?" asked Scuttle. "Those are *chips*. At the end of the game, players stack their chips. Then the dealer – the person *not* playing – "

Me? mouthed Ariel.

Scuttle nodded. "Yes. It's up to you to end the game by collecting all the chips off the board."

Ariel smiled. She would show Eric she *did* know how to play.

She walked right over to the two men. They seemed to have finished playing. They were staring hard at the board – and there weren't many chips left on it. So she bent down and swept all the pieces off the board.

Eric and Grimsby yelped. The little mermaid grinned. Eric didn't think she knew how to play his game but, from the stunned look on his face, she'd given him quite a surprise!

Ariel smiled and began to lay the 'chips' out as if they were shells in a game of Conch. This 'Stackblackbadminton' game was all right, but she couldn't wait to teach Eric and Grimsby how to play a *really* good game. She picked up the first 'shell' and showed Eric how to move it. He smiled at her, and her heart fluttered. Things were starting to go well at last.

Elsa's Gift

Everyone in the kingdom of Arendelle was preparing for the winter ball that evening. In the castle, Anna grabbed Elsa's arm. "Come on!" she said. "We have so much to do!"

While Elsa finished icing the banquet room, Anna brought in a tray full of krumkake. "Dessert table is ready! What do you think?"

Elsa smiled at Anna. She wished she could do something special for her sister.

Then Elsa had an idea and raced away. "Kristoff!" she called. "I need your help."

Elsa explained that she wanted to create the perfect gifts for Anna, including an ice sculpture.

While Kristoff went to get a block of ice, Elsa locked herself in the kitchen.

"Elsa?" Anna called, knocking on the door.

"Don't come in!" Elsa said. "It's a surprise."

Elsa was making Anna's favourite extra-gingery gingerbread men.

"Can I help?" Anna said, knocking again.

"No!" Elsa called. "Just ... go to your room."

Elsa tiptoed to her room. She brought the trinkets she had collected for her sister over the years to the banquet room and was arranging them when Kristoff arrived with a block of ice.

Soon Elsa had created a sculpture of Anna. "Where's Anna?" Kristoff asked.

"I told her to stay in her room so the surprise wouldn't be ruined," Elsa said.

"You know," Kristoff said, "I think what Anna would really like is –"

"Punch!" Elsa finished, racing out.

"I was going to say 'time with her sister'," Kristoff said to the empty room.

Later, Elsa was stirring the punch when Anna walked into the kitchen.

"Why aren't you in your room?" Elsa asked.

"I'm lonely," Anna said.

"But you'll ruin your surprise!" Elsa said.

"I have a surprise for you," Anna said. "Follow me."

Elsa went out to the courtyard, but Anna had vanished. "I don't have time –" Elsa called.

Splat! A snowball hit her in the face.

Anna giggled. "Surprise! You don't have any time for me, so I'm declaring war!" she said.

Elsa grinned. "You're forgetting which one of us has magical ice powers," she said.

The snowball fight went on until Elsa called a truce. It was time to get ready for the ball!

As Anna looked around the banquet room, she noticed Elsa's gingerbread men and punch and her lovely sculpture. "You did this for me?"

Elsa nodded. "I wanted to give you a gift."

"It's lovely," Anna said. "But the best present is being with you."

"For me, too," Elsa said and the sisters went off to enjoy the party ... together.

271

Homecoming

"**G**et them off my ship!" James the pirate captain demanded when he saw Tinker Bell and her pint-sized pirate friends. The pirates laughed as the fairies used their tiny weapons against them.

The fairies soon realized that they needed something more effective – their fairy talents! All their talents had been muddled up earlier that day, so they all had new ones.

Fawn blasted a pirate named Bonito with a sunbeam, knocking him overboard. Rosetta went after Oppenheimer on her crocodile. The creature even gobbled up the cook's ticking clock in one gulp!

While Zarina fought James, the other fairies turned the ship away from the second star. They lowered the anchor and tied it with seaweed, holding the ship in place. But James swung over the side of the deck and cut the seaweed to free the ship. Then, he trapped all Zarina's friends in a sail.

Thinking quickly, Zarina released the ship's boom, which pinned James against the mast. She snatched the Blue Dust from him and spun the wheel sharply so the ship began to tilt. James's golden dust streamed off the ship and when James reached for it, he fell.

As Zarina was freeing the girls from the sail, James, now covered in golden dust, flew up behind her and took back the Blue Dust.

But James dropped one speck. Zarina quickly grabbed it and threw it on him. "From a trickle to a roar," she said with satisfaction, as James rocketed away, out of control!

Using her new water talent, Tink put a giant wave in James's path. He crashed into it and all the golden dust was washed off. He fell into the sea, where the ticking crocodile took off after him....

"No!" James yelled. "I am not a codfish! I'm a pirate!"

The fairies had won! They took control of the ship and flew it back to Pixie Hollow. When they reached the amphitheatre, Zarina used her dust to wake up the sleeping crowd.

"Zarina?!" Fairy Gary exclaimed. "You're home...." He pulled her into a giant hug.

"She even grew a Pixie Dust Tree!" exclaimed Rosetta. Now the fairies had two.

Queen Clarion was so impressed that she granted Zarina permission to show off her talent. Colours flew as Zarina gave her friends back their original talents – the crowd was in awe!

Time passed and life in Pixie Hollow happily hummed along. But out in the seas of Never Land, things would never be the same for Captain James.

Lady and the *TRAMP*

A Rainy Night Out

"Yip!" Scamp barked at the squirrel nibbling on an acorn in the grass. His brother and sisters were taking a nap under the big oak tree, and there was nobody else around to have fun with.

"Yip!" Scamp barked again, and the squirrel darted across the lawn. Scamp gave chase. The squirrel zipped up a lamp post and leaped onto a nearby tree branch. With a whimper, Scamp sat down and thumped his tail on the pavement. That was the problem with squirrels. They always got away too easily.

Disappointed, Scamp trotted along the pavement, stopping when he got to an open space. The grass here was tall, and butterflies flitted from wild flower to wild flower.

"Yip! Yip!" Scamp raced through the tall grass. He chased the butterflies to the end of the open space and back again.

It was getting dark. Scamp decided it was time to head home. He hadn't caught a single butterfly, but he'd had fun trying. He couldn't wait to get home and tell his brother and sisters about the new game he'd invented. They'd be so impressed!

Scamp trotted up to the front porch and tried to get through the doggie door. *Thunk!* His nose hit the wood, but it didn't move. The door was locked!

"Yip! Yip! I'm home!" he barked. "Let me in!"

Scamp sat there for several minutes, barking. Nobody came to the door. Suddenly – *boom!* – thunder echoed overhead. Lightning flashed and rain began to fall.

Scamp bolted over to the big oak tree, sat down and covered his eyes with his paws. Thunderstorms were scary!

"I'm not going to cry," he told himself as his eyes started to mist over. He shivered in the dark. He'd probably catch a cold by morning!

Scamp let out a little whimper and moved even closer to the tree trunk. He buried his wet nose in his wet paws and closed his eyes.

Scamp was just falling asleep when a sound made him start. Somebody was coming up the drive!

By the time Jim Dear and Darling were out of the taxi, Scamp was dashing across the lawn as fast as he could go. He bolted through the door just as it opened.

"Scamp, you're soaking wet!" Darling declared as the puppy found his brother and sisters napping in front of the fire. And, as he lay down among them, Jim Dear came over with a warm towel to dry him off.

Home, sweet home, Scamp thought happily, as he drifted off to sleep.

Peter Pan

We're Going on a Picnic

"Cap'n?" Mr Smee knocked softly on Captain Hook's door. There was no answer. The first mate pushed his way inside, carrying a breakfast tray. "I've got breakfast, Cap'n."

"I'm not hungry!" Captain Hook replied. "Go away!"

"But, Cap'n. You have to eat." Smee was getting worried. The Captain hadn't eaten in days. In fact, he hadn't even got out of bed! "I know you feel bad about Pe –" Smee stopped himself from saying the dreaded name just in time, "– that flying boy. And the croc – I mean – that ticking reptile, too." Captain Hook was really angry about being beaten by Peter again. Even worse, Peter had set the crocodile right back on Captain Hook's trail. "But we haven't seen hide nor scale of either of them for a week. I think the coast is clear."

There was no reply from Captain Hook.

Smee thought for a minute. "I know how to cheer you up!" he cried. "We'll have a nice old-fashioned picnic! Won't that be lovely!"

Again, silence from Captain Hook.

"Ah-ah-ah! No arguments!" Smee left the breakfast tray and hurried down to the galley. A picnic on Mermaid Island was just what the doctor ordered!

Smee whistled merrily as he made herring-and-pickle sandwiches (Captain Hook's favourite) and packed them in a wicker basket. This was Hook's day! Smee carefully folded a gingham tablecloth and placed it in the basket with his tin whistle. He was going to make sure that Hook had a good time, whether he wanted to or not!

Once the picnic basket was packed, Smee called down to Hook, "It's time to go, Cap'n!"

After a while, Captain Hook finally appeared on deck, blinking in the sunlight. "Fine," he said grumpily. "But I know I'm not going to have fun!"

Smee let the rowing boat down into the water and Hook began to climb down the rope ladder. Once he was safely in the boat, Smee picked up the picnic basket.

TICK TOCK TICK TOCK TICK TOCK.

"Smee!" cried Hook. "Help me!"

Smee peeked over the side of the ship. The crocodile was about to take a bite out of the boat!

In a panic, he threw the only thing he had on hand – the picnic basket. It landed right in the crocodile's open mouth. The crocodile stared at Smee in surprise. Then, without a sound, it slipped back under the water.

"My picnic!" cried Smee. "My tin whistle!"

"Next time you have any smart ideas about cheering me up," said the Captain, glaring at his first mate, "keep them to yourself!"

Too High a Price to Pay

The evil sorcerer had managed to capture the frog Naveen! He had poured several drops of Naveen's blood into his talisman. This meant that Lawrence could continue looking like Prince Naveen.

Their plan was for Lawrence to marry Charlotte, the richest young lady in New Orleans!

"I am going to become master of the world!" the sorcerer roared with laughter. From his balcony he was watching the Mardi Gras parade go past.

The main float looked like a wedding cake, and was where Charlotte and the fake Prince Naveen prepared to get married for real. The priest had already started the ceremony.

"I haven't got a second to lose!" whispered the frog Naveen, double-locked in a sorcerer's casket. He had to stop Charlotte marrying the fake Prince!

He bravely managed to launch the casket onto the float, and at the same moment, Tiana – who was also a frog – saw that the fake Prince Naveen was about to marry Charlotte....

"Oh! I thought that Naveen loved me!" she sobbed.

"But of course he does!" cried Ray, her firefly friend. "There's something wrong. I'm going to sort this out!"

Landing on the float, Ray heard the frog Naveen calling from inside the casket. Ray quickly rescued him and, in a flash, frog Naveen jumped onto the fake prince and tore the talisman from his neck! The villain immediately changed back into Lawrence.

"Ray!" shouted Naveen as he threw the talisman to the firefly for him to look after. But the sorcerer's evil Shadows immediately sprang forward in pursuit.

As the Shadows rapidly caught up, Ray found Tiana and threw the talisman to her. Tiana tried to run away ... but the evil sorcerer blocked her way.

"Give the talisman back to me, Tiana, and I will give you the means to open your own restaurant!" he whispered. "You'll be able to honour the memory of your poor father who was never able to achieve his dream."

"My father taught me to recognize the things that are really important in life!" Tiana replied sharply. "And opening my restaurant at the cost of your success would really be too high a price to pay!"

As she spoke, she broke the talisman and the evil sorcerer disappeared into thin air.

"I will probably just stay a waitress forever now," sighed Tiana. "But at least I'm an honest waitress!"

THE LITTLE
MERMAID

In Hot Water

Ariel could hardly believe that her plan was going so well. She had convinced Ursula, the sea witch, to change her from a mermaid into a human. Even though Ariel had paid for the transformation with her voice, she had already found her beloved Prince Eric. The only problem was that he didn't recognize her. And Ariel couldn't speak to explain who she was.

But Ariel wasn't worried. She knew he would fall in love with her, voice or no voice. And then they would be happy together forever.

"Come along, my dear," a female servant said, leading Ariel into a spacious room with sky-blue walls.

Ariel almost tripped on the edge of a rug, but caught herself just in time. She still wasn't used to her brand-new legs.

She put one hand into the pocket of her sailcloth dress to make sure that Sebastian was still inside. She was glad he was with her – having him nearby made her feel more at home.

"All right, let's get you cleaned up first," the woman said. "It'll be time for dinner soon."

As the woman bustled about, Ariel had a chance to look around the room. There were large windows along one wall and an ornate lantern hanging from the ceiling. There was also a large, shell-shaped bath filled with water.

Ariel watched curiously as the servant threw some white powder into the bath. Suddenly, the water fizzed with a huge pile of bubbles! Ariel gasped, delighted, as bubbles floated up out of the water towards the ceiling. She raced forward and leaped right into the bath, splashing water and bubbles everywhere.

Forgetting that she couldn't breathe under water any more, she dived beneath the bubbles. She came up coughing and wiped the water out of her eyes.

"Ahhhh!" Sebastian sputtered, swimming out of her pocket. He spat out a mouthful of bubbles. "What do these humans do to nice, clean water?"

The servant looked alarmed. "Oh, my! Did I see something move in there?"

Ariel shook her head, quickly shoving Sebastian back into her pocket.

"Well," the servant said. "You can't take a bath in that dress. Let's hang it up to dry."

Ariel was a little worried about Sebastian, but she did as the woman said. Soon the sailcloth dress was hanging on a towel rack.

Oh, well, Ariel thought. *I'm sure Sebastian can take care of himself. Knowing him, he'll probably go and find the kitchen. I wonder what the cook is like? I hope he doesn't like seafood!*

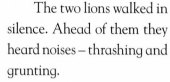

Hot on the Trail

"Over here!" Simba said, sniffing the trail. "It's going this way!"

"Yup, this way," Nala said with a nod, sniffing a stick. "And not long ago."

"I saw that stick first," Simba said. Nala was a good tracker, but Simba had learned from an expert – his mum. She was one of the best hunters in the pride.

"Hmmm," Nala said with a sniff. "So what are we following then, master tracker? Can you tell me that?"

Simba was silent. They had seen some footprints, but they weren't clear enough to read. They'd also seen some dark wiry hair on a log, but that could belong to lots of animals.

"Something that isn't very graceful," Simba said. They had seen lots of crushed grass and broken sticks.

"Mmm-hmm." Nala nodded impatiently.

"A rhino!" Simba said confidently.

"A rhino?" Nala rolled onto her back, laughing. "Simba, you crack me up!"

"What?" Simba couldn't hide the hurt in his voice. It *might* be a rhino!

"The footprints aren't big enough," Nala said. "It's Rafiki, the baboon."

Now, it was Simba's turn to laugh. "Rafiki likes the trees, he doesn't use trails like a hyena!" The giggle died in Simba's throat and he felt the fur on the back of his neck stand up. Hyenas were clumsy and had dark wiry hair....

Nala didn't say anything, but her fur was standing up a little too.

The two lions walked in silence. Ahead of them they heard noises – thrashing and grunting.

"Hey, Simba," Nala whispered, "maybe we should turn back."

"Just a little further," Simba whispered. They were almost there!

The young lions crept through the grass on their bellies as quietly as they could. The grunting and thrashing grew louder. They could see a dust cloud rising. Simba stifled a growl. Something about the smell and the sound was familiar, but Simba could not put his paw on it.

As they crept closer, two bodies came into view by the side of a termite mound. Simba pounced!

"Pumbaa! Timon!" he shouted, landing between his friends.

"Simba!" the warthog said, grinning. Termites dripped out of his muddy mouth. "Want some?"

Timon held a handful of wriggling insects towards Nala. "There are plenty to go around."

"Uh, no thanks," Nala said as she came out of the grass, giggling. She shot a look at Simba. "I think I'll wait for the master tracker to hunt me up some lunch!"

A Thank You Present

"I don't know how I can ever thank them," Snow White said to her new husband, the Prince. The two of them were on their way to visit the Dwarfs and give them a special present – a meal fit for seven kings!

Snow White looked at the dishes and hampers filled with delicious food. "It just doesn't seem like enough," she said with a sigh. "They saved my life!"

"I'm sure seeing you happy is thanks enough," the Prince said, putting his arm around Snow White. "They don't want riches, and they seem quite happy living the way they do."

Snow White had to agree and, as the cosy Dwarf cottage came into view, she perked up. She could not wait to see her little friends! "Yoo-hoo!" she called as she dashed from the coach. "Sneezy? Happy? Bashful?"

Snow White knocked on the door, but there was no answer. "They must not be home yet," she said to the Prince. "We'll have just enough time to get everything ready."

Snow White went inside and set the table and tidied the house, humming while she worked. She was so excited to see her friends, that she couldn't help checking the windows for a sign of them every few minutes. As the sun set, the Princess began to worry.

"They're awfully late!" she said.

The Prince agreed. It was getting dark.

"Perhaps we should go and find them." The Prince strode outside and unhitched one of the horses from the coach. Together the Prince and Princess set off to find the Dwarfs.

At last they reached the mine. Holding up lanterns, they saw at once what the trouble was. A tree had fallen over the mine entrance. The Dwarfs were trapped!

"Snow White, is that you?" Doc called through a small opening.

"Are you all right?" Snow White asked.

"We're fine, dear. Just fine," Doc told her.

"No, we're not," Grumpy said, rather grumpily. "We're stuck!"

"Don't worry," the Prince said. "We'll have you out in no time."

Hitching his horse to the big tree, the Prince pulled it away from the mine so the Dwarfs could get out.

Snow White embraced each dusty Dwarf as he emerged. She even hugged Dopey twice! "Now let's get you home," she said.

Back at home, the Dwarfs were thrilled to see the fine meal laid out on their table.

"How can we ever thank you?" Doc said, wringing his hat. "You saved our lives."

"Don't be silly." Snow White blushed. "Seeing you happy is thanks enough."

Bambi

Winter Nap

Bambi nosed under the crunchy leaves, looking for fresh grass. There was none. He looked up at the trees, but there were no green leaves there either. Food was getting scarce in the forest.

"Don't worry, Bambi," Thumper said when he saw the confused look in Bambi's eyes. "We'll get through the winter. Dad says we always do. We find what we can when we can, and we always make it until spring."

Bambi sighed and nodded. Thumper's dad was smart. He knew lots of things about the forest.

"Besides, it's better to be awake than napping all winter. Yech!" Thumper hated to go to bed, even at bedtime.

"Napping?" Bambi didn't know that some animals slept through the winter months.

"Sure. You know, like Flower, and the squirrels, and the bears. They hole up for months. Haven't you noticed the chipmunks putting their acorns away the past couple of months?" Thumper pointed towards an oak tree.

Bambi nodded.

"That's their food for the winter. As soon as it gets cold enough, they'll just stay inside and sleep," Thumper explained.

"But how will they know when it's time to wake up?" Bambi couldn't imagine life in the forest without all the other animals.

Thumper tapped his foot to think. It was a good question. And, since he had never slept through the winter, he wasn't sure of the answer. "Let's go ask Flower." They headed for the young skunk's den.

"Hello," Flower said.

"Flower, you sleep all winter, right?" Thumper asked.

"It's called hibernation." Flower yawned a big yawn. "Excuse me," he said, blushing.

"So, Bambi wants to know who wakes you up in the spring," Thumper said.

"You'll be back, won't you, Flower?" Bambi asked worriedly.

The little skunk giggled. "Oh, we always come back. Just like the grass and the flowers and the leaves," Flower explained. "I never thought about what wakes us up before. It must be the sun, I guess."

Bambi smiled. He didn't know the grass and leaves would come back in the spring too! He was feeling much better about the forest's winter nap.

Suddenly, Thumper started laughing. He rolled on his back and pumped his large hind feet in the air.

"What is it?" Bambi and Flower asked together.

"You really are a flower, Flower!" Thumper giggled. "You even bloom in the spring!"

The Midnight Gift

Midnight was about to strike in New Orleans! Quickly, Tiana – who had turned into a frog – hopped to St Louis Cathedral where her friend Charlotte was about to marry a valet disguised as the handsome Prince Naveen.

Fortunately, when she arrived at the cathedral, the imposter was already being taken away by the police, and the real Prince Naveen, who was still a frog too, was talking to Charlotte.

"But is it like the fairy tales then?" Charlotte was saying. "If I kiss you, will the sorcerer's evil spell be lifted, and will you become a handsome prince again?"

Naveen nodded. "Yes, because until midnight you're princess of the carnival," he explained. "And in that way Tiana will also become human again...."

Charlotte clapped.

"Oh wow! It's too marvellous for words! I have to kiss a frog, who will be transformed into a prince, and we will get married and live happily ever after, and on top of that, I will save my friend Tiana, and...."

"Wait Charlotte," interrupted Naveen, suddenly looking sad. "You must promise me that by tomorrow you will give Tiana all the money she needs to buy her restaurant.

Because Tiana's happiness is very important to me...."

Tiana had dreamed of opening her own restaurant her whole life. Prince Naveen had fallen in love with Tiana, and wanted to help her.

Charlotte was about to kiss Prince Naveen when Tiana leapt in front of them. "No, don't do it Naveen, I beg you!"

"What? But it's your last chance to achieve your dream, Tiana!"

She shook her head and replied, "There would be no point realizing my dream without sharing it with you by my side, Naveen ... because I love you as much as you love me!"

They threw themselves into each other's arms, and Charlotte burst into tears! "It's so moving," she sniffed. "Tiana ... all my life, I have hoped for a big fairytale love story. And you have found it! Of course I will kiss you, Naveen, and then you can marry Tiana!"

But it was too late – the bells chimed midnight! Charlotte desperately placed one, two, ten kisses on the lips of the frog Prince. But she was no longer a princess!

Naveen and Tiana looked at each other, madly in love. They could remain frogs forever now. What did it matter? They were contented with simply having each other.

Cinderella

The Lost Mice

One winter night, the Prince led Cinderella out to the balcony. "I have a surprise for you," he said, handing her a box. Inside was a beautiful new coat.

"Oh, it's lovely!" Cinderella exclaimed.

The next morning, the princess showed her coat to Suzy, one of her mouse friends.

A few minutes later, Jaq went into Cinderella's room. It had been a chilly night in the attic.

"Cinderelly!" Jaq called.

If he told the princess how cold the attic was, she would help them. But she was on her way out and didn't hear. Jaq sighed. He was sure she wouldn't mind if they sat in front of the blazing fire in Cinderella's room.

Soon, the new housekeeper came in. When she saw the mice, she shrieked. She didn't know that the mice were Cinderella's friends. She chased them with a broom and the mice ran straight into the castle gardener. Before they knew what was happening, he had trapped them. "Take them outside!" the housekeeper said.

Meanwhile, Cinderella and the Prince were out riding. As their horses trotted through the countryside, they saw the castle gardener in one of the fields.

"Hello!" the Prince called out. But the gardener did not answer. The Prince turned to Cinderella. "That was odd," he said. "Why wouldn't he answer?"

"Perhaps he was lost in thought?" Cinderella replied.

Cinderella was right. The gardener was thinking hard. The housekeeper had told him to let the mice go, but he was worried about them. Finally, he took the mice to the stables. "Don't tell the housekeeper," he told the stable workers. "These poor mice need warmth and a bite to eat." The mice were very grateful.

Later that night, Cinderella was starting to worry. She hadn't seen the mice all day. She was searching for them when she ran into the Prince.

"I am looking for our new housekeeper. Apparently she threw the mice out of the castle today!" said the Prince.

"Oh, no!" Cinderella cried. "Poor dears. They'll freeze outside!"

"Don't worry," the Prince said. He told Cinderella what the gardener had done.

Together, Cinderella and the Prince went to the stables. They thanked the gardener and the stable workers. Cinderella was relieved to see her little friends safe and sound. From then on, the mice always had a warm place of their own – in one of the main rooms of the castle.

The Helpful Dragon

Princess Aurora went riding on her horse, Buttercup, with Prince Phillip close behind. As they rounded a bend, a small dragon popped out from behind a tree.

"Oh, he's so cute!" Aurora exclaimed.

But Phillip was worried. "Dragons can be dangerous!" The little dragon shook his head.

Aurora laughed. "Let's take him home. I'm going to call him Crackle!"

"He does seem like a harmless little fellow," Phillip agreed.

When Phillip and Aurora rode into the courtyard, the three good fairies were hanging banners for a ball. King Stefan and the queen were coming to the castle.

Flora gasped when she saw Crackle. "Dragons can be dangerous!"

"Remember the last one!" Fauna warned.

"Oooh, I think he's sweet," Merryweather spoke up.

Just then, Crackle noticed a kitten in a basket of wool. Crackle listened to it purring. Then he tried to purr. "Purrgrr, purrgrr!" Clouds of smoke streamed from his nose and mouth.

Crackle looked sad. "Oh, Crackle," Aurora said gently. "You're not a kitten. You're a dragon."

Aurora noticed that Crackle looked unhappy, so she took him to the castle.

But King Hubert heard Crackle and rushed into the room. "Oh, my, my, my! How did a dragon get in here?" he shouted. Frightened, Crackle ran to the garden. Aurora found the little dragon sitting beside a fountain, watching a fish. *Splash!* Before Aurora could stop him, Crackle jumped into the water.

"Crackle, you're not a fish!" Aurora exclaimed. "You're not a kitten either. Do you think no one will like you because you're a dragon?" she asked. Crackle nodded.

"You can't change what you are," Aurora said kindly. "But you can be a helpful dragon."

Suddenly thunder boomed. Rain began to pour down. Everyone was gathered in the grand hallway, watching the storm.

"I'm afraid King Stefan and the queen might lose their way," Prince Phillip said.

Aurora looked at Crackle. "Please fly to the top of the tower and blow the largest, brightest flames to guide my parents to the castle."

Suddenly, gold and red flames lit up the sky. Crackle had done it! And thanks to Crackle's flame, the king and queen got safely home.

Operation Rescue

The Stabbington brothers had once been Flynn Rider's partners in crime. They helped him steal the royal crown, but things turned sour when Flynn refused to share it with them. Flynn then changed when he met Rapunzel, and tried to return the crown to the brothers.

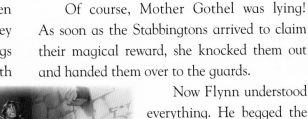

But the Stabbingtons knocked Flynn out and tied him in a small boat. They placed the stolen crown on his knees and sent the boat off towards the castle. Their plan worked perfectly – when the guards saw Flynn with the crown, they arrested him and threw him in the dungeon!

"Rapunzel!" moaned Flynn as he woke up. "I must rescue her!"

Fortunately, their horse friend Maximus had seen everything. He knew that Flynn had changed and that he didn't deserve to be in prison. He also knew that Rapunzel had been held in the tower by wicked Mother Gothel....

So, Maximus galloped to the pub full of ruffians they had visited earlier. He needed them to help Flynn escape!

Meanwhile, Flynn learned that the Stabbington brothers were locked up in jail, too – Mother Gothel had betrayed them. They had agreed to trap Flynn and give up the crown, because she had promised them Rapunzel's magic hair in exchange.

Of course, Mother Gothel was lying! As soon as the Stabbingtons arrived to claim their magical reward, she knocked them out and handed them over to the guards.

Now Flynn understood everything. He begged the guards, "Please let me go! Rapunzel needs help!"

But at that moment, the gang of pub thugs came rushing into the prison. They fought with the guards and dragged Flynn out into the main courtyard. There, one of them pushed him onto a cart tipped at an angle.

"Put your head down," the ruffian told him. "Hold your arms against your sides. Open your legs wide."

Wham! The ruffian jumped on the other end of the cart and Flynn flew into the air!

Flynn went shrieking over the prison wall and landed right on Maximus' back – the horse had been waiting for him at the dungeon entrance.

Flynn was amazed – the horse that had once been desperate to catch him was now rescuing him!

They both cared deeply about Rapunzel and wanted to save her from Mother Gothel's evil clutches.

Flynn patted Maximus, and the horse galloped off towards the tower. But would they be too late to save Rapunzel?

Disney
Winnie the Pooh

A Yummy Dream

Winnie the Pooh stepped into his house and sat down with a sigh. He and Piglet had been out on a long walk through the woods. Now Pooh was tired. And, more importantly, he was hungry.

"My tummy feels very rumbly," Pooh said aloud.

Pooh got to his feet and went over to his honey cupboard. There was only one pot of honey inside.

"Oh dear," Pooh said. One pot of honey was not very much. He sat down and began to eat. He ate every last sticky drop. But when he was finished, his tummy was still feeling a tiny bit rumbly.

"Well, I suppose there's nothing left to do but go to bed," Pooh said sadly. He put on his nightshirt and his nightcap and climbed into his cosy bed. A minute later Pooh's snores filled the air. And dreams began to fill his head – dreams of honey, of course.

Pooh stood before the honey tree. It was so full of honey, it was oozing out of the trunk!

"Yummy, yummy," Pooh said. He began to fill his honeypots.

Then, suddenly, a purple heffalump appeared behind him.

"Mmmm," the heffalump said, licking his lips. The creature stuck his long trunk into one of the honeypots and gobbled up all the honey.

"Those are my honeypots!" Pooh cried.

He tried to sound brave, even though he was just a little bit scared. The heffalump looked very big and very hungry.

The heffalump just stared at Pooh.

Pooh looked at the honeypots. There were a lot of them. Some were full, but most were still empty. Pooh looked at the honey tree. It was still overflowing with honey.

"I have an idea," Pooh said. "Let's fill the honeypots together, then share a nice snack."

The heffalump nodded excitedly. He picked up a honeypot with his trunk and carried it over to the tree. Pooh did the same, and the sweet, sticky honey dripped into the pots.

When all of the pots had been filled, Pooh and the heffalump sat down together. They ate and ate until all the pots were empty and their tummies were full.

"Thank you, Pooh," the heffalump said as he got to his feet. "That was fun. We should do this again soon."

Pooh nodded in agreement and watched the heffalump walk away. Getting to his feet, he patted his tummy.

When Pooh awoke the next morning, to his surprise, his tummy wasn't the slightest bit rumbly. Then he remembered his strange dream. It had been a dream, hadn't it?

ALICE
in
WONDERLAND

A Refreshing Cup of Tea

"*Twinkle, twinkle, little bat!*
  How I wonder what you're at!
  Up above the world you fly,
  Like a tea-tray in the sky."

The song came from just around the tall tree with the funny, mitten-shaped leaves. Alice knew it could only have been sung by one person: the Mad Hatter!

"Oh, bother!" Alice sighed. Truly, the Hatter and his friends were among the last creatures she wished to see. They were so ... so very mad, after all!

"And yet," Alice went on, again to no one but herself, "a nice cup of tea would be quite refreshing." *And who here knew where else a person might find tea?*

And so, with a bold shrug, Alice made her way around the shady bend.

In the clearing, the Hatter, the March Hare and the Dormouse were sitting, much as they had been upon Alice's last visit, around their ample tea table, singing and ranting and sleeping, respectively.

"A-hem!" Alice made her presence known to them by clearing her thirsty throat.

"Well!" exclaimed the Hatter. "If it isn't our dear, dear old friend! I say, what was your name again, dear old friend?"

"Alice," Alice patiently replied.

"Well, have a seat, Alice, dear!"

"Thank you," said Alice. "But, you know, I can only stay a minute – though I could use a cup of tea."

"And how would you use it?" the Hatter asked. "Carefully, I hope."

"Very carefully," Alice assured him.

"Ah, well, that's good. And that's also bad."

"Bad?" Alice asked.

"You heard him!" said the March Hare. "Can't you see? We have no tea!"

"No tea?" asked Alice, gazing about at the table full of empty cups and saucers.

"No tea?" sobbed the Dormouse, stirring from his sleep. "No tea!"

"There you go upsetting him again!" shouted the Hare.

"I didn't...." Alice began.

Then she remembered how useless it was to argue with a hare who was mad. Instead, she left the March Hare to his shouting, and the Dormouse to his crying, and the Hatter to his ... whatever it was he was doing ... and walked over to the stove, where a kettle was cheerfully boiling. Finding a tin of fragrant tea leaves, she dropped some into an empty teapot and filled it with hot water. Then she reached for the cleanest cup she could find and filled it.

She was tempted to offer her hosts a cup as well. But on second thoughts, she decided that perhaps it was better to just ... go.

Finding Sadness

Two of Riley's Emotions – Joy and Sadness – were lost in the Mind World and now, they had even lost each other! While trying to get Riley's core memories back to Headquarters, Joy had fallen into the Memory Dump, leaving Sadness all alone.

Down in the dump, Joy and Bing Bong were surrounded by Riley's old memories. The spheres were fading, and disappearing into thin wisps of mist.

Suddenly, Joy had an idea – if they could find Bing Bong's lost rocket wagon in the dump, they could use it to escape!

Joy started singing Bing Bong's special song, which powered the rocket wagon. They heard the sound of an engine and followed it until it got louder. They had found it!

The pair sang loudly to make the wagon fly, but each time they took off, they couldn't quite reach the clifftop above. It just didn't have enough power. Joy was ready to give up, but Bing Bong noticed his own hand was starting to fade and urged Joy to have one more go.

On the final try, Bing Bong jumped out of the rocket before it left the ground. Now that it was lighter, the rocket soared up and delivered Joy safely to the top of the cliff.

When Joy realized what Bing Bong had done, she looked over the edge of the cliff and saw him far below, dancing with happiness.

"Take Riley to the moon for me," he called. "I'll try, Bing Bong," Joy replied. "I promise."

Then Bing Bong took a final bow and disappeared. Riley didn't need him anymore. Joy felt sad, but Bing Bong had done a brave and heroic thing. She knew that her next task was to find Sadness before heading back to Headquarters. After all, Riley needed both of them.

Joy walked across the Mind World until she eventually spotted Sadness in Long Term Memory. "Sadness!" Joy called.

"I only make everything worse!" Sadness cried, running towards Cloud Town. She hopped on to a cloud and flew away. Joy tried to chase her but the cloud was moving too fast.

Then Joy spotted the Imaginary Boyfriend Generator nearby and had an idea. Joy turned on the generator and hundreds of Imaginary Boyfriends came out on the conveyor belt. Joy piled the Boyfriends up, making a huge tower. She grabbed on to a Boyfriend and made the tower swing towards Sadness's cloud.

"Joy?" Sadness said in disbelief.

"Gotcha!" Joy cried as she grabbed Sadness in mid-air. "Hang on!"

With one last swing of the tower, Joy let go of the Boyfriend. She and Sadness flew through the air towards Headquarters. *SPLAT!* They hit the back window and slid down the glass.

TinkerBell
AND THE
LEGEND OF THE
NEVERBEAST

The Mysterious Light

On a night like any other in Pixie Hollow, Iridessa, a light-talent fairy, was gathering up moonbeams. She didn't notice the mysterious green star in the sky – until it suddenly began to move. It shot through the night, trailing a bright green tail of light behind. It was a comet!

Scribble, a reading-talent sparrowman, watched it through a telescope. He knew that the last time the comet had appeared in Pixie Hollow was almost a thousand years before.

The comet's light also drew the attention of Tinker Bell, a tinker-talent fairy.

The light from the comet continued on, brightening every dark corner and crevice. And as the light spilled deep down into a cave, something began to stir; something big and hairy with bright-green eyes....

The next day, Fawn, an animal-talent fairy, began her work as usual. She tumbled happily down hills with the bugs, jumped with the bunnies and soared through the sky with the birds. Out of all the animal fairies, Fawn really embraced her job.

Later that day, Tink brought Fawn a handmade wagon. "Just as you ordered," said Tink. "But what are you up to?"

With a firm grasp on Tink's arm, Fawn led her to her home. "Just try not to scream," she said. "Deal?"

Tink didn't know what to expect, but was shocked when she peeked into Fawn's home and two big eyes suddenly blinked open. It was a baby hawk. "Hawks eat fairies!" gasped Tink.

Fawn explained that Hannah the hawk was harmless. She had fixed the bird's wing, and it was time to let her go. "We have to get Hannah out without causing widespread panic!" Fawn said.

Reluctantly, Tink helped Hannah into the wagon and covered her with blueberries. But still all the fairies and animals stared as they went by.

"What's with the berries?" asked Rosetta, a garden-talent fairy.

"Oh, we're just taking them to the forest," said Fawn innocently.

But Rosetta knew how to move the berries much, much faster! With a sprinkle of pixie dust, the fruit rose up and zoomed off to the forest, uncovering Hannah, who screeched in delight. The sight of her scared everyone, except for three adult hawks nearby. They heard Hannah's screech and decided that she needed rescuing. Hannah might have been harmless, but these adults were anything but!

Disney
Beauty and the Beast

The Enchanted Mirror

The odd sisters were in a panic. Even they could see Belle was warming to the Beast, and the Beast – well, he was experiencing something quite unique to him and utterly terrifying to the witches. It was becoming painfully clear they were falling in love!

The sisters had to do something.

"Those servants really aren't helping. They contrive romance at every single opportunity!" squealed Ruby.

Ruby, Martha and Lucinda must have looked a mess when Circe returned from her visit to Morningstar Castle to restore Princess Tulip's beauty. When they heard her come in, the three of them turned as one. "Oh! Hello!" they said together, looking tired and crazed from fretting, spying and plotting against the Beast.

"What is all this?" Circe asked.

The odd sisters just stood there. For once they had nothing to say. Lucinda's ringlets were tangled like a bird's nest, with little bits of dried herbs and candle wax stuck within them. Ruby's red skirt was covered in ash, and the feathers in her hair were sticking out at strange angles. Martha's face was smudged with some kind of orange powder.

"Spell-work, I see!" Circe scolded.

The sisters looked at each other, and with a nod from Lucinda, Ruby took a necklace out of her pocket. "We got you this!"

"We thought you would like it!" said Martha. "Try it on!"

Lucinda ran towards Circe like an excited child. As soon as she fastened the necklace round Circe's neck, she slumped into her sister's waiting arms. "That's right, little sister, sleep!"

They placed Circe on the soft feather bed. "We will wake you when it's over, and you will thank us for avenging your broken heart."

The sisters gathered again near the fire, this time tossing in a silver powder.

"Make her miss Father dear, show Belle her greatest fear," they chanted, and their laughter travelled with the winds to the Beast's enchanted castle.

They watched as the Beast asked Belle if she was happy. And yes, she was! She just wanted to see her father. She missed him so much.

"There is a way," the Beast said tenderly. He gave her the mirror Circe had given him. "It can show you anything you wish to see."

The sisters muffled their squeals of glee as Belle saw her greatest fear – her father sick, maybe dying. She had to go to him! And because the Beast loved her, he let her go.

To The Rescue

Snow White and her Prince spent nearly every day together. But one morning, the Prince told Snow White that he had an errand to take care of. The Prince saddled his trusty steed, Astor, and bid Snow White farewell.

That afternoon, Snow White spotted a cloud of dust on the road. A horse was rapidly approaching. She was excited that the Prince was home early. But imagine Snow White's surprise when she saw that Astor was alone! "Why, where's the Prince?" she wondered out loud. But the horse could not say.

Snow White's tender heart filled with dread. *Surely the Prince is in trouble*, she thought. She bravely decided she must go and find him. Astor stamped her hoof on the ground and nodded towards her empty saddle.

"Do you want me to get on?" Snow White asked. Again, Astor nodded. Goodness! Snow White thought. Maybe Astor can tell me where the Prince is after all! The Princess barely had time to sit down before Astor was racing down the road towards the forest!

Astor ran deeper into the woods with Snow White tugging uselessly at the reins. If only she knew that the Prince was safe! Then, suddenly, Snow White spotted a piece of red cloth caught on a sharp thorn. Could it be?

It was! A scrap torn from the Prince's very own riding cloak! And that wasn't all. As they continued through the forest, Snow White spotted petals from the rose she had given the Prince. Then she found his hat dangling from a tree!

Snow White gripped the reins with one hand. She clutched the Prince's hat and concentrated on thinking hopeful thoughts.

Finally, they emerged into a sunny clearing, and Astor slowed to a stop. Snow White spotted the Prince, lying on the ground. She slipped out of the saddle and raced across the clearing. Breathless, Snow White reached the Prince just as he sat up and stretched.

"What a nice nap!" he said. "I hope you're hungry!"

Snow White was bewildered. Next to the Prince lay a lavish picnic spread out on a soft blanket, and the Prince was as happy and healthy as ever!

"I knew Astor would get you here quickly," he said, beaming. "Tell me, are you surprised?"

Snow White paused for a moment to catch her breath. "Oh, yes, very surprised," she said at last, smiling. She picked up an apple and offered it to Astor.

"And," she added, "I'm very glad you have such a dear and clever horse!"

A Difficult Decision

Carl Fredricksen and Russell had flown to South America in Carl's house. Carl was an old man who had dreamed of being an explorer since he was just a boy. His best childhood friend, Ellie, had shared this same dream. They grew up and got married, and Carl promised Ellie he would take her to see Paradise Falls. But they never managed to save enough money to go, and sadly Ellie passed away.

Carl was being forced to move out of their home, so he decided to take the trip that he and Ellie had always dreamed about. But he accidentally took Russell along for the ride. Whilst walking towards Paradise Falls with the floating house in tow, they had met a strange female bird called Kevin, and a talking dog called Dug. Dug was part of a pack of dogs who wanted to capture Kevin for their leader – the great explorer, Charles Muntz!

But Charles thought Carl and Russell were trying to steal the bird from him, and he sent his pack of dogs after them. Luckily Dug blocked the other dogs' path with some rocks. But he couldn't stop the pack for long.

One dog – Alpha – shoved him roughly aside and jumped over the rocks. Up ahead, Carl, Russell and Kevin had come to the edge of a cliff. They were trapped!

Luckily, Carl and Russell were holding onto the house by the garden hose. Just then, the wind lifted the house into the air – taking Carl and his friends with it! Alpha grabbed Kevin's leg, but he lost his grip.

Carl and his friends had escaped, but Kevin's leg was badly hurt. Russell realized that the bird needed help to get back to her babies.

Out of nowhere, a spotlight appeared and shone down on the bird. Muntz had followed them in the *Spirit of Adventure*! Before Kevin could escape, a net shot out from the airship and trapped her. Carl tried to set her free.

"Get away from my bird!" Muntz snarled. Then he set Carl's house on fire!

Carl couldn't let his house go up in smoke – it held all his memories of Ellie. So he quickly made the decision to give up Kevin instead. The dogs dragged the wounded bird onto the airship. As Muntz lifted off with his prize bird, Carl ran to his house and beat back the flames.

"You gave away Kevin," Russell said.

Carl felt terrible, but what could he do? "I didn't ask for any of this!" he snapped. "Now, whether you assist me or not, I am going to Paradise Falls if it kills me."

Russell watched sadly as Carl walked away, pulling the house behind him.

Wreck-It Ralph

Something for Felix to Fix

Wreck-It Ralph, who was the Bad Guy from the computer game *Fix-It Felix, Jr*, was in a racing game called *Sugar Rush* – where everything was made of sweets. Ralph had left his own game to find a medal and prove he was a Good Guy, but had ended up far from where he belonged!

He had agreed to help his new friend Vanellope to make a new cart – she was a racer in *Sugar Rush* and wanted to win. If she did, she promised she would give back Ralph's medal, which he had lost to her.

Elsewhere, Felix from Ralph's game and Sergeant Calhoun from *Hero's Duty* were searching for Ralph. When Ralph crashed in *Sugar Rush*, he had accidentally set free a dangerous cy-bug! Felix was looking for Ralph, and Calhoun was looking for the cy-bug. Calhoun asked Felix why Ralph would leave his own game.

"I wish I knew," Felix replied. "I never thought he'd go Turbo...."

Years ago, there had been a racing game in the arcade called *Turbo Time*. Its star, Turbo, was very popular ... until a newer racing game arrived. Overcome with jealousy, Turbo left his own game and tried to take over the new one. But when Turbo appeared in the wrong game, everyone thought it was broken!

In the end, both games were unplugged and hauled away.

"I've got to fix this mess and get Ralph home, or the same thing's going to happen to my game," said Felix.

Together, the two headed further into *Sugar Rush*. Calhoun was determined to find that cy-bug before it could multiply.

Not far away, Vanellope led Ralph to the *Sugar Rush* kart bakery. The two sneaked inside and baked a kart ... Vanellope loved it!

Then, King Candy – the King of *Sugar Rush* – arrived. Vanellope and Ralph ran away! Vanellope led Ralph through a secret entrance into Diet Cola Mountain. She lived inside, near a hot spring of fizzy soda. Now and then, a few mint sweets fell into the spring, causing a boiling hot explosion.

Ralph wrecked the rocks around the lake, to create a practice racetrack. Soon Vanellope was speeding along! Ralph thought Vanellope might be a natural, if only she could stop all the twitching and glitching that she did.

Vanellope was excited. She and Ralph were heading for the big race! She was happy to have a friend, at last. The other racers thought she was just a glitch in the game, but she was going to prove them wrong!

The Real Prisoner

With a heavy heart, Rapunzel found herself back at the tower with Mother Gothel – the old woman that Rapunzel thought was her real mother.

Alone in her room, the young girl thought sadly about Flynn, who had helped her to finally leave the tower.

Even Pascal, her pet chameleon, was finding it hard to keep her spirits up. But suddenly, he changed colour to match the flag with the golden sun emblem that Rapunzel had brought from the kingdom. Rapunzel watched as he climbed along the wall, and as he passed over the pictures she had painted, the young girl was taken aback. My goodness! Without realizing it, she had painted the emblem of the kingdom all over the walls – and yet she had never seen it before she left the tower!

"How do you explain that, Pascal?"

Rapunzel thought about it. Somewhere, deep down inside her, she must have already known about this emblem, as golden as her own hair. Perhaps that was why she was so keen to find out about the lanterns that appeared in the sky every year on her birthday. Flynn had explained that the people of the kingdom sent these lanterns off in memory of their lost princess.

Rapunzel had also seen a beautiful mosaic in the town. It showed the King, the Queen and their baby before a wicked woman had stolen her away. *Look at that – I've got green eyes like the baby's mother,* Rapunzel had thought.

"Oh my goodness, Pascal! It's me. I'm the princess!" she suddenly cried out. "It all makes sense: the date of my birthday, the golden emblem...."

Immediately, Rapunzel told Mother Gothel that she knew everything.

"You're not my mother! You stole me away to make use of my magic hair! You taught me to be afraid of people who might want to steal my power from me. But all the time it was you I should have been afraid of!" Rapunzel was very angry. "I'm leaving! I forgive Flynn. I'm going to ask him to help me!"

"No point, Rapunzel," grunted Mother Gothel. "Flynn can do nothing for you. He didn't abandon you – I had him thrown in prison!"

"Locking people up is a real obsession of yours! But now I'm not a prisoner any more. I can escape from this tower but you depend entirely on the magic of my hair to stay youthful. Well, from now on I refuse to allow you that privilege. You see, the real prisoner is you!"

THE LITTLE
MERMAID

Ariel's New Move

"Whoa." Prince Eric brought the carriage to a stop. Beside him, Ariel barely managed to keep from sliding off the seat. She had been human for just a short time, and she wasn't used to her legs yet.

"Are you hungry?" the Prince asked. Eric gestured towards a restaurant and looked at Ariel expectantly.

Ariel smiled and nodded. She could not speak, and she was a little wary of eating. Humans ate fish, and she could not help but think of her best friend, Flounder, whenever she saw something scaly lying on a plate. But she wanted to please the Prince.

The restaurant was nearly empty. Eric and Ariel sat at a table for two as the owner approached.

"What'll it be, dear?" a woman with warm brown eyes and white hair asked, looking kindly at Ariel.

"She'll have ... the soup?" Eric looked at Ariel for confirmation. Ariel nodded. "And I will have the speciality of the house."

Ariel was glad that Eric didn't seem to mind talking for her, though she desperately wanted to speak for herself and tell him how much she enjoyed being with him.

When the owner walked away, the silence in the room seemed to grow. Ariel tried to communicate with gestures, but Eric didn't seem to understand and, after a few minutes, the poor girl started to feel foolish.

With a sigh of relief, Ariel noticed the owner coming back with their food. Eric seemed relieved too. After she set down the plates, the white-haired woman walked over to a tall wooden piece of furniture near the wall. She sat down in front of it and placed her hands on the black and white keys.

Ariel had never seen a piano before. And she had never heard one either. She was enchanted by the music. She let her spoon drop into her bowl. The song was lovely – happy and sad at the same time. She wanted to sing along! But, of course, she could not. Still, she could not break away. The music reminded her of the rhythms of the ocean. She stood and began to sway, but her new legs were so awkward, she stumbled.

Suddenly, Eric's strong arm was around Ariel's waist. With his other arm, he took Ariel's hand in his. Ariel looked startled. "Haven't you ever danced before?" the Prince asked.

Ariel shook her head shyly.

"I'll show you," the Prince said, smiling at her. He whirled Ariel around the floor. The Little Mermaid was a natural. She spun and smiled, glad that they had found a way to communicate without words.

101 DALMATIANS

A Helping Paw

The dairy barn was warm and cosy, and 99 exhausted, hungry pups were taking turns to drink warm milk from the motherly cows.

"We'd nearly given up hope that you would get here," the kindly collie said to Pongo and Perdita, who had just arrived with the puppies.

"We're so very grateful to you for your hospitality," Perdita murmured wearily.

"Just look at the little dears," said one of the cows. "I've never seen so many puppies in one place before!"

Pongo, Perdita and the puppies had just come in from a long and weary march in the cold. It was very late, and the pups waiting for a drink of milk could barely keep their eyes open. The puppies had recently managed to escape from the dreadful old house owned by Cruella De Vil. They had been held prisoner there, guarded by two villains named Horace and Jasper. Cruella was planning to make a fur coat out of their lovely spotted fur. Luckily Pongo and Perdita had rescued them all just in the nick of time.

The pups had their dinners and gathered around the collie, thanking him for his hospitality.

"Not at all, not at all," the collie replied. "Do you have warm milk for supper every night out here in the country?" asked Rolly.

The collie chuckled. "No, but we do eat very simple country fare. I'm sure it's plainer than the food you eat in the city, but we eat big meals because of all the chores we do."

"And is it always this cold in the country?" asked Patch.

"Well, now," replied the collie. "I suppose most of you come from the city. No, it isn't always this cold, but there are plenty of differences between living in the country and living in the city. Take leashes, for instance. We don't keep our pets on leashes here, the way you do in the city, since our pets have a lot of wide-open space to roam around in. There aren't as many dogs nearby, but there are certainly other sorts of animals that one doesn't see in the city. Take cows, for instance. And then there are sheep and horses and geese, and...."

Suddenly, the collie stopped talking. A tiny snore escaped one of the pups he had just been talking to. He looked around and realized that every one of the pups, as well as Pongo and Perdita, had fallen into a deep sleep.

"Poor little things," he said quietly, as he trotted outside to stand guard. "They've been through so much. I do hope they get home safely soon."

Not Just a Glitch

Wreck-It Ralph, from the computer game *Fix-It Felix, Jr*, had helped his new friend Vanellope to build a new racing cart, so he could get his Medal of Heroes back – he wanted the medal to prove he was a Good Guy, and Vanellope wanted to win her big race! She was a character in the *Sugar Rush* game.

As the pair headed out to race, Vanellope hit the brakes. "Forgot something!" she said. "I'll be right back."

That's when King Candy, the leader of *Sugar Rush*, arrived. He told Ralph that Vanellope was in danger – that she didn't belong in the game, and if players in the arcade saw her glitching, they'd think *Sugar Rush* was broken and switch off the game. And because Vanellope was a glitch, she wouldn't be able to escape the game – she'd be switched off along with it!

King Candy gave Ralph's medal back and asked for his help. He told Ralph he had to stop Vanellope from racing.

After King Candy left, Vanellope returned with a homemade medal, just for Ralph. On the back, it read: "To Stink Brain" and on the front, "You're MY HERO!"

Then, Vanellope saw the Medal of Heroes in Ralph's pocket. "You sold me out!" she cried.

Ralph tried to explain. He told Vanellope that she would confuse the players if she raced. And if the game were switched off, she would be doomed. Vanellope wouldn't agree, so to save her, Ralph wrecked her kart so she couldn't race.

Sadly, Ralph returned to his own game. Only a character called Gene was still there. Everyone else had fled, believing the game would be scrapped. Gene saw Ralph's medal, but he didn't care. He told Ralph that nothing had changed. Ralph would always be a guy who wrecked things.

Sadly, Ralph took off his medal and threw it against the game's front window. The glass shook and the "Out of Order" sign slipped. Ralph could see the *Sugar Rush* console ... with Vanellope's picture on it! Ralph gasped. Vanellope *did* belong in *Sugar Rush*!

Ralph hurried back to *Sugar Rush* to get some answers. He found King Candy's sidekick, Sour Bill. Sour Bill explained that King Candy had reprogrammed *Sugar Rush* and stolen Vanellope's computer code. But if she ever crossed the finish line, she'd become an official racer again!

Ralph knew he had to help Vanellope to cross that finish line. He rushed off to find his little friend.

Fawn Gets Into Trouble

In a forest in Pixie Hollow three adult hawks were on the attack. They swooped in, chasing after the fairies and threatening the animals in the nursery. They had heard Hannah the baby hawk's cry.

Fawn, the animal-talent fairy, went after Hannah. She had nursed Hannah's broken wing and they were now good friends.

Tinker Bell led the other animals towards a hollow tree for safety. "Get inside!" she yelled.

Iridessa flew away as fast as she possibly could, but something grabbed her!

It was Nyx, the head of the scout fairies. Nyx guided Iridessa to safety and then turned to face the hawks. As the protectors of Pixie Hollow, the scouts used ropes, spears and their lightning-fast flying speed to confuse the birds and chase them away.

Against Fawn's protests, the scouts then tossed a net over Hannah.

"Is everyone all right?" asked Queen Clarion, arriving at the scene. Queen Clarion was the leader of Pixie Hollow and she looked questioningly at Fawn. It wasn't the first time Fawn had looked after a dangerous animal and put them all in danger. "You've always let your heart be your guide, but...."

"But, I also need to listen with my head,"

finished Fawn. "Next time, I promise, I will."

Fawn released Hannah, and watched her friend fly away.

The next day, Fawn started the morning determined to be a model animal fairy. She greeted the bunnies: Calista, Nico and Paige. "Good morning, students," she said. "Let's see some hopping!"

Suddenly, a loud, deep moan rippled through the forest.

"I should probably check that out," Fawn said.

Following a trail of broken branches, she found an odd strand of fur. Looking around her, Fawn suddenly realized she was standing in a gigantic paw print!

She followed a trail of paw prints until she came to a clearing. Fawn had never seen anything like it before. The trees were just scorched trunks, and instead of grass there was a covering of grey ash scattered with jagged rocks. And right in the middle was a dark cave.

"Come on," she told herself. "Listen to your head. Your heart gets you in trouble."

But Fawn just couldn't curb her curiosity.

Cautiously, Fawn flew to the bottom of the cave. She had no idea that she was about to come face to face with the most extraordinary animal she was ever likely to meet!

Disney · PIXAR
BRAVE
Welcome, Macintosh Clan

Princess Merida was excited! All winter she had looked forward to the Rites of Summer, the festival that celebrated the strong friendship between the clans. The Macintosh clan were the DunBroch clan's honoured guests this year. There would be a day of dancing, games and feats of strength.

Merida's long red curls bounced wildly as she burst into the Great Hall.

"A princess must always behave with proper dignity," Queen Elinor reminded her daughter.

"You were just warming up for the races this afternoon, weren't you, lass?" King Fergus asked Merida with a wink. Merida and her father started laughing. Even Queen Elinor had to smile.

"Isn't it time to start the processional?" Merida asked.

Queen Elinor looked at her schedule. "Usually, the processional starts at half past nine … but I see no reason why we shouldn't begin a little earlier this year."

Before she could say another word, Merida was on her way outside.

Merida's family and the rest of the clan took their positions. Bagpipers played merry songs as girls from the village tossed petals into the air. The processional weaved its way to the dock.

As the mist cleared, Merida saw the Macintosh clan's lead ship! She jumped up and down with excitement.

"Oi! DunBroch!" a voice bellowed from the deck. Lord Macintosh!

"Oi! Macintosh!" King Fergus roared back.

"To the Rites!" both rulers yelled together.

Princess Merida was reunited with Young Macintosh, the tall and athletic son of Lord Macintosh.

"I see you've come to impress us with your feats of strength again," she said.

"And impressed you'll be, I'm sure," said Young Macintosh, puffing out his chest proudly. Then he remembered the last time they'd met. They'd had an archery competition and Merida had won easily.

"How about a race, then?" Merida suggested. "To the top … of the Fire Falls!"

Young Macintosh looked surprised. "You could never make it!"

"Aye, I can," Merida replied confidently. "But if you're not certain you could make the climb, we can do something else."

"I'm an excellent climber – the best in my clan!" Young Macintosh bragged.

"Then I'll wait for you at the top!" cried Merida. She looped her bow over her shoulder, headed to her horse, Angus, and raced away.

A Whale of a Tale

"Hop aboard, explorers!" called Mr Ray. Nemo, Tad and the rest of the class jumped on the back of the big manta ray. It was 'special guest' week and they were going to the Drop-off.

When they reached the reef's edge, a royal blue tang fish swam up to meet them.

"And here is today's special guest," Mr Ray announced.

"Hello, everyone," said the blue tang. "I'm Dory ... um ... am I? Yes! Just kidding! I'm Dory, and I'm very happy to be here!"

"Dory, can you teach us something about whales today?" asked Mr Ray.

"Well, let's see ... whales are very big, but they eat little creatures called krill. And I should know. One whale I met *almost* ate me – "

"So it's not true!" blurted Tad.

"What's not true?" Dory asked.

"Sandy Plankton said Nemo made up that story about how you and Nemo's dad got eaten by a whale!" said Tad.

"I did not make it up!" cried Nemo.

"Well," said Dory, "technically, Sandy Plankton is right. We weren't actually *eaten* by the whale – "

Tad smirked, until Dory added, "We were just in the whale's mouth for a mighty long time!"

"Whoa!" said the class. They were quite impressed. Tad frowned.

"You see, the whale was just giving us a ride to Sydney. I find if you talk to a whale beforehand, it clears up most ingestion issues," Dory explained.

"Excellent lesson!" said Mr Ray. "Now teach us a few words in whale."

"Oh, okay," said Dory. "Now repeat after me. Haaaaavvve aaaaaaaaaaa nnnniiiiiice daaaaayyyy!"

"Haaaavvve aaaaaa nnnniiiiice daaaayy!" the class repeated.

"Very good!" said Dory.

"This is stupid," said Tad. "You didn't...."

Suddenly, Tad stopped talking. Everyone just stared at Dory in horror.

Slowly, Dory turned around. A blue whale was right behind her!

Dory simply shrugged and told the whale, "Weeeee weerrrrre juuuuuuuuusssst praaaaactisinnnng!"

With a loud bellow, the whale wished her a nice day anyway, then swam off.

"So, Tad, do you believe Dory now?" asked Nemo.

"Wow, that was *so* cool!" cried Tad. "I can't wait to tell Sandy Plankton how I was almost eaten by a whale!"

Nemo and Dory just sighed.

Scaredy-Cat Sleepover

M innie was having a sleepover at her best friend Daisy's house!

"I've got lots of stuff planned!" Daisy told her. "First, we're making cupcakes!"

The friends got right to work mixing, baking and decorating.

"Yummy!" Daisy said.

Next it was time for a fashion show. Minnie looked at the fancy, sparkly dress she was wearing. "I look just like a Christmas tree!" she laughed.

Minnie and Daisy then changed into pyjamas. It was time to watch a film.

They settled on a scary film called *The Invisible Monster with Ten-foot Claws*. Minnie and Daisy watched as an actress entered a spooky mansion, the door slamming behind her.

"You'll never get me, monster!" the actress cried. The monster chased her all over the house.

"Eeek!" Minnie and Daisy watched the rest of the film with the lights on.

When it was over, the friends got ready for bed. But an hour later, they were still awake.

"That film scared me," Minnie admitted.

"Me, too!" replied Daisy.

Minnie suggested they drink some warm milk to make themselves sleepy. After two big mugs, they were back in bed ... and still awake.

"It's not working," Daisy groaned.

"Let's try counting sheep," Minnie replied.

They closed their eyes and began picturing a meadow full of them.

Finally, the girls started to drift off. Then, suddenly, they heard a loud SCRATCH!

"What was that?" Daisy cried.

"Maybe it was just a branch scraping against the window?" Minnie said, huddling under her blanket.

"Yes, that must be it," replied Daisy.

A few minutes later, they heard more scratching and a loud SCREECH!

"Aaah!" yelled the girls.

"What if it's the monster?" asked Daisy.

Minnie took a deep breath. "We have to investigate," said Minnie.

They tiptoed towards the scratching sound, which was coming from outside the front door.

"Let's peek out of the window," said Daisy.

Minnie pulled aside the curtain and gasped.

"Kittens!" cried Minnie, throwing open the door and bringing them inside.

"They must be lost," Daisy said.

"We'll ask around town tomorrow and find out who they belong to," Minnie replied.

"Who would have guessed that our monster would turn out to be cute?" Minnie asked as she snuggled back into her bed.

Just a few minutes later, Minnie, Daisy and the not-so-scary kittens were all fast asleep!

THE
LION KING

Hakuna Matata

"Why are you so sad?" Pumbaa asked Nala.

"I'm not sad," Nala said. "I'm just a little more on the serious side than the two of you."

"I think you could use a little *hakuna matata*," Pumbaa said.

"A whona mawhatta?" Nala asked.

"You really think she can handle it?" Timon whispered to Pumbaa out of the side of his mouth.

"Of course I can handle it!" Nala said, raising her voice. "I just need to know what it is first."

"Ahhhh, *hakuna matata*," Pumbaa said dreamily. "It's the problem-free way of dealing with all of life's inconveniences."

"It means, 'No worries'," Timon explained.

"Oh, I get it," Nala said. "Instead of dealing with your problems, you pretend they don't exist."

"*Hakuna matata* helps you relax," Pumbaa offered.

"It sounds like your *hakuna matata* is just another way of saying 'uninspired and lazy'," Nala continued.

"I think she might have just insulted us," Timon whispered to Pumbaa.

"There you are." Simba came walking towards them. "What are the three of you up to?"

"I was just learning about a strange little notion called *hakuna matata*," Nala explained.

"Isn't it great!" Simba said with a grin.

"Well, sure," Nala said. "If you don't ever want to get anything done."

Simba frowned. "It's not like that. *Hakuna matata* helps you get through things."

"Sure," Nala continued. "*Hakuna matata* – I don't have to worry. I don't have to try."

"I guess you could look at it that way," Simba said. "But, for me, it means, 'Don't worry about it right now. It's okay.' It gives me the strength to get through the bad times."

"Wow, I hadn't thought about it like that," Nala said.

"So, are you ready to join us now?" Timon asked.

"Absolutely!" Nala smiled.

"Bring on the crunchy beetles!" shouted Pumbaa.

"Let's go tease some elephants!" cried Timon.

"Everyone to the mudhole for a mud fight!" Simba yelled, and the three of them started off.

"Oh, dear," murmured Nala, "this isn't exactly what I had in mind." But she smiled, and ran after her carefree friends. "Last one to the mudhole is a rotten egg!" she cried.

Disney · PIXAR
BRAVE
A Race to the Top

Princess Merida and Young Macintosh raced towards Fire Falls on their horses. Merida had challenged him to a race as soon as he had arrived at Castle DunBroch. The first to the top would win.

They arrived at the bottom of the falls at the same time.

"You might as well stay at the bottom," Young Macintosh yelled as he started to climb. "I'll reach the top and be back down again before you've even gone halfway!"

Merida gritted her teeth and raced to catch up. Soon, she and Young Macintosh were neck and neck.

At the top of the falls, Merida used a last burst of strength to pull herself over the rocky ledge. "I won! I did it," she gasped.

"You did no such thing!" argued Young Macintosh.

Merida put her hands on her hips. "I think your head is dizzy from the climb –" she started to say, but she stopped herself. She knew that her mum wouldn't want her to insult one of their guests during the Rites of Summer festival. Instead, she knelt down by the stream to splash some cool water on her face. Young Macintosh did the same.

"This is a fine waterfall you've got here," Young Macintosh said in a friendlier tone.

"I would climb these rocks all the time, if I lived in DunBroch."

Merida wondered if he was trying to be on his best behaviour, too.

They looked down at Castle DunBroch in the distance. The Macintosh clan's brightly coloured tents were going up around the castle. They would be expected back soon.

"Where do you think the water comes from?" Merida asked Young Macintosh as she stared at the stream.

"You mean to say you don't know?" he said in surprise.

"No, I don't," Merida replied. "But today's the day I find out!"

"Where are you going?" Young Macintosh called as he scrambled up to follow her.

As they walked, the shrubs grew thicker. Soon, the bushes were so dense that it was difficult to see anything but leaves.

Then Merida stopped short. She was standing at the edge of an ordinary-looking loch. Not a bird chirped; not a beetle buzzed.

Young Macintosh's voice shattered the silence. "Just a regular loch, isn't it?"

Merida stared at the water. She was disappointed. She slumped back against a boulder – and disappeared down a dark hole!

The Crown of Diamonds

It was Aurora's 17th birthday, and she had some surprises awaiting her.

Her mother, the Queen, came in to wish her happy birthday. She led Aurora to a huge portrait hall.

"Why, Mother! Is that you?" exclaimed Aurora, pointing to a portrait. The Queen was wearing a crown with a pink, heart-shaped diamond.

"Indeed, I was 17," said the Queen. "It's a tradition that on a princess's 17th birthday, this crown is to be passed down by her mother, and worn until the princess becomes queen. However, she must answer three riddles," her mother said with a smile.

The three fairies, Flora, Fauna and Merryweather, flew in. "Happy birthday, Princess!" said Merryweather. "We're here to give you your clues!"

Flora recited the first riddle: "To the eyes, it's a treat; to the nose, a delight. To the hand it can be quite a fright. Though few think to taste it, its sweetness still shows. To this first riddle, the answer's a...."

"Let's see," said Aurora. "'To the eye, it's a treat. To the nose, a delight.' So it's pretty and smells good. 'To the hand quite a fright.' Like a thorn – on a rose. That's it!" She hurried off to the garden, and picked the biggest rose.

"Very good!" exclaimed Fauna. "And now for the second one: 'Some plant it, some blow it away. Some do it several times in a day. Some may blush getting this on their cheek'. Can you guess?"

"It's a kiss, isn't it?" Aurora laughed. She kissed each fairy, causing them to blush.

"Now it's my turn!" exclaimed Merryweather. "What only gets stronger the longer it lives? Some say it's blind, some say it's true, some simply say, 'I feel this for you.'" Aurora thought hard. Just then Prince Phillip walked by.

"Happy birthday, my love!" he called. Instantly, Aurora knew the answer. She hurried up to her mother's sewing room.

"I've solved the riddles!" Aurora exclaimed. She handed her the pink rose and gave her a kiss on the cheek.

"Very good!" declared the Queen. "And the answer to the third riddle?"

"It's love," said Aurora.

The Queen proudly placed the crown on Aurora's head.

That afternoon, Aurora had her portrait painted, so it could be hung in the portrait hall alongside her mother's.

"Happy birthday, Aurora," her mother warmly told her. "May you have many more!"

Beauty and the Beast

Gaston Gets Involved

Gaston was in his banqueting hall when the odd sisters barged in. "We have news that you might find interesting, Gaston."

Gaston slammed his knife into the wooden dining table. "First you send that foul cat to watch over me, and now this!"

Martha flew to Pflanze's defence. "She's not here to spy on you. She's here to help you."

Gaston laughed. "Help me? Why, I am the strongest, most attractive man in the village!"

"Yes, help you, Gaston. We've found Belle, and she's on her way to her father now."

Gaston fixed his gaze on the witches. "You've found Belle?"

"Yes, we've found your dearest love!" Ruby sang. "She won't be able to resist you!"

Lucinda grinned. "But on the slightest chance she can, we would like you to meet Monsieur D'Arque from the sanitarium."

Martha explained further. "Belle's father has been raving about a beast, hasn't he? Perhaps the sanitarium is just the place for him."

Ruby twittered in delight when she added, "Though I'm sure there would be no need for him to be institutionalized if Belle were to marry you."

Gaston grasped their meaning instantly, and he was thunderstruck by the brilliance of the idea. D'Arque was more than happy to help, for a fee.

When they knocked at Maurice's door, Belle answered.

"I've come to collect your father," said D'Arque.

Belle saw D'Arque's wagon in the distance and realized he wanted to take him to the asylum. She was seized with fear. "My father is not crazy!" she cried.

Meanwhile, the witches found the Beast brooding in his study. They gleefully told him that Belle was about to betray him.

"She never loved you! How could she?"

"She was your prisoner!"

"She only pretended to love you so you would let her go!"

Lucinda lifted a mirror showing Belle in front of an angry crowd of villagers. Belle was holding up his magic mirror and, to save her father, she screamed, "Show them the Beast!"

His face appeared in the mirror, ugly and frightening, his roar terrifying the mob.

"See! She's betrayed you!" Lucinda said.

"She's always loved Gaston!" chimed in Martha.

"They're to be married the morning after he kills you!" they all sang.

The Beast was defeated.

Disney
Lady and the **TRAMP**

Like Father, Like Son

Tramp had a whole new life. He had gone from being a stray to becoming a member of the Dear household. And now, he and Lady were proud parents.

But Tramp was finding it difficult to change some of his old ways.

"Tramp," Lady said gently, "you need to set an example for the puppies – especially Scamp."

Scamp had an adventurous side, just like his dad. So, it wasn't surprising that father and son often got carried away when they played together. They couldn't resist the urge to roll in a puddle of mud – and then chase each other across the clean kitchen floor.

Soon, Aunt Sarah and her two troublesome cats, Si and Am, were going to be visiting. Lady was worried.

"Don't worry. I promise to keep Scamp away from those troublemakers," Tramp said.

"And?" replied Lady.

"And I promise to stay away from them, too," Tramp added.

When the big day came, Lady and Tramp herded their pups into a bedroom and told them to stay put. But Scamp was curious. He slipped out of the room and hid behind the living room settee. Then he sneaked up behind the cats and swiped at their tails as they flicked back and forth.

The cats turned and chased Scamp up and over the settee, under a table and into a cupboard.

Well, Tramp thought, I suppose I'm going to have to chase those nasty old cats whether I want to or not!

He enthusiastically dived into the cupboard. Seconds later, Tramp and Scamp emerged. Much to Aunt Sarah's horror, Si and Am were later found inside, tied together with a scarf. When no one was looking, Tramp and Scamp shared a victory wink.

Tramp and Scamp were banished to the garden for their antics. When Lady came out that evening, she found that they had dug up the entire garden looking for bones. Father and son saw the look on Lady's face and knew that they were about to get a lecture.

Tramp looked at Lady innocently. "You want him to get exercise, don't you?" he asked.

"Try it, Mum!" Scamp cried. "It's fun."

"What am I going to do with you two?" Lady said, laughing.

Tramp and Scamp dragged a huge bone out from behind the kennel.

"Join us for dinner?" Tramp replied.

"Well, alright," Lady said. "But, as soon as we're done, we're cleaning up this garden."

"Yes, ma'am!" chorused Tramp and Scamp, looking very pleased with themselves.

Tangled
A Family Reunited

Mother Gothel was furious. Rapunzel had discovered the whole truth – that she was the lost Princess, and that Mother Gothel had stolen her as a baby. Now Rapunzel was refusing to let Mother Gothel use her magic to stay young.

"I won't sing any more; my hair will never make you youthful again!" Rapunzel declared.

Mother Gothel chained Rapunzel to a chair, but it didn't work – Rapunzel would rather die than obey her!

Just then, Flynn arrived outside the tower. Although Mother Gothel had him thrown in prison, he had escaped with some help from Maximus and rushed to Rapunzel's aid. Mother Gothel threw down Rapunzel's long hair and Flynn hoisted himself up the golden locks. But, when he eventually jumped in through the window, it was Mother Gothel who greeted him ... with a stab in the back!

"If you want me to let you sing to heal him," she told Rapunzel, "you must swear to come and live with me in the tower forever. If not, so much the worse for him!"

The young girl promised to do whatever Mother Gothel wanted in order to save Flynn. But Flynn didn't want Rapunzel to sacrifice herself for him. So, as she wouldn't listen to

him, he picked up a piece of glass from a mirror that had been broken in the struggle and he cut off Rapunzel's magical hair!

Immediately the beautiful shine of Rapunzel's hair faded away, and the golden colour turned to brown. With a yell, Mother Gothel began to grow older and older ... until she disappeared in a pile of dust!

"Rapunzel, you were my new dream," declared the dying Flynn.

Sobbing, Rapunzel tried to sing, but her hair had lost all of its magical power. But suddenly, one of her tears fell onto Flynn's face and began to glow! As they watched, Flynn's wound miraculously healed. There was a drop of magic left inside Rapunzel after all!

Overcome with happiness, the two finally exchanged their first kiss. Then, Flynn didn't waste a moment in taking Rapunzel to the castle, where the King and Queen were waiting. What joy – their beloved daughter had come home, and their family was reunited at last!

In every corner of the kingdom, the people celebrated the return of their lost Princess. They celebrated by launching thousands of lanterns into the sky – the same lanterns that had helped Rapunzel to find her way home.

A Fairytale Marriage

Deep in the Louisiana bayou, there was a lot of excitement. Naveen and Tiana – two frogs who were madly in love – were about to be married, and all of their animal friends were there to help.

Mama Odie, a good and powerful wise woman, conducted the ceremony. Naveen and Tiana had gone to Mama Odie when they'd been desperate to be human again. Now they were in love, they didn't mind being frogs so much.

"And by the powers vested in me, frogs, I now pronounce you ... frog and wife! Naveen, you may kiss your pretty little bride!" Mama Odie announced.

Naveen took Tiana in his arms and placed a tender kiss on her lips, which she returned without hesitation....

Then, a cloud of multicoloured sparks, crackling with magic, began to swirl around them – and they both became human again!

The couple looked splendid – Prince Naveen in a suit, and Tiana in a long, green dress ... they looked at each other with surprise and astonishment.

Mama Odie laughed, "I told you that the only way to overturn this evil spell was to kiss a princess!"

"But of course, Tiana!" Prince Naveen exclaimed. "By marrying me, you have become a princess!"

"And then we kissed! You just kissed yourself a princess!" exclaimed Tiana.

"And I'm about to do it again," laughed Naveen as their friends cheered.

Shortly afterwards, Naveen and Tiana married again, but this time at a cathedral in New Orleans, with all of their friends and families. It was a beautiful ceremony.

When Tiana came out of the church and climbed into her carriage, she threw her wedding bouquet into the crowd, and it was her best friend Charlotte who caught it!

Charlotte laughed, knowing this was a good sign – it meant that the next wedding would be hers!

It goes without saying that Tiana and Naveen lived together happily ever after ... and soon there was a new restaurant in town – Tiana's Palace. The happy couple had bought the old sugar mill and turned it into the best place to go for good food, lively music and fun with friends and family.

Tiana had dreamed of owning a restaurant her whole life – a dream she had shared with her father. Now Tiana had everything she had ever wished for.

The Best Babysitter

Anna was going to Troll Valley with Kristoff and Sven, to watch over the baby trolls while the adults went out for the evening.

"Sure you don't need me?" Elsa asked.

"How hard could it be?" Anna said.

On the way, Kristoff told Anna stories about growing up with the trolls.

"They'll sleep the whole time," Kristoff said.

As they reached Troll Valley, Bulda thanked them for troll-sitting. "If they get hungry, you can feed them smashed berries," he said. "They may need a leaf change, but they should be sleeping soon."

Anna waved them off. "Have a great time! Everything is going to be ..."

"... a disaster!" Kristoff finished.

Anna, Kristoff and Sven found that the toddler trolls had escaped from their pen and were climbing all over the place.

"Settle down now, guys," Kristoff said, pulling the trolls off one another.

But the more they tried to calm the little trolls, the wilder they got!

"Maybe they're hungry?" Anna suggested. But the trolls didn't want to eat.

"Maybe they need changing?" Kristoff wondered, peering into a nappy leaf. "Nope."

"Let's put them to bed," Anna suggested. "They must be tired."

But the young trolls were wide awake!

Suddenly, they heard a cheery voice. "Hello, troll babies!" It was Olaf!

"Elsa sent me to help," he explained.

"Are we glad to see you!" Kristoff said.

Anna ran to greet the snowman, but tripped and fell face first into the basket of berries! She lifted her head, covered in purple goo.

The little trolls giggled and lapped up the berry juice dripping down her cheeks.

After the trolls were finished, a strange smell floated into the air.

"Olaf, you distract them," Kristoff said.

Olaf told the little trolls stories about summer, while Anna and Sven collected leaves and Kristoff changed nappies.

Soon everyone was sweet-smelling again.

Anna saw that the trolls could hardly keep their eyes open. "Maybe Kristoff and Sven would like to sing a lullaby?" she suggested.

"Rock-a-bye troll-ys, in your small pen. Time to go sleepy for Uncle Sven," Kristoff crooned, impersonating Sven while Anna and Olaf put the trolls to bed.

By the time the adult trolls returned, the little ones were fast asleep.

"Wow, great job," Bulda whispered.

"It was easy," Anna replied.

"Piece of berry pie!" Kristoff added.

TinkerBell
AND THE
LEGEND OF THE
NEVERBEAST

The Beast in the Cave

"What are you?" whispered Fawn to the strange creature at the bottom of the cave. She tried to keep her cool, even when the enormous creature stood up.

Without warning, the beast let out a deep, ground-shaking, "ROOOOAAARRRR!" Its mouth looked as wide as the cave to Fawn, and it was full of sharp teeth.

The roar was heard all across Pixie Hollow. It alarmed Nyx and the other scouts. They questioned the other animal-talent fairies about the type of animal that would make such a sound. But they all agreed there was only one fairy who knew anything about loud, scary roars.

"Fawn," guessed Nyx.

Fawn flew out of the cave into the daylight. The huge creature followed and she was able to see it properly from a safe distance. She had never seen anything like it before. He was grey and furry, with strange markings. He had huge emerald-green eyes and a wide, toothy grin. His tail was long and fur-less. But the creature didn't look scary. He looked curious.

Fawn watched as the beast began stacking rocks in a pile. She noticed it was limping and saw a thorn stuck in its front paw.

Using a rope, she suspended a rock from a tree. As the beast stood up to reach it, she quickly yanked the thorn from his paw.

The beast howled in pain. But when he put his paw down, he seemed to understand what Fawn had done.

With a grateful grunt, he went back to work. He no longer seemed to mind that she was around.

Fawn rushed home to get her research tools. She wanted to record everything she learned about the beast. But Nyx was waiting for her.

"Did you hear that loud roar this morning?" the scout asked Fawn.

"Did it sound like an elephant?" Fawn asked innocently, imitating the sound. "Or maybe a chimp?"

"Listen, this thing might be a threat," said Nyx. "If you find out what made that roar, I need to know."

"What will you do if you find it?" Fawn asked.

"My job," Nyx responded.

Fawn knew that Nyx's job was to protect Pixie Hollow. She would trap the beast and who knew what would happen then. No, Fawn decided, she wanted to study the beast. He was far too unusual and interesting. And, besides, he couldn't be a threat to Pixie Hollow ... could he?

Disney · PIXAR

WALL·E
Finally Home

On the Axiom, the ship where all the humans now lived, little robot EVE delivered a special plant from Earth to the Captain. EVE had found it among the treasures of a robot called WALL·E.

The Captain was excited, because this plant meant he and all the humans could return to Earth. But the Captain's robot wouldn't let them. Quickly, Auto snatched the plant and dumped it down the rubbish chute.

The plant hit WALL·E. The little bot was climbing up to get to EVE! Happily he delivered the plant right back to her. But Auto electrocuted WALL·E and sent him back down the chute with EVE.

WALL·E and EVE ended up in the ship's rubbish bay. EVE rescued the injured little bot while WALL·E tried to give her the plant. He still thought she wanted it more than anything else. But WALL·E was wrong. EVE just wanted to help WALL·E now.

Soon EVE flew them up and out of the garbage bay, with the plant in hand. She wanted to get WALL·E home to Earth so she could find the right parts to fix him.

The Captain was fighting Auto for control of the ship by now. He sent a message to EVE, telling her to take the plant to a large machine called the holo-detector.

The machine would make the ship head towards Earth.

The Captain finally managed to turn off the bad robot's power. EVE fought to reach the holo-detector. At last she put the plant inside the machine. Finally they could return to Earth.

But all was not well. WALL·E had been crushed by the giant machine! Heartbroken and more determined than before, EVE wanted to take WALL·E home to his truck, where she could find the right parts to bring him back to life. As soon as the Axiom landed on Earth, EVE headed straight for WALL·E's home and repaired him. At last, he powered up … and began cubing trash. Something was wrong. He was just another trash-cubing robot. All the love was gone. He didn't even recognize EVE!

Sadly, EVE held WALL·E's hand and leaned towards him. An electric arc passed between their heads – the robot kiss. She was saying goodbye. Then … WALL·E's hand began to move. EVE looked into his eyes. He was coming back to life! He recognized her!

"Ee-vah?" he said. After following EVE across the universe, WALL·E had ended up right where he had started – home. But this time he had the one thing he truly wanted – EVE's hand clasped in his own.

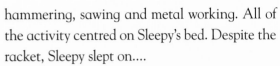

Rise and Shine!

"**A**lright, Dwarfs!" Doc called one morning. "Is everyone ready to leave for work? Let's see. We've got Happy, Dopey, Sneezy, Bashful, Grumpy and Sleepy." Doc looked around. "Sleepy?" No answer. Sleepy was nowhere to be found.

"Oh no, not again," Doc complained, leading the other Dwarfs up the stairs to their bedroom. There, just as Doc expected, they found Sleepy, dozing peacefully in his bed.

Doc walked to Sleepy's bedside. He pulled the covers off the sleeping dwarf. "Come on, Sleepy! Rise and shine!" Doc called. But Sleepy just rolled over and dozed on.

"Oh, this is ridiculous!" exclaimed Grumpy. "We go through this every single morning, dragging Sleepy out of bed, and I'm tired of it."

"Me too!" said Dopey.

"Me three!" said Sneezy. *"Ah-CHOO!"*

The Dwarfs stood around Sleepy's bed, looking down at him, wondering what to do.

"I have an idea!" said Doc. "We'll have to take the day off from the diamond mine and stay here today to work on my plan, but I think it will solve our problem – once and for all!"

The Dwarfs gathered into a huddle around Doc as he outlined the details. Then they got their tools and set to work. Soon the bedroom was filled with the sounds of hammering, sawing and metal working. All of the activity centred on Sleepy's bed. Despite the racket, Sleepy slept on....

He slept all morning. He slept all afternoon. He slept all evening. He slept through the night.

Then, bright and early the next morning, an alarm clock perched on top of Sleepy's bedside table sprang to life; its bell jangled noisily, shaking the clock.

With a rope tied to its handle, the clock bounced across the top of the table until it fell off the edge. The falling clock tugged on the rope, yanking a broomstick at the other end. When the broomstick moved, the large weight it was propping up dropped to the floor, activating a pulley that pulled up sharply on Sleepy's headboard. The head of Sleepy's bed lifted off the floor, and Sleepy slid down and off the foot of the bed, onto a smoothly carved wooden slide that carried him out of the window, down to ground level and – *splash*! – right into a wooden tub filled with cold water.

Wide awake, Sleepy sat in the tub, blinking and wondering what had just happened.

The other Dwarfs crowded around the bedroom window and peered down at him, grinning cheerfully (except Grumpy, of course).

"Good morning, Sleepy!" cried Doc. "Do you like your new alarm clock?"

THE LITTLE MERMAID

Ariel to the Rescue

"Oh, Eric! This is wonderful!" Ariel said excitedly as she twirled around the ballroom with her prince. "I can dance with you and see the ocean!"

"Do you miss your sea friends?" he asked.

"Sometimes," Ariel replied. "But I love being with you."

A few weeks later, Eric took Ariel to the lagoon. Ariel noticed that it now had a big wall around it. The wall would keep out dangerous sea creatures, but it also had a gate for Ariel's friends to enter the lagoon. In fact, Flounder, Scuttle and Sebastian were there to greet her.

Ariel was so excited that she waded into the lagoon to greet her friends. Then she saw something in the water.

"Look!" she exclaimed. As they watched, a small dolphin leaped out of the water!

"He's just a baby. I wonder where his mother is," Flounder said. He swam across the lagoon, but the baby dolphin raced away.

"Poor little guy," Flounder said. "He seems scared of me."

But the princess wouldn't give up. Soon she had coaxed the baby to swim over to her.

"I wish there was something we could do," Ariel said.

"I bet his mother is on the other side of that wall." Flounder said. "We'll find her!"

But a few days later, Sebastian and Flounder still hadn't found her. Tomorrow, Ariel would ask more of her friends from under the sea to help with the search.

Later, Ariel awoke to the sound of thunder. When she and Eric arrived at the lagoon, Flounder was trying to calm the frightened baby dolphin.

Ariel climbed onto the lagoon wall and called to the sea creatures. "Help me, please! I am Ariel, princess of the seas. I need my father, King Triton."

Below the surface, sea creatures raced to find King Triton. Suddenly there was a flash of light! King Triton had arrived.

The storm quietened down. The baby dolphin's mother was at the lagoon gate, frantically trying to get in.

"Oh, dear!" Ariel exclaimed. "The gate won't open! She can't get in!"

Eric looked at King Triton. He raised his trident and blasted down the wall. The dolphins swam to each other, then the baby went to Triton to thank him.

That night, the moon rose. But there was no royal ball at the palace. Instead, Eric and Ariel returned to the lagoon and enjoyed a wonderful night with all of their ocean friends.

Bambi

First Frost

Slowly, Bambi opened his eyes. Curled next to his mother, he was toasty-warm in the thicket. Bambi blinked sleepily, peering past the brambles. Something was different. The forest did not look the same. The air was crisp and cold, and everything was frosted and sparkling.

"Jack Frost has been here," Bambi's mother explained. "He's painted the whole forest with ice crystals."

Bambi was about to ask his mother who Jack Frost was and how he painted with ice, when he heard another voice, an impatient one.

"Get up! Get up! Come look at the frost!" It was Thumper. He tapped his foot impatiently. "We haven't got all day!"

Bambi stood and looked at his mother. When she nodded approvingly, he scampered out of the thicket. Bambi looked closely at the colourful leaves on the ground. Each one was covered in an icy-white pattern. He touched his nose to a big orange oak leaf. "Ooh, it's cold!" he cried.

"Of course it is!" Thumper laughed.

"I think it's beautiful," said Faline, as she stepped into the clearing.

"Me too," Bambi agreed.

"Well, come look at this!" Thumper hopped away and the two young deer followed, admiring the way the sun sparkled on the frost-covered trees and grass.

Thumper disappeared under a bush; then Bambi heard a new noise. *Creak, crack.*

Faline pushed through the bushes with Bambi right behind her. There was Thumper, cracking the thin ice on a puddle with his feet.

Bambi had never seen ice before. He pushed on the icy-thin puddle-covering with his hoof. It seemed to bend. Then it shattered!

Soon the three friends were stomping on the ice-covered puddles. When all the ice was broken, Faline had an idea. "Let's go to the meadow!"

Bambi thought that was a great idea. The grass would be sparkling! They set out at a run, bounding and racing each other through the forest. But when they got to the meadow's edge, they all stopped.

They looked, sniffed and listened quietly. They did not sense danger – no, the trouble was that in the meadow, nothing was different. There was no frost.

"What happened?" Bambi asked.

"Frost never lasts long," Thumper explained. "It melts as soon as the sun hits it. But don't worry. Winter is coming, and soon we'll have something even better than frost. We'll have snow!"

Orator Owl

On their way home from a leaf-collecting excursion on a cold, blustery autumn afternoon, Pooh, Rabbit, Piglet and Eeyore made their way past Owl's house. They couldn't help but notice the cheerful light glowing in all the windows – a light so warm and so inviting that the chilly group seemed to thaw just looking at it.

And so it happened that they soon found themselves warm and cosy in Owl's living room.

"Owl, thank you for having us in to warm up," said Pooh. "It's awfully windy and cold outside."

"Well, it is getting on towards winter," Owl replied. "Naturally that means it will only get colder before it gets warmer." Owl went on to explain the difference between the blustery autumn cold that they were experiencing and the winter sort of cold that was to come. He explained it in very great detail, using words like frost, frosty and frostily. It turned out to be quite a long explanation. Owl was just beginning to expound on the particular subject of frostbite when Rabbit interrupted, hoping to give someone else a chance to talk.

"Yes, Owl," he said. "I know that Piglet was very glad to have his scarf on today, weren't you, Piglet?"

"Oh yes," Piglet said. "Kanga knitted it for me."

Owl cleared his throat. "Ah yes, knitting," said Owl. "An admirable hobby. Did you know that knitting is done with knitting needles? But they aren't sharp, as one might assume. They are not, for example, as sharp as sewing needles. Or cactus needles...."

Owl continued with a comparison of many, many different types of needles. An hour later, when Owl seemed ready to jump into a discussion of pins, Rabbit again tried to change the subject.

"Speaking of pins," Rabbit began, "how is your tail today, Eeyore? Suitably secure and well attached?"

"Seems secure," Eeyore replied with a shrug, "but it always falls off when I least expect it. And I certainly wouldn't expect it to fall off now, when it seems so secure. So I suppose that could mean it's about to fall off."

Rabbit saw Owl sit up in his chair and take a deep breath – a sure sign that he was preparing another speech about tails, or expectations, or Rabbit knew not what – so Rabbit decided it was time to go.

Goodbyes and thank-yous were said, and soon the four visitors were outside, making their way home through swirling leaves.

And all the way home, Rabbit tried to decide who was windier – the great autumn wind ... or long-winded Owl!

Disney PRINCESS

Beauty and the Beast

The Curse is Lifted!

In the tall house with the witch's-hat roof, the sisters watched events unfold at the castle.

Gaston and his mob arrived and only the servants put up a fight. The Beast did nothing when Gaston found him on the roof. He wanted to die. Without Belle, he had nothing to live for.

"Kill the Beast!" the sisters yelled, but the Beast saw Belle calling him. She gave him the will to fight.

The Beast soon overpowered Gaston.

"Make the Beast remember when they were young!" the sisters cried. Their spell worked. The Beast let him go, but Gaston plunged a knife into the Beast's side.

Losing his footing, Gaston fell to his death, but he didn't matter to the witches any more. The Beast was dying in his lover's arms, heartbroken.

"Circe has to see this!"

Lucinda unfastened the necklace round her sister's neck, and Circe opened her eyes.

"We have something to show you," Lucinda said.

Lucinda led her sleepy sister into a room full of enchanted mirrors.

In the largest mirror Circe saw the Beast. "What's this?" she asked as she rushed over to the mirror. "Is he dead?"

Her three sisters stood smiling with their hands clasped, like eager little girls waiting for praise.

"How could you think I would want this?" Circe said.

"I love you," Belle was saying to the Beast, as tears streaked down her face.

Circe was also crying. "I never wanted this to happen! Look! She loves him! I'm bringing him back! I'm giving him a chance to break the curse."

The odd sisters started to protest but Circe's fury sent them flying. Their sister's powers were far greater than their own. "You say one more word and I will give your voices to the sea witch!"

Circe cast her magic. Lights showered down around the couple, lifting the Beast into the air until he was the prince once more. His face was no longer marred with anger, vanity and cruelty. She could see his soul had truly changed.

The magic cascaded down on the castle, too, transforming everyone inside.

"Lumiere! Cogsworth! Mrs Potts!" cried the prince, seeing his fondest friends for the first time in many years.

Taking one last look, Circe wiped the image from the enchanted mirror, leaving them to live happily ever after.

Tiana's Royal Wedding

After many adventures and a ceremony in the bayou, Tiana and Naveen were finally getting married properly! They welcomed Naveen's parents, the King and Queen, for the wedding.

But all too soon, the royal helpers cornered Tiana, announcing their plans for her wedding.

"We'll do this ... and this," they told her. Tiana's head was soon spinning!

"I don't want to upset the King and Queen, but their helpers' wedding plans aren't right for me!" Tiana told her friend Charlotte.

"It's your wedding! You should do what you want," Charlotte said. So Tiana made her first wedding decision – she asked Charlotte to be her maid of honour!

Just then, Tiana's mother arrived. "I'd like to make your dream gown for you," she said.

"Oh, Mama! That's perfect!" Tiana exclaimed when she saw her mother's sketch.

After everyone else had gone to bed, Tiana sneaked into the La Bouffs' kitchen to work on the menu with Charlotte.

"I want a taste of New Orleans," Tiana said. "Let's start with gumbo."

Later, Charlotte said, "Tia, every bride needs something old, something new, something borrowed and something blue. So here's your 'something blue'."

Charlotte handed Tiana a beautiful blue necklace.

The next day, Tiana told the royal helpers that she had everything she needed. Though surprised, they agreed – Tiana should have her dream wedding!

Just then Naveen's mother, the Queen of Maldonia, walked into the room. Would she be upset?

"Tiana dear, I am glad you are planning the wedding you want, but would you do me the honour of wearing the tiara I wore when I wed the King?"

Everything seemed perfect.

But Tiana missed her father. The night before the wedding, as she gazed at the Evening Star, Tiana realized that her father would always be part of her.

On her wedding day, Tiana carried her father's favourite old spoon inside her bouquet. She wore her new gown from her mother, the tiara borrowed from the Queen and Charlotte's blue necklace under her veil.

As she kissed Naveen, Tiana knew that *love* was what made her wedding – and her life – perfect.

The wedding guests loved Princess Tiana's cooking. And as Tiana and Naveen took the first nibble of their cake, they shared the sweetness of their new life together.

Small Fairies in Big Packages

Princess Aurora's wedding to Prince Phillip would take place in just a few days. The three good fairies, Flora, Fauna and Merryweather, wanted to give Aurora the perfect gift. They stood in front of an enormous box, trying to decide what to put in it.

"How about a pretty dress for Princess Aurora to wear on her honeymoon. Something pink!" Flora said decisively.

"What about a grand carriage?" Fauna suggested with a smile.

Flora shook her head. "King Stefan is already having a carriage made for them. No, let's give her a dress."

"I've got it!" Fauna cried. "A flock of doves that we'll release just as Aurora and Phillip come out of the church. Perfect!"

"A tiara to wear with her wedding gown – that's what Aurora needs," Merryweather piped up. "With three jewels: one red for Flora, one green for Fauna and one blue for me. It will remind our sweet Briar Rose of how much we love her."

"A dress is much more practical than a flock of doves, dear," said Flora firmly.

"But a flock of doves is much more romantic than a dress," Fauna insisted.

Merryweather put her hands on her hips. "A tiara! What's wrong with a tiara?"

But neither Flora nor Fauna even glanced her way. That made Merryweather mad.

"It's settled. We're giving her a dress," Flora said.

"Doves," said Fauna.

"Why can't we give her a – " Merryweather began but, as she waved her arms, trying to get the other fairies' attention, she lost her balance and fell right into the big box. Flora and Fauna did not notice.

"We'll give her both!" said Flora.

They pointed their wands at the box, showering it with sparkles. A huge piece of satin ribbon appeared, wrapped itself around the box, and tied itself into a big bow.

Flora and Fauna put on their capes, ready to deliver the gift to Aurora. But where was Merryweather?

"Oh, well, perhaps she went on ahead," said Flora. "Let's be on our way."

At the palace, Flora and Fauna placed the gift before the Princess. When Aurora untied the ribbon, Merryweather burst out of the box. She presented the Princess with a beautiful tiara that sparkled with red, green and blue jewels.

"Oh, thank you, my dears! It's perfect!" Aurora said with a gasp.

Merryweather smiled. "That's exactly what I thought!" she said.

Fawn Makes a Friend

In Pixie Hollow, Fawn began her study of the strange creature she'd discovered at the bottom of a cave. She drew him from every angle, measured him, and tried to play with him. But he completely ignored her. All he wanted to do was build his rock pile.

At sunset, the glowing pixie dust that trailed behind Fawn captured the beast's attention. He nudged her, his expression much softer now. At last, they'd found a way to get along!

Fawn sprinkled some pixie dust on a boulder and it floated magically onto his rock pile. The creature was pleased.

As night fell, Fawn curled up under a leaf and went to sleep. She knew the beast wouldn't harm her.

It was dawn when the big animal woke Fawn.

"Whoa, looks like somebody's a night owl!" she said as she studied the horn-shaped rock tower behind him. He had built it so tall that it curled up high into the sky.

Suddenly, the beast picked her up and plopped her down on top of his head. Together they marched into the forest.

"Where are we going?" asked Fawn.

The creature just grumbled.

"Well, you don't have to be so gruff about it," she complained. Then it hit her.

"I know! That's what I'll call you – Gruff!"

Gruff suddenly stopped at a clearing in the Summer Forest. He dug out another boulder and then the process of building a rock pile began again. But Fawn decided to turn it into a game this time. She sprinkled pixie dust on a boulder and Gruff knocked it into place.

"Yes!" Fawn shouted, lining up a row of boulders. But Gruff accidentally hit them too hard! They went sailing right past the rock pile towards Sunflower Meadow! Fawn yelled in alarm to the fairies below, and they quickly scattered.

Scouts rushed to the meadow. "Is everyone accounted for?" asked Nyx.

"Yes, everyone is accounted for, thanks to Fawn," answered a garden fairy. "If she hadn't shouted out that warning then we would all be flatter than pumpkin seeds now!"

"Fawn?" Nyx asked.

Meanwhile, Fawn looked over the cliff and saw the scouts in the meadow below.

She did loops in front of Gruff, pixie dust falling all around. "Okay, new game," she said to Gruff. "It's called 'chase the fairy'!"

Just as Fawn hoped, Gruff followed her golden pixie-dust trail into the woods. She wanted to keep him hidden a little while longer ... just until she could figure out what to do with him!

THE JUNGLE Book

Dawn Patrol

One day, Mowgli went to the jungle to visit his old friend Baloo the bear.

"Why so sad, Mowgli?" asked Baloo.

"It's the dry season, and the river is getting low," said Mowgli. "My friends in the village are worried about running out of water."

"Oh," said Baloo. He scratched his head. "But what about the spring in the jungle? It never goes dry."

Mowgli shook his head. "The spring is much too far inside the jungle. It would take all day to get there from the village."

Just then, Bagheera the panther padded over. "Mowgli, I have an idea – Dawn Patrol."

The next morning, Bagheera, Baloo and Mowgli all waited by the spring. Before long, the ground shook with the approach of Colonel Hathi and his elephants.

"Hup, two, three, four. Hup, two, three, four," chanted the Colonel as the herd marched behind him.

"Here they come," said Bagheera. "Dawn Patrol."

Quickly, Bagheera, Baloo and Mowgli hid in the bushes. They waited for the elephants to stop at the spring and take a long drink.

"Ready to try my plan?" Bagheera whispered to Mowgli. The boy nodded, then the two sprang from the bushes crying, "To the river! Quick! Everyone, as fast as you can!"

The elephants looked up in alarm.

"W-what's the m-meaning of this?" stammered the Colonel.

"Shere Khan is coming! Run for the river!" called Mowgli.

"Company ... RUN!" cried the Colonel, and the elephants stampeded through the jungle.

Bagheera and Mowgli watched the herd knock down every tree between the spring and the river. When Mowgli reached the river, he turned around and saw a clear, easy path straight to the big spring!

Now it was time for Baloo to play his part.

"Hey, whoa!" cried Baloo, running up to the herd. "False alarm!"

"What's that?" asked Colonel Hathi.

"Shere Khan isn't coming after all," said Baloo. "Human hunters are after him, so he's heading far away. We're all safe!"

The Dawn Patrol sighed with relief. Then Colonel Hathi called, "Forward, march!"

As the elephants marched off, Mowgli grinned. "With this new path to the spring, my friends will never run out of water."

Bagheera nodded. "Good work," he said.

"Yes, it was," said Baloo with a laugh. "And you know what was good about it? Somebody else did the work for us!"

Beauty and the Beast

A Friend for Philippe

Belle loved life in the castle with her Prince, and she loved her faithful horse, Philippe. Lately, however, Philippe had been acting strangely. One morning, Belle decided to try and cheer him up. She asked her friends for some help.

First, Lumiere helped Belle to brighten up Philippe's stall. They covered the walls with wallpaper and trimmed them with gold. They piled pillows in the corners and hung a huge chandelier from the ceiling.

"Voilà!" Lumiere cried. "What more could a horse ask for?"

But Philippe just stared sadly out of the window.

"I wish I knew," said Belle.

Next, Belle saw to it that Philippe was treated to a bubble bath fit for a king. "If this doesn't make him smile," Belle told Chip, "I don't know what will!"

But in the end, although he was shiny and sweet smelling, Philippe was just as glum – and Belle was just as puzzled. She asked the Prince if he had any suggestions.

"A good walk always used to cheer me up," the Prince said.

Belle thought that was a wonderful idea. She rode Philippe to a wide, open meadow, but he wasn't interested in galloping.

"Oh, Philippe," Belle said in despair. "I just don't know what else to do!"

Then, all of a sudden, Philippe's ears pricked up. Belle barely had time to sit up before he charged off!

Before long, they emerged into a clearing filled with wild, beautiful horses! Philippe whinnied, and several of the horses answered him. Finally, Belle realized what Philippe had wanted – to be with other horses!

All afternoon, Belle watched Philippe race and play.

Soon, Philippe had even made a friend. The two horses grazed, chased each other around the clearing, and dozed together in the warm sun.

All too quickly, the day was over, and the sun began to set. Belle put Philippe's saddle on and they started back towards the castle.

Soon, Belle heard the sound of hooves behind them. Philippe's new friend was following them home!

"Welcome to our castle!" Belle told the new horse when they arrived. Then she hurried off to fix up the stall next to Philippe's.

"There," she said when she was finished. "Now this looks like a stable where a horse (or two!) could really live happily ever after!"

And that is exactly what they did.

FAIRIES
TinkerBell
AND THE
LEGEND OF THE
NEVERBEAST

The Fairies Meet the Beast

Nyx and the Pixie Hollow scouts arrived on top of the cliff shortly after Fawn and Gruff had disappeared into the woods. They examined the clues – the rock pile, the paw prints and the leftover fairy dust.

The scouts then followed a trail of paw prints into the woods. Up ahead, the trees were shaking and they heard the snapping of branches.

The scouts flew quickly into position ahead of the noise. They tossed pouches of nightshade powder into the air and burst them open. The nightshade cloud drifted towards Gruff but Fawn turned sharply away from it and the beast followed, avoiding the sleeping powder.

Nyx raced through the trees and stopped at the edge of a cliff. Whatever they had been chasing had disappeared!

Hiding in some tree roots halfway down the cliff face was Gruff, smiling widely at Fawn. He liked this game!

Back at the Book Nook, Nyx was determined to find out what she was up against. Scribble, the reading-talent fairy, brought her book after book, but Nyx found nothing that gave her any idea, until she noticed an old piece of parchment paper on Scribble's bulletin board.

Nyx grabbed it and smiled. "Tell me everything you know about this," she told Scribble. "Everything."

In the meantime, Fawn went to collect her friends – she'd decided it was time for them to meet Gruff. But first she reminded them of her promise to Queen Clarion, to use her head to think, as well as her heart. She wanted to reassure her friends that she'd thought about what she was doing.

This worried Tink. "Fawn," she said, "what's going on?"

"Ladies, say hello to Gruff!" Fawn motioned for them to look up. Dangling from a tree was Gruff, smiling broadly.

Iridessa fainted! The others stared in amazement.

"What is that?" gulped Rosetta as she looked at the enormous creature.

"I don't actually know," admitted Fawn. "I'm going to take him to the queen and show her he's harmless."

After Fawn and Gruff had convinced her friends that he was friendly, they helped him to fly by covering him in pixie dust. They guided him to Queen Clarion's house.

"You guys keep an eye on him outside," explained Fawn, "while I work my charm on the queen and prepare her for an intro."

Tangled
The Princess Jewels

Freed from her tower and Mother Gothel, Rapunzel and her friends were travelling back to the kingdom. Soon she would meet her true parents, the King and Queen.

"I can't believe I'm the lost Princess," said Rapunzel.

Flynn smiled. "You'll be great as a princess. All you have to do is wear a huge, heavy crown...."

"Oh, my!" Rapunzel exclaimed.

"Let me start over," Flynn said. "Do you remember that tiara from my satchel? Well, let me tell you a story....

"When I was a kid in the orphanage, I read a book about a princess who said a tiara symbolized everything a princess should be. The white crystals stood for an adventurous spirit; green represented kindness; red stood for courage; and the round golden crown itself stood for leadership.

"For years, I thought of that tiara, and then one day, I actually met a gal who could wear it. She certainly was adventurous. She also showed kindness towards everyone, courage and definitely leadership. She turned every bad situation into something wonderful!"

"Flynn, are you talking about – ?" Rapunzel started.

"You!" Flynn exclaimed. "I'm talking about all those amazing things you did when you left your tower in search of the floating lights."

"But I did all those things when I had long, magical hair!" Rapunzel exclaimed. "I have no idea how to help anyone without magic."

Suddenly, they heard a noise behind them. "Nobody move!" someone shouted. "Hand over your horse!"

"Rapunzel!" Flynn shouted. "Run away!"

But Rapunzel did not run away. She ran right in to rescue Maximus. When it was over, Rapunzel scolded the bandits.

"It's all my fault," one man replied. "I need your horse to take my son to the doctor."

"Oh, my! Where is he?" Rapunzel asked. Within minutes, Rapunzel was tending to the boy's injuries. He smiled as he was hoisted onto Maximus for a ride to the kingdom's doctor.

"How can you ever forgive us?" the men asked Rapunzel.

Rapunzel thought of the tiara – adventure, kindness, courage and leadership. Suddenly, she realized she didn't need her magical hair.

"Come with me," she said.

At the kingdom, Rapunzel received her princess crown. But as she waved to the crowds, she knew that no one was as supportive as her faithful new friends!

And they always would be, too.

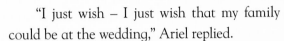

Ariel's Royal Wedding

Ariel loved Prince Eric from the moment she first saw him. And Prince Eric loved Ariel from the first time he heard her sing. And now they were going to be married!

At home in the castle, Ariel realized that there was a great deal of work to be done. The royal workers started showing Ariel lists and books and plans. She began to feel nervous.

I've never even been to a human wedding before, she thought. *How do I begin to plan for one?* Ariel knew she would need a lot of help.

Ariel asked Carlotta, the friendly maid, to help to make her dress. They worked through the night and made Ariel's dream dress.

"It's so beautiful!" cried Ariel. "I wish my sisters could see it."

The next morning, Chef Louis drew Ariel a picture of the wonderful wedding cake he would make. "It's perfect!" cried Ariel. "I wish my father could see it when it's done."

As Ariel thought about all of the wonderful wedding plans, she began to think about her family. It was Ariel's dream to spend the rest of her life as a human and as Prince Eric's wife, but she wanted her family close by on her wedding day. She began to feel sad.

Later, Prince Eric noticed a tear in Ariel's eye. "What's the matter?" he asked.

"I just wish – I just wish that my family could be at the wedding," Ariel replied.

"Hmm, I thought you might want that. So, I thought, we should have our wedding at sea!" Eric grinned. "It's all planned: we'll be married on the royal ship at sea."

"That's perfect!" Ariel cried. "Thank you!"

Soon, Ariel met her sisters near the shore. She asked all of them to be her bridesmaids. She asked Sebastian to be the ring bearer. And she asked her father, King Triton, to give her away.

The day of the wedding finally arrived. The ship was covered with beautiful pink and white flowers. The human wedding guests were all seated on deck. Ariel's father used his trident to magically lift him and Ariel's sisters up to the side of the ship. The rest of her merfolk friends looked on from the sea.

King Triton led Ariel to meet her handsome prince. The vows were read. The rings were exchanged.

"Kiss the girl!" cried Sebastian. And at last the Prince and Princess were married!

Prince Eric and Princess Ariel knew that their lives would be a joining of land and sea – this was the beginning of a life filled with joy and laughter, shared with family and friends of all kinds.

101 DALMATIANS

Special Delivery

Now that their family had grown so large, Roger, Anita, Nanny and the Dalmatians had moved to the country, or to the "Dalmatian Plantation", as Roger liked to call it. A weekly delivery of dog food came from the city. It arrived every Thursday at 3pm, and Rolly looked forward to it with eager anticipation.

One Thursday, Rolly and Pepper noticed that the back of the van had been left open. "Are you thinking what I'm thinking?" Pepper asked Rolly.

Rolly nodded. "Snack time!" Rolly and Pepper made a dash for the van and leaped into the back. Pepper clambered up onto the pile of bags and sniffed around. There had to be some loose food somewhere....

"Bingo!" Pepper cried. "Rolly, up here!"

Rolly was there in an instant.

Slurp, slurp, crunch! The two puppies were so busy eating that they didn't see the van driver come out of the house.

Slam! He closed up the back of the van. A second later it was rumbling down the drive.

"Uh-oh," Rolly whispered.

Finally, after what seemed like a very long time, the vehicle lurched to a halt. The back door opened, and the driver began unloading bags of food.

Pepper and Rolly jumped off the van while he wasn't looking. They ran and hid behind the house.

"What do you two think you're doing?" a gruff voice asked.

The puppies spun around. A big bulldog was looking down at them. "This is my property," the dog said. "It is time for you to scram."

The two puppies stared at him.

"Now!" he barked.

"You don't scare me," Pepper said boldly. "You're not half as bad as Cruella."

The bulldog's mouth fell open. "Do you mean Cruella De Vil?" he asked. "You must be Pongo and Perdita's puppies! I heard about your adventures over the Twilight Bark! You live on the Dalmatian Plantation, right?"

"Yes!" cried Rolly. "Can you take us there?"

"You bet!" the bulldog said. "Let's go!"

Luckily, Pongo and Perdita were out that day and didn't realize what a pickle Rolly and Pepper had got themselves into. But there were 97 puppies waiting in the garden as Rolly and Pepper arrived with their escort.

"Wow," said Lucky, after he had heard their tale. "Were you scared of that big mean bulldog?"

"No way!" Pepper spoke up. "That bulldog was all bark and no bite!"

Cinderella
The Sapphire Ring

It was one year since the Prince and Cinderella had married. To celebrate, the Prince was to hold a ball, and he gave Cinderella a gold ring set with a blue sapphire – Cinderella's favourite stone.

However, the ring was too large and somehow it had slipped off her finger.

"Oh, no!" cried Cinderella. "My ring! Where is it?" She checked inside her gloves, but it was nowhere to be found.

"Don't worry, Cinderelly," her mouse friends Jaq and Gus piped up. "We'll help you find it!"

"Where have you been today?" Jaq asked.

Cinderella thought. "The first thing I did was go to my bedroom to write in my diary." So, they hurried to Cinderella's room.

"No ring," Jaq said with a sigh.

"Let's try the kitchen," said Cinderella. "I went there next to make a pot of tea." But the only ring in there was a day-old doughnut.

"Perhaps we should try the library. I read there this afternoon," said Cinderella. They searched high and low, but they could not find Cinderella's sapphire ring.

"I also went to the stables to feed Frou. Perhaps I lost my ring in his stall." The three friends sifted through piles of straw. But there was still no ring.

Cinderella scratched her head. "There's one more place to look," she said. "The garden!"

The friends searched every blossom until Gus exclaimed, "Cinderelly! I see it!" He picked up a shiny, blue object.

"Sapphire, Cinderelly?" Gus asked. Cinderella shook her head. It was just a marble.

"Wait a minute," she said as they stopped by the well. "After I drew some water from the well, I noticed my ring was gone. Could it have fallen in there?"

"I hope not," said Gus, trembling.

Jaq rolled his eyes. "Don't be such a scaredy-cat. Get into this bucket!"

Cinderella lowered Jaq and Gus into the well. "Do you see anything?" she called down.

"Eek!"

Cinderella pulled up the bucket as fast as she could. "What did you see?" she cried.

"Oh, nothing," said Gus slyly. "Nothing but Cinderelly's ring!"

"My heroes!" cried Cinderella. "Wait until I tell the Prince how you saved our special day!"

At the ball, Cinderella and the Prince raised their glasses to Gus and Jaq, their guests of honour, and thought how lucky they were to have such wonderful friends.

Eeyore's New Old House

One blustery, cold November day in the Hundred-Acre Wood, the blustery, cold November wind blew so strongly that it knocked Eeyore's house right over!

So Eeyore went to Pooh's house. "Well, Pooh," Eeyore said, "it seems that November just doesn't like me. Or my house. So I'm afraid I will have to stay here with you. If you don't mind, that is."

Pooh assured Eeyore that he didn't mind and offered him some honey.

"I'd prefer thistles, if you have any, which you probably don't," Eeyore said. "Oh well. Perhaps Rabbit has some."

Well, Rabbit did have some thistles, so Eeyore settled down to stay with Rabbit. But Rabbit's house was so full of vegetables and gardening tools – rakes and shovels and baskets and twine – that there was scarcely room in the burrow for Eeyore.

"I suppose Piglet might have more room, though I doubt it," said Eeyore.

Piglet told Eeyore he was welcome to stay with him, and even made Eeyore a little bed next to the pantry, which was full of haycorns. But Eeyore was allergic to haycorns, and soon his sneezing almost knocked Piglet's own house down.

"One house knocked down today is more than – *ah-choo!* – plenty," said Eeyore. "I'll just have to try Kanga and Roo."

Kanga and Roo were happy to put Eeyore up in their house. Roo was so excited to have a guest that he couldn't stop bouncing. Soon Eeyore was feeling dizzy just from watching him. But, just as Eeyore was about to try Owl's house, Piglet, Rabbit and Pooh arrived.

"Eeyore, we've found you the perfect house to live in!" Piglet cried.

"I doubt that," Eeyore said as they led him through the Wood. "The perfect house would have thistles, and enough room, and no haycorns, and, above all, no bouncing. But where will I find a house like that?"

Soon, they arrived at a snug little house made of sticks, with a pile of thistles in it. "Here it is, Eeyore," said Piglet.

"That's *my* house," said Eeyore, hardly able to believe his eyes. "But my house got knocked down."

"Piglet and I put it back together again," Pooh said, "and Rabbit donated his thistles, so now you have a house with thistles, and enough room, and no haycorns, and, above all, no bouncing."

Eeyore looked at his house, and then at his friends. "It looks like November doesn't dislike me so much after all," he said. "Maybe, that is."

Disney · PIXAR

BRAVE
Finding the Emeralds

Princess Merida and Young Macintosh had been searching for the source of Fire Falls when Merida had disappeared down a dark hole.

"Merida!" Young Macintosh yelled with concern. "Where are you?"

"I'm here," Merida's voice echoed. "There's a cave behind the vines. And you'll never believe what I've found!"

Young Macintosh had no choice but to follow her. He stepped carefully into the cavern to find Merida kneeling near a pool of water. Her hands were cupped around something that glowed. The golden light flickered over her face.

"Look at this," Merida whispered. "Have you ever, in all your life, seen anything like it?"

Young Macintosh crouched next to Merida to get a better look. He saw a stone ledge in the middle of a shallow pool of water. Someone had carved a design along the edge of the stone.

Merida moved her hands, flooding the cave with a beautiful light. Young Macintosh blinked in surprise at two large, glowing emeralds sitting on the ledge in front of them.

"Someone must have put them here," Merida said. She cautiously reached out to touch the emeralds. "I've never seen emeralds glow like this. They must be very lucky."

"Lucky? Why's that?"

"Because emeralds bring good luck, of course," Merida replied.

Young Macintosh started to laugh. "No," he said confidently. "My father told me emeralds are a symbol of power."

"Well, your father is wrong," Merida said firmly. "Emeralds have always been lucky for our people."

Then, to Merida's surprise, Young Macintosh grabbed one of the emeralds! He jammed it into the pouch attached to his kilt.

"Put that back!" Merida ordered.

"I'm taking this back for my father. The Macintosh clan will be stronger than ever!" snapped Young Macintosh.

Merida's eyes flashed angrily, then she plucked the other emerald from the ledge. "And you can see the good luck it will bring to the people of DunBroch!"

They left the cave, arguing all the way back to DunBroch Castle.

When they arrived, the welcoming ceremony for the Rites of Summer festival was about to begin. Queen Elinor was chatting with Lord Macintosh, but she sighed with relief when she saw her daughter and Young Macintosh enter the Great Hall. The emeralds were safely hidden in their bags, but neither of them had noticed that the gems had stopped glowing.

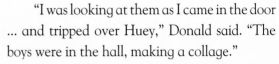

Minnie's Missing Recipe

One day, Mickey opened his door to a very worried Minnie. "What's wrong?" he asked.

"It's the annual Bake-off and I can't find my cinnamon swirl cake recipe!" Minnie cried.

Pluto dropped a rolled-up paper at Mickey's feet.

"Thanks, Pluto," Mickey said. "But I haven't got time to read the newspaper now. We have to help Minnie. Come on!"

Mickey did a search of Minnie's kitchen and noticed a postcard on the floor. "What's this?" he asked.

"Donald came over this morning to show me his postcard collection. He was so excited that he dropped them all," Minnie giggled.

Mickey had an idea. "Did Donald pick up your recipe with his postcards? Let's see!"

When Mickey, Minnie and Pluto got to Donald's house, Donald wasn't happy.

"What's wrong, Donald?" Minnie asked.

"It's my new postcards," Donald told Mickey and Minnie. "Five of them are missing!"

"My recipe is missing, too!" said Minnie.

"We were wondering if you accidentally picked it up when you were at Minnie's this morning," Mickey added.

Pluto dropped the rolled-up paper on the table, but Donald was too upset to notice.

"Where did you last see your postcards?" Mickey asked.

"I was looking at them as I came in the door ... and tripped over Huey," Donald said. "The boys were in the hall, making a collage."

"Perhaps they used some postcards in their collage," said Minnie.

Pluto dropped the paper at Minnie's feet.

"Thanks, Pluto," said Minnie. "But we have to solve this mystery!"

"Did you use my postcards in your collage?" Donald asked when his nephews got home.

"Maybe...." Dewey said.

"Where's the collage now?" Minnie asked.

"I rolled it up and put it in my backpack this morning," Louie said.

"But when we got on the bus, it was gone," Dewey added.

"It must have fallen out between Donald's house and the bus stop," Minnie said.

Everyone searched the route, but they couldn't find the collage anywhere.

Pluto barked and dropped his rolled-up paper at Huey's feet.

"This is it! We must have dropped it in Mickey's garden," Huey shouted.

The boys unrolled their collage, complete with the postcards and Minnie's missing recipe!

"You were helping us, Pluto!" Minnie said. "I'm going to bake two cinnamon swirl cakes – one for the Bake-off and one for you!"

The Real Adventure

Russell was a Junior Wilderness Explorer, and he had knocked on Carl Fredricksen's door to see if he needed help. Carl had been in a bad mood – he was being forced to move out of his home. He told Russell to find an imaginary bird called a Snipe, just to get rid of him.

Carl and his wife, Ellie, had both dreamed of being explorers and Carl had promised her they'd visit Paradise Falls in South America. But they had never managed to save enough money to go. When Ellie passed away, Carl missed her very much.

Then Carl decided he had to keep his promise and go to Paradise Falls. He tied thousands of balloons to his house and it lifted into the air. But he didn't realize that Russell was still on the porch, looking for the Snipe!

Soon the pair landed in South America. They pulled the house along as they walked towards Paradise Falls. Before long, they met a strange bird called Kevin (who was actually female) and a talking dog called Dug. There was also a pack of dogs controlled by the great explorer Charles Muntz – he wanted to capture Kevin.

Russell and Carl managed to escape with Kevin, but then Charles set Carl's house on fire! Carl couldn't let all his memories of Ellie go up in flames, so he gave up Kevin.

Russell was very upset because Carl had promised to protect Kevin. They wanted to help her to get back to her babies.

Carl told Russell he no longer needed his help, then he towed the house the rest of the way to Paradise Falls by himself. He placed the house exactly where it appeared in one of Ellie's drawings of Paradise Falls.

Russell was still angry with Carl. "Here," he said, throwing his Wilderness Explorer sash on the ground. "I don't want this anymore."

With a sigh, Carl picked up Russell's sash and went into his house. Carl found Ellie's adventure book. He had kept his promise to her, but he still felt sad. He wished Ellie was here.

Carl started to close the book, but something caught his eye. It was a photograph of their wedding day. Carl turned the page. He had never looked through the whole book before. To his astonishment, it was filled with photographs of the two of them over the years. On the last page, there was a message from Ellie:

Thanks for the adventure. Now go and have one of your own.

Carl smiled, realizing that Ellie had got her wish after all. Their life together had been the real adventure.

Disney · PIXAR

FINDING NEMO

A Real Sleeper!

"Time for bed, Nemo," said Marlin. "It's a school day tomorrow," he added. "You need to get your rest."

"Okay," said Nemo. "But can you tell me a story? How about one from when you were younger?"

"Well, just one then," said Marlin, swimming back over to his only child. He thought for a moment, then smiled broadly. "Did you know that when I was younger – much younger, actually – I wanted to be a comedian?"

Nemo's eyes widened with surprise. "*You*? A comedian? Aren't comedians supposed to be ... funny?"

"Well, you see, son," said Marlin, "life is not easy for a clownfish. You may as well realize that right now. See, when you're a clownfish, everyone you meet assumes that you are funny. It's a common mistake. Anyway, years ago, I figured that as everyone expected me to be funny, I would try being funny for a living."

"But Dad," said Nemo, "you aren't funny at all."

"Hey now! Wait just a minute!" Marlin said, a bit huffily. "In my day, I was known as quite the crack-up! Let me see. I'm sure I can remember some of my old routine, if I just think about it for a minute." He thought for a moment. "All right, it's all coming back!"

He cleared his throat. "Good evening, ladies and jellyfish! The ocean sure is looking *swell* tonight. Would you like me to give you a coral report about the latest happenings on the reef? Get it?" he said, looking down at Nemo. "You see, there's something called an oral report, and the words coral and oral sound quite a bit alike."

Nemo gave his father a pained look.

"So, the other day my appendix nearly burst," Marlin went on. "So I decided I'd better go to a sturgeon!"

Nemo blinked. "Dad, these really aren't that funny," he said with a yawn.

"A *sturgeon*. Get it? Rather than a surgeon?" Marlin sighed and continued his routine. "A funny thing happened on the way to the show tonight. I met a guy, nice fish and all, but he seemed to be a bit down on his luck. He told me he was living on squid row."

Nemo's eyes were starting to droop sleepily.

"Do you know why the whale crossed the ocean?" Marlin continued. "Now, don't try to guess. I'll tell you: the whale crossed the ocean to get to the other tide. The other *tide*."

Nemo's eyes were now completely closed, and a tiny snore escaped from him. Marlin smiled at his sleeping son.

"Works every time," he said with a chuckle.

DUMBO

A Talented Mouse

"Look, Dumbo," Timothy Mouse said, pointing to the newspaper. "There's another article about us in here!"

That wasn't unusual. Ever since Dumbo had become famous for being able to fly, everyone was interested in him.

Mrs Jumbo, Dumbo's mother, peered over Timothy's shoulder. "What a nice story," she cooed. "Too bad the picture isn't better – why, I can hardly see you, Timothy!"

Timothy peered at the paper. "Hey," he said, scanning the story. "This article doesn't mention me at all!"

"It's all right," Mrs Jumbo said soothingly. "Everyone knows how important you are."

Timothy puffed out his chest proudly. After all, he had taught Dumbo to fly!

Then he sagged again. "Am I really that important?" he said. "It's Dumbo who has the talent – not me."

Mrs Jumbo and Dumbo tried to comfort him, but he wandered away sadly. He was so smart, so talented – he should be famous too!

"I have to figure out a way to get famous on my own," he muttered. "But how?"

Suddenly he snapped his fingers.

"I've got it!" he cried. "I'll learn to fly too! Then Dumbo and I can be famous together!"

He quickly climbed to the top of the tallest circus tent. Dumbo had learned to fly by jumping off things. Timothy just hoped it would work for him too. He rubbed his hands together.

"Here goes nothing...." he muttered.

He leaped off the tent and looked down. The ground seemed very far away.

"Uh-oh!" Timothy gulped. What had he done? The ground got closer and closer. Timothy squeezed his eyes shut....

Suddenly, Timothy felt himself being whisked upwards. Opening his eyes, he saw that he was clutched in Dumbo's trunk.

"Whew!" he gasped. "Thanks, chum!"

Dumbo smiled at his little friend. He set Timothy in his cap.

Timothy settled into the familiar spot. Flying was much more fun when Dumbo's ears did all the work!

Soon they landed beside Mrs Jumbo.

"Oh, Timothy!" she cried. "You're safe! When I saw you fall, I was so worried ... Dumbo and I don't know what we'd do without you."

Timothy blinked. "Never thought of it that way," he mused. "Maybe I'm not front-page news every day. But who cares? I know I'm important, and my friends know it too. That's what matters!"

He smiled. He had plenty of his own talent, and that was good enough for him!

Disney · PIXAR

BRAVE
Clash of the Clans

"Mum, I have a question," Merida began as she joined Queen Elinor and Lord Macintosh at the welcoming ceremony in the Great Hall. "What's the meaning of an emerald?"

"Ah, lass, I can answer you that," Lord Macintosh said. "The emerald has long been a symbol of power and strength to every clan in our great land."

Young Macintosh's eyes lit up. "Just like I told you!" he jeered.

Lord Macintosh grabbed his son's chin. "You're not to be rude to our hosts on this most special day of celebration," he scolded.

Queen Elinor tried to make peace. "The emerald carries many meanings. One might argue that we've forgotten the emerald's most important meaning – as a symbol of loyalty," she said. "The Legend of the Emeralds is part of the reason we are gathered here today."

"For the Rites of Summer?" Merida asked.

Queen Elinor nodded. "Long before the peace that unites our clans, there was terrible fighting. Two great kings understood that friendship between our clans would be the only way to make peace. They each placed an emerald at the source of the Fire Falls – a worthy sacrifice to prove their loyalty to each other. From that day forth, the Fire Falls glow at sunset as a reminder of the two kings' pledge."

But just as the feast was about to begin, the doors of the hall crashed open. A DunBroch clansman raced inside. "The Fire Falls –" he panted. "They've gone dark!"

Everyone in the Great Hall gasped. King Fergus led the DunBroch and Macintosh clans outside. Something was very wrong with the majestic waterfall.

"Who has done this?" King Fergus roared. "Who has threatened the peace between our great clans?"

"I stand with King Fergus," Lord Macintosh announced. "When he finds out which one of his clansmen caused this, he will have our full support."

King Fergus turned to Lord Macintosh with a frown. Was he implying someone from DunBroch was to blame? The men started to argue and the argument turned to insults.

"Take down the tents!" shouted Lord Macintosh. "We set sail before nightfall."

"You mustn't go!" Queen Elinor exclaimed. "Our clans are still friends."

"Not any more," Lord Macintosh snapped, striding away.

Merida and Young Macintosh looked at one another.

"We've got to put the emeralds back," Princess Merida whispered.

TinkerBell
LEGEND OF THE
NEVERBEAST

Legend of the NeverBeast

Outside Queen Clarion's tree house, the fairies were looking after Gruff while Fawn, the animal-talent fairy, was inside telling the queen everything about him.

But Nyx, the scout fairy, had got there first. It was her job to protect Pixie Hollow and she knew there was a beast on the loose. She had found a piece of parchment in the Book Nook that explained everything – a comet had appeared 972 years before, and with it the NeverBeast. The NeverBeast had built towers in each season of Pixie Hollow, and when he had finished, green storm clouds had formed. The monster had destroyed everything with lightning!

Fawn knew Nyx was referring to Gruff. "Animals do not control the weather," she protested.

"Ordinary animals don't," Nyx responded.

Outside the window, pixie dust tickled Gruff's nose. ACHOO! he sneezed, spraying slobber everywhere.

Queen Clarion looked outside. Luckily, she didn't see Gruff or the girls, who were now stuck to the tree thanks to Gruff's slobber! Gruff smiled, clearly feeling guilty.

The queen turned back to Fawn and Nyx and asked them to listen with their hearts and their heads. "I trust you both to do what's right for Pixie Hollow."

Fawn and the girls flew Gruff back to the Summer Forest where Fawn explained what had happened.

"Nyx thinks Gruff is a monster. Crazy, right?" Fawn asked, but her friends backed away. They weren't convinced! "Come on, guys. I know he's not what they say he is."

"Even if you're right," said Tink, "it's not safe for him here."

Gruff went back to his tower-building while Fawn tried to think what to do next. Once he had finished the second tower, he and Fawn gazed up at the stars together.

"Rest up, because first thing tomorrow we're going to find somewhere great for you," Fawn said. "Just until things settle down."

Fawn nestled into the fur on Gruff's nose and fell asleep. But Gruff stayed awake, watching the green clouds gather.

By morning, thick green clouds blanketed the sky. As Tink stared at them, she saw scout fairies flying towards the forest with a huge net. She gasped. They were going after Gruff!

Tink rushed to Fawn and told her about the scouts. "Please tell me you took Gruff away already," she said.

But Fawn had some worrying news. "He's missing," she said.

Disney
Winnie the Pooh

Pooh Welcomes Winter

Pooh had heard that Winter was coming soon, and he was very excited about having a visitor. Pooh and Piglet decided to throw a party to welcome Winter to Hundred-Acre Wood. The two friends set off to tell everyone.

Outside, it was snowing. They met Tigger along the way, and they walked to Kanga and Roo's house together. They all decided to go by sledge to the party. Owl landed on a branch overhead.

"Winter has arrived!" he declared. "I heard Christopher Robin say so."

Pooh told Owl about the party, then they all jumped on the sledge and slid down the hill towards Christopher Robin's house.

"There's Winter!" Tigger cried. "Tiggers always know Winter when they see him. That big white face – that carroty nose. Who else could he be?" said Tigger.

"Well," said Pooh, "he looks shy. We should be extra friendly." He walked right up to Winter. "How do you do? We are giving a party in your honour." Winter did not say anything.

"Oh d-d-dear," said Piglet. "He's frozen!"

"Quick!" cried Tigger. "We'd better get him to the party and warm him up." They hoisted Winter onto the sledge. When they slid up to Pooh's house, the others were already there. Owl had hung a big friendly sign over Pooh's door – WELCOME WINTER. Pooh and Tigger wrestled Winter off the sledge.

"Give him the comfy chair by the fire!" said Rabbit. Still, Winter did not say a word. His carrot nose drooped.

Just then, Christopher Robin tramped up to the door in his big boots. "Has anyone seen my snowman?" he asked.

"No," said Pooh glumly, "but we brought Winter here for a special party. He doesn't seem to like it."

"Silly old bear!" Christopher Robin told Pooh that Winter was not a person, it was a season. A time of year for cold snow, mistletoe, warm fires and good friends.

Pooh scratched his nose thoughtfully. "Yes, I see now," he said. "Of course, I am a bear of very little brain."

"You're the best bear in all the world," said Christopher Robin. "Come on, we'd better get the snowman back outside before he melts completely."

They undrooped the snowman's nose and stuck his hands back in. They decided to have the party anyway, to celebrate Winter. So everyone sang songs and danced around the snowman until they couldn't dance any more.

Tangled

Rapunzel's Royal Wedding

Spring had sprung, and Flynn had a surprise for Rapunzel. Max kept guard, and Pascal went along to play. But Flynn wanted to be alone with Rapunzel.

Finally, dusk fell, and Flynn took his chance to jump into a boat with Rapunzel. The lovely night reminded them of times past. Flynn wanted to propose! He put his hand in his pocket, but – oops! He did need Pascal and Max, after all. They had the ring.

"Will you marry me?" Flynn finally asked Rapunzel.

"Yes," Rapunzel said happily.

On their way home, Rapunzel wanted to tell everyone their wonderful news!

The pub ruffians were delighted. It turned out they had been waiting for a wedding to organize for years! Of course, Attila helped Rapunzel to design a cake. They baked and iced and created the wedding cake of Rapunzel's dreams!

Rapunzel looked at lots of different flowers, but it took a field of wild flowers to please the Princess!

As for ring bearers, the choice was clear: Maximus and Pascal could not have been prouder to accept!

When it was time to find a dress, Rapunzel was determined to design her own.

She sketched and sketched ... but simply could not make up her mind!

The pub thugs tried to help, but their dresses didn't seem right either. Luckily, the Queen arrived. "Darling," she said. "I want to help you find the perfect dress." And she did!

On the morning of the wedding, bells rang through the kingdom. Everyone was excited to see the King and Queen happily riding in the royal coach. And Max and Pascal were thrilled – until Max sneezed and the rings flew into the air!

Max and Pascal chased the rings out of the church and up and down the streets. They finally caught them ... but then went crashing into a tar factory!

Max and Pascal made it back to the wedding just in time for the exchange of the rings – but they looked rather strange, covered in black tar!

Luckily, Rapunzel and Flynn didn't mind one bit.

Everyone helped out to make the reception as perfect as Rapunzel had planned. The newlyweds danced their first dance. They took their first taste of their wedding cake.

And as they rode away in their wedding coach, Rapunzel cried out happily:

"Best. Day. Ever!"

The Father of Invention

There was never a dull moment in the castle of Belle and the Prince. Friends came and went, Mrs Potts and the other members of the household bustled about, and Maurice, Belle's father, was always tinkering away on a new invention.

One morning, Maurice wheeled a complicated-looking contraption into the kitchen, and presented it to Mrs Potts. "Just a little something to make your life easier," he said proudly.

"Thank you, Maurice dear, but ... what is it?" the housekeeper wondered.

"I call it a 'plate pitcher'," answered Maurice. He took a pile of clean plates and loaded them onto a mechanical arm. Then he positioned the machine in front of the open china cabinet. He pressed a button and stood back proudly. With a couple of loud clangs, the machine sprang to life.

The plate pitcher began to hurl plates this way and that. They smashed against walls and onto the floor.

"Look out, Mrs Potts!" shouted Maurice as a plate whizzed by her head. He crawled along the floor, reached up and hit the off switch. "I'll just go work out the kinks," he said, wheeling the machine out of the room.

The next day, Maurice had another surprise. "It's for cleaning the carpets," he explained as he pointed to a large metal box with a big hose

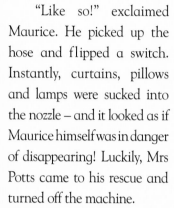

coming out of it. "No more beating heavy rugs for you!"

"Well, it looks harmless," Mrs Potts decided. "How does it work?"

"Like so!" exclaimed Maurice. He picked up the hose and flipped a switch. Instantly, curtains, pillows and lamps were sucked into the nozzle – and it looked as if Maurice himself was in danger of disappearing! Luckily, Mrs Potts came to his rescue and turned off the machine.

"Must have made it a tad too powerful," Maurice admitted.

The following day Maurice had yet another time-saving device for Mrs Potts. This one was a laundry machine that flooded the entire ground floor of the castle with water and soapsuds.

"Maurice," Mrs Potts said gently, "it is very sweet of you to want to make my job easier. But I enjoy it. By taking care of the castle, I'm taking care of the people I love." She looked thoughtful for a moment, then added, "But I have to admit, the one thing I would love is something that would make me a nice, hot cup of tea at the end of the day."

"I have just the thing!" Maurice replied with a twinkle in his eye.

Mrs Potts looked slightly worried. "You do?" she asked.

"Yes," Maurice answered. "Me!"

THE PRINCESS AND THE FROG

The Secret Gourmet

When the sun shines in New Orleans, the whole town sings and dances. And it's reason enough for Charlotte's father to want to share a meal with friends.

"Charlotte, darling," he said to his daughter one sunny evening, "what would you say to going to eat at Tiana's restaurant?"

"Fantastic!" said Charlotte happily. "I'll go and put on my pink silk dress!"

The young woman never missed a chance to go and visit Tiana. They were very fond of each other. And now that Tiana had married Prince Naveen and they had opened a restaurant together, it was even more fun to visit her!

"I hope Naveen's parents will be there!" Charlotte exclaimed shortly after getting into the car with her father. "I always enjoy chatting to a king and queen!"

As they drove down the road, no one noticed Stella, Charlotte's dog, fast asleep on the back seat.

Stella woke with a start when the car pulled up in front of the restaurant. Usually, Stella didn't like to leave the house. She was about to bark, but then she recognized the delicious smell of Tiana's cooking!

Stella suddenly didn't want to go back to the mansion after all. She sneaked quietly into the restaurant kitchen at the back of the building.

Meanwhile, Charlotte and her father were joining Eudora, Tiana's mother, who was dining with Naveen's parents. "I will serve you the new House Gumbo!" Tiana suggested.

At the back of the room, Louis the alligator and his band were playing jazz music. The atmosphere was fantastic.

Charlotte clapped her hands with joy. "We're going to have an amazing evening! All that's missing is Stella. What a shame she doesn't like going out."

Poor Charlotte! She had no idea what was happening in the kitchen....

Stella was so happy to be there and was simpering and begging so much that the chef gave her lots of food!

"We have a secret gourmet in the kitchen," he laughed. "Her appetite does me proud! Serve her as much as she wants, she's my guest!"

Stella barked with happiness. A secret passenger in the car, and a secret gourmet in the kitchen – it was good to get out of the house after all ... but only if you're a secret guest!

Hey, Hey, We're the Vultures!

"Nothing exciting ever happens around here," Buzzie complained to his vulture singing buddies.

"That's not true," said Flaps. "What about that fight we had with the tiger Shere Khan last week?"

"Blimey, you're right," said Ziggy. "That was pretty exciting."

Buzzie sighed. "What are we gonna do now?"

"Well, we could sing," suggested Ziggy.

"Hey, good idea!" said the other three vultures.

"One problem," said Dizzy. "We need a tenor."

"Awww, you're right," said Ziggy. "That little Man-cub fellow, Mowgli, would have been a great tenor. Too bad he left the jungle."

"So, what are we gonna do?" asked Buzzie.

"How 'bout we hold an audition?" suggested Ziggy.

"Good thinking," said Flaps.

So the vultures put the word out in the jungle and, a week later, there was a line of animals ready to try out for the group.

"Name?" Buzzie asked the first applicant.

"Coconut," the monkey replied.

"Alright, Coconut, let's hear ya sing," said Flaps.

Coconut shrieked for a few minutes, and the four vultures huddled together.

"He's not very good," said Buzzie.

"And he's a monkey," added Flaps.

"Next!" said Dizzy.

The vultures auditioned a lemur, two sloths, a wolf, a hippo, a toad and an elephant. None seemed like the right fit. Finally, the last animal stepped up.

"Name?" asked Buzzie.

"Name's Lucky," said the vulture. "Hey, aren't you the four fellows that helped that little man-cub scare away that tiger Shere Khan?"

"Yeah," said Buzzie. "We are."

"Then I guess you four might be called 'lucky' yourselves!" cried Lucky. He began to laugh at his own joke.

"Go ahead and sing," said Ziggy, rolling his eyes.

Lucky sang for a few minutes and the four vultures huddled together.

"He's not bad," said Dizzy.

"Plus, he's a vulture," said Ziggy.

"And he's the last one left," pointed out Flaps. That settled it.

"You're hired!" the vultures sang.

"See, told you I was Lucky!" cried the vulture.

"But only with auditions," said Dizzy.

"Yeah," said Buzzie. "When we meet Shere Khan again, we'll see how lucky you really are!"

New Friends

In South America, Carl was sitting inside his house. He had flown it there with thousands of balloons tied to it. He had promised his wife, Ellie, that he would take her to Paradise Falls one day, but sadly she had passed away. Carl kept his promise but he felt sad. That is, until he looked through Ellie's adventure book. It was full of pictures of their life together. Carl had realized their life had been the true adventure.

A boy named Russell had accidentally come along for the ride. They'd met a strange, big bird called Kevin and a talking dog named Dug. A pack of dogs were trying to catch Kevin. Their leader, the explorer Charles Muntz, wanted to capture the bird. Russell was angry at Carl. Carl had promised to protect Kevin, but he had let the bird go in order to save his house from a fire.

Suddenly, Carl heard something. He hurried outside and saw Russell gripping a bunch of balloons. "I'm gonna help Kevin, even if you won't!" Russell cried.

"No!" Carl shouted. He had to help Russell, but the house wouldn't move. The balloons had lost too much air. He had an idea. He began throwing things out of the house to make it lighter. Carl realized he didn't need the things – Russell was more important!

Carl was on his way, but then he heard a knock at the door. It was Dug. Together they set out to rescue Russell. Then they saw the boy being lowered out of Charles' airship! Carl grabbed the garden hose and, using it like a rope, he swung over to the airship and saved Russell.

Once Russell was safe, Carl and Dug went back for Kevin. They set the bird free, but suddenly Muntz appeared with a sword! Carl fought him and finally escaped. He made it back to the house when *BANG!* The balloons began to pop.

The house plunged downwards and landed on top of Charles' airship. As Carl fell out of the house, Muntz ran inside to grab Kevin. Carl knew he had to save his friends – the house was about to fall off the edge of the airship. Carl told Russell and Dug to hold onto Kevin, then he waved a big bar of chocolate – Kevin loved chocolate. The big bird jumped onto the airship, saving Russell and Dug at the same time. Muntz's foot got caught in some balloons, and he drifted away.

"Sorry about your house," Russell told Carl as they watched it disappear into the clouds.

"You know," said Carl, "it's just a house."

It didn't seem as important to him, now that he had friends. They climbed aboard the airship – it was time to go home.

The Mysterious Necklace

It was a fine morning, just right for a walk along the seashore.

With joy in her heart, Ariel strolled along the beach and soon found herself a long way from the castle.

Suddenly, she stumbled against a hard object buried in the sand.

"Ouch!" she cried, discovering a shiny object. She dug it up.

"It looks like one of those delicious things that humans are so fond of," said her friend Scuttle, licking it.

"Do you mean a 'sweet'?" laughed Ariel. "No, it's a jewel! Scuttle, go and find Sebastian. Tell him to call my father!"

A moment later, Ariel's father, King Triton, emerged out of the sea.

"Father," said Ariel. "I've just found this wonderful jewel and –"

"Where did you find it?" asked King Triton, amazed.

"On the beach," explained Ariel. "Do you know where it comes from?"

"I'm going to show you something," said her father solemnly, before transforming her into a mermaid.

Holding the jewel in her hand, Ariel dived into the water after her father. Soon, they arrived at the throne room.

"A tidal wave carried off the treasure of Atlantica," explained the king. "I fear this jewel is the only one that's left."

"I'll help you find the others!" said Ariel.

First, the princess searched the wreck of a ship and collected almost a dozen jewels!

Then, with the help of Flounder and his friends, she found even more gems in the coral reef.

Hidden among the seaweed, which was every imaginable colour, the jewels had gone unnoticed!

Soon the Atlantica treasure chest was full to the brim once more, thanks to Ariel.

"Ariel, on behalf of the kingdom, thank you," said King Triton, opening the chest to take out the wonderful precious stone that she had found on the beach that morning.

And, giving her a kiss on her forehead, King Triton fastened the necklace around her neck.

Soon it was time for Ariel to turn back into a human and return to her castle, where Eric was waiting for her.

That night, Ariel looked out at the ocean while touching the jewel hanging from her neck. Her family was never very far away, but she found it reassuring to have a little piece of Atlantica with her forever.

Bambi

The Winter Trail

One winter morning, Bambi was dozing in the wood when he heard a thumping sound nearby. "C'mon, Bambi!" his bunny friend Thumper cried. "It's a perfect day for playing."

Bambi followed Thumper through the forest. The sky was blue and the ground covered in a blanket of new snow.

"Look at these tracks!" Thumper said excitedly. He pointed to a line of footprints in the snow. "Who do you suppose they belong to?" Bambi didn't know, so they decided to follow the trail. They soon came to a tree.

"Wake up, Friend Owl!" called Thumper.

"Have you been out walking?" Bambi asked.

"Now why would I do that?" Friend Owl replied. "My wings take me everywhere."

Bambi and Thumper continued on. Next, they spotted a raccoon sitting next to a tree, his mouth full of red berries. "Hello, Mr Raccoon," Bambi said shyly. "Did you happen to see who made these tracks in the snow?"

The raccoon shook his head and began tapping the tree. "I know!" Thumper cried. "He thinks we should ask the woodpeckers."

Soon, Bambi and Thumper found the woodpecker family. "Did you make the tracks in the snow?" Thumper called up to the birds.

"No, we've been here all day," the mother bird answered.

"If the tracks don't belong to the woodpeckers or the raccoon and they don't belong to Friend Owl, whose can they be?" Bambi asked.

"I don't know," Thumper replied.

They soon reached the end of the trail, and the tracks led all the way to a snowy bush, where a family of quail were resting.

"Did you make these tracks?" Thumper asked.

"Why, yes," Mrs Quail answered. "Friend Owl told me about this wonderful bush. So this morning, my babies and I walked all the way over here."

Thumper and Bambi happily joined the quail family for a snack. Soon, it was time for the friends to go home. They'd spent all day following the trail. When they turned to leave, a big surprise was waiting for them – their mothers! Bambi bounded over to his mother and stretched his nose up for a kiss.

"How'd ya find us?" Thumper asked.

Thumper's mother looked down at the tracks in the snow.

"You followed our trail!" Bambi cried. His mother nodded.

"Now, let's follow it back home," Bambi's mother said. So that's just what they did.

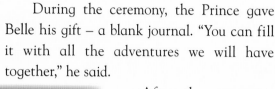

Beauty and the Beast

Belle's Royal Wedding

Belle's wedding was just days away, and everyone at the castle was busy preparing for the special celebration.

"The Prince has done so much for me," Belle told Mrs Potts. "We need to show him how much we appreciate him, and how well loved he is."

Belle thought back to when she first arrived at the castle. It was so frightening – everyone was under a magical spell. The Prince had become an angry Beast and the servants were enchanted objects. But over time, Belle became friends with the staff. Then she and the Beast fell in love.

Meanwhile, the Prince was preparing for the wedding, too. "I am the happiest man in the world!" he said to Lumiere and Cogsworth. "And I want Belle to be the happiest woman!"

When they first met, the Prince thought Belle could never love a hideous Beast. But she spent time getting to know him. When she declared her love, the spell was broken!

"How can I show Belle how much I love her?" the Prince asked. "I know! Let's find a special gift for her in the village!"

Lumiere and Mrs Potts wondered how they could show their love and appreciation for the young couple, too....

The wedding day finally arrived!

During the ceremony, the Prince gave Belle his gift – a blank journal. "You can fill it with all the adventures we will have together," he said.

After the ceremony, the newlyweds walked into the ballroom. The staff had laid out a huge banquet!

"Thank you!" said Belle. "But there is so much! I'm not sure even our whole household can eat all this food!" she joked.

Mrs Potts and the other servants smiled, and led the couple into the garden ... where the entire village was waiting to surprise them!

"I took the liberty of inviting them, on behalf of the household," said Lumiere. It was the staff's gift to Belle and the Prince.

"It's a magnificent gift!" the Prince said. "Thank you for coming!" he repeated over and over. He couldn't stop smiling. He and Belle were both thrilled to welcome everyone into their home.

When the couple shared their first dance, a shout went up from the crowd:

"Congratulations!"

As fireworks lit up the night sky, Belle and the Prince knew that their wedding had been a perfect celebration – for everyone. With so many friends gathered around them, it had been the most magical day of all.

A Visit to the Castle

"Gosh," Bashful said bashfully. "Do you think the Princess will be glad to see us?"

"Of course!" Happy chuckled.

"All right, men," Doc said. "Here we are. Now, all we have to do is go up and dock on the floor. That is – knock on the door!"

The Seven Dwarfs had just reached the castle where Snow White lived. They had been so busy in the mines that this was the first time they'd had a chance to visit since Snow White had married the Prince.

Sneezy looked up at the beautiful castle. "*Ah-choo!*" he sneezed. "Wow. This place sure is pretty."

"Time's a wastin'," Grumpy muttered.

He knocked firmly on the tall wooden door. A moment later a guard opened it.

"Er, good day," the castle guard said. "New servants around the back, please."

"Oh, we're not flu nervants," Doc spoke up. "Er, we're not new servants. We're here to see the Princess!"

"Yes! The Princess!" the other Dwarfs agreed. Dopey nodded eagerly.

The guard looked doubtful. "*You're* here to see the Princess?"

He looked them over. The Dwarfs stood up straight, glad that they'd remembered to wash that morning.

Finally the guard shook his head. "I'm sorry," he said. "You don't look like the sort of visitors that would interest the Princess."

"Oh, but we are!" Sleepy yawned. "She'll be interested in us."

"Sorry," the guard said. "You'll have to go."

But Grumpy held the door open. "Mark my words," he growled. "If you don't tell the Princess we're here, there'll be trouble."

"Who is it?" a sweet voice called from inside the castle. "Who's at the door?"

"Never mind, Princess!" the guard called. "It's just some strange little men who claim they know you."

"Little men?" Snow White cried, rushing forward. She peered around the door past the guard, and her lovely face lit up with joy. "Why, Doc – Grumpy – Sleepy – Dopey – Happy – Sneezy – even dear Bashful!"

Bashful blushed deeply. "Gosh," he said. "Hello, Princess."

The guard looked surprised. "You mean you know these fellows?" he asked the Princess. "I thought they were just riff-raff."

"Riff-raff?" Snow White cried. "Why, no – they may look a little different, but they're just like royalty to me! They're my very best friends!"

The guard apologized to the Dwarfs. Then Snow White invited her friends into the castle for a nice, long visit.

Sleeping
Beauty

Aurora's Royal Wedding

Princess Aurora dreamed many times that a handsome prince would find her, and he had! Even though their royal parents had decided years earlier that Phillip and Aurora would marry, the pair had fallen in love not as prince and princess – he was just a boy in the forest and she was a girl from the glen.

Phillip asked for Aurora's hand in marriage and she said yes. The wedding would be soon, and there was a lot to prepare!

"Everything seems well in hand, Your Majesty," said Flora.

The Queen smiled. "Yes, it does, and I couldn't be more delighted. I'll leave you now, Aurora, to enjoy the fun of choosing a dress."

"Thank you, Mother," said Aurora, but she was feeling nervous. She had yet to make any royal decisions on her own.

Just then, the dressmakers burst in with huge, lavish dresses. Aurora looked worried.

"What is it, dear?" asked Fauna.

Aurora sighed. "I don't know how to be a princess. What if I'm not a very good one?"

"Nonsense," said Merryweather. "You'll be the finest princess this kingdom has ever seen."

When Prince Phillip came by later, he had a splendid idea. "Would you like to go for a walk to get away from the wedding planning for a bit?"

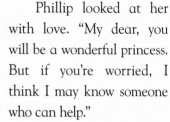

"That would be wonderful!" said Aurora.

On their walk, Aurora confided in Phillip. "I'm not sure I know how to act like a princess. I can't even choose a dress!"

Phillip looked at her with love. "My dear, you will be a wonderful princess. But if you're worried, I think I may know someone who can help."

Back at the palace, Phillip spoke to the Queen.

"Your Majesty," he said, "I think Aurora would like some help – from you, her mother."

The fairies overheard and smiled. Phillip was a perfect husband for their Briar Rose. They led the Queen to Aurora.

"Dear Aurora, I understand that you are worried, but being a princess isn't about what you do. Rather, it's about who you are. A princess is honest, thoughtful, clever and kind. And there is no doubt that you are all of these things."

"Oh, thank you, Mother!" Aurora said. "And I just had an idea about a wedding dress. Would it be possible to wear yours?"

The Queen smiled. "I married your father in a simple but beautiful gown. I think it will fit you perfectly."

On her wedding day, Aurora looked every bit a princess in her mother's dress – and she was starting to feel like one, too.

A Team Again!

Wreck-It Ralph, the Bad Guy from the *Fix-It Felix, Jr* computer game, had realized that his friend, Vanellope, from the *Sugar Rush* game, really did belong there! Vanellope had become a glitch in the game and the other racers told her it was because she didn't belong.

But Ralph had found out that the leader of *Sugar Rush*, King Candy, had reprogrammed the game and stolen Vanellope's computer code! That was why she glitched. Ralph found out that if Vanellope ever crossed the finish line, she'd become an official racer again!

Ralph had left his own game because he was fed up of being the Bad Guy. In reality, he wasn't bad. All he wanted to do was prove that he could be the hero.

But by leaving his own game, Ralph had put it in danger. The owner of the arcade would think it was broken and take it away! So Fix-It Felix, the game's Good Guy had been searching for Ralph to bring him back.

Ralph soon learned that Felix and Vanellope were being held prisoner in King Candy's castle dungeon. Ralph wrecked his way into Felix's cell and told him about Vanellope. Felix agreed to fix her broken racing kart right away. Next, Ralph crashed through to Vanellope. They were a team again!

The race had already started, but Ralph pushed Vanellope onto the track anyway. She quickly caught up to the other racers, and glitched and twitched past almost everyone. Finally, she pulled up next to King Candy.

"This is my kingdom!" he snarled.

"Race you for it!" Vanellope replied.

King Candy slammed into Vanellope's kart, to force her to crash. But she concentrated very hard and glitched away just in time!

As Vanellope glitched ... so did King Candy! The crowd watched on the screen as the king flickered, and turned into ... TURBO!

Turbo had been a very popular racing character long ago, until a newer racing game had arrived. Feeling jealous, Turbo had left his own game and tried to take over the new one. But when Turbo appeared in the wrong game, everyone thought it was broken! In the end, both games were unplugged and taken away.

Everyone gasped.

"You've ruined everything!" Turbo screamed at Vanellope.

But Vanellope zoomed forwards.

"She's going to do it!" Ralph cheered, as his friend raced towards the finish line. Finally, Ralph felt like he was the Good Guy.

TinkerBell
AND THE
LEGEND OF THE
NEVERBEAST

Lightning Strikes!

As green clouds gathered over Pixie Hollow, Fawn and Tink looked at each other. Gruff was missing and they had no idea where he was – or even what he was!

"According to the legend, he is going to build two more towers," Fawn said.

"You said the legend wasn't real," Tink said.

"Tink, in my heart, I know he's not a monster," Fawn replied.

Tink put her faith in Fawn. They knew he had built rock towers in both Spring and Summer, so Tink headed to Winter while Fawn flew towards Autumn.

In the Autumn Woods, Fawn found the tower already complete. Gruff had to be in Winter. She ducked out of sight as Nyx and the scout fairies arrived. It was their job to protect Pixie Hollow and, right now, Gruff appeared to be a serious threat. They had to capture him before he could finish the fourth tower and bring devastating lightning to Pixie Hollow.

Nyx looked at the rock tower. "Just like the other two," she said, shaking her head.

Suddenly, the scouts heard tree limbs cracking. The noise sounded like it was coming from the Summer Forest.

"Let's go!" yelled Chase.

But Nyx wasn't fooled by the trick. Fawn had wanted to draw the scouts away from Gruff by sending them in the wrong direction, but Nyx knew Gruff wouldn't be in Summer. She'd already found the tower there. The last tower had to be in Winter!

Tink was already in the Winter Woods, and she approached Gruff as thunder rumbled and lightning flashed.

"Gruff!" yelled Tink. "The scouts are coming for you! You have to hide."

But Gruff looked different – bigger and fiercer. Did he even recognize her?

"It's me, Tink," she said. "Fawn's friend."

A jagged bolt of lightning shot through the air. Gruff lunged at Tink and swatted her with his tail!

When Fawn arrived, she saw Tink lying on the ground with Gruff looming over her. "Gruff, what did you do?"

At that moment, lightning struck the tower. As Fawn watched, huge horns grew out of Gruff's head and a hump formed on his back. He looked just like the monster in the drawings!

"No!" cried Fawn. Had she been wrong about him? Had he meant to hurt her friend? Was he the monster Nyx thought he was, trying to destroy Pixie Hollow?

Lady and the TRAMP
Sledging

Lady stood on the porch as Jim Dear and Darling walked up the front path. Jim pulled a sledge and Darling held their son. They were all covered in snow, rosy cheeked and smiling from ear to ear.

"That was fun! Wasn't it Darling?" Jim asked.

"I don't know the last time I had so much fun," Darling agreed, patting Lady on the head.

"But we should get out of these wet clothes before one of us catches a cold," Jim said, leaning the sledge against the side of the house.

"I agree," Darling said. And the three of them hurried inside.

Just then, Tramp came walking up the front path. "Hey, Pidge," he said to Lady. "What do you say we take this old thing for a spin?"

"What is it, anyway?" Lady wanted to know.

"A sledge!" Tramp told her.

"What do you do with it?" she asked.

"You ride down hills," Tramp explained.

"That sounds dangerous," Lady said hesitantly.

"Nah, it's fun!" Tramp cried. "So, what do you say?"

"It's awfully cold out here," Lady said. She wasn't convinced at all.

"Oh, come on," Tramp said. "It'll be great! You saw how much fun Jim Dear and Darling had." Tramp grabbed the rope in his teeth and pulled the sledge across the porch and down the steps.

Lady took off after him. "Wait for me!" she cried anxiously.

"Come on, Pidge!" Tramp encouraged her. "Jump on!"

Lady jumped onto the sledge, and Tramp pulled her down the snow-covered street and up to the top of a nearby hill. "What a view, huh?" he said.

"What a view indeed," Lady agreed. "What now?"

"Now, we ride," Tramp said. He pushed the sledge forward and took a running leap onto it, sending them racing down the hill.

"Oh, dear!" Lady yelped as they went down the hill, the wind blowing her ears back.

"Just hold on!" Tramp instructed.

Lady squeezed her eyes shut, and Tramp barked with excitement. But suddenly they hit a patch of ice, the sledge spun and they went flying – right into a snowbank!

Tramp jumped to his feet. "Pidge, are you okay?" he asked anxiously.

"Okay?" Lady asked. She was already pulling the sledge back up the hill. "Hurry up, Tramp! Let's do it again!"

Disney
Winnie the Pooh

A Bounciful Friendship

Tigger was having a bounciful day in the Hundred-Acre Wood. He decided to bounce over to Winnie the Pooh's house. Pooh was cleaning out his cupboards and carrying his honeypots outside. As he was placing a full honeypot on the ground, Tigger bounced straight into him. Pooh lost his grip and the honey spilled!

Tigger looked at the mess. "Would you like some help? Getting out of sticky situations is what tiggers do best!"

Pooh decided it would be better to clean up the mess himself, so Tigger bounced off.

Tigger bounced over to Rabbit's next. Rabbit was busy in his garden. Tigger didn't notice the rake right in front of him – until he bounced on it and fell on Rabbit's plants!

Next, Tigger bounced straight into Piglet and knocked him right off his feet – making Piglet spill all the haycorns he'd collected. Then Tigger bounced to Owl's house and ended up knocking Owl's teapot to the floor.

Next, Tigger bounced off to see Eeyore. But Tigger bounced in so suddenly and loudly that Eeyore fell into the side of his house.

Tigger helped Eeyore up. Just then, Rabbit, Pooh and Piglet arrived.

"Tigger, your bouncing is out of control!" cried Rabbit.

"But tiggers are bounciful when they're happy to see their friends!" Tigger explained.

Rabbit knew that was true. But he was still annoyed. "You need to be a little more careful with others and their things!"

Tigger looked at his friends. He couldn't understand the idea that his bouncing could made them unhappy. He walked away so he could think.

Tigger soon came across Christopher Robin. Tigger told the boy about what had happened.

"I'm sure you can fix whatever needs fixing," said Christopher Robin.

Suddenly Tigger bounced up. "That's it! I'm going to fix everything!"

Tigger gave Pooh a new pot full of honey. He collected a basketful of haycorns for Piglet and planted new seeds for Rabbit. He carefully glued Owl's teapot back together and rebuilt Eeyore's house all by himself.

"I must say I am feelin' pretty tiggerific!" said Tigger, seeing his friends' happy faces.

"Why aren't you bouncing then?" Christopher Robin asked.

"You want me to bounce?" asked Tigger.

"Wouldn't be you if you didn't," Eeyore said. And so Tigger bounced – because it turns out that bouncing *and* being careful is what tiggers do best!

347

Tinker Bell
LEGEND OF THE
NEVERBEAST

Tink Reveals the Truth

Nyx arrived in the Winter Woods just as Gruff was running away. He looked every bit a monster – with raging green eyes, huge horns and lightning crackling around him. She raised her spear, but Gruff leaped over her head. She turned to give chase, but Fawn's words stopped her. "Nyx, help!"

Nyx hurried to Fawn and Tink as Gruff escaped into the forest.

Tink was lying on the ground, lifeless and pale. They took her straight to the fairy hospital.

While Tink was being cared for, Fawn sat outside. She was cross with herself and very sad. Yet again, she'd listened with her heart not her head. And because of it, her best friend was hurt.

"She needs to rest for a few days. But she'll be all right," the healing-talent fairy assured Fawn and her friends, who had all gathered to help.

Everyone breathed a sigh of relief.

"See, Fawn," Rosetta said, in an effort to reassure her friend, but Fawn was already gone.

Fawn was searching for Gruff. She found him sitting on a ledge, looking sad and in need of a friend. "Come here," she called, feeling guilty about what was about to happen.

As soon as Gruff jumped down, the scout fairies suddenly threw a net over him.

"Nightshade powder!" called Nyx, leader of the scout fairies. Five pouches exploded over Gruff. He fought, then collapsed as the sleeping powder took effect.

"Okay, that's mission accomplished!" shouted Nyx before turning to Fawn. "You did the right thing." Thinking that Gruff had hurt Tink, Fawn had led him into a trap!

Leaving Gruff behind, Fawn returned to check on Tink. When she arrived, happily Tink was awake. "I'm so sorry," said Fawn.

"There's nothing to be sorry for," Tink replied.

Tink explained what had happened. She said that lightning had split a tree and Gruff had pushed her out of the way to save her life.

Fawn couldn't believe it. "I betrayed him!" she cried. Just as she'd thought, Gruff wasn't a monster. He had saved Tink, not hurt her! She had to go back to help him.

Fawn rounded up her friends, and together they flew to set Gruff free. They used pixie dust to remove the net and Gruff staggered to his feet.

His eyesight was blurry, but he could see the light of Fawn's pixie dust.

"Don't worry, Gruff," she said. "I'm going to get you out of here."

Disney
WRECK-IT RALPH

How Bad Could He Be?

Wreck-It Ralph was the Bad Guy from the *Fix-It Felix, Jr* computer game. But he was fed up of playing the Bad Guy. He wanted to be a hero! So, he left his game and found the Medal of Heroes in the *Hero's Duty* game. But Ralph accidentally freed a dangerous cy-bug, which had multiplied.

The cy-bugs were now attacking the *Sugar Rush* game, where Ralph's new friend Vanellope was trapped! She couldn't leave because she was a 'glitch' – an old game character called Turbo had stolen her computer code. The only way Vanellope could be an offical *Sugar Rush* character again was to cross the game's finish line. But the cy-bugs had attacked just before she reached it!

In *Sugar Rush*, everything was made from sweets. Ralph knew that he needed a bright light to beat the cy-bugs – that was what killed them in their own game. Ralph had an idea! He headed straight for Diet Cola Mountain. On the way, though, a cy-bug attacked him....

Ralph fell and smashed into the mountain. Under him, a Mentos stalactite broke loose and fell towards the hot diet cola below ... along with Ralph. But just in time, someone appeared and grabbed him. It was Vanellope!

The sweets from the mountain hit the cola and ... KABOOM!

A glowing tower of cola spewed out of the mountain. The cy-bugs turned and flew into the light! Not even the Turbo-bug could resist. ZAP! ZAP! All of the bugs were destroyed.

Once the cy-bugs were gone, Fix-It Felix – the Good Guy from Ralph's game – repaired the broken *Sugar Rush* racetrack. Ralph pushed Vanellope gently across the finish. The whole game glitched then returned to normal. But one thing had changed – Vanellope had transformed into a princess!

At last, everyone knew the truth. Turbo had stolen Vanellope's royal identity, and now she had it back.

It was almost morning, and the arcade was due to open. Everyone needed to return to their games. Vanellope gave Ralph a hug.

"You could just stay here and live in the castle," she said.

"I'm already happy," replied Ralph, "because I have the coolest friend in the world."

Back in the arcade, Mr Litwak was just about to unplug *Fix-it Felix, Jr* when a little girl shouted that the game was working. The kids lined up to play. Ralph was back and the *Fix-It Felix* game was saved! Ralph still worked as a Bad Guy, but now he knew he didn't need a medal to be a Good Guy. A little girl like Vanellope liked him ... how bad could he be?

Cinderella

Cinderella's Royal Wedding

Prince Charming had found the woman he loved, and he wanted to marry her. He asked, "Will you marry me?" and waited for the answer. Of course, Cinderella said yes!

The King was thrilled. In the hall, he pointed to a portrait of a beautiful woman. "This was my wife on our wedding day. And Cinderella shall wear the same thing. It is royal family tradition," said the King. "There is nothing more important than family traditions!"

Cinderella quietly looked at the Queen's portrait. She didn't want to disappoint the King, but following family tradition wasn't easy! The Grand Duke brought her a huge pile of books about royal traditions. She read until eventually she fell asleep and began to dream.

In the dream, Cinderella's mother gave her a special gift. "Cinderella my love, this necklace will remind you that whenever you have a problem, if you listen to your heart, it will lead you to the answer."

When Cinderella awoke, she began to search through some of her old trunks. She soon found what she was looking for – a portrait of her mother on her wedding day.

Cinderella showed the portrait to the royal dressmaker. "Would it be possible for you to make me a dress like this?"

The dressmaker bowed his head. "I would be honoured."

Next Cinderella visited the royal jeweller. "Do you think it would be possible to work with my mice friends and combine two necklaces into one?"

"For you I shall create the finest necklace in the Kingdom," he replied.

The royal wedding day arrived. The King came to see Cinderella.

"I hope you don't mind. This is a copy of my mother's wedding dress," said Cinderella. "It honours my family tradition. And with my necklace and veil, I also honour yours, your Majesty."

The King saw that his Queen's pearls had been used to make the wedding necklace and veil. "Oh my dear girl, this is a great honour. You have blended the treasures of two families – and created a new tradition for our family."

The King proudly led Cinderella down the aisle. The guests were thrilled. The Prince was entranced. Even the Grand Duke wiped a tear from his eye.

The Prince and Princess answered the question that all brides and grooms must answer. "They do! They do!" shouted Gus-Gus.

And so, by following tradition – and her heart – Cinderella had the wedding of her dreams!

Tangled
Rapunzel's Heroes

I remember the day started nicely enough. It was the morning of my eighteenth birthday and the birds were singing. Just the day before, I'd taken a huge step – I had left the tall tower that had been my home all my life! And soon, if all went well, I'd be at the kingdom for the first time, watching the floating lights that were released there every year on the same date ... my birthday.

It should have been a lovely morning. But instead, there I was, trying to rescue my guide from a horse!

I'd only known Flynn a short while, but I already knew he was trouble!

After I yanked Flynn free, I stepped in front of the horse and stroked his nose. The name on his chest plate read MAXIMUS.

Maximus thought Flynn was a thief. Still, I hoped the horse wouldn't turn him over to the guards.

"Today is kind of the biggest day of my life," I explained. "It's also my birthday, just so you know."

Together, we set off for the kingdom. Maximus wouldn't let Flynn ride on his back – he threw him off, into a puddle!

"I don't like this horse!" Flynn howled. "And this horse doesn't like me!"

As we walked, Maximus and Flynn wouldn't stop annoying each other.

I sighed. Those two just had to get along, or my special day would be ruined. Luckily, I had an idea. "I know!" I told Flynn, "I'll teach you how to get along with Maximus!"

Flynn grumbled, but watched as I stroked Maximus under his chin.

"See?" I said, nuzzling Maximus's face. "Now you do it."

"Ugh! No way!" Flynn protested. But I asked him to try.

Getting into the kingdom was a little tricky, because Flynn was wanted by the palace guards. Maximus and Flynn managed it, though, by working together. Those two were making good progress!

I think Maximus was a little surprised as he watched Flynn that day, being kind and gentle. Maybe he realized Flynn wasn't so bad after all....

That evening, Flynn gave a bag of apples to Maximus! I was proud of them for making an effort to be friends.

That night, Flynn was put in prison and I was captured by cruel Mother Gothel! Maximus raced to free Flynn. The two of them then hurried to my rescue! They were a team.

After they saved me, I told them how grateful I was. Flynn and Max were heroes. But just as important, they were friends.

Disney
101 DALMATIANS

Having a Ball!

"Ten days until Santa!" the spotted puppies barked, bouncing into one another as they tumbled down the hall.

"Ten days until presents!" Penny barked.

"And ten days until Christmas dinner!" Rolly added.

"Ten days to stay out of trouble!" Pongo said with a smile.

"Do you puppies know what comes before Santa and dinner and presents?" Perdita asked.

"Umm ... stockings?" Lucky asked.

"No, before that," she said.

Patch wasn't sure. He sat down on the hall rug to think.

"We have to decorate and sing carols," Perdita said, wagging her tail. At that very moment, Roger and Anita threw open the door to the study and invited all the dogs inside.

Patch blinked. He couldn't believe his eyes. "What's a tree doing in the house?"

"Just watch." Perdy gave Patch a quick lick.

While the dogs looked on, Roger and Anita began to decorate the tree. They hung lights and angels, snowmen and tinsel. Of all the decorations, Patch liked the glittering glass balls best. Balls were one of his favourite things! He could not take his eyes off them.

When the tree was ready, Anita brought in cocoa and dog biscuits. Munching on a biscuit in front of the fire, Patch didn't think the evening could get any better. Then Roger sat down at the piano, and everyone began to sing.

Patch howled along with the others, but he could not stop looking at the balls on the tree. A large red one was hanging near the floor.

Patch reached over and gave the ball a pat with his front paw. It swung merrily above him. Looking at his reflection, Patch started to laugh. His nose looked huge!

"What are you doing?" Penny stopped singing to see what was so funny. Then Freckles joined them, then Lucky. The puppies took turns knocking the ball and watching it sway, then – *crash*! – it fell to the floor, shattering.

The singing stopped. Poor Patch was sure the special evening was ruined.

"Oh, dear." Anita scooped the puppies out from under the tree. "Careful, now," she said. "Those balls aren't for playing with."

While Roger swept up the glass, Patch cowered. He knew he was in trouble.

"Maybe I should give you all one gift early," Anita said with a grin. Patch couldn't believe his luck. Instead of a firm talking-to, each puppy got to rip open a small package. Patch tore off the paper. Inside was a brand-new red rubber ball!

FROM THE MOVIE DISNEY·PIXAR **INSIDE OUT**

Reunited

Joy and Sadness had finally made it back to Headquarters after their long and difficult journey through Riley's Mind World. The problem was, they couldn't actually get in!

Riley's other Emotions, Anger, Fear and Disgust, ran to the window. Then Disgust had an idea. She taunted Anger until he got so mad that fire burst from his head. Then she picked him up and used the flames to cut a hole in the window! Joy and Sadness climbed inside.

"You're back!" cried Fear, feeling relieved.

While Joy and Sadness had been gone, a lot of things had gone wrong, and Anger had decided Riley should go back to Minnesota where everything had been perfect.

"Joy, you've got to fix this," Disgust pleaded. "Get up there!"

"Oh no!" Joy exclaimed, as she looked up at the screen and saw that Riley was on the bus, ready to run away. Then Joy looked at Sadness. "Sadness," Joy said, "it's up to you."

"Me?" Sadness replied. "Oh, I can't, Joy!"

"Yes you can," said Joy. "Riley needs you."

Sadness took a deep breath and stepped up to the console. Joy, Anger, Fear and Disgust watched the screen and waited.

On the bus, Riley's face changed from totally blank to very sad. She stood up. "Wait!" she called to the driver. "I want to get off!"

When the bus screeched to a standstill, Riley jumped off and started running.

At Riley's house, Mum and Dad were worried sick. Suddenly, the front door flew open and Riley burst in.

"Riley!" her mum cried.

In Headquarters, Joy handed the core memory spheres to Sadness. The spheres all turned blue, and Riley's mind was filled with memories of her old life.

Riley began to cry. "I miss Minnesota," she told her parents. "I want my old friends and my hockey team … I wanna go home. Please don't be mad."

"We're not mad," said Dad. Then Mum and Dad explained they missed Minnesota, too.

They fell into a big, warm family hug and, in Headquarters, a brand-new multi-coloured core memory was created.

After a while, Riley was back to normal – and so was her Mind World. The Islands of Personality had reappeared, with a few new ones, too. The Emotions stood in Headquarters, looking out of the window at their new view.

"Whoa!" the Emotions said, excitedly.

"We've been through a lot lately, that's for sure," said Joy. "But we still love our girl. She has great new friends, a great new house … things couldn't be better. After all, Riley's 12 now … what could possibly happen?"

Who Ate the Brownies?

Minnie had just baked a batch of butterscotch brownies because Daisy was having a party. "The gang will gobble these up," she said, wrapping the brownies in tinfoil and tucking the package into a bag.

When Minnie arrived at Daisy's house, the others were already there. Daisy was taking food out of the fridge while Donald looked on hungrily. Goofy, who had bandages on both thumbs, was carefully petting Pluto.

"I was trying to hang up some pictures," Goofy explained to Minnie.

"Want to dance, Minnie?" Mickey asked.

"Yes!" Minnie said, putting her bag on the table and following Mickey to the living room.

Minnie was still dancing with Mickey an hour later when she remembered the brownies.

"The butterscotch brownies!" she exclaimed. "I forgot to unpack them."

"Great! Let's eat!" cried Goofy.

Minnie ran to the kitchen and found the bag empty on the table. The butterscotch brownies were gone!

Minnie went back to the living room. "My brownies are missing!" she cried.

"I haven't seen them!" said Daisy, Donald, Goofy and Mickey, one after the other.

"Well, they were in this bag when I got here," said Minnie. "One of you must have sneaked out to the kitchen and eaten them."

"I didn't take your brownies," Daisy said. "I don't like butterscotch."

"Really?" Minnie asked.

Mickey laughed. "Daisy would sooner eat spinach than butterscotch," he said. "And it wasn't me. You and I have been dancing."

"True," Minnie said.

Goofy gulped. "Well, I sneaked out to the kitchen and ate a few things. But I didn't touch that bag."

"It wasn't you, Goofy," Minnie realized. "You couldn't have unwrapped the tinfoil with your thumbs in bandages!"

When Minnie turned to Donald, he squawked, "It wasn't me! I might have unwrapped the tinfoil to take a peek. But I did not taste your brownies, not even one crumb."

"Come on," Minnie said, deciding to trust Donald. "Let's look in the kitchen for clues."

"Hey, I found some footprints," called Mickey, pointing at the floor below the table.

They followed the trail of footprints up the stairs and into Daisy's bedroom. They disappeared beneath the bed....

Pluto let out a groan. He had butterscotch crumbs all around his mouth.

Minnie smiled. "We shouldn't be too tough on him," she said. "Looks as if he's already paying for it – with tummy ache!"

DUMBO
The Show Must Go On

The wind whistled around the Big Top, pulling the canvas tent that Dumbo was holding out of reach of his small trunk. "I'll get it," Dumbo's mother said as the tent flapped over their heads.

If the weather hadn't been so terrible, Dumbo thought, he could have flown up to grab the edge of the tent. But the whipping wind was too much, even for Dumbo's wing-like ears.

At last, standing on her back legs, Mrs Jumbo caught the canvas in her trunk. She pulled it taut and let the roustabouts tie it off. But Dumbo noticed several new rips in the fabric.

"Quit your clowning!" the Ringmaster barked at the clowns. He noticed the rips too. He ordered the clowns to sew them up. "The repairs must be finished by showtime!"

Dumbo felt terrible. All the circus performers, animals and roustabouts were working hard in the storm. He had gone and made even more work, by letting the canvas get torn. And now the Ringmaster's mood was as foul as the weather!

Just then, Dumbo noticed another blast of cold air whirl the Ringmaster's black top hat off his head.

"That does it!" the Ringmaster shouted. "There will be no show tonight!"

Dumbo could not believe his ears. The announcement was even enough to wake Timothy Q. Mouse from his nap in a nearby bale of hay.

"No show? I can't believe it!" Timothy cried. The rest of the circus folk couldn't believe it either. They silently continued to set up.

"What a fuss over a hat." Timothy shook his head. "The show must go on."

Dumbo nodded. Then something caught his eye. The Ringmaster's hat was caught on the flagpole, high over the Big Top. Perhaps he could get it for him?

Bravely, Dumbo took off. The wind was strong, but he tucked his head down and flapped his ears hard. When the wind calmed for a moment, the small elephant saw his chance. He grabbed the top hat and flew quickly to the ground.

Shyly, Dumbo held out the hat to the Ringmaster.

"Thank you, Dumbo." The Ringmaster took his hat gratefully. He looked around at all the people and animals still hard at work. He looked a little embarrassed. Then, as he placed the hat on his head, he shouted, "The show must go on!"

Everyone cheered.

"What'd I tell ya?" Timothy asked, winking at Dumbo.

Disney·PIXAR
FINDING NEMO

Old Man Octopus

"**Y**ou're it!" Nemo tagged Sheldon, who was hiding next to a mollusc.

"Aw, man!" Sheldon swished his tail. "I'm going to get you next time, Nemo."

"Only if you can find me," Nemo teased. Then he called louder, "Ollie, ollie, all swim free!" The rest of the fish, who were playing hide-and-seek, returned to the giant barnacle they were using as base. When they were all there, Sheldon began to count again.

Nemo swam away, scanning the reef for a good hiding spot. Sheldon would be out to get him for sure. Nemo swam past a large empty abalone shell. "Too easy," he muttered. He darted into an anemone. "Way too obvious." Finally he came to a dark cave in the coral. "Too dark," he shivered, looking into the spooky opening. "It'll be perfect."

Mustering his courage, Nemo swam inside. At first he couldn't see anything. Then, as his eyes adjusted to the dark, Nemo saw a large eye open on the cave wall. What could it be?

Another eye opened. Then the entire wall began to move.

"O-O-Old Man Octopus!" Nemo stammered as eight long arms oozed off the cave wall. Nemo and his friends told stories about Old Man Octopus at sleepovers. In the stories, Old Man Octopus sneaked up on little fish and gave them a terrible scare.

"S-sorry to disturb you, sir." Nemo swam towards the cave entrance. Then he noticed something amazing. The octopus's arms were changing colour ... and texture! Instead of matching the brown bumpy cave wall, now they looked more like the reddish coral at the bottom of the cave.

"You didn't disturb me, boy. Tell me what brings you to this corner of the reef?" The octopus's voice was slow and kind, and Nemo's fear melted away.

"Hide-and-seek, sir," Nemo answered politely. "But I wouldn't need a cave if I could camouflage myself like you!"

Old Man Octopus laughed. "Hide-and-seek, eh? One of my favourites. The camouflage does come in handy, but nothing beats a cloud of ink when you want to make a break for the base!"

"You can shoot ink clouds too?" Nemo was so excited, he forgot to be quiet.

"I hear you, Nemo!" Sheldon shouted.

"Are you ready to swim for it?" Old Man Octopus whispered with a wink.

Nemo nodded. He high-fived one of Old Man Octopus's tentacles. Then, in a burst of inky blackness, he darted out of the cave, past Sheldon, and all the way back to the barnacle base. Safe!

Snow White
and the Seven Dwarfs

The Magic of Friendship

One day, the Seven Dwarfs were visiting Snow White and the Prince at their palace. They were all having a picnic.

"Please, help yourselves," said Snow White, as she passed out china plates. "One for you ... and you ... and ... Oh, my! Where is Dopey?"

Snow White and the Prince and all six Dwarfs searched everywhere for Dopey. Finally, Snow White spotted him – he had found a caterpillar! Everybody came to look.

"Enough lookin' already," huffed Grumpy. "The Princess has made us a picnic. Besides, caterpillars ain't nothin' but trouble, if you ask me."

"Oh, Grumpy," said Snow White sweetly. "I don't think this caterpillar will be any trouble. Come," she told the Dwarfs. "Let's go back to the picnic. And Dopey, why don't you bring your new friend along?"

Everyone enjoyed the picnic, and ate and ate and ate, until every crumb was gone. Then it was time for the Dwarfs to go. Dopey took his new friend with him.

Before long, Snow White visited the Dwarfs at their cottage. She found poor Dopey in tears! Sadly, Dopey took Snow White's hand and led her outside. Then he pointed to a hard, shiny shell hanging from a branch.

"That old caterpillar went in there a few days ago," said Doc. "But he won't come out."

Snow White shook her head and then wrapped Dopey in her arms. "Oh, Dopey," she said gently, "didn't you know? The caterpillar is changing!"

"Er...." Doc began. "Changing into what?"

Snow White saw a pair of bright-coloured wings flutter by. She pointed to the butterfly and smiled. "Into that!"

Sure enough, the Dwarfs turned and looked just in time to see the little shell crack open. A creature – Dopey's caterpillar – began to push out. Slowly, but surely, the small wings began to open.

"It is a butterfly!" cried Happy.

Dopey smiled a big smile and held out his finger to his caterpillar friend, now a fancy-looking butterfly! But instead of climbing on to it, the butterfly flew away!

Snow White tried her best to comfort little Dopey. "Don't worry," she assured him. "Remember, I went away, too. But I still come back and visit. Being a good friend sometimes means letting your friends go ..."

"... and letting them return for lots and lots of visits!"

Just then, the butterly landed right on Dopey's nose!

THE LION KING

All Wet

Timon pounded his tiny chest and gave a mighty yell as he swung out over the lagoon. He let go of a vine and threw his arms out wide, hitting the water with a small but very satisfying smack. He popped to the surface, shouting: "Ta-da!"

Pumbaa was next. "Look out below!" he called. He backed up on the rock ledge, then charged. The warthog's splash sent water flying high into the air. The lagoon was still rippling when he surfaced.

"Not bad," Simba said. "But I bet Nala could do better." The Lion King looked up at Nala, who was sunning herself on a rock as far from the water as possible.

"Ha!" Nala laughed. "You know I don't like to get wet."

"Oh, come on, Nala. Give it a try. The water's fine!" Simba said.

"The water *is* fine ..." Nala replied slowly, rolling over and licking her paw " ... for drinking."

Pumbaa and Timon sniggered. Simba frowned. Nala was making him look silly in front of his friends. Was he King of the Pride Lands or not?

Using his most commanding voice, Simba gave Nala an order. "You will come swimming with us right now, or else!"

Nala did not even lift her head. She closed her eyes. "Or else what, Your Mightiness?"

Simba couldn't come up with anything, so the argument was over. And Nala, as usual, had won.

Accepting his defeat, Simba ran to the edge of the rocky ledge, sprang high in the air and tucked his paws in for a royal cannonball.

Pumbaa and Timon were drenched. Slinking slowly out of the water, Simba signalled to them. He pointed at his dripping mane and then up at Nala's rock.

Timon winked, and he and Pumbaa began a noisy mock water fight to distract Nala. While they hollered and splashed, Simba climbed up to Nala's warm spot in the sun. He walked quickly but silently. Drawing closer, he crouched, his legs coiled to pounce. Nala did not move.

Then, with a triumphant roar, Simba jumped onto Nala's rock and gave his sopping mane a mighty shake. Nala was drenched.

Nala leaped to her feet with a snarl. Simba rolled onto his back, laughing.

"You're all wet, Nala!" Timon guffawed. Pumbaa was laughing so hard, he could barely breathe.

Nala tried to glare fiercely at Simba, but she couldn't. She had to laugh too. "King of the practical jokers," she said.

Bambi
Night-time is for Exploring!

As the moon rose above the forest, Bambi snuggled close to his sleeping mother. What a day it had been! Exploring new places, learning new words and meeting new friends. Bambi yawned and closed his eyes....

"Bambi! Oh, Bambi!"

Bambi slowly opened his eyes. "Thumper?" he whispered. "Why aren't you asleep?"

"Asleep? Come on!" cried Thumper. "Sleep is for the birds! How can you sleep when there's so much to see and do at night?"

"But everybody knows that night-time is for sleeping," Bambi said.

"Oh, brother," Thumper said. "Do you have a lot to learn! Follow me, Bambi, and I'll show you how the night is a whole new day!"

And suddenly, at the prospect of a new adventure, Bambi's sleepiness disappeared. Quietly, he stood up and let Thumper lead the way.

Thumper was right – the forest was as busy at night as it was during the day, but with a whole new group of animals. Owls, opossums, raccoons and badgers – all those animals that Bambi thought spent most of their lives asleep – were now as lively as could be.

"Wh-wh-what's that?" Bambi exclaimed, as a dot of light landed on his nose.

"Don't worry, Bambi, it's just a firefly," Thumper said with a giggle.

"'Firefly'," Bambi said. Then suddenly, the little light disappeared. "Hey, where'd it go?"

"There it is!" cried Thumper, pointing to Bambi's tail. "No, wait. It's over there."

Happily, Thumper and Bambi chased the firefly as it flitted from one friend to the other. "I think he likes us!" Thumper cried.

But their game was soon interrupted by a flurry of sound. Thousands of leathery wings were suddenly beating overhead.

"Duck, Bambi!" hollered Thumper, just as the whole group swooped around their heads.

"Boy, that was close!" said Thumper.

"Were those fireflies too?" Bambi asked.

"Naw," Thumper laughed. "They didn't light up! Those were bats."

"'Bats'," repeated Bambi. "They're really busy at night."

"You can say that again," agreed Thumper, trying to stifle a yawn. And, since yawns are contagious, Bambi's own yawn was not far behind.

"This was fun," Bambi told his friend. "But what do you say we go home and go to bed?"

But there was no answer ... for Thumper was already fast asleep!

The Jewel of the Bayou

One morning, Tiana, Naveen, Eudora and Charlotte were discussing Tiana's birthday party. Prince Naveen was worried – he still hadn't found the perfect gift for his princess!

Nothing had seemed special enough for Princess Tiana. But luckily, Naveen had overheard Tiana and Charlotte in the kitchen.

"When my daddy and I used to go fishing in the bayou, we'd sometimes find a piece of swamp amber," said Tiana. "It was the most precious thing!"

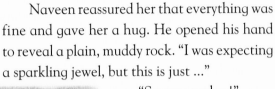

"That's it!" whispered Naveen. Naveen met with the jazz-loving alligator, Louis. They were going to find Tiana some swamp amber!

As the birthday party was about to begin, Tiana couldn't find Naveen anywhere. A guest said he saw the prince down by the old, mossy tree in the bayou. Tiana was afraid Naveen was in trouble.

She ran to the river and climbed into a rowboat. She saw Naveen in the distance. He dove into the water by the old tree.

"Naveen!" Tiana called out. When the prince didn't reappear, she dived into the water!

She found Naveen in a tangle of roots. Tiana grabbed his hand and pulled him to the surface.

Naveen reassured her that everything was fine and gave her a hug. He opened his hand to reveal a plain, muddy rock. "I was expecting a sparkling jewel, but this is just ..."

"Swamp amber!" Tiana exclaimed. "What a wonderful birthday surprise!"

Later, when Charlotte saw the birthday gift she screamed in fright. But Tiana explained that the rock brought back loving memories of her father. "That is the most precious gift of all," said Tiana.

Mama Odie picked up the swamp amber. "A little sparkle couldn't hurt," she said, tossing the rock into a pot of gumbo. "Gumbo, gumbo in the pot, we need some sparkle. What you got?"

In a puff of magic, the swamp amber became a dazzling golden jewel set in a fine necklace.

"Mama Odie!" Naveen exclaimed. "How did you do that?"

Mama Odie winked at Tiana.

"Oh, it's just a talent we have down here in the bayou. We like to take things that are a little slimy and rough around the edges and turn 'em into something wonderful!"

"Like turning a frog into a prince!" Naveen agreed, as he and Tiana danced the night away.

December
24

FAIRIES
TinkerBell
AND THE
LEGEND OF THE
NEVERBEAST

Save Pixie Hollow!

Suddenly a lightning bolt struck. Gruff pushed Fawn aside so the lightning wouldn't strike her, and he took the full force himself. Fawn and her fairy friends watched in awe as huge wings grew out of Gruff's back.

Fawn now understood Gruff's purpose. "The towers … they draw in the lightning … so he can collect it. He knew the lightning strikes were coming and he's been preparing for it the whole time!" Fawn explained. He was saving Pixie Hollow. Not trying to destroy it!

"We're going to the towers," Fawn shouted. "All right, big guy," she called to Gruff. "Just follow my glow!"

Fawn led Gruff to the Autumn tower, which glowed from a constant stream of lightning hits. Gruff charged at it and the lightning jumped to his horns. Then, the tower crumbled and the lightning cleared from the area.

Fairies on the ground watched in amazement as Fawn led Gruff overhead.

At the Winter tower, Gruff twisted and turned as he again absorbed the lightning.

"One more to go!" shouted Fawn.

As Fawn and Gruff reached the final tower, Nyx struck it and knocked the tower down. Gruff fell to the ground. The lightning, no longer contained by the tower and Gruff's horns, split into hundreds of bolts.

"Nyx!" cried Fawn. "What are you doing?"

"Saving Pixie Hollow," Nyx yelled back.

But the lightning was everywhere. Trees burst into flames as they were struck, and a stray bolt of lightning arced towards Nyx.

Gruff stepped in to absorb the strike.

"Don't you get it, Nyx?" shouted Fawn. "He was saving Pixie Hollow!"

Gruff desperately tried to rebuild the tower. "It's too late," said Fawn. "How can we catch it all?"

Glancing up into the sky, Fawn realized the lightning was coming from the eye of the storm. She and Gruff knew they had to reach the source to stop it.

"Follow me," said Fawn.

Gruff followed Fawn's glow as they flew up to the storm's vortex. As they got closer, Gruff pushed Fawn behind him. Through his horns, Gruff gathered up all the storm's energy until the clouds were drained.

In one enormous blast, Gruff shook off the energy waves, sending them far out over the sea.

The storm was over. Fawn and Gruff had done it. But now they were falling from the sky, and they needed their fairy friends' help.

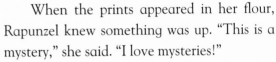

Rapunzel's New Friend

Long before Rapunzel knew she was a princess, before she left her tower for an adventure across the kingdom, she was a lonely little girl.

Mother Gothel often left Rapunzel alone. And the only creatures that crossed her path were butterflies, bees and the occasional bird.

But butterflies are notoriously skittish, bees do not like hugs and no matter how many seeds Rapunzel gave them, the birds never stuck around very long.

Since friends were scarce, Rapunzel did the next best thing. She filled each day with an exciting new activity.

She tried painting, but her artwork never looked as good as what she had imagined.

Then she tried baking, but her cakes came out burned and black.

Finally, Rapunzel tried gardening, but her seeds weren't sprouting.

"That's it!" shouted Rapunzel. "I can't paint, I can't bake and I can't even grow one strawberry. I give up!"

But just as she was about to throw away her gardening gloves, Rapunzel noticed a strange pattern in the dirt. Taking a closer look, she realized they were footprints.

A few days later, the same prints showed up in her paint!

When the prints appeared in her flour, Rapunzel knew something was up. "This is a mystery," she said. "I love mysteries!"

So, from then on, whenever Rapunzel painted a picture, she spilled a little paint on purpose.

Whenever she baked, she scattered a little flour.

And whenever she gardened, she sprinkled a little dirt.

She wanted to see if the prints would reappear … and they always did! But Rapunzel still didn't know who was making them.

Meanwhile, she got really good at painting, baking and gardening!

One day, as she was picking strawberries, Rapunzel spotted an odd-shaped berry.

As she reached for the berry, it changed colour! Before her was a small green chameleon, curled in a ball and frozen with fear.

"So you're the one who's been leaving the funny little prints!" said Rapunzel.

The chameleon seemed to nod. Rapunzel hadn't been alone in her tower after all! But how would she convince him to stay?

"My name is Rapunzel," she said. "I'll call you Pascal. Would you like some cake?"

Rapunzel learned that Pascal never said no to cake. And Pascal learned that Rapunzel was the best friend a chameleon could ever ask for.

A Frozen Festival

Just before spring was a special time for Elsa and Anna. It was their mother's birthday.

"Let's have a festival in her honour," Anna said, "just like we used to before the gates closed."

"Lovely idea!" Elsa cried. "We'll start planning it in the morning."

The next day, Elsa made an announcement: in three days there would be a week-long Winter's End Festival in Arendelle in honour of Queen Iduna. Everyone was invited!

"Mother believed in fresh air and exercise," Anna said. "So we need to decide on some outside activities."

"I love fresh air!" yelled Olaf. "I'll come."

"Kristoff said he'd organize reindeer rides on Sven's back," said Anna.

"We'll need carrots," said Elsa. "Let's buy them at Wandering Oaken's Trading Post!"

"I know what Mother would have liked," Anna said, as they walked. "Snowshoe games!"

"Good idea," said Elsa. "Let's hope Oaken has enough pairs for the whole kingdom!"

They ordered snowshoes and carrots for all the races and games they were planning.

"Now let's go home," said Elsa. "We still have a lot to prepare, like –"

"The menu!" Anna exclaimed.

Back at the castle, it didn't take Anna and Olaf long to decide on the menu: desserts!

Later, Anna went to find Elsa, but the ballroom door was locked. "Elsa?" Anna asked. "What's going on in there?"

"I'm practising," Elsa said.

"Ice sculpting?" Anna said when Elsa opened the door. "That's brilliant, but you can't compete because it wouldn't be fair. Mother wouldn't have used magic."

Elsa smiled. "This is just for decoration."

"Great! Now, let's go outside. I have a surprise for you!" Anna smiled.

SPLAT! A snowball landed on Elsa's head.

"You'll be sorry," said Elsa, giggling and gathering up a big pile of snow.

The sisters sent snowballs back and forth until they were red-cheeked and out of breath.

"I think I hit you about six hundred times," said Anna. "But I wasn't really counting."

"I ran out of snow," said Elsa. "And I was doing it the non-magical way."

The next morning, Elsa woke up Anna. This time, she had prepared a surprise. They walked over to the window.

"How did this get here?" Anna asked, delighted by a freshly iced pond for skating.

"I wanted everyone to have as much fun at the festival as we had planning it," said Elsa. "So I decided a bit of magic might be in order."

"Mother would be proud," Anna said. "Let's kick off the festival!"

Disney · PIXAR

BRAVE

Rites of Summer Begin!

Princess Merida and Young Macintosh had to return the emeralds to the source of Fire Falls to reunite their clans. To do so, they had to climb the waterfall again, but the rocks were too slippery!

They worked together. Merida pulled her strongest arrow from her quiver. Young Macintosh tied his rope to the arrow. Merida even saved Young Macintosh when he almost fell, but as she did so, she dropped one of the emeralds.

"Maybe this emerald will be enough to fix the Fire Falls, even without the other one," Young Macintosh said hopefully.

When they reached the cavern, Young Macintosh put the emerald back where it belonged but it wouldn't stay put, not without the other emerald to balance against.

Merida racked her brain for a solution. She reached for her lucky thistle charm – she had never needed luck more. Suddenly, her face lit up. "We need to follow the legend!" she gasped. "Two leaders … a symbol of loyalty … a worthy sacrifice…." They both had to sacrifice something that truly mattered to them.

Merida placed her charm on the ledge. Young Macintosh put his family's crest from his kilt sash on the other side of the emerald.

The flash that burst from the emerald was so blinding that Merida and Young Macintosh had to shield their eyes. Crystal-clear water began to pool around the emerald, and golden light made the water glitter like shooting stars.

"It's working!" Merida cried.

"Hurry – to the docks!" Young Macintosh cried.

The Macintosh clan were still loading up their ships when Merida and Young Macintosh arrived. King Fergus and Lord Macintosh were shouting at each other.

"Wait!" Merida and Young Macintosh cried as they dismounted their horses.

"The Fire Falls are sparkling again!" Merida exclaimed.

The crowd gasped in surprise. Merida and Young Macintosh explained everything. They wanted their clans to be friends again.

King Fergus and Lord Macintosh exchanged glances. "Of course our clans are the dearest of friends," King Fergus finally said. "It would be a dark day for DunBroch to lose the friendship of the Macintosh clan."

"Aye, but it would be a darker day for us!" replied Lord Macintosh.

"Tonight, we will celebrate," King Fergus announced. "And tomorrow – let the Rites of Summer begin!"

Merida and Young Macintosh smiled at each other. This year, there was more to celebrate than ever.

Roo's New Babysitter

"**I** don't want to be babysitted!" cried Roo. Roo's mama, Kanga, was going shopping and Pooh was going to babysit.

"I want to go shopping!" cried Roo. He had a large bag and was filling it when Pooh arrived.

"Hello, Pooh," said Roo. "I'm shopping!" He put more tins in his bag, partly because he didn't want his mama to see how much he minded being left behind.

Roo and Pooh said goodbye to Kanga. Then Pooh gave Roo a hug and tried to feed him a nice smackerel of honey.

"I want to go shopping," squeaked Roo. "I don't want to eat."

"Hmmmm," said Pooh. "NOW what do I do?"

"You don't know how to babysit?" asked Roo. "I'm good at babysitting. I'll tell you how. The first thing a babysitter does is climb!"

Pooh, who was starting to think there was not much SITTING involved in babysitting, said, "Okay, let's find a good climbing tree."

They climbed the old apple tree in Roo's back garden. Roo hopped from branch to branch, and Pooh climbed up behind him.

"Mmmm," said Roo. "Look at those apples. Babysitters always pick apples for supper."

So Pooh climbed up to the highest branch, picked four bright red apples and then inched back down using one arm. They sat side by side and swung their feet and ate the sweet apples.

"This is the best supper ever!" cried Roo.

Next, Roo showed Pooh how babysitters pour a whole bottle of bubble bath into the bathwater. Roo disappeared under the bubbles. *Wfffffff.* Pooh blew on the bubbles but he couldn't see Roo!

"Look at me jumping," squeaked a little voice. Roo was jumping on his bed, all wet! Pooh dried Roo off, then helped put on his pyjamas.

"Time for your Strengthening Medicine," said Pooh, a little more sternly than when poohs usually say such things. But Roo didn't want it. He folded his arms across his chest.

"Oh well," said Pooh, slumping in a chair. "Why don't you give ME a spoonful? I think I could do with it!"

"Now, Pooh, dear, here's your medicine," said Roo in a cheerful, grown-up sort of voice.

"Ahhh!" said Pooh. "Thank you, Roo. You are a good babysitter."

Just then, Kanga opened the door and saw Roo and Pooh snuggled together in the chair.

"Mama!" cried Roo. "I'm babysitting Pooh!"

"Of course you are, dear," said Kanga.

Tinker Bell
AND THE
LEGEND OF THE
NEVERBEAST

Goodnight, Gruff!

Fairies flew from everywhere in Pixie Hollow to catch Fawn and Gruff as they fell from the sky. Gruff had taken the full force of the storm, absorbing all the lightning in order to keep the fairies safe from harm. He hadn't created the storm; he'd woken from his hibernation to save Pixie Hollow from it.

With his scorched fur and broken horns, Gruff was weak, but he was all right. Fawn, however, was motionless. The beast nuzzled her cheek, and as he did, one last tiny bit of electrical energy sparked into Fawn.

Her eyes fluttered open and she smiled. "Hey, there's my big furry monster," she said looking up at him.

Everyone cheered!

Before long, Gruff and Fawn had both made full recoveries. Gruff was a hero to the fairies. He helped repair the damage from the storm, fixing trees and using his size and strength to help his new friends. The fairies no longer feared him.

But it wasn't long before Gruff became tired. Fawn listened to his heartbeat. It was slowing down. Fawn realized it was time for him to go back to his cave to hibernate.

"How long are we talking about?" asked Rosetta.

Fawn held back her tears. "About a thousand years," she said.

The girls understood. "So we'll never see him again," said Tink.

Fawn and the girls led Gruff back to his cave. Hundreds of fairies lined the route to wish him well, lighting his way with glowing lanterns and fairy dust. It was a beautiful fairy farewell to a trusted friend.

Inside the cave, Tink had made him a special bed. Rosetta had given him a fluffy pillow. Silvermist had put in a spring-fed water bowl. Iridessa had brought a night light. And Vidia had added a gentle breeze.

Nyx gave Gruff something, too. "The enduring respect of a grateful scout," she said.

And then it was Fawn's turn to say goodbye. "Hey, big guy," she said. "I won't see you again. But I know you'll always be there when we need you."

Gruff settled into his bed and smiled. Fawn kissed him on the nose. "I'm really going to miss you," she whispered as he fell asleep. "I love you, Gruff."

And with that the legend of the NeverBeast had changed forever.

Disney

Beauty and the Beast

A Wintry Walk

"It's so beautiful," Belle murmured as she gazed out of the castle window. Snow had been falling for hours and hours, covering everything in a deep blanket of white. "You know what would be nice? A wa –"

Suddenly, a heavy red cape was draped over her shoulders. "How about a walk?" the Prince asked.

Belle smiled into his blue eyes. "I was just thinking that!" she said.

"Aha," he replied mischievously. "But were you thinking of a walk on these?" He pulled a pair of large snowshoes out from behind a chair.

"Snowshoes!" Belle cried, clapping her hands together. She and her father used to go snowshoeing together in the woods when she was a little girl, and she loved it. No matter how deep the snow was, the special shoes allowed her to walk over the huge drifts.

Minutes later, the pair were in the castle courtyard, strapping the snowshoes onto their boots. Belle walked forward gracefully, heading through the gate towards the forest, pausing to scatter birdseed for the neighbourhood birds.

But the Prince was having trouble, tripping over the giant shoes with every step.

"When I was a beast, I just walked through the snow," he said, panting. "I didn't have to bother with silly contraptions like these!" He stepped forward and tumbled headfirst into a deep snowbank.

Belle laughed. At first, the Prince scowled but soon he was laughing too.

"You're thinking too much," Belle said. "It's actually a lot like walking in regular shoes. You just have to keep your feet a little further apart so they don't get caught up in each other."

"Hmm," the Prince said. He stepped forward. But, when he lifted his other foot, it caught on the icy top layer of snow, and he fell again.

Belle stifled a giggle as she helped him to his feet. "Step lightly," she suggested.

"I'll say," the Prince grumbled. He stepped more lightly this time, and moved easily across the snow. Soon he was keeping up with Belle, who led him all the way through the forest. It was a wonderful, wintry walk. And, when they got back to the castle, they found hot chocolate and biscuits waiting for them in front of the fire!

"Oh, good," said the Prince. "Eating! This is one thing I'll always be good at." He picked up a biscuit, which broke and fell with a *plop*! into his cup.

"Aw," he said, crestfallen.

"You know," Belle said with a teasing smile, "you aren't so different from the clumsy beast I fell in love with!"

Lilo & Stitch

Countdown to Midnight!

"No sleep till midnight!" Lilo and Stitch chanted, bouncing up and down on Lilo's bed. It was New Year's Eve, and Nani had agreed to let them stay up late.

"Okay, okay." Nani held her hands out. "It's only five o'clock now. Don't wear yourselves out. You still have seven hours until the new year."

Lilo and Stitch looked at each other. Wear themselves out? Impossible!

"Look, Stitch," Lilo said. "We only have seven hours. What do you want to do first?"

"Surfing!" Stitch cried.

"Sunset surfing it is!" Lilo gave the little alien a high five before turning to Nani. "Okay?" she asked sweetly.

Nani shook her head again. I must be nuts, she thought. "I'll go get my suit." She sighed.

The three surfed until sundown. Then they headed for home.

"So, what's next?" Lilo asked Stitch.

Stitch smacked his lips. "Dinner!"

"Don't worry," Lilo said. "We'll cook."

"And I'll clean," Nani muttered.

When they got home, Nani lay down on the couch with her arm over her eyes. Five hours until bedtime. She switched on the TV and tried to ignore the crashing noises coming from the kitchen.

"Ta-da!" Lilo emerged with a huge plate of something steaming and cheesy.

"What is it?" Nani asked cautiously.

"Pizza, Stitch-style!" Lilo said. "With anchovies, peanut butter and fruit cocktail!"

Nani cringed. "Don't worry, Nani," said Lilo. "We left the toothpaste on the side this time. Plus, there's a milkshake for dessert!"

The three ate the gooey mess, while Lilo and Stitch discussed what was next.

"How about that milkshake?" Nani suggested before Lilo could come up with a noisier, messier or more dangerous idea.

Stitch grabbed the blender and dumped the milkshake on his head. Nani shooed the two into the living room and began to tackle the mess in the kitchen.

The washing-up took forever. Nani could not figure out how they'd managed to use so many pots and pans. She was still elbow deep in suds when her eyes grew wide with alarm. Something was wrong. It was too quiet! Nani rushed into the living room. Lilo and Stitch were sound asleep! Nani looked at her watch.

"Five-four-three-two-one," Nani counted down. "Happy New Year," she said softly, as she covered the pair with a blanket.

She smiled as she looked at the clock. It was only 10pm!